ALSO BY
KATEE ROBERT

Dark Olympus
Neon Gods
Electric Idol
Wicked Beauty
Radiant Sin
Stone Heart (prequel novella)

Court of the Vampire Queen

CRUEL SEDUCTION

KATEE ROBERT

Cruel Seduction *contains explicit sex, attempted murder, murder, violence, blood, child abuse (historical, non-graphic), and attempted sexual assault (historical, off-page).*

Published by Sourcebooks Casablanca, an imprint of Sourcebooks
P.O. Box 4410, Naperville, Illinois 60567-4410
(630) 961-3900
sourcebooks.com

Cataloging-in-Publication Data is on file with the Library of Congress.

Printed and bound in the United States of America.
LSC 10 9 8 7 6 5 4 3 2 1

To everyone who loves MESS. This one's for you.

THE RULING FAMILIES OF
Olympus

CHILDREN OF THE THIRTEEN

THE THIRTEEN

APHRODITE
(née Eris)
Alliances

ACHILLES
Lover of Ares

PSYCHE
Daughter of
Demeter

APOLLO
(née Linus)
Lore

HERMES
Communication

ZEUS

ADONIS
Former lover
of Aphrodite

ARES
(née Helen)
Security

HERA   **POSEIDON**

HEPHAESTUS
(née Theseus)
Inventor

PERSEPHONE
Daughter of
Demeter
Co-leader of
Lower City

HADES

CASSANDRA
Daughter of a
fallen house

ARTEMIS
Huntress

DIONYSUS
Entertainment

PATROCLUS
Lover of Ares

ATHENA
Special Forces

DEMETER
Supply lines

EROS
Son of Aphrodite

PANDORA
Friend of Hephaestus

EURYDICE
Daughter of
Demeter

ORPHEUS
Brother of Apollo

THE INNER CIRCLE
HADES: Leader of Lower City
HERA: (née Callisto) Spouse of ruling Zeus, protector of women
POSEIDON: Leader of Port to Outside World, Import/Export
ZEUS: (née Perseus) Leader of Upper City and the Thirteen

MUSEWATCH

Previously in Olympus...

OLYMPUS'S SWEETHEART GONE WILD!

Persephone Dimitriou shocks everyone by fleeing an engagement with Zeus to end up in Hades's bed!

ZEUS FALLS TO HIS DEATH!

Perseus Kasios will now take up the title of Zeus. Can he possibly fill his father's shoes?

APHRODITE ON THE OUTS

After publicly threatening Psyche Dimitriou for marrying her son Eros, Aphrodite is exiled by the Thirteen. She chooses Eris Kasios to be successor to her title.

ARES IS DEAD...

A tournament will be held to choose the next Ares...and Helen Kasios is the prize.

...LONG LIVE ARES

In a stunning turn of events, Helen Kasios has chosen to compete for her own hand...and she won! We now have *three* Kasios siblings among the Thirteen.

NEW BLOOD IN TOWN!

After losing out on the Ares title, Minos Vitalis and his household have gained Olympus citizenship...and are celebrating with a house party for the ages. We have the guest list, and you'll never guess who's invited!

APOLLO FINDS LOVE AT LAST?

After being ostracized by Olympus for most of her adult life, Cassandra Gataki has snagged one of the Thirteen as her very own! She and Apollo were looking very cozy together at the Dryad.

MURDER FAVORS THE BOLD

Tragedy strikes! Hephaestus was killed by Theseus Vitalis, triggering a little-known law that places *Theseus* as the new Hephaestus. The possibilities are...intriguing.

APHRODITE

EVEN AS A CHILD, I KNEW I WOULDN'T MARRY FOR LOVE. Love is a fairy tale, a fantasy built on lies as fine as gossamer wings. Normal people marry for love. They settle down, do the white-picket-fence thing, have two-point-five children and a dog named Spot. Maybe they're happy in the end. Maybe they're not.

That isn't my path.

I'm marrying for power. For duty. For Olympus.

I tighten the tie of my silk robe and fight the urge to pace around the bridal suite. Just fifteen minutes before, it was filled to the brim with bridesmaids and hair and makeup people, but I sent them away to give myself time to breathe. Two weeks is nowhere near long enough to pull together a wedding worthy of my title, but desperate times call for desperate measures.

My new husband is an enemy to the city that I love. A murderer, who killed the last Hephaestus to gain his title. He and his family are a danger unlike this city has ever known, and with the barrier around Olympus failing, the stakes have never been higher.

Even if I have no doubts about taking this course of action, that doesn't mean it's without cost.

I press my hand to the spot on my hip where a small tattoo is hidden, the skin still tender from the fresh inking yesterday. An anemone flower. I'm not normally so sentimental, but the physical pain alleviates the ache in my chest a little. Or at least that's what I tell myself as I turn to the window overlooking the courtyard where I'll walk down the aisle and sign my life away to Olympus's new Hephaestus.

The rows of seats are half-filled with all the important people in this city. My family is nowhere in evidence; likely they're having some kind of hushed meeting right about now to ensure my groom doesn't attempt to leave me at the altar.

He didn't choose this marriage, after all.

I smile. I don't know what Theseus Vitalis thought he'd accomplish by taking the Hephaestus title by force, but he's a small fish in a big pond here, even if he *is* now one of the Thirteen. He tried to argue against the marriage, but with the rest of the Thirteen in agreement on this course of action, he was essentially out-voted.

I chose this. I will continue to choose this. Growing up as the daughter of one Zeus—and now the sister to another—there was never any question that my marriage would be one of politics.

It also means I'm no stranger to violence and death. And if Minos's people decide they're better off trying to take my title by making him a widower...

I ignore the frisson of something almost like fear slithering down my spine. Ruling Olympus means we're all swimming in blood up to our necks, even if some of my peers pretend otherwise.

I've never had the luxury of a soft fantasy, and I'm not about to start now.

I'll do anything to keep this city safe.

Even this. Especially this. I was *made* for this.

A knock on my door has me turning from the window. I tighten my belt again, pause to ensure my makeup is pristine, and walk to the door. "I said I need some time. Why are you—" I stop short when I see who's on the other side. I thought the ache in my chest was inconvenient earlier. It's nothing compared to the pure agony that flares as I look up into Adonis's dark eyes.

He looks good. Of course he looks good. He always does, even when he's obviously been missing sleep. His dark-brown skin is warm in the early afternoon light, but there are exhaustion lines around his eyes. He doesn't smile. It's fine. I don't deserve his smiles any longer, but I still mourn the loss. "Adonis," I say softly. "What are you doing here?"

"I was invited." I belatedly register that he's wearing a perfectly tailored pale-gray suit. He always dresses well, but this is clearly *event* clothing.

I didn't invite him. I have plenty of capacity for cruelty, but I don't level it at those I care about. At those I...love. I swallow past the awful sensation in my throat. "You shouldn't have come."

He doesn't deny it. Instead, he seems to drink in the sight of me. "It should have been me, Eris."

He's the only person outside my family who uses the name I was born with instead of my title. It used to feel like a secret just between us, but now he might as well have pulled out a knife and stabbed me. Gods, why does this hurt so much? "It was never going to be you." Pain makes my voice harsh. "My brother never would have allowed it." Except that's a cop-out. Zeus didn't force me to marry Hephaestus. *I* decided on this course of action. I square my shoulders. "*I* never would have allowed it."

If I could marry for love, I would have married Adonis without a second thought. Our relationship has never been particularly smooth, but it has been consistent in its inconsistency. He makes me laugh more than any other person in this city, and he makes me feel seen, even if he doesn't always like my more chaotic impulses.

But I am Aphrodite, formerly Eris Kasios, daughter of one Zeus and sister to another. My fate was written the moment I was born.

Adonis's jaw goes tight. "Come with me."

"*What?*"

"Come with me," Adonis repeats. He holds out a broad hand. "I've already bribed Triton. We just have to get to the boundary and he'll see us through. You don't have to do this, Eris. We can leave. We can start a life somewhere outside this fucking city and be *happy*."

The space behind my eyes burns, but I am a Kasios and I learned from a very young age to control my tears. I will not cry now, even if it feels like the broken shards of my heart are grinding to dust against each other. "No."

He doesn't drop his hand. "It doesn't have to be like this."

How can I love him even more now, knowing that he would sacrifice everything for me, even though I would never have asked it of him?

I shake my head slowly. "No," I repeat. "We had something

special, Adonis. Don't ruin it with theatrics." The words are cruel, intentionally so. I swallow hard and push through. If I have to hurt him to keep him safe, then I will.

This is why we could never be endgame. Adonis insists on seeing the best of me, without acknowledging the depths I will descend to in order to keep my people and my city safe. He will always balk about doing what needs to be done, and I don't have the luxury of hesitation.

"Eris—"

"Aphrodite." My grip goes white-knuckled on the door. "I am *Aphrodite*, and you'd damn well better remember it. I chose this, Adonis. I chose...him."

"Don't lie to me. You hate him."

"I would rather take a knife to his throat than slip his ring on my finger."

He flinches. "Then *why?*"

"You know why." I have to pause and lower my voice. "Your parents didn't raise a fool, so stop playing the innocent. Minos has a foothold in the Thirteen now; he isn't going to stop. What happens if we tuck tail and flee, leaving everyone else to pay the price of his ambitions?"

"That's not fair."

"No, it's not. Neither is you showing up here and asking something from me that we both know I can't give." My chest aches so much, I can barely draw a full breath. I refuse to let it show on my face. "What I do, I do to protect this city and everyone in it. Including you."

This marriage is the only way. Friends close and enemies closer and all that. I want Hephaestus to *pay*, and the best way to ensure that happens is if we're sharing a life, a home, a bed. He and his little fucked-up family won't be able to slither about unnoticed when we're in such close quarters. He'll slip up, and when he does, I'll be there to gather all the information I need to ensure Minos doesn't succeed.

In the meantime, I'll keep my new husband so busy chasing his tail that he won't have time to worry about plotting his next move.

I lift my chin. "I am marrying him, Adonis. Nothing you say or do will change that." It's on the tip of my tongue to apologize, but if I'm sorry this is hurting him, I'm not sorry that I'm taking this necessary action. "I think you should leave."

His broad shoulders slump. "You're serious. You're really going to marry him."

"Yes." It hurts to watch him crumple, but it hurts more when he straightens and shakes it off. Anyone with a drop of power in Olympus learns to lie early and often, with word and action and expression.

Adonis has just never bothered to lie to *me* before.

He does it now with a bright grin that doesn't quite reach his eyes. "Point taken, Aphrodite."

Gods, but it hurts to hear *that* name on his lips. "Adonis—"

"See you around. Or not." He turns without another word and walks away.

I tell myself to close the door, to not watch him and hope against hope that he'll turn back and look at me. That this thing between us won't be over, once and for all.

I know better. Despite how he sometimes seems, Adonis is no

innocent. We grew up together. He knows exactly what it takes to grab power in Olympus—and what it takes to keep it.

"Eris?"

I jolt at my sister's voice. I hadn't even heard her approach. "I'm fine," I say automatically. I almost sound like I believe it.

"Was that—" She looks past me to where Adonis is disappearing around the corner.

"I don't want to talk about it." I step back into the room. It takes a full five breaths before I have my emotions under control. The new tattoo on my hip feels like it's beating in time with my heart, but that's just my mind playing tricks. "Help me get into this dress."

Helen—Ares, she's called now—follows me into the room with worry in her hazel eyes. She's already ready, dressed in the tasteful red bridesmaid dress I picked out last week. It took a bit of doing to get our dresses tailored and ready in time, but the designer pulled it off. Not the legendary Juliette—she doesn't like me much—but another recommended by Psyche Dimitriou.

My sister unzips the cover around my dress. "You don't have to do this."

We've had this same conversation half a dozen times since I announced I would marry our new Hephaestus, making our union a condition of the rest of the Thirteen accepting him and the power-hungry Minos into our inner circle.

But Helen is an idealist. I'm still not sure how she managed that while growing up in the same household I did. Having an abusive megalomaniac as a father has a way of bringing things into perspective. Helen has spent her whole life fighting against the role she was assigned at birth.

I've embraced it.

I don't bother to answer her as she takes down the dress and holds it for me to step into. I've planned my image carefully for this event, from the dress that dips low between my breasts and skims the rest of my body, to the lace layered over fabric panels the same color as my skin. It's meant to tease, to tantalize.

This marriage won't be in name only. I won't give my new husband a single piece of ammunition to say it's anything less than legitimate in order to claim an annulment. That includes consummating, no matter how distasteful I find the idea. Hephaestus is attractive in a rough kind of way, but he's crude and about as subtle as a brick through a window. Mutual hate can lead to intense chemistry in the bedroom, but in this case, with how he keeps looking at me like he'd love to see my blood paint the walls, I'll be lucky if we both make it to tomorrow alive.

Helen finishes zipping me up and steps back, her expression unreadable. When we stand side by side, it's achingly clear that we're closely related. We have our mother's coloring, though Helen's hair is lighter than mine with little bits of red catching the late afternoon light. She's prettier, too, though *pretty* isn't the right word. Helen has traffic-stopping beauty. On me, the same features are a little too sharp, a little uncanny.

I prefer it that way. My beauty makes people uncomfortable. Wary.

My new husband won't know what hit him.

HEPHAESTUS

"I DON'T WANT TO DO THIS."

"It's too late for that, my boy." Minos, the foster father I owe everything to, stands before me and adjusts my collar. Almost as if he's a real father at his real son's wedding. The pride on his face is real enough, even if everything else about today is a farce. He pats my shoulder. "With great power comes great responsibility."

Funny how he only remembers the last part of that saying when it suits him. When we came to Olympus, things seemed simple enough. Take the Ares title and secure a spot for the rest of my family in this cesspool of a city. Except nothing has gone to plan since we arrived here. I was eliminated in the second round instead of going on to win the whole tournament. More, that little bitch left my knee permanently fucked up. Not even surgery could fix it.

If we were anyone else, that would have been the end of it.

We're not anyone else, though. *Minos* isn't anyone else. He's a powerful man beholden to someone even more powerful.

A single failure isn't enough to set someone like that back. I'm not convinced he didn't plan for us to miss the mark in the Ares tournament, because he pivoted fast enough afterward.

"You never said that taking the title like this would sink me up to my neck in political bullshit." Political bullshit like marrying that witch Aphrodite. From the moment I saw her, I've hated her and wanted her in equal measures. She's too smart, too gorgeous, too good at getting under my skin. A marriage would be bad enough—it's not something I've ever wanted—but with this pairing, every day will be a battlefield.

"If you'd succeeded at claiming the Ares title, you would have married Helen." An edge creeps into Minos's voice. "You failed, so here we are. Helen would have been a more biddable wife, but the dice have been rolled."

I highly doubt the woman who maimed me would ever be described as *biddable*, but I'm not about to argue. It doesn't matter, anyway. I'm not marrying Helen. I'm marrying Aphrodite. "I didn't fail twice," I snap.

I'm one of the Thirteen most powerful people in Olympus now, but since I killed the last Hephaestus and stepped into his place, there's been nothing but strings tying me down. Can't do this. Can't do that. Have to marry *her*. In all this shit, no one mentioned that I'd lose all free will the moment I lost my name. I fucking hate it.

Minos draws himself up. He's a big man, nearly as broad as me and an inch taller. He's aged in the time we've been here, the lines deeper around his eyes and mouth. All my life, he's been a godlike figure. He's the one who rescued me from that orphanage, the one who taught me everything I know and carved me into the warrior I am today.

I might not agree with all his shit, but I owe him everything.

I start to drag my hand through my hair, but he catches my wrist. "You'll muss yourself."

"I could give a fuck."

His mouth thins. "Appearances matter here, Hephaestus. That's a lesson you need to learn, and fast."

Hephaestus. Not Theseus. The only person who uses my real name anymore is Pandora, and I haven't seen much of her in the last two weeks. My *fiancée* is holding her hostage in the wedding party, though Aphrodite would never be so plain as to say as much. "My name is Theseus."

"Not anymore." Minos looks me up and down. "You're no use to me if you can't do your job. We're not done here in Olympus, not by a long shot, and I can't waste time babysitting you. I have things to take care of."

Things to take care of. Right. Not that he tells me much anymore. My name isn't the only thing I lost when I became Hephaestus. The title put me on the other side of the line from Minos, or at least it feels that way. I can't shake the feeling he doesn't trust me now. "I got it," I finally manage. "I won't disappoint you."

"I know you won't, my boy. Not again." He glances at his watch. "It's time."

A protest rises up my throat, but I swallow it back down. It's too late to turn back. It was too late the moment we came to this fucking city. I follow Minos out into the hallway where my groomsmen are gathered. My foster brothers, the Minotaur and Icarus...and the two men I didn't choose. Eros, a fucking fixer for Olympus. And Zeus, my future brother-in-law. They couldn't have spelled out the threat more clearly than if they'd written it in blood.

Zeus is a white guy with blond hair and blue eyes so cold, they give even me pause. He raises an eyebrow. "Problem?"

"Not at all." Minos is all projected good cheer. "No cold feet to speak of."

"Good." So much threat in four letters. "Let's go."

We file out of the building and into the yard or courtyard or whatever the fuck this space is. It's packed with people and there are flowers everywhere. As if this is a real wedding, instead of a charade.

The rest of the Thirteen are here. I easily pick them out in the first few rows. Artemis, who looks like she wants nothing more than to strike me down where I stand for killing her cousin. Athena, Dionysus, Apollo, Poseidon, all of them serious and stern. I notice that Apollo brought his little girlfriend along.

Every single one of them wants me dead, and here they are, attending my wedding. Have to keep up appearances. This city loves that shit. Demeter, Hades, and Hera round out the guests. Soft. All of them are so fucking *soft*.

The music swells, and the guests turn as one to look back at the fancy door at the back of the space. First comes Ariadne, my foster sister. I don't have much experience with weddings, but I thought the point was to pick ugly bridesmaid dresses so they don't show up the bride. Aphrodite hasn't done that. The deep red looks nice against Ariadne's light-brown skin and the cut is flattering on her curvy body.

My gaze tracks to the reporters clustered just off to the side. Their snapping cameras are audible even with the strange little melody the wedding planner picked for this part of the event.

Pandora follows, and fuck if that doesn't piss me off even more. She looks great. She always looks great. Her dress is a little different from Ariadne's and fits her curves to perfection. She gives me a big smile, as if this whole thing is real instead of a political marriage to my enemy. But then, Pandora has a habit of only seeing the bright side of things. She's my perfect balance in that way because fuck if I can see anything bright about this situation.

I wish I'd had a chance to talk to her in the last couple days. She always has a new perspective to offer, and maybe she knows some secret that will make this marriage anything less than open warfare.

Except that's a fool's dream.

Hermes and Ares follow. Hermes is a petite Black woman wearing an honest-to-gods jumpsuit with her natural curls on full display. She's cute, but I've seen exactly how dangerous she is. Only a fool would see the impish smile and think she's harmless.

Ares is last: a white woman with auburn hair, each move showcasing the kind of grace that she used against me in the Ares competition. I hadn't known she was a gymnast before entering the tournament. Maybe if I had, I wouldn't have underestimated her. I watch her approach with narrowed eyes. She's the reason I walk with a limp now, and I'd like nothing more than to return the favor.

Ares lifts her gaze and catches me staring. She's absolutely stunning, even when glaring. If Aphrodite didn't want to be outshone on her wedding day, she shouldn't have put her sister in the wedding party. Ares is the kind of beautiful that makes me a little sick to my stomach. Features too perfect to be real.

I could fix that for her.

Her gaze flicks to my knee and her smile widens. It's everything I can do to stand perfectly still as she walks past to take up her place on the other side of the altar instead of wrapping my hands around her long throat.

The music changes and then it's Aphrodite's turn.

The air goes charged as she steps through the doors and makes her way slowly down the aisle. She doesn't have the same otherworldly beauty that Ares does, but I can't tear my gaze away from her. Her dress is almost indecent, or at least hints that it could be with one wrong move, and her mass of dark hair is piled on her head in a fancy design that looks like it took hours.

She holds my gaze boldly. It strikes me that she's walking down the aisle alone. Shouldn't her brother be giving her away instead of standing at my back like he wants nothing more than to sink a knife between my ribs before I can say my vows?

There's probably some symbolism here. Olympus seems to love that shit. Nothing is straightforward and no one says what they mean. It wasn't like that back on Aeaea. I won't pretend it was some nice life without pitfalls, but at least people didn't smile to your face and then murder you the first chance they got.

It isn't lost on me that I did exactly that two weeks ago.

Aphrodite stops in front of me. She's already tall, but wears heels that make her even taller than my six feet, two inches. She smiles and it's not a happy expression. I once again have to fight not to tense. I've read the headlines of that gossip site they call news—MuseWatch. No one believes this is a love match. It's a relief in a way.

I don't have to pretend to like my wife.

The priest, an old white guy with all of three hairs on the top of his head, starts going on about the principles that guide a good marriage, but I ignore him and stare at the woman I'm linking my life to.

Not for long. Not if Minos and the others have their way. I can see him out of the corner of my eye, all smiles and pretend joy. My foster father doesn't share my difficulty with lying in both expression and body language. The memory of his words has me straightening.

This is what's required to keep the rest of them thinking we're cowed. Play the part, Theseus.

I follow the priest's instructions to place my left hand under Aphrodite's right. Her skin is soft and smooth, free of the calluses that mark mine. I'm not fool enough to think that means she's not dangerous. She's already proved otherwise.

"Cold feet, Husband," she murmurs.

"No colder than your heart," I snap.

The priest ignores us as he wraps a piece of golden cloth around our hands, binding us together symbolically. He drones on about binding our lives together. It seems to go on forever, the late summer sun beating down on us and making my suit feel too tight. I want to get the fuck out of here, to move until I stop feeling like an animal in a trap.

He finally lifts our hands high. "What the gods have bound, no one should separate."

And then it's over.

We'll have to wear the bindings until the reception, which seems like a good time to attempt an assassination, when both parties are awkwardly tied to each other and at least one's dominant hand is out of commission. Another useless Olympus tradition.

My skin prickles as we walk back down the aisle together. None of the people watching us seem overly happy with this event. That's to be expected, but I didn't anticipate it making me feel so fucking vulnerable. I hate it.

We step through the doors, but Aphrodite doesn't stop there. She practically drags me through the hall, past the ballroom where part of the reception will be held, and through a nondescript door.

My eyes are still adjusting to the dimness when she spins and shoves me against the wall. It's awkward because our bound hands mean she comes with me, landing against my chest.

"You fucking bastard," she snarls.

Just like that, I know exactly why she's pissed. Apparently my little invitation found its home. *Good.* I relax back against the wall and look up at her. "Problem, Wife?"

"You know exactly what the problem is." She grabs for my chin, but I catch her wrist before she can make contact. She narrows her eyes. "Release me."

"Call it an overabundance of caution." I tighten my grip a little when she yanks on it. "Wouldn't want you clawing up my pretty face with those nails." Now that I have a better look at them, I'm not at all surprised to see that they're sharp enough to serve as weapons in their own right. She's not going to be ripping out any throats, but she could probably take an eye or two.

Aphrodite flips a switch so fast it makes my head spin, all her fury tucked away between one heartbeat and the next. She goes soft against me, her smile still cold as ice. "You're not pretty, Hephaestus. You never know; a few scars might be an improvement. They've certainly served the Minotaur well."

"Pass." My wires are getting crossed by this interaction. She came in like an attack, but now she's pressed against me like a lover, her breasts nearly spilling out of her dress. Our faces are even, close enough to kiss. I don't like how fast she changed things up on me. I don't trust it. "Back off."

"Why, Husband? We'll be consummating this marriage shortly. We could get started now."

Just like that, I get it. The anger was the slip, not this weird sexual tension that flares between us like poison. I lower her arm and pin it to the small of her back, pressing us closer yet. It's a fight to keep my body from responding to her. I'm only human, and Aphrodite might be a snake, but she's a gorgeous one.

She's also just confirmed exactly what I suspected...and handed me the ultimate weapon in the process.

I lean down a little to speak directly into her ear. "Did your little boyfriend pay you a visit, Wife?"

She tenses for half a beat and then relaxes. A quick recovery, but we're pressed too tightly together for me to miss it. "I don't know what you're talking about."

"Liar." Being this close is a mistake, but I like that she can't lie effectively like this. It makes me want to press my advantage. "Did he offer to save you? To take you away from big, bad me?"

Again, a quick tensing following by a forced relaxation. Aphrodite releases a slow breath. "Adonis was a fun little fling who let his emotions get the best of him. He doesn't matter."

I laugh. "Cute story. I saw the way you looked at him at the house party. Seems like love." If I have to be in this marriage—and I do—then I fully intend to make Aphrodite pay for cornering me in the first place. Political machinations may have forced me into this, but I'm determined to end up on top. No matter how formidable she is, she's got one glaring weak spot.

And I fully intend to exploit him.

APHRODITE

The reception stretches on for an eternity. Even though I carefully hide what I'm feeling, I can't stop the sinking in my stomach. I played right into my new husband's hands. A mistake, and one that will be costly. I can't afford to underestimate Hephaestus, and reacting to Adonis unexpectedly showing up before my wedding to the enemy? I might as well have waved a red flag in front of a bull. My husband will be charging in no time. I wish I could trust Adonis to avoid that pitfall, but emotions make everything messy and I hurt him badly by making this move.

He's not the only one.

All through the speeches and cake cutting and first dance, Hephaestus keeps that satisfied smirk in place. It makes me want to...

I manage to extract myself and part ways with my husband to grab a glass of champagne off a waiter's tray. Now's the time to follow him back to our seats at the center of the bridal party table, but I need a moment, so I drift over to the doorway leading back outside. The air has cooled with the sun setting, giving the first hint of the bite winter will bring.

I close my eyes and inhale deeply. The desire to strike back at Hephaestus after that little altercation is nearly overwhelming, but I haven't made it to where I am now by acting impulsively. Mostly.

Right now, the only thing that matters is getting through the rest of the reception and then managing to resist the impulse to make myself a widow on my wedding night. Hephaestus is an enemy, but he's a known one. If Minos thinks he's getting his way, he will let his guard down. Hopefully.

Worrying about Minos and his plans can wait for tomorrow.

Even knowing that is the smartest course of action, I can't help searching the faces of the guests gathered in the ballroom. Adonis isn't here—I *know* he isn't—but that doesn't stop me from looking despite myself.

He won't have left Olympus; not without me. His life is here. His family and fortune and a whole city's worth of admirers. He has a way of drawing people to him wherever he goes, his charm and beauty making him the darling of MuseWatch and a good portion of the legacy families. Not enough to help him secure one of the titles of the Thirteen for himself, but Adonis lives a charmed life.

None of that really excuses what I've done.

Or the fact that I didn't talk to him about it first.

I smother the guilt trying to take root in my chest. Adonis knew what he was getting when we started this ill-fated on-again, off-again relationship several years ago. I was a Kasios before I became Aphrodite.

I drain my champagne glass and tuck all the messy emotions away. It doesn't matter what could have been because this is my reality. I will not give my new husband and his family even an ounce of satisfaction from thinking that I'm heartbroken.

Being heartbroken would require me to have a heart.

I make my way toward the table with the wedding party. It's slow going because everyone wants to stop the bride and wish me congratulations or use thirty seconds of their time to try to weasel closer to the power Aphrodite holds. My title's responsibilities include making marriage matches, and arranged marriages are one of Olympus's favorite ways to consolidate power.

Again and again, my attention is drawn back to the bridal party. They've mixed up a bit. My people—Hermes, Eros, and my brother and sister—on one side and Hephaestus's—the Minotaur, Icarus, Ariadne, and Pandora—on the other. It's the latter who interests me.

In the brief time I've known their cursed household, Pandora seems to be the only one whom my lovely husband does more than tolerate. Even now, he's leaning over Icarus to speak to her and there's an actual smile on his face. It's strange and soft, and it makes me want to grab the nearest piece of silverware and gouge his eyes out.

Instead, I focus on Pandora. She's a pretty little thing—short and soft with the kind of curves a person can sink their hands into. Smooth light-brown skin and a thick fall of wavy black hair complete the picture. But what really sets her apart is the way she lights up a room when she walks into it. Her laugh fills a space in a way I've never experienced before. I added her to my side of the wedding party out of spite because I knew it would bother Hephaestus, but I actually found myself enjoying being around her.

If her attitude is a mask, it's the best I've ever seen.

Hephaestus sees me coming and sits back abruptly, his smile falling away and clouds gathering in his dark eyes. I dislike how attractive he is. Medium-brown skin and dark-red hair that's actually trimmed properly for this event. His muscular frame marked him as a warrior before his injury, and I have no doubt that even with his injured knee, he can do plenty of damage.

He killed the last Hephaestus, after all.

I slip around the table and take my place at his side. I can do this. I chose this. The reception is all but over, and then all that's left is to consummate the marriage. After that, I can put the next stage of my plan into motion. For the next hour or two, I simply need to endure. Even knowing it's coming, the rest of the reception passes in a blur of congratulations.

And then it's time to see us off.

Hephaestus has only just moved into the penthouse he inherited with the title—likely because his predecessor's people made the transition difficult—and I have no intention of letting him into *my* home. As a result, we've booked a hotel room for the night.

It was the simplest solution, but I'm regretting the short trip now. The remaining wedding guests line the hall, tossing flowers before us, a perfect blend of red—roses and carnations and poppies. It creates a beautiful stage for us to walk down, holding hands as if we're a real husband and wife, instead of enemies. Distantly, I note the photographer taking pictures furiously. Helen will go over which to release tonight, and the rest will be sent to me afterward.

What's the point in a wedding as a distraction if everyone isn't talking about it?

My sister appears at the end of the hall and pulls me into a quick hug. "Be safe," she whispers. Something cold presses into my hand.

I glance down and nearly laugh. It's a small knife, wickedly curved and designed to fit perfectly in the palm of my hand. "What am I supposed to do with this?"

"He's a murderer, Eris." She hugs me again, speaking directly into my ear. "Do what you have to."

I don't tell her not to worry. Truthfully, this wedding was a gamble. It could be as much a trap for me as I intend it to be for Hephaestus. If one of his family decides to kill me and trigger the assassination clause—the carefully guarded, fucked-up bit of old Olympian lore that gained Hephaestus his place in the Thirteen—they would be entitled to my title. Being alone with him is asking for an ambush.

But that danger goes both ways.

"I'll be safe."

"Don't make promises you can't keep." She steps back and

then our brother is there. He doesn't hug me; he's not really the hugging type.

He just looks at me and nods. "Do what you have to do."

Helen makes an angry sound, but she's never really understood Perseus—now Zeus—the way I do. He's ruthless to a fault and clinically cold, both traits our bastard of a father encouraged, but he's never railed against his role in this city. Not like Helen. Not like Hercules. I wince a little at the thought of our youngest brother. He's not here. He was invited, of course, but he's made it clear he's not returning to Olympus, even if our father is gone.

I try not to hold that against him. He's happy and that's enough for the others. It has to be enough for me, too.

"I always do what I have to." I turn away from what remains of my family and walk with my new husband to the elevator that will take us up to the honeymoon suite. The doors close and I'm alone with Hephaestus for the first time.

I don't know what I expect. Threats or more taunting, perhaps. He says nothing. The silence unnerves me, but this is a weapon I'm familiar with. My father didn't use it often, but when he did, it was so bad I almost preferred his fists. He would ignore us when we made him a special shade of angry, would act as if he couldn't see or hear us for hours and sometimes days. Perseus always seemed to find that almost a relief, but it made me wild with fury. When I was fifteen, I destroyed an entire room while shrieking at my father, and he sat there staring mildly out the window and drinking his coffee the entire time.

I shudder. I'm not fifteen any longer. Control has been hard-won, but it exists. The doors open before I can make a liar out of myself, and I charge forward, leaving Hephaestus to follow behind.

The honeymoon suite is lovely. Everything about this historic hotel is lovely; it's why I picked it for the wedding. That and the fact that every member of my family going back generations has been married here.

In my father's case, multiple times.

I stare at the tasteful cream decor and my stomach twists. Best not to think about that. Or the fact that my brother and sister-in-law occupied this same room for *their* political marriage back in May. I shudder. Tradition is a trap, but I've gone too far to back out now.

Hephaestus steps around me and makes a beeline to the kitchenette. There's a bottle of whiskey there with a jaunty bow around it that seems to be made entirely of glitter. Even before he picks up the card and snorts, I know who it's from.

Hermes. Up until two weeks ago, I considered her one of my best friends in this world. Now, I don't know what to believe. My brother thinks she's a traitor, and she hasn't done much to disabuse him of the belief. I still can't quite believe that she means this city harm or that she's really allied with Hephaestus's family. Surely there's some game afoot. Surely she didn't feed Minos information with the intention of bringing Olympus and the Thirteen down.

Maybe that belief makes me naive. I've been accused of worse.

I swallow past the complicated feelings the thought of her brings and cross to join Hephaestus at the counter. "Give me that."

"I've got it." He rips at the bow almost violently.

I barely resist the urge to snatch the bottle out of his hands and pick up the card instead. Hermes's sprawling handwriting greets me.

Enjoy the wedding night, you two lovebirds!

I sigh and toss it aside. "Always playing games."

"She's an Olympian. It's what your people do." He finally gets the bow off and drops it to the counter with a disgusted grunt. The bottle top soon joins it. Hephaestus takes a long pull directly from the bottle. Another time, I'd make a biting comment about his manners, but right now I need the same fortification he obviously does.

No. Damn it, *no.*

I am not some weak princess, married off against her will. This wedding is by my design. If this were a story, I'd be the cunning queen, or even the evil witch. I am not helpless and I am not innocent.

If Hephaestus needs liquid courage, that means *I'm* the one coming out on top of today, no matter his nasty little trick with Adonis earlier. I still take the bottle from his hand and lift it to my lips, holding his gaze all the while. One swallow, then two. I stop myself there and set it on the counter with a clink. "Shall we, dear husband?"

He shakes his head slowly. "You really are Olympus's wh—"

"I'm going to stop you there." It takes everything I have to resist clenching my fists...and perhaps driving one right into his face. "This marriage can be as awful or as pleasant as you choose." Lies. I have every intention of making each day a new torment for my *dear husband.* Any information I gather is valuable, and my brother has more plans in place to find out exactly what Minos is up to. We will attack this problem—this enemy—from several different directions.

If I can make my new husband suffer in the process? All the better.

He looks at me as if he'd like to toss me out the nearest window. The feeling is entirely mutual.

I resign myself to a torturous experience and turn for the bedroom. "Let's get this over with."

HEPHAESTUS

I TAKE ANOTHER LONG PULL FROM THE WHISKEY BOTTLE before I follow Aphrodite down the hall to the ridiculously lavish bedroom. Everything about this place reflects Olympus as a whole. Wealth invested in useless things to create an aesthetic. Appearances are all that matter to the citizens of this city, and the longer I'm here, the less connected with reality I feel.

It doesn't matter. I don't need reality. I have Minos's plans. It should be a victory beyond measure that a pissed-off orphan is now one of the thirteen most powerful people in one of the world's most untouchable cities. I expected that feeling, anticipated it. This is what I've always wanted, after all. Power enough not to be fucked with.

I didn't anticipate that power would feel like a steel trap closing around my leg.

Growing up, I always thought power meant freedom. Being brought into Minos's household as a teenager only cemented that belief. He answers to one person, and even then, it's rarely. I wanted that for myself, wanted it so desperately, I could taste it.

The last two weeks have shown me how wrong that belief is. I haven't made a choice for myself since becoming Hephaestus. There's more red tape than I could have dreamed, and it all culminates with this fucking marriage and this fucking night.

Aphrodite takes her hair down from its fancy design, pin by pin. She doesn't look over, doesn't even act like I'm in the room.

Now's the time to take charge of the situation, to show her that I'm not some weakling that she can manipulate and steamroll. But I can't quite make my body move as I watch dark strand after dark strand fall. Her hair is long, reaching halfway down her back in a faint wave. It's not naturally wavy. Or at least it wasn't during the house party Minos threw two weeks ago.

She sets the last pin on the dresser and runs her fingers through her hair. "That's better. Now, come unzip me."

I jolt. "The fuck?"

Aphrodite turns to face me, a mocking smile on her crimson lips. "Darling, look at me. In case you didn't notice, this dress hardly allows for much movement."

Against my better judgment, I drag my gaze over her body. The dress truly is a masterpiece. It leaves little to the imagination, and if she's built just as sharp in body as she is in face, even I can't deny that Aphrodite is beautiful. The lace flows over her body, drawing my attention to the curve of her small breasts, the slight flare of her waist, the miles and miles of legs.

"Turn around." I hardly sound like myself.

She gives me one last long look and then turns. It's not better without her dark eyes on me, because the mirror over the dresser hides nothing. She should be afraid of me, should be wondering what I might do now that we're alone, and yet I'm the one who's almost tentative as I move to stand behind her.

The zipper is a tiny little thing, but I'm used to this sort of shit after growing up with Pandora as a best friend. Women's clothing is fucking impractical, and Pandora likes to pick the most impractical of all. I hope she listened to me about going home with the family tonight. She was a little tipsy when we left, and she gets mischievous when she drinks. So far, I've managed to keep her out of trouble since we came to Olympus, but this is the first night we won't be spending together in longer than I can remember.

Fuck, I can't think about that.

She's smart. She won't do anything dangerous. After the media frenzy that's followed us around since I became Hephaestus, she has to know better than to be caught out alone. The reporters and paparazzi are unrelenting. I don't know how these fuckers live like this.

Pandora isn't part of Minos's plan, which means she's expendable in his eyes. Or she would be if her safety wasn't so fucking important to me. He'll have a security detail on her. He promised.

"Problem, Husband?"

Godsdamn it, but I can't afford to think about Pandora right now. She'll make it through the night and I'll clean up any mess tomorrow. Right now, I need to focus on the danger closer at hand.

My wife.

It feels unbearably intimate to grab that ridiculous zipper and drag it slowly down the line of Aphrodite's spine. The fabric parts, revealing smooth pale skin unmarred by scars. It's nice to be an Olympian princess, apparently.

The dress slithers off her, and she makes no move to stop it.

She's wearing a pair of white lace panties beneath it and nothing else. Aphrodite turns to face me and leans against the dresser. "Your turn."

I've never found the sweet, shy virginal thing particularly attractive, but her brazen attitude still sets me back on my heels. She's been driving this encounter from the beginning. The wedding was all her doing, right down to the little details. And now this.

I'm fucking done.

"We do this my way." I close the distance between us, pinning her between me and the dresser. She's still wearing her heels, and fuck if it doesn't irritate me beyond all reason to have her face even with mine.

Maybe that's why I kiss her. It's pure instinct, wanting to put her in her place, to remind her that she's not the one in charge of this shit.

I should have known it wouldn't be that easy.

She meets me halfway, our kiss immediately turning into a war of tongue and teeth. I dig my fist into her hair and wrap my other arm around her waist, jerking her against me. Fuck, but she feels good. I *hate* how good she feels.

I spin us around and half carry her to the bed. My instincts are all fucked up. I want to punish her, to make this fast and rough and selfishly chase my own pleasure...but I can't quite make myself stop kissing her.

Aphrodite snakes a hand between us and cups my cock through my pants. She breaks the kiss long enough to say, "Someone's happy to see me."

No use arguing. I'm hard enough that I'm half-surprised I haven't split the seam. My wires always did get crossed with anger and fucking. "Don't let it go to your head."

"Too late." She strokes me slowly, a wicked grin curving her lips. Again, trying to take control of this. Again, it's far too tempting to let her.

Instead, I drop her on the bed.

She lets out a startled yip, but I'm already moving, grabbing her around the hips and flipping her onto her stomach. I drag her back until her feet meet the ground. This view isn't any less distracting. She's got a tight little ass that makes me want to…

I yank her panties down her legs, cursing a bit when she lifts her hips to help me. The heels keep her ass high in the air. I can't quite stop myself from palming her, squeezing her flesh. She moans a bit and spreads her legs. "Now."

It would be simple as fuck to free my cock and take her like this. Hard and fast. Part of the wedding preparations were both of us getting tested and her providing evidence she's on birth control.

But a piece of paper is easy enough to forge. I've done it myself in the past, though not with *this* kind of shit. Marrying this woman is one thing. Having a child with her? The thought makes me take a step back.

I don't want kids. I'm self-aware enough to know I'd be a shit parent. Fuck, look at all the horrific shit Pandora and I went through in that orphanage before Minos swept in like some fucked-up fairy godfather. Most importantly, I don't even *like* kids. It's not worth the risk that she'd trap me like this.

"Condom," I manage.

Aphrodite huffs out a breath. "Now you're just stalling." She continues before I can tell her in no uncertain terms that I'm not fucking her without one. "Top drawer."

I don't ask how she knows that. It doesn't matter. I stalk to the dresser and yank it open. Sure enough, there's a sealed condom box there. I look it over, trying to think clearly even through the blood rushing through my head and cock. My concentration takes a nosedive when I glance at Aphrodite and find her hand between her thighs, working her pussy. I can see the glisten of her wetness coating her fingers from here.

Fuck this, I'm done waiting.

I tear open the package and rip one of the condoms off. It takes all of a few seconds to get my cock out and roll it down my length. I don't take off the rest of my clothes. This situation is out of control enough without losing that last bit of a barrier. It's already clear I won't put Aphrodite in her place like this, but I'll keep my word and consummate this sham of a marriage.

Back at the bed, I lift her hips higher and grab her hand. She tenses. "What...oh." I press it to my cock, letting her feel the condom.

"You won't trap me like this."

She laughs, low and throaty. "As if I need to. We're already married, *Husband*."

She's right. I hate that she's right.

I knock her hand away and press against her entrance. Once again, Aphrodite doesn't give me a chance to decide how I want to play this. She shoves back against me, sheathing me to the hilt.

A choked curse escapes despite my best efforts. She clamps around me, tight enough that I almost lose it right then and there. It's been too long since I was with someone. That's the only reason I'm in danger of coming so fast. It's not because of the sexy as fuck flare of her waist that seems made for my hands. Or the way she tilts her hips up to take me deeper yet.

I grab her hips, holding us sealed together, as I fight for control. This is only the first battle in a war that might last years. I can't let her defeat me. "Feels good, doesn't it?"

"One cock is as good as another." The words are harsh, but her voice is too breathy to really pull it off. "You could be anyone."

Smarter to think of it that way. To pretend she's some stranger I will never have to see it again. To let myself enjoy this pleasure, even a little bit. Almost against my will, my attention lands on the diamond on her ring finger. This isn't a stranger. This is my wife. I'd be a fool to forget that. "But I'm not just anyone, Wife. It's your husband's cock you're about to come all over." I thrust a little, vindicated when she gives a choked curse in response.

I really should know better by now. She's not one to take any kind of dominance passively, because of fucking course she isn't. She might be pinned on my cock, but that doesn't stop her from wresting the control right out of my hands. "Yeah, I am about to come. No thanks to you," she gasps. She still has her hand between her thighs, stroking her clit even as her pussy flutters around me. Little moans slip free, the sounds surprisingly sweet for such a vicious witch.

Holy fuck, she really is coming.

My body takes over, even as my mind grapples with this surreal experience. I drive into her, needing to get deeper, to take her harder. Her moans grow louder, and she's arching her back, angling to take me the same way I'm taking her.

Three strokes in, I realize I don't give a fuck about lasting. She's ensured her own pleasure. I'm a sap if I do anything else. I curse and jerk her back onto my cock, giving in to the pressure building in my balls. I come so hard, it makes me dizzy. I want to keep fucking her, to drive into her again and again until...

Until I don't know what.

I stare down at the point where we're joined. Sex is sex, and its importance begins and ends with having a good time. Except this isn't sex. I just passed the point of no return. There can be no annulment now.

We're well and truly married.

I withdraw from her, careful to keep the condom in place, and stagger into the bathroom. I'm no steadier once I've cleaned up, so I splash some cold water on my face. There's the rest of the night to get through, and though I have no intention of fucking my wife again, I still have to learn to live with her.

Except when I step back into the bedroom, it's to find her pulling on a different dress. It's a vibrant red and barely covers her ass and tits. It's also tight enough that I can tell she's not wearing a thing under it.

"What are you doing?"

She brushes past me, still wearing those damned heels, and finger-combs her hair in front of the mirror. "Our business is done for the night, dear husband. I'm off to have some fun."

Alarm bells peal through my head. This isn't going at all like I thought it would. She doesn't seem affected by the fact we had sex at all.

Not that *I'm* affected by the sex at all. More that past partners have usually wanted to talk or cuddle or some shit after the fact. Maybe go for round two or three. They aren't dressed after fucking and taking off the first chance they get. "Running away?"

She pauses. "It's really cute that you think you scare me."

"Don't I? We're alone. No big brother to protect you." I don't know why I say it. Minos gave me clear orders, and those orders don't include making waves with my new wife. I'm supposed to settle into Hephaestus and secure this power base.

Aphrodite watches me in the mirror, her gaze mocking. "Aw, you think I need protection. Cute." She turns, and I'm only human. My attention drops to where the top dips until I can almost see her dusky-rose nipples. She snaps her fingers by her face to drag my eyes up. "If you planned on murdering me, you would have done it before the wedding and that lackluster sex."

Lackluster—

She tugs on the hem of her dress, and I'm distracted by the possibility of her breasts popping free. She smooths her hands over the slick-looking fabric. "There."

"You can't go out like that."

I realize my mistake the moment she smiles. "On the contrary, I can do whatever I damn well please." She flicks a glance at my hips. At my *cock.* "Or did you think that sad little performance was enough to leave me comatose? Sorry, darling, but I have entirely too much energy to stay cooped up here with you."

She blows past me again, leaving me to hurry after her, feeling like a fool. "Stop."

"I don't think I will." She pauses at the door and blows me a kiss. "Have a good night, *Husband.* I certainly plan to."

PANDORA

THE RECEPTION CONTINUES AFTER THESEUS—
Hephaestus, I have to remember that—and his new bride go
upstairs. I'm worried about him. He's always been too locked
down, and Minos fostering him hasn't done anything but make
that worse. Not that he listens to me when it comes to his fucked-up
little family.

I'm sure I'm supposed to be somewhere, but like every other time
Theseus is occupied with Minos's tasks, I'm immediately ignored.
Normally, I appreciate the reprieve. Minos doesn't like me and he's
not very good at hiding that fact, for all that he's an excellent liar.

I've never felt so adrift before this moment, though.

I drain my champagne glass. Too much alcohol, but I think I
can be excused. It's a *party*, after all.

"Pandora?"

I turn, tipping a little, to find a pretty Black woman standing
a few feet away. She's wearing a deep-purple dress that flatters her
light-brown skin. It takes my brain a second to place her familiar

face. "Eurydice." She was one of Minos's guests at that ill-fated house party. At least *she* survived it. I look around. "Where's your handsome shadow?"

"Ah." She tucks a loose curl behind her ear. "Charon is around here somewhere. He's my ride back to the lower city when this is over."

"Your ride," I repeat slowly. I could have sworn they were dating, but apparently I was wrong. "Right."

She stalls for a moment, but gives herself a shake. "Actually, that's why I came over. I know you're relatively new in town. I thought you might want to see the lower city."

Well, if that's not a trap, then I don't know what is. I snag another glass of champagne. I know I should stop, but the last two weeks have been a special kind of torture. Theseus barely has time to talk to me, and while I don't have a problem with his new wife in theory, the reality is that she didn't agree to marry him because she's madly in love with my best friend. She did it because he's made himself Olympian Enemy Number One. Theseus is going to get himself killed and he doesn't seem to care.

If I go back to Minos's home—not my home, it will never be that—all I'll do is pace my room and worry. There are far too many hours until dawn, and each promises to be filled with fears about everything that could go wrong on this wedding night.

I try to sip this glass slowly, but give up before it touches my lips. "Thanks, but no thanks."

Instead of leaving in a huff, she smiles. "I'm not talking about the tourist route, Pandora. I'm talking about the kind of stuff only locals know about." She steps closer. She's wearing a light floral perfume that is just as lovely as she is. "I'm talking about a very special kind of club that caters to people with very special tastes."

I blink. Of all the pitches I expected to hear, this didn't make the list. "You're talking about a kink club."

"Well..." She looks around, but there's no one paying us the least bit of attention. That, in and of itself, is suspicious. During the last two weeks of whirlwind wedding planning, I have existed under a microscope. I could have told them it's a lost cause; I don't know anything useful about Minos's plans, let alone have an acting role in them. Instead, I endured the stares and just smiled harder.

Eurydice leans down. She's very tall, nearly as tall as Theseus's new wife. Just as pretty, too, though Eurydice's beauty is more traditional and less feral than Aphrodite's. "Yes, it's a kink club. Very exclusive. Very expensive."

If this is a trap, it's the strangest trap I've ever encountered. I finish my glass and reach for another. Eurydice catches my wrist. "I think you've had enough. If you drink too much, you can't participate."

I laugh. I can't help it. "Honey, I'm buzzed, but I'm nowhere near drunk enough to agree to a sex party with a bunch of people who'd like to run me over with a car."

"That's fair." She releases my wrist. "Participation is absolutely optional. You can come watch, if you like. See if it's your kind of thing."

She's being too insistent. I peer up at her. "Are you coming on to me?"

"No." She looks away and then back at me. "I mean, you're really attractive, but I'm not exactly over my ex, so I'm not great

company these days. But, if you'll forgive me for being blunt, you
don't seem like a total asshole like the rest of your household.
You're obviously sticking around for the long term, so there's no
reason we can't get to know each other."

Yeah, it's still a trap.

The problem is...I'm not sure I care. It's a distraction, and at
this point, I'll take what I can get. I'm reasonably sure that the
Olympians won't hurt me, not when they still think they can coax
secrets with honey.

Besides, I'm curious about this kink club.

"I don't know anything useful." I peer around, searching for
another waiter with champagne. "If you're going to, like, throw
me in a kinky dungeon and torment me for information about
Minos and the rest of them, it's a waste of everyone's time. I'm not
part of the family." The words taste bitter, but that can't be right.
Minos only pulled me out of that orphanage alongside Theseus
because that was Theseus's condition for allowing the fostering.
We were a package deal, and Minos has barely tolerated me in the
years since. He puts a good face on it for Theseus's benefit, but
I see the way he looks at me when he thinks no one is watching.

If he can find a way to remove me to gain full control over
Theseus, he will do it in a heartbeat.

"I don't know how you think we do things here in Olympus,
but torture is a bit extreme." I give her a long look and she sighs.
"Okay, I won't pretend the people in power here aren't capable
of that kind of thing, but I honestly just thought you could use
a friend."

Damn it, I'm going to say yes. This is so ridiculous. "You've convinced me. But only if we go now and only if there's alcohol there." I'm not normally a big drinker, but I think I can be forgiven tonight. It's the only thing that numbs the pit of worry that opened up in my stomach when Theseus agreed to marry Aphrodite.

No, that's not the truth. It started earlier, when Minos announced his plan to take us all to Olympus, to use the Ares title to secure a spot among the Thirteen for either Theseus or the Minotaur. Something that seemed simple enough on the surface, but nothing Minos does is ever simple. Sure enough, look at us now.

Eurydice's eyes go wide. "Sure. Okay. Let's go."

The champagne is really starting to kick in, which is the only excuse I need to snag a full bottle on our way out the door. Charon, a tall white guy with dark hair, broad shoulders, and the suspicious look of bodyguards everywhere, falls in behind us as we leave. He manages to get in front of us to open the back door of a nondescript black town car, though.

It's only when we're driving away from the hotel that I wonder if I should have told someone where I was headed. Not Minos, but Ariadne or Icarus. *Whoops.* I dig my phone out of my tiny purse and shoot off a text to both letting them know about my poor choices. I don't know if either have their phones on them now, but they will before the end of the night.

Eurydice keeps up smooth small talk that requires little of me as I drink my way through the bottle I took. I slump back against the seat. "I'm not normally like this." I feel downright morose right now, instead of my normal sunny self. It will come back. It always does. But not until I see for myself that Theseus is okay.

"I, ah, kind of noticed." Her hazel eyes are kind. "Are you in love with him?"

That surprises a laugh out of me. "What? No. Not like you mean. I mostly prefer women." I take a long drink from the bottle. "But Theseus is my best friend and I love him. It's just not like *that* with us." We did try it once when we were teenagers, since it seemed a natural progression of how much we care about each other, but it was a disastrous experience and we both agreed that there is no *next level* for our friendship.

"I see." She motions and I hand her the bottle. "You aren't like the rest of them."

"Sweet words will get you everywhere." The farther we travel from the hotel and the mess contained there, the better I can breathe. This is fine. This is better than fine. "Look, you're cute and this is a fun little field trip, but I meant it about not knowing anything worthwhile. Also, not a single one of them will give even a penny in ransom." Theseus doesn't believe in ransom, though he'd come for me and kill everyone responsible.

Eurydice laughs. "Again, not kidnapping, torturing, or otherwise harming you. You just looked like you needed to get out of there. I understand that urge, so I thought I'd help you out. That's all."

She's lying, but I don't mind. Everyone lies. Once you accept that, you get really good at reading between the lines. "So you're taking me to Hades's famous sex club?"

"It's hardly *famous*." She makes a choked sound. "And that's my brother-in-law you're talking about."

I twist in the seat to face her fully. I'd much rather talk about this than about myself. "You know, your sisters seem the

overprotective sort, and that's not even getting into your mother."
Talk about a nightmare. "I'm surprised they let their precious
baby sister attend a place like that."

"Oh. That." She waves it away. "They don't know."

"*What?*"

"They don't know," she repeats. Eurydice smiles. "So, you
see, now you have a secret of mine."

Sharing simple secrets to promote the sharing of deeper secrets
is a trick as old as time. I ignore the impulse to do exactly that;
it's just the alcohol talking. "Rumor has it that you're living in the
same house as your sister and Hades. How could they possibly not
know that you're playing tourist in his sex dungeon?"

She shoots a look at the back of Charon's head. He doesn't
appear to be paying us the least bit of attention, but he's too close to
miss any of it. Eurydice clears her throat. "I'm not allowed to participate or go into the club without Charon as an...escort. I just get
to watch on the nights Persephone and Hades aren't down there."

"I see," I say slowly. That's an interesting piece of information that I don't bother to file away because I have no interest in
helping Minos do whatever he plans to do to Olympus. Murder
and mayhem and chaos. He's a bastard and a half, and I have no
doubt that he'd sacrifice Theseus at the altar of his ambition.

Theseus already got hurt. I don't want him to get dead, too.

I take another long drink of the champagne bottle. My stomach
isn't feeling too great. Or maybe that's because we're crossing over
the bridge to the lower city. Apparently there's a barrier here similar
to the one that surrounded Olympus, keeping it separate from the
rest of the world. Magic or some fancy tech that might as well be

magic? I have no idea. I suppose it doesn't matter. The alcohol fuzzes my brain, making it hard to tell if it's the same sensation I felt entering the city or if I've just drunk too much.

I mean, I've definitely drunk too much.

It doesn't take long for the car to roll to a stop in front of a nondescript gray building. I frown out the window at it. "This looks like a place you take people to murder them."

Eurydice gives a choked laugh. "The other entrance is in my sister's house, and *that* will create more questions than I want to answer. Come on." She slips out of the car, leaving me to follow.

I'm distantly aware of Charon coming around the car and following us up to the large door. I'm so far past buzzed that I start to list to the side, and he has to move fast to catch me. He slips an arm around my waist and keeps me on my feet. "You sure about this, Eurydice?"

"Yes." She opens the door. "Come on."

The room is kept atmospherically dim in a way I might appreciate on a different night. Not right now, when the strangely reflecting light on the ceiling makes me dizzy. I try to focus on Eurydice's back, but *everything* is a bit watery right now. "I drank too much."

"You're safe here, Pandora." She leads the way through a series of couches and chairs, circling a low dais in the center of the room. The place is packed, and the couples and throuples and moreples in various states of undress and sexual revelry only add to my dizziness. I'm pathetically grateful when Eurydice stops in front of a private booth tucked back against a wall. Charon helps me slide into it, but I keep sliding, slumping down against

Eurydice. She laughs a little and helps me right myself. "She'll be here soon. But let's get you some water in the meantime."

She?

Time ceases to have meaning. Water appears at some point, and Eurydice coaxes me to drink a little, but my stomach is still swirly in a really worrisome manner. Damn it, I shouldn't have drunk so much. I never do this. I have fun, but never recklessly. Even before I came to Olympus, I knew better, but these days the stakes are so much higher.

My blinks are getting longer and longer when the room seems to darken. I blearily look up, only to realize it hasn't. There's a woman standing over our table in a gorgeous red dress that screams *sex*. It coats her lean body lovingly, kissing the curves of her breasts and hips. As she shifts, it presses to the mound of her pussy in a way that makes my mouth water. From this angle, with her height, I can almost see beneath the short hem, and that's probably wrong, but I can't quite remember why.

Then my gaze reaches her face and my stomach drops. This isn't some stranger. No, the woman I was just ogling is Aphrodite.

Theseus's wife.

APHRODITE

"DID YOU DRUG HER?" I PEER DOWN AT A NEARLY PASSED out Pandora. When I pulled Eurydice aside at the reception—wanting a little revenge after the stunt my husband pulled with Adonis—I told her to get Pandora to the club. I didn't expect *this*.

"No, I didn't drug her." Eurydice rolls her eyes. She's nursing a glass of white wine and surveying the people in the club behind me. It's late enough that there are plenty of people in various stages of fucking, putting on quite the show. She meets my gaze. "She drank too much because she's worried about Hephaestus."

I refuse to feel even a twinge of guilt. Best I can tell, Pandora exists outside Minos's cozy little family unit and is only there because of her connection with Hephaestus. It doesn't matter. She's here, which means she's the enemy. All's fair in love and war. "We're all worried about Hephaestus."

"Not like that and you know it." She brushes Pandora's dark hair off her face. "I like her."

"Eurydice." I sigh. "Don't go soft on me now."

She drops her hand and takes a sip of her wine. "No danger of that. I know what's at stake. I'll reach out to Ariadne tomorrow and get that moving."

"Good." I'm still not entirely convinced of Apollo's report that said Minos's daughter might be turned to our side, but at this point we can't afford to overlook any potential foothold.

I turn to where Charon is leaned against the wall nearby. He's always haunting some space near Eurydice. She seems to find it comforting. I feel it's disconcerting. With someone as dangerous as Charon, I prefer to have him where I can see him. "Help me get her into the car." I had planned to come here and get her sloppy drunk, so her managing it on her own skips a few steps.

Sometime later, I corral a nearly passed out Pandora in my apartment and help her get out of the bridesmaid dress and into my bed. Guilt threatens to rise again, but I swallow it down. She's not an innocent, no matter how sweet she's been since I met her. She's part of Minos's household, which means she's part of the plot to bring down the city I love.

That doesn't stop me from pulling the covers up around her shoulders. It's cold in here and she's already asleep. There's no reason for her to freeze. It might make her wake before I'm ready for her to. That's all.

I watch her sleep for a few moments. She's got to be the only person in existence who doesn't look more innocent like this. Not that she's *innocent* when she's awake, but there's something about Pandora that invites the kind of delight that only exists before the world shows exactly how cruel it can be. I don't understand it.

It must be a mask, but I've never seen it so much as crack in the hours we spent together for the wedding planning.

That means nothing.

My mask doesn't crack, either.

Satisfied that she's not somehow faking sleep, I head for my bathroom. I need to take a quick shower and wash the events of the day off me. I'm mildly irritated to discover I'm sore after having sex with Hephaestus. I press my fingers to my pussy and shiver. It was fast and cruel and, damn it, I came. I shouldn't have bothered, but in the moment I couldn't resist.

I love pleasure too much to miss an opportunity to take it.

It's tempting to take a long shower, but I have my task to keep in mind. It will be dawn soon enough, and there's no time to waste. I'll sleep later. Probably. Maybe.

It still takes another thirty minutes to dry my hair and put on enough makeup to hide the exhaustion starting to make my body feel heavy. It doesn't matter. Sleep is something that evades me even under normal circumstances. Except with...

No. No use thinking about him.

A black silk robe completes the picture. I run my fingers through my hair a bit to give it a messier look and head back into the bedroom. Pandora is exactly where I left her, snoring softly. Cute. Her dark hair is spread out over my red sheets, creating the perfect contrast.

I move to the window and lift the blinds just enough to give some natural light in the room. One of the things I learned early was how to manipulate the public. With the current situation in Olympus, that skill is needed now more than ever. If we have a chance to avoid an all-out war, we have to fight the first battles through public perception.

Right now, all the headlines are screaming about the secret assassination clause that can catapult anyone who manages to kill one of the Thirteen into their newly vacated position.

The city's opinion of the Thirteen is a fickle thing. They love to watch us, fish in an aquarium for their entertainment, and some of them flat-out love us. But that sort of thing can turn on a dime. Power is a heady thing, and if there's one thing Olympus idolizes even above the Thirteen, it's power itself.

No matter how much they enjoy watching our dramas play out in the gossip sites, it won't take long until they start wondering what it would be like if *they* held the title of one of the Thirteen.

If we don't give the people something else to talk about, every one of our lives will be in danger. Even with all our security measures, there's no guarantee someone won't succeed.

My husband did.

And that chaos will only spread. It's exactly the thing my brother was worried about when we had three title changeovers in a single year. A destabilized city is ripe for the picking, which is no doubt what Minos wants. Throw in a faltering barrier, and we might not be able to muster up a defense if and when the enemy comes knocking at our door.

Well, fuck that.

If I have one skill, it's giving people something to talk about. I intend to keep them so busy gossiping about my bullshit marriage that they won't bother to sharpen their knives. Entertainment is king, after all.

I grab my phone, ignoring last night's increasingly irate texts from my husband, and carefully snap a few selfies. I flip through them, picking the one that has me looking soft and mischievous... and has the tiniest hint of Pandora in the background. She's turned away from the camera, only her mass of dark hair and one soft arm in the frame. She could be anyone...

But Hephaestus will know exactly who she is.

And the rest of Olympus will drive itself into a frenzy speculating why there's someone who isn't my husband in my bed on my wedding night.

I post on social media with a string of emojis—sun, heart, coffee, lips—that could mean anything and will add more fuel to the fire as people try to decode the secret message. Then I wander into my kitchen and take my time with my espresso machine. This is the favorite part of my day, the careful ritual of putting together the perfect latte.

I get five minutes of peace before my phone starts blowing up. A quick glance shows Hephaestus's name. I grin and go back to the espresso machine.

Three calls later and Pandora's phone starts ringing. I left it and her purse on the counter, so I grab it. The photo displayed is an old one with Pandora and Hephaestus—Theseus, then. He's got his arm around her and he's looking down at her with a smile that's so relaxed, I almost doubt this is the man I married. She, of course, is her customary sunny self, beaming at the camera. It's cute.

"Gross." I swipe to answer the call. "Hello, Husband."

"What the fuck did you do to her?"

"Hmm?" I drizzle caramel on the inside of my cup. "I'm not sure what you're accusing me of, but I do believe I'm insulted."

"I swear to the gods, Aphrodite, if you've harmed one hair on her head—"

"That's *your* role, dear husband. I prefer softer methods." I pause and pour the espresso into the cup. "And Pandora is *very* soft."

He's silent for a beat. Two. "I'll kill you."

A shiver of dread goes through me at the sheer menace in his voice, but I shake it off. I knew what he was capable of when I offered to marry him. Marrying murderers is practically a family tradition at this point, though I have no intention of suffering the same fate my mother did.

Even in my head, the thought falls flat. Dark humor has kept me going through some nightmarish experiences, and it will continue to do so. I add milk to the cup, then ice, and finish it off with more caramel.

"You won't." My voice doesn't so much as quiver. "You need this marriage, and you're no Zeus to survive the reputation of being a spouse-killer. I am Olympus's darling little rebel, and if the people of this city think you've hurt me, they'll tear you limb from limb." Probably. If they don't whip out some popcorn to cheer on the fall of one of the Kasios family. Truly, it could go either way.

Public opinion is a fickle beast, but I don't expect Hephaestus to know that. He's shown absolutely no skill at manipulating the press to date, so I don't expect him to start now.

When he speaks again, his tone hasn't lost its quiet menace. "Leave her alone. She has nothing to do with this."

"Then she shouldn't have come to Olympus. Have a nice day,

Hephaestus. I certainly plan to." I hang up and turn the ringer to silent. A quick check of my social media confirms the post is already blowing up. The comments are all gleeful speculation. *Good.*

"Aphrodite?"

I turn and freeze. Pandora stands in the doorway to my kitchen, her curvy body framed by the morning light. She's wearing a bra, panties, and little else. Her body is... I swallow hard. Gods, I have the most inappropriate desire to pull her into my arms, to press my mouth to the soft line of her shoulder, to follow it down—

Stop that.

I smile slowly. "Good morning, Pandora."

Her makeup has smudged a bit, and it's truly unfair that it only makes her dark eyes more prominent and pretty. She gives me a long look. "What am I doing here?"

This, at least, I have a ready answer for. "Oh, you drank too much last night and Eurydice called me because she was worried you wouldn't make it home safely."

"So your solution was to bring me to *your* place?"

I shrug and sip my coffee. "It was closer and I was tired. I'm sure you understand."

She gives me a look that says she sees through my bullshit but isn't ready to call me on it. "Where is Theseus?"

"His name is Hephaestus now. He's earned that." I can't quite keep the bite out of my voice.

Pandora shakes her head slowly. "Maybe to the rest of this city, but he'll always be Theseus to me."

That's precious and sadly innocent. I sigh. "Would you like some coffee?"

"Yes."

I expect we won't be alone for long, but I don't rush through my process. "Caramel?"

"Sure."

I can feel her watching me, but I keep my movements smooth and slow. A few minutes later, I slide her cup to her. "Let me know how that is."

She has the strangest expression on her face. "You look different when you're like this." She sips the coffee before I can decide how I'm supposed to respond to *that*. "Oh, this is good. Thank you."

"Of course." I lean against the counter and reclaim my cup. "You should be more careful in Olympus. If Eurydice hadn't called me, you could have gotten into trouble." True, she only called me because she and I arranged this little meetup ahead of time, but Pandora doesn't need to know that.

I didn't have a firm plan to use Pandora against Hephaestus at the start of this, but she's too good a lever to overlook. *And turnabout is fair play.* If he thinks I have my hands all over her, it will twist the knife and he'll be so busy chasing his tail, he won't have time to enact whatever plan Minos has put together.

And if it doesn't distract him? Well, I'll deal with that when the time comes. I'm adaptable like that.

"She's the one who invited me to the lower city." Pandora makes a face. "Though I didn't get to enjoy it very much."

It's exactly the opening I need. *Come into my parlor, said the spider to the fly.* I smile. "I'm more than happy to take you there sometime if you want."

Pandora leans back against the counter, mirroring my position. "I was under the impression that Hades didn't like the rest of the Thirteen all that much. Why would he give you unlimited access to his private club?"

Apparently she's been paying closer attention than I realized. Oh well, I planned for this possibility, too. "He and I have an understanding." Unlike some of my peers, Hades can see the writing on the wall. If Minos gets his way, then the murder of the last Hephaestus is only the beginning of the trouble we'll see.

It doesn't mean he likes my methods, but he's agreed to stay out of my way as long as I don't endanger any of the precious citizens of his lower city. He wouldn't thank me for including Eurydice in my plans, but what Hades doesn't know won't hurt him.

And what Persephone doesn't know won't hurt *me*.

For a moment, Pandora looks tempted, but then she shakes her head. "No. I appreciate the offer, but Theseus wouldn't like it, and I'm not going to be the instrument you use to hurt him."

She's smarter than I gave her credit for, which should frustrate me, but instead a strange sort of delight unfurls in my chest. I like that she's not a complete pushover, even if it's inconvenient.

"Of course," I agree easily. "You're *friends*, after all."

Her dark brows draw together in a frown. "Why do people keep putting that kind of emphasis on it? Is it really so hard to believe we're just friends?"

"Darling, it's hard to believe he has any friends at all. Don't take it personally." I lean forward a little and lower my voice. I'm delighted when she mirrors the movement, her forehead nearly touching mine. It's enough to bring back the memory of that little game at Minos's house party where we shared a kiss. Two, actually. Her lips were particularly soft. Not that I've been thinking about it at all. "But you? I believe that *you* have a lot of friends."

"Now you're just being mean."

I shrug and force myself to straighten. "It's what I do."

She opens her mouth to say something, but never gets the chance. My front door booms open hard enough to echo through the whole apartment and Hephaestus's roar fills the space. "*Aphrodite!*"

I hide my grin. *Right on time.* "In here, dear husband."

He's limping a bit more than normal as he comes around the corner and stops short. Being on his feet so much of yesterday must have taken its toll. Either that or the little sex we had was too much for him. The thought makes me chuckle.

Hephaestus looks from me in my robe to Pandora in her underwear, his rage something truly outstanding to behold. I lean forward, wondering if he might give himself a stroke from the rise in his blood pressure. Unfortunately, that would be too easy, and he manages to regain control of himself. "Pandora, put your clothes on. We're going."

I expect Pandora to hop to obey. She might not be one of Minos's children—foster, biological, or otherwise—but she's a part of the household, and the household dances to the tune of the patriarch. Hephaestus is an extension of that will right now.

She doesn't move. Instead, she frowns. "You don't get to use that tone with me, Theseus."

He shoots a look at me, and I'm delighted to see a thread of unease filter through his dark eyes. When he turns back to

Pandora, he's obviously made a small attempt to moderate his tone. "Let's go."

"I'm good."

It takes everything I have to keep my surprise off my face. I've underestimated her stubbornness. That shouldn't delight me. The stakes have never been higher, and my perverse curiosity has gotten me into more trouble than I care to admit. I absolutely cannot afford to have the impulse sink its teeth into me and hold tight.

"Pandora—"

"I'll get a ride back to the house later." She walks out of the kitchen and, over the sudden silence that permeates the room, I hear her heading back down the hallway to my bedroom.

Hephaestus levels a murderous look at me. "If you touch her, I'll kill you."

"What makes you think I haven't already touched her?" I permit myself a slow smile. "She's such a luscious little gem, isn't she? I'm only human, Husband. I can't be expected to resist such tempting fruit." He opens his mouth and I lift a finger. "Ah-ah. She made her choice. Leave."

For a long moment, I don't think he will, but he finally curses and exits my apartment. I make my way to the front door and throw the dead bolt. He was so panicked at the thought of me having Pandora, he didn't even stop to wonder how he was able to get past my doorman *and* my door.

Foolish man.

He's playing in the deep end now, and he obviously doesn't know how to swim.

HEPHAESTUS

MY KNEE IS A BALL OF FIERY RAGE AS I TAKE THE ELEVATOR
back down to the lobby. I screwed up. Pandora has always been too
stubborn by half, and going in there yelling orders was only going to
ensure she dug in her heels out of sheer stubbornness. Which she did.

I make it three steps out of the elevator before reality sinks
in. I'm not going to make it across the lobby without stumbling.
Yesterday was trying, but the thing that fucked me was attempting
to run here. I know better, but sometimes I forget my new limits.

No, that's bullshit. The truth is sometimes I intentionally
ignore my new limits.

And I always pay the price.

This place is all black marble, black metal accents, and large
windows overlooking the street. As tempting as it is to just push
through and not worry about the people who will no doubt witness
my weakness, the last two weeks have proven that someone is
always watching.

There are a trio of benches in the lobby, separated by tasteful bush things that are undoubtedly real despite their cost to maintain. Olympus is so obsessed with appearances—but only where the rich and powerful spend their time.

I've seen the upper warehouse district and some of the more far-flung parts of the city where the Thirteen never roam. It's not pretty. It's also familiar. Aeaea is the same, at least in this. The rich control every aspect of their surroundings, and everyone else is left with the castoffs…if they're lucky.

I make my way to the bench farthest from the windows, each step sending a hot poker of agony through my knee. My phone buzzes before I can attempt to make myself comfortable.

Minos: What the fuck happened last night?

My stomach takes an instinctive plunge in the face of his anger, but no one's around to see it. Not that there's anything to see. Showing hurt or guilt or anything other than stone-faced coldness is a good way to make Minos go nuclear. He prizes control over all things, and last night more than proved that I don't have control of shit. Certainly not my wife.

Still, I'm not about to confess anything.

Me: What are you talking about?

A link appears. I already know what I'll find before I click it. If someone's always watching in Olympus, MuseWatch is always reporting. We knew that early on, of course, but even Minos underestimated its power initially.

The citizens of Olympus treat it as gospel, and they're the ones we need on our side if we don't want to get knifed as news of the assassination clause spreads like wildfire. Minos is riding that wave like he's born to it, and why not? He's the most charming motherfucker I've ever met. He could sell a drowning man water, and the public seems to adore him.

Unfortunately, manipulating public opinion isn't a lesson Minos saw fit to teach *me* during all my training.

It's even worse than I feared. The top headline splashed over the site screams:

HEPHAESTUS: DISAPPOINTING OLYMPUS AND HIS NEW WIFE.

"Fuck," I breathe. It doesn't get better as I read the actual text of the article.

Hephaestus and Aphrodite might have left their reception together, but they didn't stay there. After what we can only assume was an underwhelming performance, Aphrodite was seen slipping into a certain club in the lower city. If you know, you know! Then this morning she posted a sultry pic with a mystery lover in the background who's most assuredly not her husband. Can anyone blame her?

"Fuck," I say again, this time with more force.

"She brings out that reaction in people."

I don't startle, but it's a near thing. I glance up to find Adonis standing over me. This morning, he's not dressed to perfection, wearing a plain white T-shirt and a pair of dark jeans. For all that, they're clearly expensive. He's the kind of man who clothes himself in wealth thoughtlessly because it's all he's ever known.

He's got nothing to compare it to. He's never gone hungry, never gone without. His privilege is written all over his perfect features and easy smile.

It's enough to make me hate him, except hating him is exactly what Aphrodite would want.

With that in mind, I try for a smile. "I didn't realize it'd be like this." There. That's a nice neutral statement.

Adonis, of course, takes the bait. He sinks down gracefully next to me on the bench. "It was cruel of you to invite me to the wedding."

I consider and discard several responses. After what Aphrodite pulled with Pandora, I want to strike back, to put her in her place. The one thing I've always been shit at is dancing the careful choreography of speaking in layers. It's easier to scare people into doing what I want, and that won't work with Adonis.

Instead, I tell the truth.

"Yeah, it was." I lean back until our shoulders brush. "But I didn't choose to get married and I wanted to hurt her." My wife doesn't have many obvious weaknesses, but this man is one of them. I learned that well enough at the house party Minos hosted a few weeks back; the one that ended in blood and death. During one of the headfuck games Minos played, Adonis won a "date" with me.

I never did get a chance to collect on that.

"It's just like at the party," he says, mirroring my thoughts. "You're both using me as a bone to taunt the other with." Adonis shakes his head. "I came here to check on her, to make sure she's okay. But after seeing that social media post, I feel naive. It's not a comfortable feeling."

I eye him. "You just called me cruel and now you're oversharing."

"I guess I am." His smile is bright and as false as fool's gold. "I'm very angry with her right now, and I suppose I'd like to give her a taste of her own medicine."

Surely he's not playing right into my hands and calling it his own idea? I've never been lucky, and it seems to defy belief that he'd present me with such an opportunity. I hold perfectly still. "Meaning?"

"Do you want to go get a drink, Hephaestus?"

When I took the title from the last fucker who held it, I never thought I'd miss my own name. Hearing *his* name on everyone's lips makes me feel invisible. It's too late to go back, though. I've made my devil's bargain and now I have to live with it.

I nod slowly. "It's ten in the morning."

"As if that's enough to stop us. I know a place." He rises to his feet. Gods, he's a handsome fucker. Smooth dark-brown skin, cheekbones sharp enough to cut, and broad palms that speak of strength beneath the polished exterior. He holds out a hand. "What do you say?"

Even knowing this is an opportunity I'd be a fool to pass up, I can't help eyeing his face for any sign of the pity or derision I've come to expect from the people in this cursed city. It'd be hard enough to adjust to my new mobility limits without them seeing my fucked-up knee as an unforgivable flaw. They react more to *that* than to the fact I'm a proven murderer.

It could be a trap. The Thirteen have promised to leave me alone if I married the witch, but there's nothing stopping Adonis from taking matters into his own very capable hands. He seems like a genuinely nice guy without a murderous bone in his body, but that doesn't mean it's the truth.

Going with him is a risk, but the potential gain is too tempting to ignore.

Adonis merely maintains his smile and waits.

Ultimately, what decides me is the trio of people all but pressed against the glass, watching us. My knee has started to stiffen up, and if I try to get up on my own, I'm going to give them something to laugh about.

I slip my hand into Adonis's. I'm a good four inches taller and have to weigh quite a bit more since I'm not built lean like him, but he pulls me to my feet with no apparent effort. He keeps my hand for a beat too long and then steps back. "Come on. My car is out front."

He easily matches his stride to my slower one, and ignores the people snapping pictures of us as we step through the door and out onto the sidewalk. I can't tell if he's just that used to being a tiger in a cage or if he's got a better poker face than I realized. Each click of the cameras make me want to smash them into a thousand pieces. I can't. I know enough to recognize that, even if I chafe against the constraint.

Adonis presses a hand to the small of my back. Not urging me faster, just angling his body between mine and the press. It shocks me enough that I'm still processing it a few minutes later when we're safely in the back of his town car.

He...protected me?

I shake my head sharply. No, this is another game. There's no way this guy is as guileless as he seems. This fucked-up city would have eaten him alive if that were the case.

Not to mention my wife would have chewed him up and spit him out without missing a step.

He gives an address that's only a few blocks away. When he catches my glare, he shrugs. "I'm not going to make you walk it when you're obviously in pain. I don't think I like you very much, but cruelty for cruelty's sake isn't how I operate."

Again, I search his expression for pity or some kind of judgment, and again there's nothing. He states it as fact and that's that. I don't know how to feel about it, so I ignore it completely. "You seem like a nice guy." He huffs out a laugh, but I continue before he can get a word in edgewise. "What are you doing chasing after that witch?"

"Eris is a lot of things, but she's hardly a witch."

My wife's birth name fits her far better than her title. We did our research before coming here, so I know what the last Aphrodite was like—blond and gorgeous and selling an image of perfection. She's nothing like the woman I married. *My* Aphrodite is all too happy to be messy in public and make a spectacle of herself, all to humiliate *me*. Yeah, Eris fits her a whole lot better than Aphrodite, but I'll never call her by that name. It feels like a capitulation, though I can't begin to say why.

I shift on the seat. I can't stretch out my knee in this position. "She's doing a damned good impression of being a witch right now."

"Yeah." Adonis sighs. "I guess she is."

The car stops outside a building that looks just like every other building in the center of the upper city. Chrome and glass and concrete. Back home, the buildings have more character. Even the rich like to put their own stamp on their businesses and residences. No one would mistake Minos's house for any other, not with its copper roof tiles that have aged to a pleasing green or the brilliant coral door that is twice the size a normal door should be.

I rub my chest. I might have come here at Minos's command, but part of me misses that house. Everything is *wrong* in this city, from the people to the buildings to how it's affected my friendship with Pandora, rot already worming between us.

Adonis climbs out and again offers his hand. "Come on. No one will bother us in here."

Again, I consider ignoring his offer for help, and again, my need not to fall flat on my face overrides the pride demanding I do it on my own. This time, his palm doesn't linger against mine, and I tell myself I don't mind the lack at all.

The door he guides me through takes us to a small half-circle lobby with a trio of doors leading deeper into the building. Stylized lettering frosts each of them, all in the same font and the same style. Only the words set them apart.

This city truly lacks soul.

Adonis heads to the far left one. He slips a key out of his pocket and unlocks the door. When he catches me looking, he shrugs. "As you said, it's ten in the morning. They won't be open for hours yet."

I pause meaningfully. "If you're looking to get some revenge, I'm not going to be an easy mark."

"If I wanted to hurt you, I would have won the moment you got into the car with me." His lips curve, though the expression still hasn't reached his dark eyes. "I want to talk, Hephaestus. That's all. We'll have privacy here, which is something you'll find in short supply in this city."

"Theseus." I don't know why I say it. But once it's out of my mouth, I don't want to take it back. "My name is Theseus."

"Not anymore."

"Still, I'd rather you use it." I follow him through the door and into a surprisingly charming little bar. It's nothing like the pub I used to spend my time in before leaving Aeaea, its walls plastered with signed dollar bills, its floors permanently sticky and the jukebox stuck on some weird-ass band no one but the owner had heard of. But...this place *does* have more soul than most of the city I've interacted with so far. There's black and red art hanging on the walls, the style abstract in a way that feels almost violent. I look at the painting nearest us for a long moment, trying to figure out what's causing the effect. It makes me vaguely uncomfortable.

"Maybe one day I will." Adonis moves past me to the long bar that stretches down one wall. When I met him, I would have wagered he'd never worked a day in his life, but he slips behind the bar with a level of comfort that suggests he's slung drinks here plenty of times.

Interesting.

I follow more slowly, still taking in the space. Black marble tabletops and black leather chairs and stools. Bright-red shelves that house a truly impressive selection of liquor. It should feel like the whole place is trying too hard, but somehow it forms a cohesive whole.

Adonis doesn't ask me what I want. That should irritate me, but as I slide onto a stool, I find myself fascinated by the graceful way he creates two identical drinks in front of him. He moves fast enough that I can't quite catch everything—sure as fuck not enough to recreate it.

"This is your family's place?"

"Yes." He adds a cherry that's so dark it's almost black to each drink and slides one over to me. "It's more a hobby than anything else, but my family likes to pride themselves on being a *working* family, so it's tradition that each of us work here for a bit as adults."

An entire business that functions as a hobby. That sounds like some rich people shit. Technically, I'm one of the rich now, have been ever since Minos pulled me out of that orphanage at fifteen. But half a life among the privileged doesn't erase that my first half was spent with nothing of my own.

Nothing except Pandora.

I should have known better than to yell at her. She's never liked that shit; it's a guaranteed way to ensure she does the exact opposite of what I want. Like stay with *Aphrodite*.

The thought of my wife anywhere near Pandora has me clenching a hand around my glass. No matter what Aphrodite wants me to think, Pandora would never jump into bed with her... I pause. Well, she wouldn't jump into bed with my wife on our wedding night, at least. I've seen the people Pandora is attracted to, and to a person, the only thing they have in common is that they're beautiful, dangerous, and bad for her.

Like my wife.

I take a drink, mostly for something to do, and am surprised to find it light and refreshing. I examine the liquid in the glass. "What *is* this?"

"Old family secret." Adonis smiles and leans forward to prop his elbows on the bar. "Now, let's talk."

ADONIS

"ERIS WOULD LOSE HER MIND IF SHE KNEW I WAS HERE alone with you."

"What my wife doesn't know won't hurt her."

His wife. Not mine. Never mine. She was never going to be, as she reminded me yesterday.

Most of my life, I've gone with the flow. I live a charmed existence and I'm aware enough to realize that, but I also realized pretty early on that I'd never hold one of the thirteen titles. My mother takes after *her* mother in being too outspoken and too stubborn to bend when others think she should. Old money has a way of thinking the world revolves around it instead of the other way around, and my mother reflects that.

My other parent isn't that much better. They like to poke their nose in when they're not welcome and have a nasty habit of sharing gossip a little too freely. Everyone does it, of course, but my parent doesn't bother to pretend they're not. It gets people's hackles up.

So, no, I was never going to become one of the Thirteen.

I never wanted it, frankly. Hard to go with the flow when you're the one directing it. It's a lot of responsibility and I've seen the toll it takes on those who hold those positions. The power might be nice, but I have everything I could ever want. Why do I need more?

I know better now.

Hephaestus watches me like he's not sure if I poisoned his drink. Honestly, it's not a completely irrational fear. I wouldn't do it, but there are others in the upper city who wouldn't hesitate. But if Eris wanted him dead, he'd be dead, and I might be so furious at her that I can't think straight, but I won't trample on her plans.

"But you do want to hurt her. Hurt us, really."

Hephaestus shrugs. "I got what I wanted. I'm one of the Thirteen."

Surely he doesn't expect me to believe that line. I've seen Minos's kind before; Eris's father, the last Zeus, was a lot like him. Charismatic enough to have the people of Olympus enraptured, and all the more dangerous because of it. Minos didn't come to Olympus to place one of his children among the Thirteen.

He came for Olympus itself.

Which is why Eris is doing what she's doing. The best and worst thing about her is that she will always put this city first. Her father was Olympus's monster and raised his children to be the same. Somehow it got twisted into this messed-up sense of responsibility because of the family she was born into. Now that she's Aphrodite, that feeling of responsibility has only gotten stronger.

Her brother is leaning hard on her. Probably her sister, too.

Three of the Kasios family. It's never happened even once in Olympus's history.

"Why did you invite me for a drink?" Hephaestus asks abruptly. "Be honest with me."

Honesty is a risk, but it's all I have. I take a breath and lay my cards on the table. "I don't want you to hurt Eris."

He studies me. Hephaestus is a big man. He looks every inch an old-world warrior with his broad shoulders, square jaw, and callused palms. Based on the final Ares trial, his foster brother is trained with a sword, and I suspect Hephaestus is as well.

He's dangerous. The kind of dangerous we don't see in Olympus. Here, battles are fought with bladed words and shady alliances. Or they used to be. The assassination clause was virtually unknown until a few weeks ago.

Until Minos came.

Until Theseus murdered the last Hephaestus.

He smirks. "She dumped you and married me. Why do you care what happens to her?"

I shrug, forcing my body language to remain light and uncaring. "I am angrier at her than I've ever been, but that doesn't mean I want her hurt." I love her. That love might have twisted and morphed into something unrecognizable, but we have too much history to ignore. "You obviously didn't want this marriage, and your family has more than proven that they're willing to kill to get the titles. Killing her would give them the Aphrodite title and end your marriage in one move."

"I won't pretend I haven't considered it." He shakes his head. "But you're missing a vital part of negotiations, Adonis."

Hephaestus leans forward. He's tall enough that we're almost even like this, tall enough that the bar between us suddenly doesn't feel like much of a barrier. "What will you offer me to ensure her protection?"

I blink. "That wasn't very subtle."

"Neither was your statement."

He's right, but I'm merely matching his energy. Since he took over the title, it's never been clearer that he isn't from around here. Minos might know how to talk to the press, but he hasn't passed on that skill to his foster sons. Hephaestus's brusque attitude has already set people on edge and created a problem with how people perceive him. Eris's antics this morning are just one more nail in the coffin. "We do things a certain way here. Trying to go against that isn't going to earn you any friends."

"I'm not here to make friends."

Yeah, I know. "That's the problem." I catch a faint thread of some woodsy scent he's wearing and have to tell myself not to inhale deeply. Hephaestus is attractive enough to turn heads if one is willing to risk their safety in his bed. He's the enemy, but this is Olympus. Sleeping with your enemies is practically a professional sport. No, the more important truth is that he's Eris's husband. No matter how angry I am at her, that's a line I shouldn't cross.

That's a line I *refuse* to cross.

I lean back and busy myself putting away the bottles I pulled to make the drink. "You're losing the battle of public perception on multiple fronts. People don't like you, and they *do* like your wife. Normally, you might have been able to garner sympathy that she's cuckolding you, but people are actively rooting against you at this point. They want you humiliated. They're downright gleeful at the prospect."

His brows draw together in a truly fearsome glare. "This city is fucked."

"You came here and put a target on your back." I sip my drink even though I don't feel like drinking anymore now that my anger is fading. "You don't respect the rules of this place. From the moment you came here, you've acted like you're better than them—than us. Did you honestly think people would thank you for it?"

"You're not telling me anything I don't already know." A dangerous edge has come into his voice. He hasn't bothered to pretend to be anything other than what he is—a predator—but he dampened it a bit in our previous encounters. This man, though? I fully believe he beat another human to death.

An idea comes to me slowly. It's a terrible idea, one that will have a good portion of my peers turning against me. I'm not sure I care. I might not want Eris hurt physically, but that doesn't apply to her reputation. Ultimately, Hephaestus being a member of the Thirteen that the public actively hates weakens the entire ruling body when they need most to project strength.

All for the love of Olympus, right?

I know my smile has taken on an edge, but I can't quite reclaim the easy expression I normally wear. "I propose a bargain."

He narrows his eyes. "I'm listening."

Now's the time to turn back. Nothing will come from this except more misery. I should be focusing on picking up the pieces of my life created when Eris shattered our relationship. I might garner more pity than I can stomach, but it will pass. Olympus has a long memory on some subjects, but broken relationships are a dime a dozen. No one believed Eris and I would go the distance.

No one except me, apparently.

Admitting how naive I was feels like swallowing acid. "I'll help you fix your image. In return, you'll promise not to harm her."

He sits back slowly. The movement brings into attention the shift of his muscles beneath his button-down shirt. It doesn't fit quite right, not having been tailored for his sheer size, and even as I notice that, I can't help the heat that rises in response to his strength. I've always been attracted to strength in its many forms; to my detriment, most of the time.

Hephaestus considers me for a long moment. "Why?"

I know better than to hand away a weapon for free, but this is hardly a normal situation. Hephaestus obviously wants to use me against Eris, and I'm angry and hurt enough to be used, but he's too smart not to check for strings. I cross my arms over my chest. "I don't care what your foster father has planned; you're weakening the entire body of the Thirteen, which is weakening Olympus as a whole. You need the public on your side now more than ever."

"I couldn't give a fuck about what the public thinks."

"You can't afford to be that reckless." And neither can the city. I don't think for a second that the Thirteen will come together, join hands, and fix things. It doesn't matter. A stable Thirteen translates to a more stable Olympus.

"You aren't doing this for the good of the city, or at least that's not the whole reason."

He's not wrong, but he already knows Eris is my weak spot—and I'm hers. No reason to remind him. "Are you worried that you can't handle anything I can bring to the table?"

He smiles, slow and languid. It completely transforms his face. Oh, he's still got the brutal beauty, but his smile softens it into something truly devastating. "I can handle anything you throw at me, Adonis. In fact, I look forward to it." The sheer insinuation in his low voice gives weight to the air in the room, and suddenly it's hard to draw a full breath.

Gods, he's dangerous.

I knew that, but he's been such a blundering, prideful fool since taking the title that it was easy to tell myself I imagined his rough charm from the house party. That I imagined my response to it. "I'm not offering that."

"Not as part of the bargain," he agrees easily. Too easily. Before I can reiterate that I'm not, under any circumstances, having sex with the person who's married to my ex, he continues. "How do you plan to fix my image?" The words have a sarcastic edge, but he looks genuinely curious. "Fight fire with fire?"

I laugh. I can't help it. "That's a losing game. Eris has been playing the press since she was a teenager. Earlier, even. No, you have to go in a different direction."

Interest lights his dark eyes. "Okay, you have my attention."

I haven't spent any time thinking about this, but I was trained the same as Eris. I'll never have the same media spotlight that she does, but my parents taught me early that perception is a weapon at our disposal. It's easy enough to come up with a solution that has a chance of working. "You play the doting husband."

"Pass." Hephaestus's face twists. "Everyone knows I didn't choose the marriage. No one will believe I'm following my unfaithful wife around with hearts in my eyes."

"Not if you keep standing next to her and glowering like you want to murder her." I set my glass down. "You need to make them root for you. The only way to do that is to play on their pity."

"I do *not* want their pity."

Pity is obviously a sore spot for him, but I don't care. "Let me paint you a picture." I lower my voice, forcing him to lean in. "The steadfast, loyal husband and the philandering wife who flaunts her lovers in public. Who do you root for?"

"Pick another option."

"You're not capable of any other option and Eris is too beloved, even if it's that they love watching her spectacle. You have no chance of being more charming than her. You don't have her connections. Minos is tolerated right now the same way people tolerate an amusing jester, and he shows every evidence of building that amusement into goodwill, but *you* don't have his skill. People do not like you."

"Tell me something I don't already know."

I eye him. "If you'd played it the way I suggest from the start, pretending to be in love with her, or at least besotted with her, then people would empathize with you. Half the city wants to be in Aphrodite's bed, and the other half wants to be her. You're a newcomer to Olympus, so it'd be easier to project their feelings onto you...except you keep being an asshole, which turns that empathy to hate. If you'd started things this way, she never would have been able to pull that stunt this morning."

His mouth thins. "I don't like it."

"You don't like any of this, so that's hardly news." I catch my tone going playful. I am *not* going to flirt with him. I don't even like him. "That's my offer. Take it or leave it."

He considers it. I like that he doesn't simply take me up on it without thought. Finally, he says, "If you're trying to get close to me to spy, it's a waste of time. I'm not soft enough to share pillow talk, and Minos certainly isn't going to let anything slip."

My skin flares hot at the idea of pillow talk with Hephaestus. I want to say desiring him is just a side effect of a broken heart, but there was a spark when we first met, too. Not enough to indulge in, not when I was with Eris.

But I'm not with Eris anymore.

That's enough. You said you didn't want her hurt, and now you're fighting not to flirt with her husband. What do you think that would do if she found out?

Not that hurting *me* was enough to give her pause before moving forward with her plan.

"Then I suppose you have no reason to say no."

His smile widens. "Guess you're right." He reaches out a big hand and I do my best to ignore the zing that surges through me when I slip my hand into his. "Okay, Adonis, you have yourself a bargain."

APHRODITE

PANDORA OBVIOUSLY HAS NO INTENTION OF LINGER-
ing despite not leaving with Hephaestus, but I'm not about to
waste this opportunity. I watch her pull the rumpled bridesmaid
dress over her wide hips and have to fight not to lick my lips. She
really is delicious. "Eurydice said you were interested in the club."

"I was drunk." She tugs the fabric up around her stomach and
then breasts.

I'm already moving. "Let me."

She huffs out a breath, but turns to present me with her back.
I would like to say it's my mercenary streak that has me dragging
my knuckles up her spine as I zip her up, but really I just want
an excuse to touch her. Adonis and I were always so aware of
appearances that when we were "on," we never stepped out of the
respectable, monogamous box Olympus put us in. As a result, it's
been a long time since I touched anyone else like this.

Too long.

Even thinking that feels like a disservice to him. Being with him was hardly a chore. I loved—love—him. But there's always been a secret part of me that felt stifled by what we had. I'll never admit as much aloud, and certainly never to him, but it's the truth.

I finish Pandora's dress and can't stop myself from touching the bare spot just above it. "There."

She releases a shaky breath and turns to face me. "I'm not some club you can beat Theseus with. He's my best friend, and I won't hurt him."

"Of course not," I agree easily. "I would never ask that of you." I don't need her to agree to hurt him when her presence will serve the same purpose.

That's not the full truth, though. I am curious about this sparkling woman who lives among the snakes of Minos's household. She caught my eye at the disastrous house party a few weeks ago, a bloom that stands apart. I doubt she knows much about Minos's plan, but that's fine. I want to know about *her*.

Best our information can tell, she was raised in the same orphanage as Hephaestus. Apollo couldn't find much info about it, other than that it was named after some historical figure from Aeaea, and it was shut down abruptly a few years ago.

When Minos brought Hephaestus into his household, Pandora came with him. I had thought maybe something insidious was going on there, but Minos appears to mostly ignore her and no one has found evidence to contradict that. Which means she's there for Hephaestus.

And *that* is just as interesting as the fact that my husband seems to genuinely value her above all others.

I give her my most charming smile. "I would like to get to know you. Show you around."

She laughs and starts for the door. "Don't lie to me. You want to parade me around and stir up trouble for him."

Well, yeah. I can appreciate that she sees right through me, even if it's inconvenient. I follow her down the hall. This will be my only chance. If I don't hook her here...

What?

There are other people I can leverage in Olympus. The important part is humiliating Hephaestus and undermining his power. I don't need Pandora, specifically, to do that. Yes, she's the most likely to drive my dear husband into a blackout rage, which is personally entertaining for me, but as far as the public is concerned, the identity of my lovers matters less than the fact they exist.

None of that makes any difference right now. I want her. I'm not willing to let her walk away just yet.

"There are no cameras in Hades's little playground." I'm speaking too fast, but she's almost to the front door. "We'll arrive separately and leave separately. No one talks about what goes on in there unless they want to run the risk of never being invited back." The exception, of course, is when Hades or Persephone *wants* to spread information about a certain pairing or activity, but they use that power sparingly.

Pandora slows. "Why are you so invested in this?" There's something there, a thread of curiosity in her voice.

"Isn't it obvious?" I wait for her to twist to look at me. That same curiosity is there on her face, and it's the only motivation I need to take one step after another, closing the distance between us. I don't stop until her back hits the door and one deep breath will press her breasts against me. "I want you."

Her jaw drops, but she recovers quickly. "I told you not to lie to me."

"I never lie when pleasure is involved." I twist a strand of her hair around my finger and laugh a little at her disbelief. "Okay, *that* was a lie, but I know you felt that little zing when we kissed at Minos's party." I lean down, gratified when she tilts her head back, almost as if she can't help herself. I lower my voice. "I bet if I kissed you right now, we'd feel that zing again."

She shakes her head, but her response is slower this time, her gaze lingering on my mouth. "I appreciate the offer, but—"

"Do they have kink clubs in Aeaea?"

"They have kink clubs everywhere, Aphrodite. They're not mythical places."

The fact that she's still here, arguing with me, is promising. She knows she shouldn't say yes, but there's something in her that wants to. I force myself to slow down, to look at the angles.

I want her. I think she wants me, too. But she's too stubborn to say yes for something as simple as lust. Even if it's clear she's fighting not to reach for me right now. Yes, she felt that connection. I'm sure of it.

The only way forward is to incite her curiosity. "Hades's club is very exclusive. He barely lets me in there, and I'm allowed to go wherever I please."

Her lips quirk. "Poor thing."

I ignore her amusement and continue. "Some nights, he brings in professionals for the shows, but while those are like watching living art, they aren't my favorites."

Pandora hesitates, but finally says, "What's your favorite?"

"Amateur night." I smile slowly. "Not as perfect a show, but they have so much fun with it, it's infectious in the best way." I lean forward until our exhales mingle in the bare space between us. "Tonight is amateur night, Pandora. Are you sure you don't want to join me? Not to participate. Just to watch."

I see the exact moment her curiosity gets the best of her. "Fine. Tonight." She licks her lips, her voice breathy and filled with desire. "But only because I want to see the club."

I take a slow step back and allow myself to look her up and down the way I've wanted to since meeting her. Pandora is one of those people who is beautiful, but for the life of me, I can't tell how much of it is physical beauty and how much of it is pure presence. Either way, I wasn't lying when I said I wanted her. "Tonight, then. Your invitation to the lower city will hold." A favor from Hades, though if he thinks for a moment it will endanger his people, he'll withdraw *both* our invitations.

She looks like she wants to say something else, but finally nods. "Okay."

I let her get her hand on the door before I speak again. "Pandora." She glances at me, something almost like hope in her dark eyes. "There's a car waiting for you in the parking garage. Go to the second level. No one will see you leave."

She hesitates. "Oh. Right. Uh, thanks."

This time, when she opens the door, I don't call her back. I allow myself to feel a deep satisfaction that things are going to plan, but only until I get a text from my driver confirming she got to the car. Then I head back into my room to get dressed properly.

It's time to see my allies.

———————

My siblings have told me to see to my husband and leave the rest to them, but I am who I am. I won't interfere with the layers and layers of plots they have going on, but I read the last report Apollo sent.

He might have seen promise in turning Ariadne against her father at the house party, but he hasn't been able to get close to her since. Her father is actively blocking her access to any of the Thirteen, and that includes Apollo. One could argue that he's doing what any devoted father would do for his beautiful daughter when faced with the circling sharks of Olympus, but considering he auctioned off a date with her at his party, I'm with Apollo on this. Minos knows she's a weak spot and he's trying to keep her locked down.

That's fine.

Some things just require a softer touch than the Thirteen can manage.

My destination is a little bar right on the edge of the upper warehouse district. It's far too early for it to be open, but this is one of Dionysus's personal businesses, so he let me borrow the keys for this meeting. Not even our friendship is enough to get him out of bed before noon.

I'm still turning on the lights when Eurydice slips through the door, followed by her ever-present shadow. I give Charon a long look, but they're a package deal, and neither of them seem to have much sense of humor when it comes to people asking questions about their relationship.

Eurydice, of course, looks fresh and lovely and like she had a full night of sleep instead of being out all hours of the night at a kink club. She's also not wearing one of her customary pretty dresses, opting instead for a pair of cutoff shorts that leaves her long legs bare, and a slightly oversized T-shirt.

I barely manage to resist asking if it's Charon's. If I do, she might leave in a huff. "Thanks for coming."

"Of course." She walks up to the bar and leans against it, looking around with interest. "Dionysus owns this?"

"You've never been?"

"No." Her mouth twists. "My mother and sisters have strong opinions about what is appropriate entertainment for me, and this hardly qualifies." She motions at the wallpaper filled with pinups, their mostly bare bodies on display.

I don't comment on that, though I have my own thoughts on how the Dimitriou women treat Eurydice. No one stays sheltered in Olympus for long, and trying to make that happen does a disservice to the person in question.

Look at what happened with Eurydice's ex, Orpheus. Or, rather, the stunt my father pulled in order to draw Hades onto the wrong side of the river. She never would have fallen for such a trap if her family didn't insist on wrapping her in gauze to keep her safe.

"You're here now. Want a drink?"

"No." She starts to look back at Charon, where he's taken up a spot against the wall near the door, but stops herself. "Let's get down to business."

I almost poke at her a bit more, but ultimately business is why we're meeting. "You did wonderfully with Pandora."

"I hadn't planned on her getting that drunk." She makes a face. "I feel bad."

"It served its purpose. She slept it off in my bed and was none the worse for wear."

Eurydice gives me a long look. "And you upheld your end of the agreement."

It's not a question, but I roll my eyes. "I didn't touch her. Gods, who do you think I am?"

"I think you're one of the Thirteen and you'll do anything to serve Olympus."

She's not wrong, but it still makes my face burn. "I draw the line at sexual assault, thank you very much."

"But not murder."

"Oh, please." I wave that away. "If you came here to be self-righteous, we can end this right now."

She glares, but gives herself a bit of a shake. "I got Ariadne's number out of Pandora's phone. I'll reach out later today. I plan to take the commiserating approach—both of us younger daughters who have been locked away by our families."

"Smart." I cross my arms over my chest. "Though she's not a fool. She won't respond."

"Yes, she will." Eurydice lifts her chin. "I know you had your own trials growing up the way you did, but what she and I have experienced is unique enough that I would bet good money she's climbing the walls right about now. She was flourishing at that house party with so many people around, and now her father has essentially locked her up and thrown away the key, all in the name of her safety and his ambition. She'll respond, even if it's to get some interaction with someone who isn't family."

If she's wrong, then we'll try something else…but I don't think she's wrong. I nod. "Keep me updated. If you need anything, I'll provide it."

Eurydice pauses, shoots a glance at Charon again, and blurts, "Why me?"

"What?"

"Why did you ask me for help with Pandora?" She speaks quickly, words tumbling over each other. "And then again with Ariadne? Surely you have people on staff who could do this sort of thing. You could have picked someone else to avoid pissing off my sisters and mother."

She's not wrong. The Dimitriou women were formidable when they were just daughters of Demeter. Now Psyche and Persephone are both married to dangerous men, and Callisto has become Hera. Even without that, Demeter is one of the most terrifying people I've ever met, and I take great pains not to cross her.

Or I did until now.

Should she find out about this little scheme Eurydice and I are running, she would undoubtedly consider it a betrayal that needs to be punished. Her daughter Psyche took down the last person to hold the Aphrodite title, after all.

But I grew up in Zeus's household, and frankly all four of those women do Eurydice a disservice by trying to swaddle her up to protect her. The woman I interacted with at Minos's party—the one standing before me now—has a *backbone*.

She deserves a chance to use it.

I shrug. "You're smart, beautiful, and perfectly placed for this kind of thing. I think we can both agree that you're being underutilized at the moment, and you're obviously itching to do more or you wouldn't have been so receptive to my offer." I jerk my chin at Charon. "And you're hardly unprotected."

She smiles slowly. "You know, I think you're the first person to see me as valuable instead of just a pretty thing to be admired."

I glance over her shoulder to where Charon watches her with molten eyes. He catches me looking and shutters the expression quickly, but not quickly enough. *I don't think I am the first person to see you as valuable.*

I pat Eurydice on the shoulder. "Keep me in the loop." I pause. "Oh, and stay out of the club tonight. I'm bringing Pandora and I don't want her thinking about anything but me and the show."

"Okay." She turns toward the door, but pauses. "Thanks for this. I mean it. Olympus is my home, too, no matter how flawed, and I want to help."

"You are helping, and I appreciate it." I inject warmness into my tone, but for once I'm not lying. Not really, anyway. I like Eurydice, and she's useful. Win, win from where I'm sitting.

Everything is going according to plan.

PANDORA

I ALMOST DON'T GO BACK TO MINOS'S HOME. RETURNING there always feels like stepping into a cloud of noxious gas, except the very air has weight. Minos mostly ignores me, which means the Minotaur mostly ignores me as well, and I prefer it that way. But that doesn't change the fact that I can't ignore either of them. I learned early on that knowing the most dangerous people in the room might save my life one day, and they are both *dangerous*.

There's nowhere else to go, though.

For all Minos's show of buying a house outside the city proper, it's not convenient for day-to-day life, so he's rented a penthouse a few blocks away from the city center. I think he tried to get closer, but all those buildings are owned by families that can trace their origins back to Olympus's conception. They might not be giving him the cut direct currently, but none of them wanted a new, ambitious stranger living so close.

I bet they're all happy about that after what went down two weeks ago.

I push the thought away, just like I have every day since the house party ended in violence and death. I know what Theseus is capable of. I've always known it.

That doesn't make it easier to stomach.

It's not the death that bothers me. Death is a part of life, and murder is far more common among the powerful than anyone wants to admit.

What bothers me is the fantasy Minos spun for Theseus. The one where doing this would fulfill all his dreams of stability and power. Judging by the last two weeks, all of that is one big lie. He's got power, but stability is in short supply, and he certainly doesn't have the freedom he craves.

Coming here was a mistake.

I'm only in Olympus because Theseus refuses to cooperate if I'm not a package deal with him, and Minos resents me intensely because of it. I'm the one relationship in Theseus's life that predates everyone here. The chosen family that Minos cannot manipulate or control. The one person who's known Theseus since we were barely out of diapers.

Not that Theseus listens to *me*. If he did, he wouldn't be in his current predicament. The fact he thinks he can dictate my actions, though? It makes me want to put him in his place all over again the way I did this morning.

I wish I could pretend that's why I accepted Aphrodite's invitation.

The hook in my gut is attached to a string of pure desire, and I'm terribly afraid she might hold the other end of it. She's beautiful and magnetic, and I'm only human. Being the primary recipient of all her attention is a heady thing. I won't act on it...

Probably.

"Pandora!"

I give myself a shake and look up as Ariadne and Icarus wave me into the living room. It's a wide-open space with cold leather couches, a glass coffee table, and massive floor-to-ceiling windows that give me vertigo when I stand too close.

Ariadne is lounging on the couch with her head in her brother's lap. She's about my size with light-brown skin and long dark hair. Truly, we look enough alike to almost be real sisters, or at least that's what everyone says. She's in her home clothing—leggings and an oversized hoodie that must belong to the Minotaur. I wouldn't dare even take a piece of food off his plate, but his sweatshirts have a habit of magically finding their way into her laundry and she never seems to return them.

It's weird, frankly.

Icarus is the opposite of Theseus and the Minotaur in every way. He shares his sister's coloring and is lean to the point of being skinny, with delicate features and dark curly hair that somehow always seems to misbehave. It must be intentional, if only because it irritates Minos to have even a thread out of place, but Icarus is a study in underachieving. While it's entirely possible that keeping his hair regularly trimmed and styled is merely too much effort, I suspect it's one of a long string of rebellions against his father.

"What are you two doing?" I glance around.

"We're the only ones here." Icarus's lips quirk in a sardonic smile. "No need to run and hide."

"Icarus." Ariadne smacks his knee and sits up. "Don't be mean."

"Just speaking the truth."

Yeah, I'm not going to touch that. Icarus was dancing to his father's tune when we first arrived in Olympus, going so far as to attack Pan at the party. I could have told him it's no use. He might be Minos's son by blood, but he's not what Minos *wants* in a son.

Now, it seems he's back to his old self. He's got a sharper tongue than anyone I've met and he doesn't hesitate to use it. I don't dislike him the way I do the Minotaur and Minos, but being friends with Icarus isn't a comfortable experience. "I'm exhausted so I'm going to take a nap."

Icarus takes me in, dark eyes narrowing. "Our new sister-in-law posted the most interesting photo this morning. Seems Theseus didn't do a good job of exercising his wedding night duties." He leans forward. "If I don't miss my guess, that was *you* in her bed."

It takes everything I have not to flee. Doing so will confirm his suspicions and will give him something to needle Theseus about. I might not be entirely happy with *him* right now, but I'm not going to hand over ammunition to Icarus. "I spent the night in the lower city."

"Told you so." Ariadne twists her hair around her fingers. "I saw her leave with Eurydice Dimitriou." She worries her bottom lip. "Honestly, I was a little jealous. Father had *us* herded directly back here as soon as the reception was over."

"Gods forbid we do something further to embarrass him." Icarus rolls his eyes. "I want to see the kink club."

Ariadne blushes a bit and looks away. "I'd like to see it, too. I'd like to see *anything* that isn't these four walls."

Guilt sparks. I might resent Minos in more ways than I can

count, but his apathy for me translates to freedom these two don't have. We've snuck out together before, back on Aeaea. There was a little bar Theseus introduced me to, and I would bring Icarus and Ariadne there whenever Minos was away on business. Everyone was afraid of Theseus, so they never messed with me, even if he wasn't there every time I was.

There isn't anywhere like that in Olympus.

"Maybe we could—" I start.

"We don't need you to babysit us. If I want to see the kink club, I'll see the kink club." He flops back against the couch. "Maybe I'll ask Aphrodite. She seems to enjoy sowing discord, so she'd probably say yes."

"*Icarus.* You can't!"

I cross to Ariadne and cover her hand with mine. It's been years since she was in danger of ripping out her own hair because of anxiety, but seeing her twist her curls makes my scalp twinge in sympathy. "Don't let him get to you." I shoot a look at Icarus. "And you. Behave."

"Many have tried to get me to behave; all have failed." He grins suddenly, the expression is pure delight. This right here is why I can never hate Icarus. As sharp as he is, he's just as quick to trade insults for a mischievous invitation to get into trouble. He proves me right when he leans in. "You went to an infamous kink club with Eurydice Dimitriou last night. Did you seduce Demeter's youngest daughter? Tell us all the details."

I smile and lean forward, enjoying the way they both mirror my movement. I wait until they're practically quivering with anticipation to say, "A lady never tells."

He groans. "That's no fun. Eurydice is pretty, but her shadow is even prettier. I don't suppose Charon joined in the fun?"

Ariadne covers her face with her hands. "For gods' sake, Icarus, can you just be *normal* for two minutes."

She doesn't see his flinch in response to her words. His family never seems to. He catches me looking and we share a heartbeat of commiseration. I, at least, have a reason to be on the outside of this fucked-up little family unit. Icarus is Minos's biological son. I can't imagine how it must have felt for his father to go seeking two more and then turn around and show them such blatant favoritism.

So, yeah, I don't love Icarus's cutting remarks, but I don't hate him for them.

"I didn't sleep with Eurydice *or* Charon. And I have to question your taste if you call *him* pretty." Like so many people in the upper tiers of Olympus, Charon is attractive, but it's a more salt-of-the-earth attractiveness than some of the peacocks who strut around the upper city.

Best I can tell, Eurydice is oblivious to the way he looks at her even as she watches him when she thinks no one is paying attention. I don't really know her, but it makes me want to give her a sharp elbow and sharper words. Life is too short to pass up something that's obviously founded in more than pure lust.

It's not my business.

Frankly, *nothing* in this city is my business. The whole thing exhausts me, especially after yesterday, last night, and this morning. "I'm going out tonight."

Icarus perks up. "Out? Where?"

"I have an invitation—and it's exclusive." I can't stand the way he wilts the tiniest bit. "I hear there are some lovely shows in the theater district. Why don't you two try to check one of those out? Surely Minos can't object to *that* activity."

"He objects to all activities right now. We're under strict instructions to stay here and out of trouble." Ariadne won't quite meet my gaze. "But have fun tonight."

Gods save me, but I almost offer to take them with me right then and there. Only the knowledge of their reaction to it being *Aphrodite* issuing the invitation stops me... That, and the fact that I kind of want her all to myself tonight.

I refuse to think too closely about that.

Still, I hesitate. "Let me check this place out. If it's on the up-and-up, I'll see who I have to talk to in order to convince them to issue you invitations, too." It's not, strictly speaking, a lie. But it's not quite honest, either. I feel a little bit of a monster for the way they both beam at me.

I'll ask Aphrodite about it tonight. No matter what else she's said, the only reason she's getting close to me is to suss out information about Minos and his plans. Surely she'll want access to Icarus and Ariadne, too. They don't know anything more than I do, but she won't believe it. It's as good an excuse to get them out of here as any.

———

My confidence that I know what I'm doing dwindles with each floor the elevator passes on its descent to the parking garage. I check my phone for the sixth time, rereading Aphrodite's brief text again.

Aphrodite: My car will meet you in the parking garage.
Be there at nine.

It's not until I open the door and slide into the back seat that I realize I've made a mistake. I'm not alone. Aphrodite lounges in the seat next to me, wearing a masterpiece of a red dress. Its silky fabric leaves her shoulders bare and drapes horizontally across her chest in a way that should be modest...if not for the corset boning just below it that emphasizes her thin waist, followed by more draped fabric around her hips that leaves one long leg completely bare to the upper thigh.

It's a dress meant to seduce.

I know better than to let my gaze linger on the smooth skin of her thigh, to let my curiosity tease out what she might or might not be wearing beneath the dress. She looks like a present just begging to be unwrapped, the top of the dress barely clinging to her upper arms. One tug and I could know if she's bare there, too...

I jerk my gaze away.

Gods, what am I thinking?

"Pandora." Aphrodite's voice is lower than normal, a faint edge there that makes my skin prickle in a way that's far too pleasant. "You dressed up for me."

I swallow hard. "I dressed up for the club."

"Of course," she agrees easily. She leans over and drags her gaze over me in a sweep I can almost feel. I have to fight not to shift, to press my thighs together.

Truth be told, I *did* dress up for her. I wanted her to look at me just like she's doing right now. I just...wasn't prepared for my reaction to it. I'm not normally so reckless when I choose my lovers, but there's something about Aphrodite that sweeps away all common sense.

I give myself a mental shake. Surely I'm not actually considering letting her seduce me? Of all the people in Olympus, she's the one most off-limits. She's my best friend's wife. Yes, it was a forced marriage and yes, he appears to hate her, but honestly that just makes her an even more inappropriate choice.

Not to mention, she's dangerous. Possibly to me. Definitely to Theseus.

Aphrodite leans back, but it's no easier to breathe in the close space. Her perfume is faint but intoxicating. She's styled her dark hair up in a way that's artfully messy and makes me think of sex.

For her part, she seems equally affected. She clears her throat, and when she speaks, her voice still has that edge of seduction. "There are some ground rules for your admittance to the club. Hades and Persephone are unaware of our presence there, but Charon is a stickler for the rules. No drinking on your first time."

"Last night was my first time and I was most definitely drunk." I refuse to feel shame for that. They obviously had a plan for me, so I suspect I would have ended up sleeping it off in Aphrodite's bed no matter what choices I made leading up to arriving at the club.

"Special circumstance," she says breezily. "As I was saying, you can observe the other people in attendance, but you can't participate with anyone outside your party." She gives a sharp smile the same cherry red as her dress. "If you're a good girl, then you'll likely be invited back with more freedom."

Good girl.

The two words go through me like a gunshot. I press my lips together and fight not to shake. What is *wrong* with me? I won't pretend I haven't lost myself to lust more times than I care to count—I love life too much to turn down either fun or pleasure—but this is different.

This feels weighted in a way I'm not prepared to deal with.

I think I made a mistake agreeing to this.

APHRODITE

I'VE ALWAYS BEEN ONE TO MIX BUSINESS AND PLEASURE. Life's too short to deny yourself, and if it has the added bonus of sending the men of my family spinning out? Well, I'm an overachiever like that.

This feels different.

Pandora is practically vibrating with tension by the time we pull up outside the club, and while part of me enjoys the fact that she's obviously so deeply affected by me, the rest of me has the strangest urge to comfort her.

I don't like it.

Sex is simple. It goes into a neat little box and stays there. Relationships are in a different box. With Pandora, there's room in one box but not the other. I can't afford to care. She came to the city with Minos and the rest of his fucked-up little family. If she's not an active part of their plan to harm Olympus, she's also not speaking up against them. She's a passive enemy, but an enemy nonetheless.

I take down my enemies with a single-minded focus that they never see coming.

Except how am I supposed to focus when she's climbing out of the car in *that* dress? We really do match. Hers is a fitted black creation that covers her from wrists to throat, but the fabric is sheer under its geometric pattern, giving tantalizing glimpses of a black bra and panty set beneath. It leaves her curvy body on full display and I fucking love it.

But the real kicker is the zipper. It runs from hem to neckline and she's unzipped it enough to leave one soft, round thigh exposed. My fingers tingle with the desire to touch her there, to follow the line of that dress and undo the zipper with my teeth.

I take a shaky breath and follow her out onto the sidewalk. My body takes over, slipping my hand into hers. Pandora gives me a surprised look, but doesn't snatch her hand back.

No reason to look into that, but my determination to seduce her is only rising with each charged moment that passes between us. I would do it even without the added bonus of it pissing off my dear husband.

She's too sweet a fruit not to be plucked.

Tonight isn't about pressing her for information; she's far too smart to give away the goods so quickly. I have to seduce the information out of her, and I am only too happy to rise to the cause.

I tug her along with me to the entrance and then out of the night's chill and into the club. It's still relatively early as such things go, which was intentional on my part. I want time to get Pandora settled into a booth before the atmosphere of the place takes over.

Truly, I can't believe Hades was hiding out here in the lower city and keeping this little gem tucked away from everyone on the other side of the river. It's more of an open secret now, but the mystique hasn't dampened. If anything, the way people whisper about this place has only added to its allure. Everyone wants an invitation and only a select few get one. Add in the fact that the press are *not* welcome in the lower city and even the most foolhardy of them won't dare piss off Hades...

It's a perfect setup for a little private fun.

Nothing stays secret for long in Olympus, of course. But the only thing that comes out of this club are verbal rumors. Hades doesn't allow the rest of the Thirteen free rein, but I've convinced him to make an exception for me. The exception only lasts for as long as our alliance does, but that's fine. I plan to take full advantage of it.

"Would you like something to drink?" I catch Pandora's sharp look and smile. "No alcohol, but there are plenty of other options."

She shakes her head slowly. "I'm good."

I lean back in the booth, watching her watch the room. In the next thirty minutes, people will have taken seats on the variety of chairs and sofas and love seats scattered around the main floor and the show will begin. I would pay good money to witness one of Hades and Persephone's coveted floor shows—they're both sexy as sin and watching them fuck would be a true delight—but Hades curates those audiences. He's overprotective of his little wife, even though she doesn't need protecting. It's cute.

Pandora studies the dais in the center of the room, a round

stage that is a foot or two off the ground. Not high, but high enough to ensure everyone in the space can get a good look. "When the lights go down, it's rather magical." I don't exactly mean to speak, but her curiosity is practically shouting and I want to hear those thoughts racing behind her big, dark eyes.

"The lighting is fascinating." She eyes the ceiling, where the water reflections from the cleverly hidden trough circling the edge of the room paint glimmering ribbons of light against the black.

"You're going to hurt Hades's feelings talking about the lighting when there's so much else to look at." A playful edge works its way into my tone. "Did you know the first time he brought Persephone here, he fucked her on that throne right there?" I jerk my chin at the gleaming black throne positioned against the wall opposite of us. It's empty now, and will remain so tonight, but it's a showstopper. I don't know if he meant to create this place as the polar opposite of my father's domain—all gold, all the time, the tackier the better—but it's hard not to compare the two.

Thankfully, my brother has subtler taste.

"For a place that boasts no media, everything that happens in this club seems to find its way to the upper city." Pandora's lips twist, though the curiosity in her eyes doesn't dim. "I'm not going to fuck you on that throne."

I laugh. I can't help it. "Honey, no one is allowed on that throne except them. It sits empty on the nights they aren't down here." From the rumors I hear, it sits empty more and more often lately. It's enough to make one wonder if their honeymoon period has worn off so quickly.

The lights dim a bit and the small amount of chatter from the

people gathered dies away. We all watch a pair of white men step
up onto the dais. I've never seen them before, but that doesn't
mean anything; I don't spend much time in the lower city as a
general rule, and it is amateur night, so they don't work here. They
obviously know each other, though. They move in the easy way of
a couple who've done this before enough times to know the steps
by heart.

"I don't understand."

I tear my gaze away from the dais to refocus on Pandora.
"What's there to understand?"

"I've been in Olympus long enough to know the way things
work here." She tucks her long dark hair behind her ears. One
curl immediately breaks free, and I find myself catching it and
smoothing it back. Pandora shivers, but doesn't move away. She
narrows her eyes at the dais. "The upper city is very focused on
their thin veil of purity. Then people act like this the moment they
get a chance. It's hypocritical."

"How naive." I shift a little closer and lower my voice so I'm
speaking directly into her ear. "Power is a game. The shape of it
might look different in other cities, but don't pretend Olympus is
unique in its hypocrisy." Purity and innocence were two things my
father tried to beat into my bones. He should have known it was
a lost cause from the moment I turned fifteen and laughed in his
face when he told me to change my dress before a party. My sister
is more like our mother; she wants to believe the best in people,
even when she knows better.

Me? I take after our bastard of a father. I'm stubborn to a fault
and I will do whatever it takes to reach my end goal. It's a silly

twist of fate that it took me becoming Aphrodite for our goals to align, and by that point, he was dead.

What I do, I do for Olympus.

Even if he wouldn't approve of my methods.

"It's different," Pandora whispers. "Everything about this place is different."

"Not so different." It's difficult to remember that I need to keep a careful distance between us, to not push her too hard. Seduction is an art and I'm normally very good at it, but there's something about Pandora that overrides my normal strategic instincts. "We're human, you and me. No matter how different cultures dress it up or don't, humans are...earthy."

She turns her head, kissably close. "Earthy." She shivers. "That's one way to put it."

I have a plan. It's a very good plan if I do say so myself. I fully intend to edge her to the point where she's panting after me and will do anything I ask. It's worked in the past with other people.

But with her breath ghosting against my lips, the thought of maintaining the distance between us is abhorrent to me. Unnatural. "I'd like to kiss you."

"Not so chaste." She smiles a little, but it's a real smile. It makes her eyes light up. They crinkle at the edges. I never noticed that before. Even in the low light, she takes my breath away.

I lift my hand slowly, giving her plenty of time to react, and cup her soft jaw. Gods, everything about her is soft. I want to drag my mouth over every inch of her skin and see if she tastes as sweet as she smells. "I'm Aphrodite. Chaste is for others. It's not for me." I run my thumbnail lightly over the dip below her bottom lip.

She shivers again, but she leans into my touch. "This is a bad idea."

"Undoubtedly." I grin. "But you knew that when you agreed to come here with me. Are you really going to turn away before you satisfy your...curiosity?"

She looks down, and it takes everything I have to hold perfectly still and let her come to the proper conclusion on her own. We both know tonight will end with my mouth on hers. I don't need to rush her about it. She exhales slowly, and when she raises her gaze, her jaw is set. "Show me."

I kiss her. I've seduced more than my fair share of people—it's practically a hobby at this point—but this feels different. Pandora is no innocent, but kissing her almost feels like it's my first kiss *ever*. I don't know how to explain it. I just want more.

She reaches a shaking hand up to sink into my hair and tug me closer. I use the shift to tilt her head back and deepen the kiss. I don't even have to tease her mouth open. She parts her lips for me eagerly, her tongue sliding against mine in an almost teasing way that goes straight to my head.

A loud moan from the dais makes Pandora jerk back a little. We're both breathing hard, our exhales shared in the minuscule distance between us. "We shouldn't," she whispers.

"I know." I force myself not to kiss her again. She has to be the one to resume this. I had every intention of steamrolling her a bit...later on...but tonight I want her to choose this. To choose *me*. I lean forward and flick the shell of her ear with my tongue. "But that's what makes it so hot, don't you think? Knowing we shouldn't...and doing it anyway."

Her breath shudders out. A pause, barely more than a heartbeat, and then her hands are in my hair, sending it cascading down my back. Pandora kisses me like all the answers of the universe are on the tip of my tongue.

I don't make a deliberate decision to move. One moment I'm awkwardly angling my body at her side, and the next I have one knee between her thighs and I'm pressing her back against the booth. She tugs my hair harder, kissing me deeper, even as my knee slides higher. Offering her what she obviously needs.

I brace one hand on the booth behind her and drop my other to the soft curve of her hip. The fabric of her dress infuriates me. I want it gone, want nothing between us, but this isn't the time or place for that. I urge her to roll her hips and close the last bit of distance between us so she can grind on my thigh. I go still at what I feel. "Pandora."

"Yes?" The word is barely more than an exhale.

I kiss her jaw, her throat, the spot behind her ear. "You're so wet. Is that just for me?"

She shivers as if struck by a live wire. "Aphrodite—"

"Eris," I say sharply. Adonis has been my only lover since taking the title, and he's only ever called me by my actual name… but I can't think about him. Not right now. Not ever again. The thought sinks into my chest, as heavy as an anchor. I have plenty of experience compartmentalizing, though. Dear old Dad taught me.

Not thinking about *him* right now, either.

"Eris." Pandora's little moan scatters all the thoughts in my head. She kisses me again, and then she's moving against me, following my urging. Chasing her pleasure.

I want to give her more. So much more. Desire beats through me with a strength that makes me dizzy. I want to touch this woman with nothing between us, to taste her, to lose myself in making her orgasm so many times the world ceases to spin outside of us.

Hades's club is not the place to do so.

Still...

I catch the back of her knee and lift her leg up and out the tiniest bit, opening her for me. I taste her moan and then she's sliding against my thigh faster. She's so wet, I can feel it through her panties on my bare thigh. Close. My pretty little Pandora is close.

In the end, I just can't help myself. I tug the zipper of her dress open a few precious inches and delve my hand between her thighs. She gasps, but I don't stop palming her pussy. I slide a hand under the silky fabric and... "Fuck, Pandora." She's slippery and wet against my fingers. My nails are too long, so I focus on her clit instead of pressing into her the way I want. "Come for me, beautiful."

It takes less than thirty seconds for her to spasm against me, her cry loud enough that I kiss her again to muffle it. I can't quite stop myself from sliding my fingers over her folds, exploring her carefully. I plan to do it with my tongue at the first opportunity.

Not yet.

Her head lolls against the back of the booth, and she blinks up at me as if she's never seen me before. "Wow."

"Yeah." My voice is nearly as shaky as hers. "That about covers it." I can't stop myself from kissing her again, more lightly this time. "You are a gift."

"Eris." The lovely, glazed look in her eyes clears between one blink and the next. She licks her lips. "Don't use this against him. Please."

The plea is like icy water dumped over my head. Him. Hephaestus. My husband. The person I'm supposed to be seducing Pandora to work against. Except I wasn't thinking about him at all once her mouth met mine.

"I won't," I lie. I like Pandora quite a bit more than I expected to, but in the end my only allegiance is to Olympus. I love Adonis and I still cut out his heart to sacrifice to this city. I'll do the same to this woman, even if it pains me to think of dimming the soft happiness in her dark eyes.

It takes more restraint than I would have guessed to ease back and fix her dress. It takes even more to urge her out of the booth and walk through the dark room to the exit.

And putting her in a car to send home alone?

That takes the most restraint of all.

HEPHAESTUS

I HEAR MY WIFE WALK THROUGH THE DOOR A FEW
seconds before I see her. It's dark in her apartment, so she doesn't
notice me standing in the living room at first. Obviously she forgot
she gave me access in the first place—and then forgot to revoke it.

She looks like she's been out fucking. Her hair is a tangled
mess, as if someone dragged their fingers through it, and her come-
fuck-me dress is sliding dangerously low on her breasts.

Then I see the lipstick smeared at the base of her jaw. Even in
the shadows, I know that shade. It's the only one Pandora wears.
"What did you do?"

To Aphrodite's credit, she doesn't jump or scream. No, the
damned witch goes right for the gun she had fastened to the underside of the coffee table. She curses when she finds the spot empty.
"What the fuck are you doing in my house?"

"I'm your husband." Following Adonis's instructions, I made
sure I was seen coming here. Waiting for my wayward wife while
she was off doing gods-alone-know-what. The poor sap of a

husband. The skin of that role feels too tight, but Adonis was right before... In a game of perception, Aphrodite is a heavy hitter, and I don't know what the fuck I'm doing.

Seeing her infuriates me. She was born with everything at her fingertips, and that privilege is there even now in the way she rises gracefully to her feet. This woman has wanted for nothing, and every second in her presence is an itch I can't scratch, one designed to drive me mad. She's the one who took over my life and trapped me in this marriage I don't want.

She is my enemy.

"Husband or not, you're trespassing." She starts pulling pins out of her hair and moves to the side table, dropping them there, one by one. "I'm not in the mood to play with you. Come back during normal business hours."

"You're my wife," I growl.

She stops and smirks. "Please. You're not naive enough to think that means anything." She runs her fingers through her dark hair and it cascades down around her bare shoulders.

Aphrodite looks good, which just pisses me off further. I stalk to her. Even with taking it easy this afternoon, my knee fucking hurts and I can't keep the limp out of my step. Rationally, I know my wife isn't to blame for that particular sin, but her sister *is* and that's enough to have me catching her jaw and turning her face away from me. I swipe my thumb over her skin, smearing the lipstick. "I'm going to ask you this once more—where have you been?"

"Here and there," she says airily. "You know how it is. Too many places to be, too little of me to go around."

I rub the lipstick between my fingers. It *is* Pandora's shade. I'm sure of it. Now that I'm thinking of it, there's a scent in the air...

Aphrodite curses when I pin her to the wall and press my face to her neck. I inhale deeply and, yes, there it is. Pandora's perfume. It's the first gift I bought her after Minos put me in the ring at eighteen, bought with my winnings from that fight. Ever since then, I buy it for her for birthdays and whenever I notice she's running low. It always makes her smile, and that brightens my day no matter how shitty everything else is going.

"I told you to leave her alone."

To her credit, Aphrodite doesn't play coy. The tension melts out of her body, and she leans back against the wall to look at me. She's wearing those ridiculously high heels again, so our faces are even. She smiles, her dark eyes cold and fearless. "I *am* leaving her alone, dear husband." She runs her hands up my chest and loops them around my neck. Her lips brush my ear. "But who's going to tell *her* to leave *me* alone?"

It was a mistake touching her, allowing her this close. Aphrodite muddles my brain and gets my wires crossed. Half of me wants to shove her away, but the other half wants to grab her tight little ass and haul her more firmly against me. "You're such a bitch."

"Guilty." She sounds so pleased with herself it might make me laugh if I didn't want to strangle her. "Face it, Husband. You're outclassed on every level. If you were smart, you'd roll over and play dead and hope I wander off to torment someone else."

As if giving up has ever been an option for me.

Not in the orphanage, dealing with shit no kid should ever deal with. Not when we moved into Minos's house and suddenly had everything we could ever hope for…but not without cost. There's a price to every action and inaction. I know Pandora thinks I idolize Minos, and maybe she's right, but the truth is that I wouldn't have trusted a free ride. I understand what he wants from me, and he's been nothing if not consistent in those demands.

It's a price I'm more than willing to pay for safety and security. And, truth be told, I'm just monstrous enough to enjoy the work.

"I'll kill you before I let you use Pandora in some sick game."

She laughs in my face. "You don't get to have the high horse, *murderer.*" Aphrodite tilts her head to the side, her hair tumbling over my arm. "She's a smart woman. She knows what I am."

I highly doubt that. I don't even know what Aphrodite is. Every time I think I have her nailed down, she twists out of my grasp and does something to make my life more complicated.

I met her two weeks ago. We've only been married two days. I don't like to think what kind of damage she'll do with more time at her disposal. "Leave her alone."

"Leave her alone," she mocks. "If that's the only argument you have, it's no wonder you need Minos pulling your strings. Ironic that you're Hephaestus now when you never could have gotten the title with your smarts."

I push her back against the wall, using my bigger body to hold her in place. "You keep running that fucking mouth, Wife. You're right. I'm a murderer. What's to stop me from snapping that pretty neck of yours?"

Even in the face of a serious threat, she's undaunted. Aphrodite is relaxed in my arms, as if we're in an intimate embrace instead of half a breath away from a physical fight. It confuses me. My brain knows she's dangerous, but my body is all too eager to remember how good it felt to sink into her wet heat. I strain for control, but my cock isn't listening.

"I don't understand what she sees in you."

The words don't make sense...until they do. I glare. "Don't talk about her."

"Why not?" She kneads the base of my skull with her nails. It doesn't quite hurt, but it doesn't entirely feel good, either. Aphrodite lowers her voice. "Now, what you see in her? I get that. She's a sweet little thing, isn't she?"

"Stop it." I'm playing right into her hands—again—but I can't seem to stop.

"Selfish, though." She smiles, slow and sinful. "She came all over me and then got in a car and went home." Aphrodite laughs. "Woman knows how to leave you wanting more."

She's lying. She has to be. Pandora can be reckless and wild, but she'd never betray me like that...

Though I did find her here this morning, looking hungover and faintly embarrassed. That doesn't mean anything, though. She said nothing happened, and Pandora and I don't lie to each other. Nothing happened.

Last night. That doesn't mean it's true for tonight, though.

"Pandora would never fuck you," I say through clenched teeth.

"Why not? *You* did."

I don't know who moves first. One moment we're glaring at each other and Aphrodite looks like she wants to rip my throat out with her teeth, and the next our mouths meet in a clash.

She tastes of sex. The realization is almost enough to stop me in my tracks, but Aphrodite wraps one bare leg around my waist, and control slips through my fingertips. I run a rough hand up her thigh and cup her ass under the slit of her dress. "No panties. What a little slut."

"Your girlfriend likes it," she gasps against my lips.

I kiss her again to shut her the fuck up. Gods, but I hate this woman. That alone should be enough to ensure I never touch her again, but my body hasn't gotten the memo. I lift her and take one step...

Which is the moment my knee decides to remind me that it's not on board with this abuse.

It buckles and then we're falling. I manage to catch the back of Aphrodite's head to ensure she doesn't bounce it on the marble floor, but that means I take the brunt of the impact.

Godsdamn it, that hurts.

She doesn't pause, one clever hand delving between us to make quick work of my pants. The witch is already trying to take control of this. She doesn't give a fuck that my knee is one blazing starburst of pain or that I saved her from the worst of the impact. The only thing she gives a damn about is winning.

Yeah, fuck that.

I brace myself with a hand on the floor by her head and catch first one wrist and then the other. She curses a little, but I'm not in the mood to play. "Spread your legs."

"You're not in charge."

"Right now, I am." I press her wrists to her stomach, pinning them there. "Spread your fucking legs, wife."

Her slow smile makes what little reasoning I have short out. Her words sweep away the rest. "Make me."

"Never the easy way with you." I should stop this now. There's no way I come out on top of this situation; our wedding night more than proved that. I don't care. I need to put her in her place, and if I have to drive her out of her mind with pleasure to do it, then damn it, I will.

I shift down her body and use my shoulders to force her legs open. For all her smart mouth, she doesn't fight me, letting her legs fall wide. I spare the thought to wish for better lighting to see her properly, but there's no time to pause with lust and rage in the driver's seat.

"If you don't—"

I cover Aphrodite's mouth with my free hand. "You want me to stop, tap my wrist with your fingers." I ignore the mocking look in her dark eyes. I might be a right bastard and a murderer, and I might fantasize about killing my wife more than is healthy, but I don't want to force her. Some lines shouldn't be crossed.

With that boundary clearly defined, there's nothing holding me back from settling between her thighs and dragging my tongue over her pussy. She's *soaked*, and the fact that I don't know if it's for me or leftover from Pandora drives me out of my mind.

I need her to lose control. It's the only way I can regain it.

Another lick. How dare she taste this good? She whimpers against my palm, and that spurs me on. My wife is not infallible. It doesn't matter why she's hanging on the edge, only that I'm there to exploit it. I have to force myself to slow down, to not let her know how much I'm enjoying this. I rub her clit with the flat of my tongue, back and forth, back and forth, testing her reaction.

She might be a liar in every other way, but she can't lie to me like this. Her thighs shake and clench around my head. Her pussy is so wet, I can't resist dipping down and shoving my tongue into her. Too good. Everything about her is a nightmare in how perfect it is.

A harpy in the body of a nymph.

She was sent to destroy me, but I'm going to destroy her first.

APHRODITE

I'VE MADE A MISCALCULATION. I THOUGHT I COULD control this interaction with Hephaestus just like I controlled it last night. He knew I didn't need foreplay, and I didn't peg him for the type to enjoy it anyway; more like he gets in, gets out, and rolls over to snore his way through the night.

Apparently I was wrong.

The man between my thighs, currently fucking me with his tongue, is a stranger. He's obviously furious with me about Pandora, but his solution was to eat me out? It doesn't—

Hephaestus moves back to my clit, working me with that slow, intentional stroke. Even as I tell myself to be still and silent, a whimper slips free. I didn't lie before. Getting Pandora off had me so turned on I couldn't see straight. I fully intended to come home, strip down, and give myself as many orgasms as it took to exhaust me.

Maybe then I'd be able to sleep.

Hephaestus sucks my clit into his mouth and it's too much.

My back bows. My thoughts flicker out. I come so hard, it scatters the world around me.

He releases my hands slowly, as if he expects me to be able to move. "Keep them there."

I can only blink down at him, this furious husband of mine. There isn't a single response ready to deploy, even if he wasn't still covering my mouth with his wide palm. He shifts a little and then his fingers are there, pressing into my pussy.

I thought I was done.

I thought *he* was done.

Apparently I was wrong on both accounts.

He goes back to my clit, pressing remarkably soft kisses there even as he fucks a third finger into me. I'm almost too full, but my body can't decide if it hates it or loves it, not with the conflicting signals being sent. Hard and soft. Rough and gentle.

Oh fuck, I'm going to come again.

I start to lift my hand, to tap out. A denied orgasm isn't ideal, but neither is letting my husband know he's got my number down. People get cocky when they think they have your pussy on a leash. Sex has never been enough to cloud my judgment, and it won't be now, but no reason to give him ideas.

It's too late.

He curls his fingers inside me, testing. His growl of satisfaction is the only warning I get. He zeroes in on my G-spot. Even after the last orgasm, I'm too tightly wound. Too on edge. I come with a scream I'm relieved is muffled.

I think I black out. One moment, I'm lying there, staring at my ceiling and wondering what the fuck just happened.

The next, Hephaestus is flipping me onto my stomach. "You done?"

I should be. It's the smart thing to do. This isn't going at all like I expected, and that means it's time to retreat and recalculate. I open my mouth to confirm that I'm done, but those aren't the words that emerge. "Finish what you started, Husband." I manage to choke out a laugh that's *almost* mocking. "Unless you came in your pants already."

"So quick-witted." He hesitates and then his weight is gone. I hear him hefting himself to his feet with a faint pained groan. "Bed. Now. This floor is killer on my knee."

I watch him walk toward my bedroom. This is my chance to put an end to this. All I need to do is call security and have him escorted out. Married or not, this apartment is *mine*.

But I don't.

I stagger upright and follow my husband into my bedroom. I stop short in the doorway. He's stripping down as if he has every right to be here. Despite myself, I can't help drinking in the sight of him. A warrior, through and through. It's written across his medium-brown skin, there in the scars that line his back and pepper his chest. The scar on his knee is still the bright pink of the newly healed, a mess of tissue that indicates just how bad the injury was.

My sister didn't pull her punches. Or, more accurately, her kick.

"Take off the dress."

I bristle at his command, but my body still shakes from the two orgasms. Last night was fine, but things are different between us right now. Even though I know better, I want to see what he'll do.

I unzip the dress and work it down my body. His attention follows the fabric, and he snorts when I step out of it. "No bra, either." Hephaestus leverages himself down onto the bed.

"It doesn't go with the outfit." I strut over to him and place my foot on his upper thigh, the spike heel bare inches from his hard cock. To his credit, he doesn't so much as flinch, though the muscle flexes beneath my shoe. I bat my eyes at him. "Undo me, Husband?"

"You really are a damned witch." He moves before I can process that, hooking a hand behind my knee and hauling me down astride his lap. "Condom?"

I don't know if I'm irritated he doesn't trust me or proud of him for that same lack of trust. Instead of answering with words, I lean over, letting him catch my hips to keep me in place, and pull one out of the top nightstand drawer. I dangle it in front of his face. "Shall I?"

"No."

Again, that reluctant admiration flares. My husband is taking no chances, and even if it's inconvenient, he's smart not to. I lean back as he rips the packet open and rolls the condom down his impressive length.

He inches back onto the mattress, taking me with him. Hephaestus stares at my breasts for a long moment. "Turn around."

"Excuse me?"

"You heard me." When I don't move fast enough, he hooks

me around the hips and drags me back as he reclines. We end up on our sides, with his arms wrapped around me. He moves me like a fucking doll, draping one of my legs up and over his hips, opening me so he can press his cock to my entrance. "I'm going to fuck you now, Wife."

For such a brutal motherfucker, he really is a softy when it comes to ensuring I'm right there with him. If I was any less determined to make him suffer, that might make me waver. I can't afford to.

My husband is my enemy. My city's enemy.

"You're talking so much, you almost sound like you're working yourself up to it. If you're too scared, just go home. I can finish myself." The words feel too sharp, but I can't help it. I *have* to remember that we're on opposite sides of an uncrossable line.

Instead of getting pissed, he relaxes against me and chuckles. "There she is. You had me worried."

What the fuck is he talking about? "I—" A horrifyingly delicate whimper slips from my lips at the invasion of his cock. I'm wet enough that he doesn't have to fight quite as hard as he did last night, but it's still a tight fit.

He doesn't give me a chance to catch my breath, though. Hephaestus palms one breast with his hand and the other winds around my thigh, hitching it higher in the process, to press lightly against my clit. I'm so oversensitized that any touch stronger than that would be too much, and damn him, he knows it.

"I'll tell you a secret." He fucks me slowly, as if he has all the time in the world. I'm not certain he doesn't. He pinches my nipple lightly, earning another of those godsawful whimpers. He drags his mouth along my throat up to my ear. "You're much more pleasant when someone is playing with your clit."

"You son of a—"

Another nipple pinch steals my words. Hephaestus changes his angle a little and, oh fuck, this feels good. I'm melting for him, and even as I try to fight it, my body has taken over. He keeps up that light touch on my clit, fucking me right to the edge of a third orgasm.

How did I lose control so thoroughly?

I'm a shaking, whimpering thing, and all I can do is cling to him and take what he gives me. Later... Later, I'll make him pay for this.

After he makes me come again.

His voice is rough with pleasure, lower than normal and gravelly. "Gonna be a requirement for every talk going forward. Spread those thighs and put you in an agreeable mood. If you're very good, I'll even give you this cock again."

I need to push back against this. I *have* to. Because the picture he's painting isn't disagreeable. I can envision it all too clearly. Us trading barbs while he's fingering me... While he's going down and putting that vicious tongue to work. "Oh fuck."

"That's right, Wife. Come on your husband's cock."

I don't want to. I desperately don't want to give him this. But it's too late to go back. I cry out as I come, clenching around his cock. He barely waits for my orgasm to ebb before he picks up his pace, fucking me roughly for several long minutes, and then coming with a curse that makes me shiver.

Then the motherfucker pulls out of me and slaps my ass.

I'm still trying to find words when he returns from my bathroom, drops down next to me with one heavy arm draped over my waist, and passes the fuck out. I blink in shock. The asshole is *snoring*.

My thoughts are too scattered after this hard pivot to fully comprehend what just happened. That was...good sex. Really good. It doesn't mean anything, and it certainly won't divert me from my goals, but it's more than a little shocking. I don't know why he's *staying*, though. It doesn't make sense. He hates me as much as I hate him, and while he might be wholly outclassed for his title, that doesn't mean he's a complete fool. There's no way he'd sleep in my bed without good reason.

Surely the reason isn't because he slept as little last night as I did?

A yawn catches me by surprise. I'm going on forty-eight hours without sleep. Not my longest stretch, not by a long shot, but the longest in years. Even when Adonis and I were on our off times, he was always there for me to crash in his bed, the familiar cadence of his breathing enough to send me under. That's not an option anymore, and I have no one to blame but myself.

I yawn again. Hephaestus is heavy, his arm a solid weight pinning me to the mattress. I try to shift away, but he tightens his hold on me, tucking me against his larger body. I curse. "You've *got* to be joking me." I poke his shoulder. "Hephaestus. Hephaestus, you can't stay here."

He doesn't move. He doesn't respond at all, other than letting out another quiet snore. I sigh. Some soldier he is. I could claw his eyes out or smother him right now; he might wake up to prevent me from killing him, but I could definitely maim. Surely he doesn't think so little of me?

It's definitely not that he trusts me.

I certainly don't trust him.

I don't mean to close my eyes. I have every intention of wrestling my way out of Hephaestus's hold, showering the scent of sex off my body, and then brewing some coffee to keep the mental cobwebs at bay. He just... He smells really good. And my body is relaxed from the orgasms and the feel of him half holding me down. Like my very own cranky weighted blanket.

Dangerous thoughts.

I'm going to get up.

In just a moment...

"Eris?"

I jolt awake. There's something wrong in the room, and it's not just the man sleeping at my side. The light is all strange. It was dark just a moment ago, only the lights of the city playing through the windows of my bedroom. Now it's bright.

I slept.

I *slept*.

"Eris."

I belatedly register it's not my husband talking to me. I look up and go still. *Adonis.* I wish I could say he looks great, but it would be a lie. His pants are creased and his shirt is buttoned haphazardly. He also hasn't shaved recently, so a shadow of a beard darkens his jaw. "What are you doing here?"

"I..." He shakes his head sharply. "I was worried about you."

Gods, it hurts to look at him. It hurts even more that both

of us are very carefully not looking at my husband lying naked on the bed between us. There's no way he's still sleeping, but he hasn't opened his eyes, and this moment feels too fraught to call him out on eavesdropping. I drag in a shaky breath. "I told you we shouldn't see each other anymore."

Adonis's dark eyes take on a look I've never seen before. On anyone else, I would call it cruelty. "And yet you didn't revoke my permission to your apartment or take your key back. Seems like you're sending mixed signals."

I didn't do either of those things because deep down, I'm a sentimental fool. Not that I'll ever admit it. I lift my chin. "An oversight on my part. I've only been married two days, after all." I'm being an unforgivable bitch, but *why is he here?* Surely it hurts him to look at me as much as it hurts me to look at him?

Adonis shakes his head. "I didn't come to fight with you, Eris. I came to make sure you're okay."

"What are you talking about?"

"There was an attack." He looks away. "Someone tried to kill Athena."

ADONIS

ERIS WAS *SLEEPING*. WITH HEPHAESTUS.

Even as she stares at me in shock, rattled by the attempt on Athena's life, I can't erase the image of her sharp features relaxed, her body tucked into his embrace. They look good together. I knew that, of course; photos from their wedding were splashed all over MuseWatch. Her in that gorgeous gown standing next to his broader form, them both the same height with her heels. His brooding attractiveness and her sharp beauty.

A matched pair.

Eris slaps Hephaestus's shoulder. "Stop pretending to sleep. I know you're awake."

He rolls onto his back, seeming completely uncaring that he's as naked as she is. Eris has always stopped my breath in my lungs. She says I'm the beautiful one, but she's the kind of devastating that brings down cities and leaves a trail of broken hearts behind her.

Hephaestus is different. He draws me in a way that's all too earthy, his massive body peppered with scars and the kind of muscle definition that makes me want to trace the lines with my tongue. Despite myself, my gaze snags on his hips, where his cock jerks as if in response to my attention.

"See something you like?" he drawls.

Eris flicks the sheets over his hips. "Stop showing off." She snaps her fingers. "Adonis, focus. What happened to Athena?"

Right. The reason I came. I clear my throat. "It was a sniper. They shot at her from a building across the way. She received minor injuries from shattered glass, but is otherwise fine."

"A sniper." Eris frowns. "But that won't trigger the clause, even if they were successful."

"You know that. I know that. The greater Olympus population doesn't." Somehow, in all the chaos after the house party, *that* piece of information was never made public, which just proves that Minos is smart. He leaked enough information to cause problems, but not enough to actually change power.

If Athena was killed without the proper steps being followed, her murderer would be executed and her successor would be appointed by Zeus, just like every Athena before them.

"I bet you're happy." She glares down at Hephaestus. "This is what you wanted, isn't it?"

"I wanted to be one of the Thirteen." He pushes off the bed and carefully stands, but on his first step, his knee buckles.

I move on instinct, catching his elbow and keeping him on his feet. It brings us startlingly close. Close enough that I can smell Eris and sex on his skin. Jealousy and something infinitely more complicated sink their fangs into me.

I love her. I'm quickly having to admit that I'm attracted to him. The thought of them fucking, of them *sleeping together*, claws at my insides, knowledge I can't escape.

Hephaestus's gaze drops to my mouth for one charged moment and then he shakes me off. "I got it."

We watch in silence as he moves slowly into the bathroom and shuts the door firmly behind him. I turn back to Eris almost reluctantly. I didn't think he would still be here, or I never would have come.

Except that's not the truth, is it?

When I heard the news about Athena, I didn't stop to think. I was already walking through the lobby to Eris's building by the time my brain caught up with my body. I can barely process the relief I feel over her being okay when *this* is what I found. It feels like she stabbed me in the gut, and I don't know what it says about me that I can't just be happy she's alive and well in this moment. I can barely look at her. "You slept with him."

"He's my husband. I'm allowed to fuck him."

She's being intentionally difficult. I clench my jaw. "That's not what I mean and you know it. You *slept with him*, Eris. What the fuck?"

"Adonis—" She stops short and sighs. That sigh feels like a hook in my chest, dragging what's left of my jagged heart out into the open between us. It's only been a couple weeks since she broke it off, and it's never been so final between us. My brain knows that it's over. My heart hasn't quite caught up.

"Don't." I don't know what I'm protesting, only that I'm already the walking wounded and I can't take her kicking me in the teeth right now. "Just don't."

"It doesn't mean anything." She speaks so quietly, none of her normal sharp edges present. "We fought and we fucked and I haven't slept in days. That's all it was."

Except we both know better.

Eris doesn't sleep well. She hasn't for as long as I've known her, which is most of our lives. She's given dozens of answers over the years to explain it away, but I suspect the truth sources back to growing up in Zeus's household. It's bad enough to know her father murdered her mother—and got away with it—but he put all his children through trauma I can barely imagine. My parents can be difficult and stubborn and strict, but my home was a safe space. It still is a safe space.

She never had that.

She still doesn't, though she'd fight me to a standstill if I suggested it. Eris doesn't see what she and Zeus are doing as anything other than necessary, but marrying the enemy and going through torment to bring them down? That's not normal, even for Olympus. It's certainly not safe.

"Eris." I catch myself. Eris might be who I fell in love with, but she's not that person anymore. "I suggest you expand your security detail, Aphrodite. Maybe your husband won't dare hurt you, but there are plenty of people in Olympus who are willing to kill for your title."

"Adonis..."

She starts to rise, but I shake my head. "No. I'm done. Coming here was a mistake." I keep expecting the pain of losing her to dull, but it's as sharp as ever. Before, even when we were on a break, we were still friends. That isn't true anymore. I can't be just friends with this woman. We've been ingrained in each other's lives for too long. Maybe we could never quite make it work in a permanent way, but we had our history binding us together.

Or at least we used to.

"I'll leave my key on the kitchen counter."

"Wait—"

I walk out of the bedroom before she can find the words to keep me there. She will. She always has in the past. What I need to do is leave immediately, but I find myself moving through the rooms of the apartment. There are so many good memories here from over the years. Evenings spent trying to cook whatever new dish Eris found on the food blogs she refuses to admit to anyone else that she loves. Lazy mornings strategizing on the political moves others are making and how she wants to either disrupt or assist. Nights where she fell asleep on my chest, her dark hair silky against my skin.

Never again.

I leave my key where I told her I would. It feels like a final goodbye. The elevator ride down to the lobby is even worse, to the point where I'm relieved when my phone buzzes in my pocket.

Less so when I realize who it is.

Hephaestus: Meet me at my place.

I stare at the text for a long moment. Agreeing to help him was a mistake. I knew it going in, and what I found this morning only confirms it. I can't take this man's word for anything. Continuing this charade where I give him advice to help him undermine

Eris's—no, *Aphrodite's*—plan to thwart the enemy? It skirts the line of making me a traitor.

In this moment, I'm not sure I care.

I type back a quick agreement and keep going. There are a pair of photographers huddled across the street, and I force my expression into my customary relaxed grin. They'll already have enough to talk about with my rush into the building; no reason to give them more ammunition.

My mother calls as I head back to my apartment. I sigh and check my pace. "Hello, Mom."

"Adonis, honey, why are you outside that woman's apartment?"

My mom loves Eris. She genuinely hoped we'd get married at some point and pop out half a dozen grandchildren for her to dote on, despite the fact that neither of us are overly inclined to be parents. But ever since the marriage was announced, Eris has become *that woman* in conversation. As much as I appreciate the unrelenting support, it doesn't change the fact that it makes me want to defend Eris. "I had to drop off my key."

Her beat of silence lets me know what she thinks of that poor excuse. "That girl has her sights set elsewhere, Adonis. She always has. It's time to stop following her around like a lovestruck teenager and find someone to settle down with."

We've had a variation of this conversation a dozen times in the last dozen days. I can almost recite it by heart. "Mom, you've got to give me time."

"Your parent and I only have so many years left. You won't have us dying without knowing you're happy, will you?"

I don't roll my eyes, if only because my mother has a sixth

sense when it comes to anything resembling disrespect. "You're only in your fifties. You were just saying you're still in your prime last week. You'll be around for another forty years at least and you know it."

"Maybe. Maybe not."

There's no reasoning with her when she gets like this. She means well, even if her idea of a reasonable timeline to get over a broken heart leaves something to be desired. "I'll considering dating at some point. That's all you're going to get out of me right now."

"I suppose that will have to do." She sounds so pleased, I can't help grinning. Mom laughs. "You're a good boy, Adonis. Anyone who doesn't see that isn't worth your time. Come by for dinner Sunday."

"Yes, ma'am. I'll see you then."

"If you decide to bring someone, I wouldn't be sad about it."

I chuckle. "Goodbye, Mom. Have a good rest of your day." I make a quick stop at my apartment to fix my appearance. I had no thought of that when I rushed to Aphrodite's side earlier, but now that I'm going to be circling Hephaestus, it's important to keep up every barrier possible.

My fingers still in the middle of buttoning my shirt. I knew he was attractive, of course, but seeing him naked was something that never should have happened. My family and friends don't think I have much in the way of canniness, but even I know better than to sleep with this man.

But I won't lie and say the temptation isn't there. For a multitude of reasons.

I find Hephaestus waiting for me outside his building, leaned up against the wall as if he doesn't notice the paparazzi trailing him. They're further away than I expect, but then I wouldn't want to risk a known murderer's wrath if I were them, either.

He sends me a searching look. "You're still torn up over her."

"No shit." I know better than to let my emotions get the best of me, but there was no closure this morning. If anything, it tore open a brand-new wound I wasn't even aware of until now. "She *slept* with you."

"You keep saying that." He narrows his eyes. "What does that mean?"

I open my mouth to reply, but my brain catches up before I have a chance to. He has enough ammunition against her without me giving him more. I don't want to actually hurt Aphrodite—just her public image. It's a bone in my throat to know she was able to sleep with *him* in her bed, that she was never going to come to me for that again, not now that she's married.

She needs to sleep.

I just hate the source of her relief.

"Nothing." I turn back to where my car idles at the curb. "Let's go."

"Where are we going?" Even as he asks the question, he moves to follow. He really is a cocky bastard. I could have murdered him several times over.

Unlike the greater Olympian population, *I* know what's required to trigger the assassination clause. If I killed Hephaestus and took his place, *I* could marry Eris. There would be no one standing between us...

Even as the thought crosses my mind, I discard it. I'm not

a murderer. I'm capable enough, even years after training with Athena, but I've always lacked the coldness she requires in her people. It's why I didn't last more than two years with her before she sat me down and gently—for her—told me that I'd be better suited for another line of work.

The assassination attempts on the Thirteen won't go away. If anything, they're going to get worse as time goes on and people become bolder. Too many people saw the attack on Athena. It's being actively televised right now, a spray of glass and her people pulling her down to the ground and covering her with their bodies.

There will be another attack, and soon.

Maybe it's naive, but I don't want to be part of the problem.

"Adonis?"

Gods, but I like the rough way he says my name. I open the car door for him. "We're going to your building and seeing your people."

"They aren't my people." He glares, but he slides into the seat all the same.

I shut the door and circle around to the driver's seat. "Yes, they are, and the sooner both you and they make their peace with that, the better."

HEPHAESTUS

I DON'T WANT TO GO TO MY BUILDING. *MY BUILDING.* The very label makes me want to curse. It's not *mine.* Of all the titles I could have taken, Hephaestus is the one least suited to me. Everyone who works for the title is so damned smart, and the few times I've darkened the doorway of this building, I've felt like a lumbering oaf.

"This is a mistake."

"You can't keep ignoring your responsibilities." Adonis doesn't look at me. He's tense, almost angry, and I find it interesting that he's obviously trying hard not to direct it at me. What a novel concept.

I deserve his anger, I guess. I married his woman, and I'm sleeping with her, which seems to be the more upsetting development. There's a thread there to tug on, but I'm weirdly reluctant to do it. At the end of the day, there's only our deal holding Adonis to me, and there's nothing real stopping him from walking away.

It'd be better for him if he did.

I cross my arms over my chest. "They're doing just fine without me."

"Undoubtedly."

I glare. "Then why bother going in there? It's a waste of time."

Adonis sighs, a nearly soundless exhale. "Because you are Hephaestus."

"Theseus." I don't know why I argue. He's not wrong, but I hate that fucking title in his mouth.

He finally turns to face me, and I'm struck all over again by how beautiful he is. More than any other person I've met, except maybe Helen. Certainly more beautiful than my wife.

Adonis snaps his fingers. "Stop looking at me like that. This is business."

Right. I should know better than to forget. There might be a spark of attraction between us, but I'm an enemy of Olympus and Adonis is its beloved son.

When he seems satisfied with how I'm looking at him, he continues. "You are Hephaestus," he repeats. "You took the title, and now you have to own it. That means dealing with the responsibilities that come with it."

"Seems like there's nothing but responsibilities with this shit."

"Now you're beginning to understand." He smiles grimly. "The Thirteen might be the most powerful people in the city, and they might abuse that power regularly, but they are also the ones who keep the city running. *You* are now responsible for keeping the city running. You can't do that if you're hiding from your people."

I know what he's attempting. He's trying to leverage my pride to get me to do what he wants. I'm fucking irritated to discover it's working. "It's not that easy."

"Of course it's not. The last Hephaestus was hardly universally beloved, but he *was* good at his job."

I'm not beloved *or* good at my job.

I glare up at the building where all of Hephaestus's work is done. I want to get the fuck out of this car and away from this place. The problem is I can't pretend that if I'd been successful taking Apollo's title, things would've been any better. Really, I'm suited for Ares, and no other.

But there's no getting out of this.

Adonis leads the way through the sliding glass doors and into what could be every other building in downtown Olympus. Glass and marble and steel. Don't these fuckers ever get tired of this decorating scheme? Apparently not.

We take the elevator up to the tenth floor. I've only been here a handful of times, but it always plays out exactly like this. I'm a little surprised to feel humiliation sink in as we step through the elevator doors. Several people look up from the cubicles scattered through the space. The instant they recognize that it's me, the whispers start.

The feeling of humiliation grows when Brontes approaches from the back office. Xe is a short person with light-brown skin and a haircut that looks like a toddler got ahold of some scissors. Xyr straight black hair is all different lengths and I can grudgingly admit that it looks good despite myself.

Xe is also a giant pain in my ass.

Brontes stops in front of us. Xe manages a bright smile for

Adonis, and I can't say I'm surprised. The man seems to walk in a permanent beam of sunshine wherever he goes, and people react accordingly. The look Brontes gives *me* is significantly less pleasant. "So. You're here."

I glance at Adonis, but he seems content to let me take the lead now that he's dragged me here. Traitor. I clear my throat. I don't even know what to ask, which just makes the feeling beneath my skin worse. "I need an update on all current projects."

Brontes raises xyr eyebrows. "All of them?"

I've made a mistake, but I can't admit it now without admitting I don't know what the fuck I'm doing here. "Yes. All of them. I need to be brought up to speed."

If I hadn't known I'd fucked this up, xyr delighted smile would have informed me. Brontes gives a neat little bow that somehow manages to make me feel like even more of a lumbering fool. "Of course, Hephaestus. If you'll wait in your office, we should have that ready for you in about, oh, three or four hours."

Three hours.

Fuck me.

Brontes doesn't lead us to the office, and I've only been in there once, so it takes me three tries to find the right one. All the while, that fucking terrible feeling at the back of my neck gets worse.

I can barely look at Adonis as I drop into the chair behind the desk that will never be mine. "You happy now?"

He sighs. "We have a lot of work to do."

———

That evening, I slam the door hard enough to shake the house and stalk down the hallway into the living room. It's empty except for Pandora, and as much as part of me is relieved to see her here and safe, I can't forget her lipstick on my wife's jaw and her perfume coating Aphrodite's skin. "What the fuck do you think you're doing?"

Pandora sets down her e-reader with exaggerated slowness. Her sunny smile is nowhere in evidence. "If you want an actual answer, I'm going to need you to check your tone and try that again."

I have to muscle down the urge to roar out all my frustration and anger at her. It's not her fault I had a shitty day in a long string of shitty days, but I thought she was in my corner and now I'm not so sure. I succeed in moderating my tone. Barely. "You fucked my wife."

She doesn't tend to blush, but I don't need to see it when she's shifting on the couch like someone poured itching powder into her leggings. "I wouldn't call it 'fucking.'"

"Don't play semantics with me, Pandora."

Her dark brows crash down. "Why are you really mad?" She waves a hand before I can respond. "Oh, I know you'd be pissed about that little indiscretion no matter what, but not *this* mad."

Damn her for knowing me so well. I move into the living room and drop down next to her on the couch. "Adonis and I went to my office today."

"Adonis," she says slowly. "As in Aphrodite's ex, Adonis? Someone's a hypocrite."

"That's not what I'm talking about right now."

She turns to face me on the couch, curling her legs in a position that makes me wince in sympathy for her joints. Her expression is all feigned calm, but her eyes are just as angry as I feel. "By all means, Theseus, let's not talk about anything *you* don't want to talk about right now."

She's pissed and she probably has a right to be, but I'm so fucking frustrated, I can barely focus. "I should have killed literally anyone else. I'm not cut out for this fucking job. All the people who answer to Hephaestus—"

"*You're* Hephaestus now."

I ignore that. "Every single one of them is a fucking snooty asshole who graduated with some obscure college degree that I've never heard of. Even with Adonis there, they all played innocent while they updated me on shit that doesn't even make sense. They made me wait *four hours* for a bunch of reports I can't even read. I know they're written in English, but they might as well be Latin for all I understood it. And, those fuckers, they know it." I am smart enough when it comes to the things I care about, but I never did well in school and college wasn't even on the agenda.

Minos didn't pick me because I can talk fancy and invent shit.

He picked me because he looked at me and saw a capacity for violence that he could hone into a weapon. I made my peace with that a long time ago. I don't try to be anything but what I am.

Except now my very role in life is something that I'm not.

"Oh, Theseus." Pandora squeezes my arm. "We're basically invaders. Of course they weren't going to welcome you with open arms."

I know that. Of course I fucking know that. "It would have been better if I'd become Ares. Or even Athena or Artemis."

Unlike the Minotaur, *I* wouldn't have fucked up that kill. At least then I'd be in charge of a realm that made sense to me.

"It will get better."

I give her the look that deserves. It's not going to get better. Minos hasn't shared the details of his plans going forward, not now that I've served my role, but if he gets his way, I doubt Olympus will be standing by the end of this. That should be comforting. I am Hephaestus, but who knows what that will mean in six months, or a year. I should be *happy*.

Instead, it's hard not to feel like I've sacrificed so much for shit-all.

"It won't get better for them," I snap.

"It doesn't have to be that way. We don't have to act this way." Pandora shifts and tucks her hair behind her ears. "I know what we were taught, but maybe they aren't as bad as all that. Really, they're not that much different from us."

She's not wrong. The way the center city lives is still alien to me, but the same could be said of Aeaea before Minos took us in. The orphanage might as well have been on the moon for all our lives there had in common with how we lived in his house. But that doesn't make a difference. "We came here for a purpose, and we're going to see it through."

"What if the purpose is wrong?"

I sink down next to her on the couch. We've had variations of this conversation for months. Longer, even. Pandora doesn't feel beholden to Minos the way I do. She doesn't understand that I will do anything to keep us from going back to a place without power, helpless to the whims of those around us.

Even if lately I feel more in common with that child in the orphanage than I do with the man I've worked so hard to become. "It's not for us to question the purpose. Minos has a plan." A plan that seems to require sacrifice from everyone but him.

He hasn't felt the weight of all the strings that tie me in place.

Or if he does, he hides it significantly better than I do; another lesson he never bothered to teach me.

"You have more faith in him than I do." Pandora shakes her head, her dark eyes holding things I'm not ready to see. "I wish you would listen to reason, Theseus."

No matter the shared history we have, Pandora will never look at Minos the way I do. To her, he's a vicious man who ruthlessly adopted two teenagers to enact a plan fifteen years in the making. And she's not wrong. But what she fails to acknowledge is where we would've ended up if not for Minos. He saved us, whether she wants to admit it or not. Without him, we would've been turned out onto the streets the second we turned eighteen.

And the streets of Aeaea would've eaten us alive.

I don't know if I could've protected Pandora, not at eighteen, not without the skills that I've learned since joining Minos. She doesn't want to hear that, though. We've had this argument more times than I care to count. I know exactly how it will go from here. We will circle round and round until we're yelling at each other, and then one of us will storm off, only to crawl back and apologize within an hour or two.

Instead I change the subject. "Where is everyone?"

Pandora shrugs as if it doesn't actually matter. "Icarus is off doing…whatever it is that Icarus does when no one else is around.

I saw Ariadne typing away at her computer awhile back, but that's all she seems to do these days."

"I wasn't asking about them."

She gives me a look filled with censure. "You never ask about them."

Why would I? They're soft, coddled creatures. Even with Minos as their father, they haven't acquired the hard edge that Pandora and I were born with. And the Minotaur? Well, he's another story altogether. But Ariadne and Icarus have been kept safe and sheltered, and it's spoiled them to the reality of the world. Ariadne spends all her time online, indulging in the privilege of a digital life and ignoring the blood staining the hands around her.

Icarus doesn't hide, but his relationship with Minos is complicated. Instead of keeping his head down and obeying, he flounces and makes passive-aggressive comments, dramatic to the bitter end.

"If you'd just—"

I shake my head sharply. "No. They aren't like us."

"Theseus." She touches my forearm. "It doesn't have to be this way. You have the title now. I might not love the way you got it, but it's done. You don't have to keep doing the awful things he asks of you." She hesitates. "Aphrodite isn't all that bad. If you'd stop fighting her and start working with her, maybe we could put a stop to all this before it truly spins out of control."

Hearing my wife's name on Pandora's lips banishes the warmth in my chest. I straighten, shifting my arm from her touch. "She's using you. I thought you were smarter than that, Pandora."

"Oh no, you don't get to do that." She narrows her eyes. "I grew up in the same place you did, and I learned the same hard lessons surviving that nightmare. You do *not* get to act like I'm some naive fool being led along by my curiosity. The Thirteen as a whole are monsters. I've never argued with that. But they are still made up of people. People with scars who have seen things just as horrible as what we grew up with. And that's not even getting into the people who don't live in the center city. There are people like *us* here, Theseus."

"We're not going after the people like us."

Pandora tosses up her hands. "I wish you would stop and *think*. If Aeaea had the equivalent of the Thirteen, then Minos would sit on that board. He's the very thing you claim to hate. You are, too, now that you've become Hephaestus."

I push to my feet, driven by the need to get the fuck away from this conversation, from hearing *that* name on my best friend's lips. "Whatever. I'm going to find Minos and update him."

"Oh yes, do run away like a damned coward."

I spin on my heel. My knee buckles, but I manage to keep my feet and resist wincing as pain shoots up my leg. I point at her. "That's where you and I are different, Pandora. You can drag your bleeding heart all over this city, wasting it on people who wouldn't piss on you if you were on fire. I don't give a fuck about them, just like I don't give a fuck about anyone back in Aeaea. I give a fuck about *you*, and I can't keep you safe if you're off gallivanting around with one of those monsters."

She sits back, her expression sad. I hate that I made her sad, that it seems to be the rule rather than the exception these days. I disappoint Pandora. I disappoint Minos. I'm fucking up. Pandora picks up her e-reader, but her voice follows me as I leave the room. "I've always had a monster at my side, Theseus."

No reason for her words to plague me. I know what I am. I'm not the good guy. That was never going to be my role, and damn Pandora for pretending like I've ever had a choice.

In our world, you're either predator, or you're prey.

I had to be predator enough to protect us both. Apparently I still do.

I make my way through the penthouse to where Minos's office is. The door is cracked, so I can hear his deep voice as he speaks to someone on the phone. I lean against the wall, waiting.

"Things are proceeding according to plan, more or less. The shipments are currently waiting in the harbor, but Poseidon has no reason to question their contents." A pause. "No, I haven't been able to get to the lower city. The outer barrier might be faltering, but the one on the River Styx is still strong enough to repel us if he decides to make it so, and he's not my biggest fan."

That's the understatement of the year. Though, honestly, it's a toss-up who among the Thirteen wants us dead the most. Zeus or Hades, perhaps, but we can't discount Hera, Artemis, Athena, and my darling wife. All are formidable in their own way—even Hera, despite our reports saying it was all but an empty title. That may have been true with past Heras, but it's not with *this* one. I would hesitate to give her my back, for fear of ending up with a knife slipped between my ribs.

Minos clears his throat. "The public is responding exactly as you anticipated. They're doing most of the work for us. One of them even tried to kill Athena this morning, which is significantly more ballsy than I expected so early in the process." A beat. "Yes, the timeline is intact. It's a waiting game until the ship docks and our...packages...are unloaded. I'll, of course, keep you updated." A pause. "Stop lurking in the halls and get in here." He's lost the false cheer in his voice, but I prefer him this way.

When it's just us, Minos never pretends to be anything other than what he is. A predator, just like me.

I step into the office. It's nearly identical to the one he set up in the country house he bought from Hermes. A large, dark wooden desk dominates the space with a floor-to-ceiling window overlooking the city behind it. The other two walls are lined with bookshelves, though in all the time I've known him, I've never seen him read. Ariadne is the reader of the family, but Minos would never allow her bent and dog-eared romance novels to populate the shelves of *his* space.

"Shut the door."

My stomach drops, but I obey. I clench my jaw and keep the limp out of my stride as much as possible as I cross to sink down in the chair across the desk from him. Even with that effort, his gaze lingers on my injured knee and distaste flickers across his features. He grabs a tablet and his fingers sweep over the screen. "I'd like you to explain this to me."

He spins it to face me, and the sinking feeling in my stomach gets worse. It's a MuseWatch article on the home page. The photographer caught me right as I was walking up to Aphrodite's building, and I don't know what the fuck I was thinking in that moment, but I can't deny that I look...lost. The headline is even worse.

POOR HEPHAESTUS. AT HOME WAITING FOR HIS WIFE WHILE SHE'S OUT PHILANDERING.

I skim the article, which is pitying, but significantly more sympathetic than previous ones. Adonis's plan is working, but it doesn't make me feel any better about being painted as some poor sap waiting with his heart in his hand while his wife runs around town with anyone who will have her.

With Pandora.

"I—"

Minos talks right over me. "Because it *looks* like my foster son is playing the part of a pathetic weakling who can't control his wife. It's been less than a week, and she's already been photographed with four separate people who aren't you. The entire city is laughing at you. At *us.*"

That's the crux of the matter. Pandora might think I follow Minos without question, but I know what he is and what his priorities are. How he's acted with me since the Ares competition has more than proved that. I'm no use to him if I'm not in perfect health and the very picture of obedience. "I'm working on it."

"Are you? Because it appears you're pining." He spits it as if it's a dirty word. "You look weak, which makes us look weak by extension. I have put too much effort into garnering favor with the Olympian people to have you undo it in a few short days. It's unacceptable."

Frustration sinks its roots into me. "If you have a better idea to gain public favor, I'd love to hear it."

"Watch how you speak to me, boy." His tone goes sharp and dark. "I pulled you out of the gutter and I can put you right back into it. You've failed me one too many times already. Do it again, and I'm going stop being so nice."

"I'm sorry. I'll fix it."

"You'd better. You won't like how things fall out if I'm required to step in."

You're Hephaestus now.

"I'll take care of it." I shake my head sharply, trying to banish Pandora's voice. It doesn't matter if I'm technically one of the thirteen most powerful people in the city. So was the last Hephaestus, and look where he is now.

Six feet underground, food for the worms.

The same can happen to me.

The same *will* happen to me if I don't fix this.

PANDORA

I DON'T MEAN TO GO TO APHRODITE.

After that disastrous conversation with Theseus, I actually follow him down the hall to apologize…which is when I overhear Minos's not-subtle threat. Theseus doesn't challenge him, doesn't tell him to fuck off with that nonsense. He rolls over and shows his stomach. I hate that. Minos doesn't deserve his loyalty.

But telling Theseus that will just result in a continuation of our fight.

He thinks I don't understand why he follows Minos around like a whipped dog. I do. I was in that same orphanage he was. I suffered the same punishments, ranging from skipped meals to forced isolation to beatings. *I* am the reason Theseus committed the act of violence that brought us to Minos's attention.

I never faulted Theseus for taking Minos's deal, but we aren't fifteen anymore. We don't have to stay with him. *That's* what Theseus doesn't seem to understand.

I flee before they finish their little meeting. I just need some air.

That's all. Maybe that will help me find a way out of this impossible situation. Minos sees Theseus as a pawn; he always has. And what's a pawn good for but sacrifice? Being Hephaestus won't save Theseus if Minos decides he's outlived his usefulness.

The worst part is that I'm not sure Theseus would fight. He might just kneel, bow his head, and accept his punishment as if that's something he deserves.

I've known the man my entire life. I *should* be able to come up with the right sequence of words to get him to listen to me. Except every time I try, we end up in the same damn fight. I don't know what to do. I've never felt so fucking helpless in my life.

I leave Minos's penthouse and walk the streets. I'll never get used to this place—or at least the city center where the rich and powerful make their homes. It's all metal and concrete and glass. Soulless. Back on Aeaea, the rich don't congregate in one place. It's a point of prestige to have a massive house with even more massive grounds, all hidden away behind stone walls.

Gods forbid one of the rabble should dirty up the space with their presence.

It was one of those homes that Minos brought us to after slipping enough money to the right people to ensure he got exactly what he was looking for—two teenaged boys, their strength only matched by their rage. It's just his bad luck that one of them came with me attached, but he wanted Theseus too badly to balk at my presence.

And now look at us.

We're the bad guys. I might not have committed any violence with my own hands, but I stood by and let it happen. How could

I do anything else? If the Olympians knew Minos's plan to insert Aeaeans into the Thirteen through the assassination clause, they would have killed Theseus outright, and *that* I won't be party to.

I slow and stop in front of familiar glass doors. Walking through them is in direct conflict with what Theseus wants, but at this point, I don't know that he's thinking clearly. I don't know if any of us are. Things have changed too quickly, and despite all the preparation, it's clear Minos didn't actually know the full extent of what becoming one of the Thirteen means. He has his end goal, whatever it is, but he's not offering Theseus any support in the meantime.

If I could get Theseus out from under his thumb...

I'm moving before I can think of how flimsy that excuse is. The lobby is exactly how I remember it from the other day—just as soulless as the rest of downtown. I smooth down my shirt and walk to the desk with the snooty-looking white woman behind it. She eyes me as if I'm a piece of trash that blew in off the street, but her expression changes as recognition rolls over her pretty features. "You're Pandora."

This is something I'll never get used to. I might not be in the spotlight as much as the rest of Minos's household, but strangers are still starting to recognize me. I don't like it, but I manage a smile all the same. "Is Aphrodite in?" It's on the tip of my tongue to spin some lie about why I'm here to see her, but overexplaining won't do me any favors. This woman isn't the one I need to convince to help me.

"I can check. Just a moment." She's perfectly polite now, though I catch her watching me beneath her fringe of blond bangs.

A few seconds of murmured conversation later, she carefully hangs up. "You can go on up. I'm assuming you know the floor number?"

"I do. Thanks." Now's the time to turn back, to put a stop to this impulsive urge to see her. Aphrodite is not my ally, and she's all but admitted that she's using me to hurt Theseus.

But... What if she *could be* an ally?

That's the question that drives me to walk slowly to the elevator and take it up to her floor. Or that's what I tell myself. The truth is far more tangled.

Aphrodite meets me at the door. She looks similar to how she did the morning after her wedding, her hair hanging in careless waves, her face with only the barest hint of makeup, her long legs in fitted lounge pants. Her sweater looks comfortable, thin and soft; I have to clench my fists to keep from testing it for myself.

I don't understand the hold this woman has on me.

"Well, don't just stand there. You look like you could use a drink. Tea or tequila?" She steps back and holds the door open for me.

"Um. Tea would be great." I step into the penthouse and follow her into her kitchen. I fully expect her to launch into an interrogation as to why I'm here, but she busies herself getting an electric kettle going and pulling out a tray with the most bougie tea setup I've ever seen. I eye it. "No store-bought brands for you, I see."

"I'm a spoiled brat." She shrugs. "I like my indulgences, and tea should always be an indulgence."

I slide onto one of the barstools and watch her brew the tea. She doesn't ask me what kind I want, which is just as well. I'm more of a coffee drinker normally, but I can't deny how relaxing it is to watch the almost ritualistic way Aphrodite moves through the process. By the time she slides a cute little cup and saucer in front of me, along with a tiny tray with milk and sugar, most of the tension has melted out of my body.

"How do you do that?" After the slightest hesitation, I dose the tea liberally with both milk and sugar.

"I find it calming." She doesn't add anything to her tea. She just picks up the cup and leans against the counter across from me. "Now, tell me what's wrong."

"Why would anything be wrong?" The words are too sloppy, too quick. "Maybe I came here to seduce you."

Her smile is knife-sharp. "I'd love to be seduced by you, Pandora, but the fact remains that you seemed almost afraid when you showed up on my doorstep unexpectedly, and as much as I want you in my bed, I don't want fear driving you there. So why don't we try this again? What's wrong?"

It's so tempting to spill everything. There's something about this woman, about the connection strumming between us even now, that makes me want to trust her. I'm not so foolish as that, though. "I don't want Theseus hurt."

She makes a face. "Oh. Him."

"Yes. Him. He's my best friend, Aphrodite. I love him, and I hate seeing him dragged through all this." I take a cautious sip of my tea and am surprised to find that I like it. It's not as bitter as coffee, but it's got a delightful layering of flavors. "This is good."

"You don't have to sound so shocked. I made it; of course it's good." She sips her tea for several long seconds and finally sighs. "Look, I like you."

"Yes, you've said that."

"But it changes nothing. The man you came all this way to defend is a violent murderer. You can't spin some tale about him being a good person who's in over his head. He would have killed my sister in the Ares tournament without hesitation, and he *did* kill Hephaestus at that cursed house party. He's been an active participant in Minos's plans every step of the way, and if he has his way, he'll destroy the city I love." She sighs again. "I feel for you. Truly, I do. I know it's not easy to be subject to a family ruled by a man who puts ambition above all else. But the fact remains that my husband has made his choices. I have to make mine, too."

She's being remarkably frank in a way I find refreshing. But then, she's always seemed to be frank and downright honest when we speak. Maybe that's all a ploy to gain my trust, but my instincts don't think so.

I sip my tea. "You're talking about your father. The last Zeus."

Aphrodite hesitates, almost as if she's arguing with herself. Finally, she shrugs. "My father wasn't much different from Minos, best I can tell. Ambition and power didn't turn him into a monster, but they gave him the ability to be monstrous without worrying about consequences. He formed me and my siblings into tools the same as Minos has done with his children and foster children. So, as I said, I sympathize."

I hadn't given much thought to the last Zeus, seeing how he's dead. But it's impossible to escape his shadow in Olympus. People still talk about him in whispers, and when I got curious and looked him up in MuseWatch, I was a little shocked to find rumors that he killed *three* of his wives.

Including Aphrodite's mother.

"That must have been hard for you having a father like that."

"I survived." She's obviously trying for an irreverent tone, but she doesn't quite pull it off. "He didn't break any of us, though he drove one of my brothers out of this city and now he'll never return, even though the old bastard is dead and gone."

This openness has to be a tactic of some kind, but if I want Aphrodite's help, I have to offer her something. I drink half my tea while I debate how much to tell her. I know Minos—or his benefactor—has put significant resources into burying any mention of them and their history...which includes records of us and the Minotaur from before he fostered us.

That history can't touch us now, but it might not hurt to share to see if it tips Aphrodite in a more sympathetic direction. "Theseus and I were both dropped at the same orphanage when we were babies. It was..." I stare into the remains of my tea. "It was bad. It could have been worse, I suppose, but we learned early to watch each other's backs and that we could only trust each other. I'm not proud of some of the things we did to survive, but the alternative?" I shrug, fighting to keep tension from my shoulders. The alternative was death or being forced to barter body and soul to those more powerful for protection. Drugs ran rampant through the older kids, an intentional funnel between getting them hooked and then feeding them into the underground of Aeaea.

Theseus and I managed to evade that fate, but I can't help feeling like he bartered body and soul, just in a different way. For me. "I can't regret what he's done to secure our safety." Regretting it means devaluing his sacrifice, and I won't do that.

"I'm sorry." Aphrodite sounds like she even means it. I can't help checking her expression, searching for pity I don't want.

It's only the absence of it that keeps me going. "We were fifteen when Minos heard word of us and came calling." Gods, this shouldn't be so hard. I clear my throat. "The reason he found out about us was, well, one of the adults at the orphanage was taking too keen an interest in me. He came to my room one night and Theseus beat him nearly to death."

"Pandora..."

I keep going. I've committed to this, and I'll see it through. "He kept me safe. Against all odds and even though he was just a kid himself, he's always kept me safe. Minos seemed like a gift from the gods, but neither of us was naive enough to believe it came without strings. That's why Theseus negotiated to ensure Minos took me, too."

It's my fault he took that deal. I don't say the words. I've never said the words. Theseus would argue me to a standstill if he knew I felt like that. To him, protecting me is second nature. He never counts the cost to himself.

"So, yeah, I won't argue that Theseus —or I—are good people. I know we aren't. But surely you can understand why he's given Minos his loyalty. If you could offer something even greater, you might win his loyalty for yourself." It's a long shot, an impossible ask. If Theseus won't turn away from Minos for *me*, what can she possibly offer that would sway him?

Aphrodite considers me for a long time. "I'm sorry for what you've gone through. I'm even sorry for what he's gone through, though Theseus hardly has the market cornered on suffering. But, Pandora, you have to understand. My first loyalty will always be to this city. I've sacrificed people I like and people I...love...for Olympus. Theseus—Hephaestus—doesn't even rank. I can't afford to hesitate or let my emotions make choices for me. As long as he's a threat to Olympus, I'm a threat to him."

"But—"

"I appreciate your loyalty to him." She smiles a little. "He doesn't know you're here, does he?"

I could lie, but I have a feeling she'd see right through it. "No."

I expect her to gloat. Or make a snide comment. Something to celebrate this little victory over her husband.

She doesn't. Aphrodite's dark eyes are sympathetic. "Would you like some more tea? I was just about to settle in for the night and read a book. You're welcome to join me."

Longing hits me hard enough that I sway. I shake my head, trying to focus. "No cavorting around town and making a fool of Theseus?"

"Ah, but there's a method to my chaos." She grins. "You have to give the press time to rest in between rowdy, scandalous acts. Otherwise, they lose their impact."

I stare. Always three steps ahead. No wonder Theseus is struggling so much with her. None of the weapons he's trained with work in the arena where he finds himself fighting. "You're terrifying."

"It's been said before. It'll be said again." She shrugs, but the move is a little too tense to be fully uncaring. "Choose, Pandora. Stay or go?"

I drain the rest of my now-cold tea. Really, there's no choice at all. I desperately don't want to go back to Minos's place, and I have nowhere else to go.

Excuses to take what you want.

I ignore the little voice inside me and set my cup down on the saucer. "I'm staying."

HEPHAESTUS

PANDORA IS LONG-GONE BY THE TIME MINOS FINISHES lecturing me on all the ways I've failed him. It's just as well. I don't have it in me to keep fighting right now. I've never been so fucking exhausted in my life. Everywhere I turn, I'm falling short of people's expectations. Minos. Pandora. Brontes and the rest of Hephaestus's people. Even my cursed wife. I shouldn't care about the latter two, but when they become part of a larger problem? That shit is a trend, not an exception.

I stop by Minos's library to snag a bottle of whisky and tuck it into my jacket. I turn toward the door and stop short.

Icarus leans against the wall. He's wearing slacks and a shirt that looks like he started unbuttoning and got distracted. He doesn't look much like his father, aside from his coloring. Light-brown skin and wavy dark hair. But his eyes are wider and doe-like, his features fine and delicate. Like Ariadne, he apparently takes after his poor, dead mother.

He lifts a single brow. "Stealing liquor. How pedestrian of you."

"I don't have time for this." I shoulder past him. The last thing I need is a reminder of everything I'll never have. Icarus and Minos rarely see eye to eye, but Minos never threatens to disown *him*.

Not even after that fuckup where he attacked Pan instead of Dionysus at the house party.

No matter how often Icarus disappoints his father, he's still Minos's trueborn son. No one can take that away from him, not even his father.

"Crown sitting heavy, Theseus?"

I don't answer, and his mocking laughter follows me all the way to the front door. Down on the street, I dig out my phone and press *Call* before I can talk myself out of it.

Adonis answers almost immediately. "Yes?"

"Where are you?"

A hesitation. "I'm at home. Why?"

I hang up without answering. The positioning of the pathetic husband is Adonis's fault. I agreed to it, but it was his idea in the first place, and clearly, it's not helping me. I can't push back against Minos, can't get a handle on my wife, but I can put Adonis in his place.

It's not until I'm standing at his front door, feeling like I'm about to come out of my skin, that I can admit that I also just want to see him. I bang on the door. Too hard. Too angry. I don't know how to be any other way.

He opens it a few seconds later, and the sight of him relaxes something inside me. I fucking hate that he has this effect on me...almost as much as I crave it. It's worse now. Stronger. He's obviously in for the night, wearing gray lounge pants and nothing else, his smooth brown skin showing off clearly defined muscles.

Adonis smiles briefly. "Hephaestus. What a lovely surprise."

"Theseus. I told you to call me Theseus."

"We're not in private."

I walk past him without an invitation and barely wait for him to shut the door to continue. "Now we are."

"Did you need something?" He leans against the door and crosses his arms over his chest. The move makes his biceps flex, and I have the almost overwhelming impulse to sink my teeth into them.

"I needed to talk to you," I say faintly, still staring at his body. I shake my head once, sharply enough that it should shake some reason back into my brain. It doesn't work.

"You could have talked to me on the phone. You hung up and came here in person." He doesn't move, though his gaze coasts slowly over me. "Why are you really here…Theseus?"

The low way he says my name feels like he reached out and ran his hand over my bare skin. I take a step closer to him on instinct alone. "I wanted to see you." I pull the bottle out of my jacket. "Thought we could have another drink."

"Liar." His smile widens, taking the sting out of the word.

I take another step closer to him. "I came to yell at you. I look foolish in the media. Minos is furious."

"Mmm." Adonis's focus narrows on my mouth. "Closer, but still not the full truth."

Another step. We're almost chest to chest now. A deep breath would bring us flush together. When I initially reached out to

Adonis, it was to use him as a weapon to strike at my wife. That's not why I'm here now. It's not even because Minos is pissed.

I'm here because, out of everyone in Olympus, Adonis is the only one I've ever really relaxed around, even a little. He reminds me of Pandora, a bright exterior that camouflages a clever mind and a core-deep kindness that might as well be a different language for all I understand it. He might have helped me for his own reasons, to hurt Aphrodite, but our initial chat would have covered that and then some.

No, this is something else.

"Theseus." His voice is low and full of things I can't define.

"Adonis." Slowly, almost reluctantly, I lift my hand and place it against the center of his chest. Gods, his skin is soft. I clear my throat. "You feel it, too."

His deep inhale presses his chest more firmly against my hand. "This won't end in anything but heartbreak for both of us."

One has to have a heart for it to be broken. I lift my gaze to his. "Do you care?"

"I should." Another of those deep breaths that feel like he's reaching out to me without moving his arms. "My heart is already shattered. Another blow might be the end of me."

I bite down on the strangest impulse to reassure him that I won't break his heart. It's not a promise I can make. Even if we weren't on fundamentally opposite sides of the coming conflict, I am who I am. I can't offer soft words and softer landings.

I only know how to destroy.

Still, I can't leave his comment hanging. "I don't want to break your heart." The heart currently racing beneath my palm. I inhale deeply. I can't place his scent, but it wraps around me all the same, muddying my thoughts.

"Which isn't the same thing as promising not to." His smile falters. "Though I wouldn't believe you even if you made that promise."

"Adonis—"

"Theseus." His eyes go serious. "Either kiss me or get your hand off my chest."

I know the smart move, but I don't give a fuck. I can't be his soft landing...but maybe he can be mine. Just for tonight. It doesn't matter what my original plans were when it came to him. I want him. That's reason enough.

I kiss Adonis.

His lips are soft. So fucking soft. He makes a sound in his throat and opens for me. It's the most natural thing in the world to drag my hand up to bracket his throat, tilting his head back to give me better access. His hands find my hips and jerk me forward until I'm pinning him to the door.

Fuck, he feels good.

In the back of my mind was the thought to keep this kiss light, to control this encounter, but all my intentions are swept away in a wave of need. Need to get him closer. Need to get his fucking clothes off so there's nothing between us.

With that in mind, I start to go to my knees.

He stops me. "Theseus, wait."

I freeze. "What?"

"Your knee."

Shame coats me, nearly drowning out desire. I try to shove it down, with only moderate success. "Fuck my knee. I want your cock in my mouth."

He leans his head against the door and closes his eyes. His pulse races against where I have my lips pressed to his throat. "I would very much like my cock in your mouth," he finally manages. "But not if it hurts you in the process."

There it is. That softness I should despise. He's all but offering me a fault line to expose, an admission that saving me from pain is a lever I can pull to manipulate him.

Except I don't want to.

I don't even want to throw his caring back in his face. I want to indulge it, to luxuriate in it. Unforgivable. I don't give a fuck. I'm not going to stop.

I stagger back from him and catch his hand, dragging him behind me. "Couch. Bed. I don't give a shit, but tell me where to go."

"First right."

I follow his muttered instruction, which leads into a living room with leather couches, a big-screen TV, and three different video game consoles arranged in the entertainment center below it. It's the vase of flowers that gives me pause. "Are those foxglove?"

Adonis gives a strangled laugh. "Good eye." He nudges me toward the couch. "They're not real. Just decoration."

I don't have to ask where they came from. It seems like the kind of perverse gift my wife would send a lover. A small, strange part of me doesn't like that he still has evidence of her in his home, but it's none of my business.

She's not here.

I am.

I grip the back of Adonis's neck and drag his mouth to mine. I love the way he gasps against my lips. There are no games here like with Aphrodite, no power plays and worrying that each move, each touch, gives away more than I intend. There's just pleasure with a man I'm quickly coming to crave.

One who cares if I hurt myself, even a little. I don't know what to do with that. I start to sink onto the couch and Adonis catches my elbows, lowering me slowly. I break the kiss long enough to say, "I sit down all the time. I don't need you to treat me like a child."

He grins against my lips. "Maybe I just like touching you."

I don't know what to say to that, so I don't say anything at all. I press him back a little and hook my fingers into the waistband of his pants. His cock is a hard imprint against the fabric, but I purposefully avoid it for now. One tug brings him between my thighs. Close enough that I give in to the urge to drag an open-mouthed kiss over his abs. "Spend a lot of time in the gym?"

"You would know," he rasps. He grips my shoulders and kneads lightly. "You have more than enough muscle to spare."

Because I thought I'd be a warrior. Not a hero—never that, not with the skeletons rattling around in my closet—but someone who commanded respect and fear in those around him.

Instead, I'm a failure. I failed to take the Ares title and bring Helen Kasios under our thumb. I failed to kill one of the other titles that would have been a good fit for me. I failed to avoid a marriage to a damned witch who comes far too sweetly for my peace of mind.

I'm failing at being Hephaestus.

Adonis sifts his fingers through my hair and tugs gently. "That feels good."

I exhale slowly. I might have failed at everything else, but I'm succeeding at seducing this man. I'm going to make him feel good, make him come so hard he won't be thinking of anyone but me.

That, I can do.

"I'm not done yet." I lick my way down his stomach, but stop short of his pants. I want his cock in my mouth, but even more than that, I want to see him without a single thing hiding his body from my sight. A few tugs on the pants and they slide off his narrow hips, pooling around his ankles.

My mouth literally waters at the sight of a naked Adonis. I don't know if I believe in perfection, but it's hard to argue against its existence with this man standing before me. His brown skin is smooth and unblemished by the scars that pepper my body. Even his cock is perfect, long and broad with a wicked curve.

I draw a single finger down his length. "You're like a fucking piece of art. Are you sure you're real?"

"Real enough." His hands spasm in my hair. "If you don't stop looking at me like that..."

It's only sex. A release for both of us. Or that's what I tell myself as I dip down and take his cock into my mouth.

I ignore the fact that those reassurances have the flavor of lies.

ADONIS

THERE IS NO SCENARIO WHERE FUCKING THESEUS IS A good idea. I should have turned him away when my doorman called up. I certainly shouldn't have answered the door without a shirt just to see if he's as affected by me as I am by him.

Even then, I'd half convinced myself that it would end with a conversation...then with the kiss.

Until that look in his eyes when I wouldn't let him hurt himself to bring me pleasure. That shocked and almost awed expression. As if no one has ever stepped in for his benefit before. It doesn't make sense. Surely he has people who care about him.

I can't afford to be one of them, but that doesn't stop me from wanting to guard this soft part of him I've been shown unexpectedly.

Now, standing before him while he sucks down my cock, I'm lost. I half expected him to go about this the same way he seems to go about everything—quick and efficient. Instead, he teases me as he explores my length with his mouth. Sucking me down one moment, easing to achingly light movements around the head of my cock, then licking down to my base and back up again. The pleasure leaves me helpless to do anything but dig my hands into his hair and hang on. "*Fuck.*"

Hephaestus—Theseus, whoever the fuck he is right now—eases back the tiniest bit. I don't have a chance to protest. He catches my chin and drags me down until our faces are almost even. "I like you. I have no fucking business liking you."

Before I can respond, he shoves two fingers into my mouth. Theseus holds my gaze as he fucks my mouth with his fingers, pressing deep enough to have me gagging around him. My grip spasms in his hair. Gods, why is this so sexy?

Just when I think I can't handle it another moment, he eases his fingers out of my mouth. "Say my name when you come. My real name." He descends on my cock again and, this time, he's not playing around. He presses his fingers, wet from my mouth, into my ass.

My brain shorts out. All intentions to be careful disappear. My body takes over, my hips rolling to fuck his mouth, to fuck myself on his fingers. "Oh gods." I can't catch my breath, can't slow down, can't stop. My orgasm is coming too quickly, but there's not a single thing I can do about it. "*Theseus.*"

He growls around my cock, the vibrations only making me come harder. My knees buckle, but I manage to keep my feet through sheer desperation. If I fall now, I lose the feeling of him drinking me down.

Theseus lifts his head slowly and presses a kiss to my stomach. "Good boy."

The praise spoken so gruffly by this scarred warrior buoys me in a way I'm not prepared to deal with. He eases his fingers out of me and leans back. "That was a good start."

"I…" There's nothing to say, is there? "Bedroom."

"Yeah." He nudges me back and rises. "Let's go."

We take a quick detour to the bathroom for him to wash his hands, and then I lead him down the hall toward my bedroom. I pause long enough to wonder what he thinks of it. My apartment isn't particularly large. There's only me here, and I don't care to keep up with cleaning a bunch of rooms I don't spend time in.

I'm a bit of a snob when it comes to my bedroom, though. My mattress is top of the line and my sheets have the kind of thread count that used to make Eris tease me with a wicked look in her eyes.

No.

I'm not thinking about Eris right now.

I ignore the ache in my chest and start for the window to close the curtains. Theseus's hand closes over my shoulder. "Wait." His free hand skates down my spine, stopping at the small of my back. "I want to fuck you, Adonis."

"I want it, too."

"Do you need to prep?"

I flush when I realize what he's asking. Part of me wants to pretend I don't understand, to deny that I even considered it a possibility we might get to this place tonight. I swallow my pride and rasp, "We're good."

Theseus gives a low laugh that makes my skin tighten. He steps closer, pressing against my back, his cock a hard length against my ass. "You really are a good boy, aren't you?" He kisses the back of my neck. "Got yourself all ready for me."

The contrast between his mouth soft on my skin and his fingers digging into my shoulder makes me moan. "Yes."

He coasts his hand from the small of my back to my hip and jerks me closer. "Tell me what you like."

I don't exactly mean to lean back against him, but it's like he's got a gravitational pull of his own and I'm helpless to resist it. He drags his hand from my shoulder and down around to my stomach, splaying his fingers out and holding me in place as he keeps kissing my neck. I'm hardly in my early twenties, recovering in the space of seconds, but my cock twitches all the same.

"Adonis," he murmurs against my skin. "Tell me."

The truth is that I'm not entirely certain I'd dislike anything he does to me. I don't know how I got to this place, but it feels so good to let my brain click off and my body take over. To submit, just a little, and let someone else shoulder the worries that have plagued me for weeks.

Even if they're still there, lingering at the edges of my mind, along with my broken heart and far too much anger.

I will *not* think about her. Not now. Not in the midst of this.

He nips the spot where my shoulder meets my neck and the words spill out. "I want it slow."

Theseus's hand on my stomach shakes, just a little. "You really are the little romantic, aren't you?" I can't help tensing, waiting for derision or mocking, but he just sounds as faintly wondering as he looked earlier. He sets his teeth against my skin. Not quite a bite, but it makes me jump all the same. "You want me to fuck you like I love you."

"I didn't say—"

He spins me around and then his mouth is on mine. Gods, but I could get addicted to the way this man kisses me. This time it's soft and slow and, yes, like he loves me. I know it's a lie, but I can't stop myself from sinking into it. Theseus will never be mine, not in reality, but I'm so damn tired of reeling after Eris's moves that I'll take the illusion of it.

Even if it's only for tonight.

Theseus backs me toward the bed, keeping us tightly pressed together. It's a little awkward, but that only heightens the way he takes my mouth like he owns me. My legs bump the mattress and he presses me down. "Lube?"

"Nightstand."

The weight of him is gone in an instant. He moves to where I indicate and pulls out the bottle of lube and a handful of condoms. When I raise my brows, he shakes his head slowly. "This might not be true any other time, but tonight you're safe with me."

A lie.

He's just playing into the *fuck me like you love me* thing. That's all. But that doesn't stop my chest from going soft in a truly worrisome way. "Okay."

He pushes me back onto the bed, flips me onto my stomach, and settles on top of me. The weight of him does funny things to my head. Theseus, in general, does funny things to my head. I know he's not for me, could never be for me, but he's so refreshing in a way I never expected. Blunt and harsh and, strangely enough, awkward and kind.

"You're thinking too hard." He presses an open-mouth kiss to the back of my neck. The scrape of his beard against my skin makes me shiver. "Second thoughts?"

"No, nothing like that." I reach back to where he has one hand braced on the bed beside me and lace my fingers through his. "Don't stop."

"Okay." He trails kisses down my spine. I know this isn't real—or at least isn't anything realer than lust—but Theseus's touch feels downright worshipful.

This is what I asked for.

I know. I *know.* But that doesn't change the fact that it *feels* real.

"You really are perfection, aren't you?" He blows lightly on the skin damp from his mouth. It's such a light touch, a direct counterpoint to his weight pinning my lower body to the mattress, that I have to bite back a moan. Theseus skims his fingers over my side. "Gorgeous and strong and loyal. Enough ambition not to be boring, but not so much that you're trampling over the people around you."

Each word feels like he's reaching into the direct heart of me. "Theseus—"

"Too much?" There's a smile in his voice, and I suddenly want to see it on his face.

I twist and he moves back enough to allow me to turn over. And there it is, a faint curve of his lips. This smile is different than any he's given me to date, though. It warms his dark eyes, twinkling in their depths. I lift a shaking hand and cup his jaw.

This isn't real. It isn't—

He kisses me, sweeping away what's left of my resistance. I

cling to him as he retreats a little, but he's only grabbing a condom. He sits back on his heels and looks down at me as if he wants to memorize this moment, imprint it right down to his bones.

This man, this monster, this enemy...

He's all business as he rolls on a condom and picks up the lube. He pops the cap and pauses. There's a question in his gaze, but he doesn't voice it. He doesn't have to. The pause is inquiry enough. I cover his hand holding the lube and guide him to squeeze a bit onto his free hand. His resulting smile is more of a grin—and a crooked one at that.

Oh gods, he's charming when he's not snarling and glaring.

"A gift," he murmurs.

"For me or for you?"

"Haven't decided yet." He coats his cock with lube and then spreads a bit more down my ass.

Theseus calls me perfect, but the sight of him leaves me breathless. I feel like so much of my strength is in theory, marked out in clear boundaries to keep me safe. I work hard...in the gym. I'm ambitious...but only to a point that doesn't put me or the people I love in danger. I grew up in a loving home with two parents who would cut off their own hands before they raised them to me. What discipline I received was tempered with love.

Not like Eris, who might be physically unmarked, but wears her scars on her soul.

Not like Theseus, the things he's survived written across his brown skin. And those are only the things I can see on his physical body. There are more beneath the surface; I only had to have a single conversation with him to know that.

All that strength to keep moving, to keep surviving...

He leans forward and presses his cock to my ass. Slow. So devastatingly slow. This time, he doesn't ask me if I'm good. He doesn't need to. I'm moaning and writhing for him, trying to take him deeper even as he controls the pace.

It seems to take forever for him to sheath himself to the hilt. Theseus caresses my thighs, a gentle stroke that makes me whimper. He grins in response. "I like it when you make that sound. I like that I'm the one to do it."

Not real.

The words feel as insubstantial as mist. I can barely keep my eyes open, but I refuse to miss a moment of this. It won't last. It *can't* last. But we have right now, and right now is more perfect than I could have dreamed. "More," I whisper.

He doesn't answer with words. He simply starts moving inside me, one smooth withdrawal followed by an equally smooth stroke. It's so good and yet not enough. I reach up and grab his sides. It's on the tip of my tongue to beg him to kiss me, to not stop, but I don't manage to get the words out before he anticipates my needs.

Theseus hooks an arm under my hips, lifting me to him even as he descends to me. Our chests are slick with sweat and the delicious friction is almost unbearably good. I wrap my legs around his waist and kiss him.

Time ceases to hold meaning. There's only the thrust of his body into mine, the slide of our bodies together, his taste on my tongue as our breath mingles with each broken kiss.

When we finally collapse to the bed, spent and exhausted, the line between reality and a pretty lie has blurred until it's unrecognizable. Especially with the way he strokes a hand down my side and presses a kiss to my temple.

It might not be real...

But it feels a whole lot like love.

APHRODITE

I DON'T END UP READING. INSTEAD, I HOLD MY BOOK open and watch Pandora circle my living room. She's as curious as a cat, touching the little trinkets I have arranged on the floating shelves by the door, sifting through the books on my bookshelf, even testing out each of the couches and chairs. She does it all without a smidge of self-consciousness. I like that a lot.

I should be seducing her right now. She knows more than she's saying just by virtue of being Hephaestus's best friend and living in Minos's household. If I've learned anything through the years, it's that even the most steadfast asshole will forget themselves when they're doped up on good sex. It's a tactic I've used more than a few times, with great success.

It would work on Pandora.

Our little interlude in Hades's club all but proved it. I spent far too much of today thinking about how sweetly her lips had parted and how lovely the lust-glazed look was in her dark eyes. "I want to keep you."

Pandora stops in the middle of flipping through a book filled with monster-fucking art. "Excuse me?"

I hadn't meant to say it aloud, but now that I have, I'm not about to backtrack. "You feel this connection, too. I realize we're somewhat on opposite sides of things, but I've never let a little thing like a person being an enemy stop me from taking what I want. I want you."

She slowly turns another page. "Even if I admitted to feeling a connection with you... Eris, I'm not for keeping. I'll never be the type of person who feels comfortable with monogamy."

I laugh. I can't help it. "No, I don't imagine you would be." I lean forward, drawing her gaze from the book to my face. "You're too invested in new experiences to limit yourself to one person."

She eyes me as if testing for a trap. "Even if you were fine with that, there's still Theseus between us. I like you quite a bit, Eris, but he's my best friend. If you two can't come to some kind of peace, then there can be no you and me."

I lean back and shut my book. I'm not normally one to let my emotions get the best of me, but I want more time with Pandora. Not just to get whatever information out of her. Not just to use her to hurt my husband.

I feel parts of me unwind in her presence. She's gone through so much and still manages to keep a light about her that feels downright magical.

It could be that I'm playing right into her hands—into Minos's hands—by indulging this attraction, but... "What about a compromise?"

"What compromise?"

This is a fool's bargain. I don't care. I lean forward and prop my elbows on my thighs. "When it's just you and me…it's just you and me. No politics. No mining for information. No public power plays. Just us."

Pandora laughs. The sound fills the room like afternoon sunlight. "Come now, Eris. I may not know you well, but even so, I'd put good money on you sticking to that agreement for only as long as it suits you."

She's right. I shrug. "We'll have plenty of fun in the meantime."

"You're unrelenting." She purses her lips and flips another page. "It's not a good idea."

No, it's certainly not. I push to my feet and cross to slide the book out of her hands. "Nothing about this has been a good idea. That hasn't stopped either of us yet."

"If you're trying to get into my pants, there are easier ways."

It would be simpler if that was all I wanted from Pandora. I *do* want that, but I've also enjoyed the time we've spent together in the last two weeks. I like that she laughs too loud and doesn't care who else is in the room. I love the way she seems perpetually willing to see the glass as half-full, no matter the circumstances. She's soft and she's sweet and yet she's not weak. I can't steamroll her. I like that, too.

Part of me whispers that the only reason I'm pushing so hard for this is because I've lost Adonis, but it's not quite the truth. That relationship was worlds different than what Pandora and I might have. Even if she's technically part of Minos's household, she stands outside the power structure. She's not Olympian. She's enemy by association, but not actively working to hurt the city I love.

With Adonis, things were never simple. Even when we were alone, part of me was always aware of what our relationship looked like from the outside. What it *meant*. He might not have ambitions to be one of the Thirteen, but his proximity to me, especially after I became Aphrodite, made him a power player.

And power players are not to be overlooked or underestimated when it comes to the damage they can cause, even unwittingly.

Even in our relationship itself, he and I were always so intense, hot and cold and never anything in between. Before meeting Pandora, I would have said that something warm and easy and *simple* would be the antithesis of what I wanted.

I was wrong.

For the first time in weeks, I'm not thinking about my next move or how to manipulate those around me into cleaving to my end goals. I'm just...relaxed. Because of *her*. "How about this?" I tuck a long strand of her dark hair behind her ear. An excuse to touch her, and it takes far more effort than I would like to admit to withdraw my hand instead of cupping her jaw and tilting her face up. "We won't have sex."

"*What?*"

I nod, even though I have my doubts about this plan. "We know we fit there, even if we haven't indulged nearly as much as I'd like. Give me a chance to prove we fit elsewhere. No monogamy. Open communication." This is probably a mistake. It might feel simple when we're alone, but I'm Aphrodite. Who I take to bed is anything but uncomplicated. It will give Pandora power...if she chooses to take it.

She narrows her eyes. "You're serious."

"Yes." I hope to the gods I'm not making a mistake, but it's too late to back out now. I've lost Adonis. I'm playing out an intense game of political chess with my husband, which isn't helped by the fact that last night's sex confused the situation more than I want to admit. Adonis was right to freak out about my sleeping with Hephaestus. I don't know how to deal with the fact I did, so I'm just ignoring that it happened in the first place.

Pandora is still staring at me like I've grown a second head. My skin heats in something like embarrassment, so I grab her hand and pull her toward the couch. "Let's start now. We'll watch a movie."

"A movie."

"Yes, that's what normal people do on dates." I'm pretty sure. I tend to prefer ridiculously expensive dinners and dancing, interspersed with sowing chaos in the political parties the Thirteen host on a semi-regular basis. It's always more fun to do it with a partner in tow, even if they're only there to observe. The shared experience is fun to deconstruct later that night after we've fucked all the restless energy out of ourselves.

But sex is currently off the table with Pandora.

A movie seems like a safe enough bet. I'm sure I can manage to keep my hands to myself and prove that I'm serious about this with her. Probably.

"Okay, fine. Let's watch a movie." She points at me. "But only because I really don't want to go back to Minos's place."

"You really aren't a fan of his, are you?"

"That is severely understating things."

I almost offer to set her up in her own place, but that's too much, too soon. She's not even sure if she wants to watch a movie with me, and I'm standing here wondering if she'll let me pay for her rent. I give myself a mental shake. "Let's see what's streaming."

In the end, I let Pandora pick, though I have cause to regret it when she lands on a horror movie about a haunted house. I don't mind gore and I've sat through more thrillers with Perseus than I care to admit, but there's something about ghosts that gets beneath my skin.

Maybe because I have my own haunting me. Some living, like my little brother. Some dead and gone, like my mother. I don't think of her most days, but when the old grief rises, dull and throbbing like a poorly healed wound, it always catches me unaware.

And my father? He haunts me in an entirely different way. The longer I hold the Aphrodite title, the more I see why he did some of the things he did. When you have so much power at your disposal, it's so easy to trample those around you. My aims might be slightly more noble than his—protection of this city, rather than personal gain—but that doesn't change the outcome.

I've hurt people, just like he hurt people. Without hesitation. Without regret. I'd do it again if the situation required it.

Growing up, I never thought I'd be in danger of becoming the monster who terrorized my childhood, and yet it's a future that feels inescapable now.

"Eris?"

I glance down to find Pandora watching me with a worried expression on her face. "Are you okay?"

"I'm fine." It's even the truth. I *am* fine. My heart hurts over losing Adonis, but not enough to change my path. I'd probably shed a tear if I had cause to trample Pandora, but I'd do it without blinking if Olympus required it.

Gods, I really am a monster.

"Do you have a blanket around here? It's a little cold."

I'm pathetically grateful to get up and pull out one of the throw blankets I keep in the chest under the television. I pause to flip off the overhead light and then walk back to the couch.

Pandora takes the blanket from me and shakes it out. "This will work." I barely have a chance to sit down before she's cuddling up against me and tossing the blanket over us both. She exhales gustily. "Perfect."

The comforting weight of her stills the worst of my circling thoughts. There's no point in worrying about what cruelties I'll be required to enact in the future. It's not right now.

Right now, I have a beautiful woman half-draped over me. I relax by inches. Pandora smells lovely, and she snuggles more firmly against me when I drag my fingers lightly through her hair.

I've just decided that maybe I *should* seduce Pandora properly when she gives a light snore. I shift back enough to see her face. Sure enough, she's sleeping. I'm not prepared for the protective urge that surges up inside me with enough strength to steal my breath. She trusts me enough to sleep on me. Not because she's drunk, but because I'm here and she feels safe.

I settle back against the couch and tuck her more tightly against me. "I'll keep you safe, Pandora. I promise." I hope to the gods I'm not going to make a liar out of myself.

The movie ends with everyone dying in increasingly horrific ways, and I switch on a sweeping period piece that I like to watch when my mind needs a break. Occasionally, it's even enough to coax me to sleep, but after a full eight hours last night, my tiredness doesn't evolve into anything other than gritty eyes and a cranky temperament.

Morning comes far too soon and Pandora shifts against me and lifts her head. She blinks those big, dark eyes at me. "I fell asleep."

"You seemed to need the rest." I ease to my feet. My arm is asleep and my hips feel a little wonky, but it's worth it. "You're more than welcome to stay, but I need to go in to work today."

She yawns, as cute as a kitten. "I won't overstay my welcome. I should check on Ariadne and make sure she's left her room sometime in the last twenty-four hours. Sometimes she gets hyperfocused on a project and forgets little things like food and showering."

It's on the tip of my tongue to ask what kind of projects, but I just got done promising to keep prying questions away from this relationship. "You like her."

"She's a good girl." Pandora stands and stretches. "Sheltered and a bit spoiled, but it hasn't soured her. Minos mostly ignores her and I think she prefers it that way."

I can't understand that, but then, I'm a very different person than Ariadne. I make a mental note to touch base with Eurydice and see if she's made any progress prying Ariadne out of that shell. "I'll text you later."

Pandora bites her lip and shifts a little. "Okay." She hesitates and then rushes forward to press a quick kiss to my mouth. Before I can change my mind again, she's gone, slipping out of my living room. A few seconds later, I hear my front door shut.

Normally, after a sleepless night, no matter how used to them I am, it takes a truly outstanding amount of coffee to put a little pep in my step. Not this morning. I feel strangely buoyant as I get ready to go into the office. The nature of my title means I don't have giant holdings like Demeter or soldiers like Ares or a team of engineers like Hephaestus. I prefer it that way.

I wonder what my dear husband was up to last night?

I push the thought away. He managed well enough on his own, and I wouldn't trade that quiet time with Pandora for anything. I'll worry about him later. Right now, I'm going to enjoy my good mood and the good weather.

The morning is nice, the air crisp with just a tease of winter's chill. Far too nice to take the car. Besides, after what happened to Athena, it's especially important that the Thirteen don't hide. We have fought our battles in the court of public perception, but the stakes have never been higher. The average Olympian won't stoop to murder, no matter how delightful they find the fantasy of being one of the Thirteen, but it would take very little for the tide of public opinion to turn against us and for the people to start rooting for our assassins.

We're facing down a rabid creature; one flinch and it will tear out all our throats.

There aren't many people out and about, just a scattering of professionals making the trek to work. Several of them eye me, but I'm used to that. I've grown up under the watchful eye of the entire city. Paparazzi were snapping photos of me on the grade school playground. There was a particularly disgusting set of people who did countdowns to when Helen and I turned eighteen.

As an adult, there's always someone staring or, if they're brave, asking for a picture or an autograph. There's even a particularly robust fanfic community devoted to shipping me with anyone I look sideways at.

It's just how my life is.

I make it to my office without having to directly deal with anyone. It's a small building compared to the ones that tower around it, but I like to think that's because we have nothing to prove. People who come through my doors need a service only I can provide.

I took the Aphrodite title because I wanted the power, even if the last bitch who held it only gave it to me to sow discord. I never expected to enjoy the work.

Sele looks up as I slip through the door. They're a petite person with medium-brown skin, truly outstanding cheekbones, and black hair they keep in a funky short style. Today they're wearing a long-sleeved black garment that I don't clock as a jumpsuit until they move around from behind the desk. "Morning."

"Morning."

They eye me. "You look...oddly happy."

"Thank you, Sele, I'll take that backhanded compliment." I shake my head. "Especially when you usually tell me that I look tired."

"Because you usually *do* look tired. Really, there's a reason I gave you those sleepy-time teas." They arch an eyebrow. "Also, there's someone here to see you."

That gives me pause. "Already? We just opened the doors a few minutes ago."

"He was waiting outside. Kind of sad, really. You should cut the poor guy a break." They move back behind the front desk and tap a button of their keyboard. "Also, there are a bunch of requests for matches that came in overnight. I just sent them to you."

"Thanks." I sense movement behind me and turn to find the very last person that I want to see on this morning. My promise of a very good day goes down the drain before my eyes.

My husband is here.

HEPHAESTUS

MY WIFE LOOKS GOOD. FAR TOO GOOD. SHE'S PULLED her long dark hair back from her face in a sleek ponytail, and she's wearing a red dress that's slightly too sexy for the office. Everything about her is a temptation, and even knowing how poisonous her touch is, part of me wants to do it anyway.

I glance at the receptionist. They've been nice enough, allowing me into the lobby to wait for her, but I can feel their curiosity. More proof of Adonis's plan working, no matter what Minos thinks. I had fully intended to tell Adonis to fuck off with the plan last night, but now I'm not so sure that's the right call. People are starting to look at me with interest and sympathy, rather than suspicion and rage. I hate the sympathy, but it serves my purpose.

For now.

"You've been avoiding me." I'm playing for an audience of one, but with how closely the receptionist is watching, this is going to be recounted somewhere later. I'm fucking betting on it.

Aphrodite rolls her eyes. "I just saw you a little over twenty-four hours ago. I never expected you to be clingy."

"Again with the smart response."

She flicks her ponytail off her shoulder. "Of course. I'm both smart and quick. Really, you should be used to it by now."

I don't know what it says about me that her stinging words are starting to be less infuriating and more intriguing as time goes on. I step closer. My body is sore as fuck after last night. No matter how careful Adonis was with me, it was still more stress on my knee than it's had in a while, and I'm paying the price this morning.

Now's the time to throw what happened last night into my wife's face. I fucked her ex, the one she still watches with her heart in her eyes when she thinks no one is looking. Pandora might be my best friend, but Aphrodite was romantically in love with Adonis. Still is, if I don't miss my guess.

But it feels...weirdly wrong. I didn't sleep with Adonis last night with the intention to hurt my wife. I didn't even think of her once I started kissing him. I'm still not sure why I went to him in the first place. It doesn't make any sense.

"Have dinner with me tonight." I say it before my brain has fully processed that I was going to speak.

She blinks. "Excuse me?"

"Dinner. It's a meal people eat in the evening. Have it with me tonight."

"I know what dinner is." She shoots a look at her receptionist, steps closer, and lowers her voice. "What game are you playing at?"

I don't know. I wish I could say this was all part of some grand plan Minos and I devised, but the truth is that I'm acting on impulse. I hadn't even thought about the invitation for a moment before it was coming out of my mouth, but now I want her to say yes. It's...strange. "I'll see you at seven."

"I never agreed to dinner, you ass."

I catch movement behind her as someone walks through the door. They're wearing a trench coat and a hat pulled low over their face. Too warm for this weather. They slip their hand into their coat.

Gun.

I move on instinct. One step brings me to Aphrodite, and I fully intend to spin us around and put me between her and this person, but my knee buckles. "Fuck!" I go down, taking her with me. We hit the floor, and I barely manage to make sure she lands on me instead of under me. It happens so fucking fast.

The person sprays the space where Aphrodite just stood with bullets. Too many fucking bullets. The ridiculous etched glass divider shatters into a million pieces over us. I try to curl around my wife, but there's no time. The receptionist shouts, and the attacker turns and flees. I didn't even get a look at their face.

My blood roars in my ears and I can't tell if it's me or Aphrodite shaking. That was close. Too close. It's not over yet, though. I keep one arm around my wife and point at the receptionist. "Call Ares's people. Now!" I'm not going to be able to chase some fucking gunman through the streets. It's already too late, anyways— they're gone. But Ares should be able to pull the footage or some shit and track the fucker down.

The receptionist nods and grabs the phone with shaking hands.

I sit up slowly. "Are you okay? Did the glass get you?" Even as I ask, I see the cuts on her legs. "Fuck."

"I'm fine." She's not quite steady as she pushes off me. I grab for her, but she's too quick to her feet. Aphrodite stumbles to the door and flips the lock.

"Get away from the window." I tense, but no more gunfire meets her.

She tries to smirk, but all the color is gone from her face. "They're still running. They won't be back." Her lower lip quivers but she shakes her head. Hard. "It was only a matter of time. This is the reality we live in now."

I don't know if she's trying to convince me or her, but I struggle to my feet all the same. My knee hurts like a motherfucker, but I don't let that stop me from limping to her side. I take her shoulders. "Come away from the window."

"What do you care? I know you don't give a fuck about committing murder, but surely you would be relieved if someone else took care of the wife you never wanted. Gods, maybe Minos stopped plotting in the dark and finally decided to take more direct action. He'd like to rid you of me."

"He's not behind this. Look to your own people for that."

"Of course. Why would he get his hands dirty when everyone else is all too willing to spill blood for him?" She blinks rapidly, her eyes too wide. "You certainly didn't hesitate to do it."

Her accusation rolls right over me, absent of the sting her comments usually contain. Her voice *shakes*. Aphrodite always seems larger than life, like she's walking around bulletproof, but right now every sign says she's scared shitless.

Again, I'm not thinking things through as I wrap an arm around her shoulders and snarl at the receptionist, "We'll wait for Ares's people in her office." It's a token of just how fucked up my wife is that she doesn't argue as I guide her around the broken glass to the hallway leading farther into the building. She must be going into shock, though she manages to stir herself and point to the gilded door that's obviously her office.

I sweep a look around the room as we enter, not remotely surprised to find the space just as gilded as the door. It's subtler in here, though: gold accessories on the meticulously organized desk, gold foil on the books in the small bookshelf to the right of the door, a faint hint of gold in the patterned rug beneath our feet.

I guide Aphrodite toward one of the fancy chairs. "Sit down before you fall down."

"I'm not going to fall down." But she doesn't shrug out from beneath my arm. "I hope you're happy," she says faintly. "This is what you wanted."

"You keep saying that. It's not true. It's what Minos wants." I don't know why I say it. She's not wrong. We had a plan when we came to Olympus, and this destabilization is part of it. If we had won Ares, Minos still would have played out his little house party and taken over as many of the Thirteen as possible via the assassination clause.

He might not be actively behind the assassination attempts now, at least not to my knowledge, but all that means is that we've moved on to the next stage of whatever his plan is.

I move back from her, just a little. The cuts on her legs drip blood, but none of them seem particularly deep. Still, they'll have to be checked for glass before they're bandaged.

What am I thinking?

Why the fuck do I care if Aphrodite is bandaged properly or just straight-out murdered? Yes, the bullets would have hit me, too, but that's not what I was thinking when I went for her. I wasn't considering the danger to myself at all. "Do you have a first aid kit?"

She lifts a shaking hand and stares at it. "What must you think of me? Sheltered Olympian princess, right? Never seen violence once in her life." Aphrodite laughs bitterly. "If only that were the truth." She waves a hand at her desk. "Bottom drawer."

Now's the time to leave. Her sister will arrive with her people, and the last thing I want is to face down Ares again.

Except I don't leave.

I round the desk and pull open the bottom drawer. I snort at the sight of the perfectly normal first aid kit. "I half expected it to be gold."

"Themes are important." She watches me come back with dull eyes. "My brother might prefer simpler things, but my father liked his gold. I'm Zeus's daughter, and there's no point in having survived what I did without reminding everyone of that fact. The gold in this office serves its purpose."

There's no way I can crouch, so I drag the other chair closer. "You're Zeus's sister now. Why not give up the gold shit if it reminds you of your father?" Minos has a file several inches thick on the last Zeus. He was corrupt and violent, covered in a thick, honeyed charm that this fucking city ate up.

I'm nearly certain Minos crafted his approach to the press by using Zeus as an example.

"I'm my father's daughter." She says it likes she's pronouncing a curse.

I lean down and grab her ankle, carefully lifting her leg to drape over my thighs. "I need to see if there's glass in the wounds."

"Hephaestus." She pauses. "Theseus."

Hearing her say my real name in such a serious tone gives me pause. "Yes?"

"Why?"

She doesn't have to elaborate. It's the same question I've been asking myself since the adrenaline started to wane. "I don't know." I carefully clean the scattering of wounds and then prod them gently. "Any sharp pain?"

"No."

Good. "You'll need to get these checked by someone who actually knows what they're doing, but at least I can bandage it."

I can feel her watching me as I take care of the first two cuts. Even without looking, I can sense her shock fading. Sure enough, she sounds sharper when she finally speaks. "You seem to know what you're doing. Then again, I've seen you naked. Your scars speak for themselves."

I glance up, fully expecting to see some kind of vindictive expression, but there's only a soft understanding. I shrug, trying to keep the tension from clinging to my shoulders. "I've seen some shit. It's nothing to write home about."

"You would say that." She gives a broken laugh. "I have my scars, too. My father valued perfection too much to ever leave a permanent mark, but sometimes I'm sure I can see the ghosts of bruises from his fingertips." Another laugh, quieter this time. It almost sounds like a sob. "I guess after this, I'll finally have some physical ones. Can't hide the violence anymore."

I'm not prepared for the sheer rage that hits me. This woman is as much a monster as I am. Different, yes, but no less dangerous. She was meant to be an opponent met on equal ground. And yet...

"Yeah, well, that fucker is dead and you're still here being a pain in my ass." I say.

The thought of what her father must have done to put *that* tone in her voice makes me want to break something. The knowledge that I'm at least partially responsible for the state of Olympus...for the fact that its people are now turning against the Thirteen, against *her*...

I don't know how to feel about that. I don't know how to feel about any of this shit. I can't fight a fucking ghost, and I'm already doing a shitty job of fighting myself when it comes to everything about the last few days.

"Yeah, I guess I am, aren't I?" Her laugh is a little ragged, but warm enough that I find myself smiling in response. I keep my head down. There's no point in letting her know I'm worried about her. She might get the wrong idea.

Instead, I finish cleaning her leg and shift to the next. I repeat the process, again finding no glass in the wounds. We fall into an almost companionable silence, at least until I guide her foot to the ground and sit back with a slow exhale. "There."

"If you're petitioning for a blow job, I might actually be convinced."

Just like that, I'm back to the moment last night when Adonis wouldn't let me go to my knees. I don't want Aphrodite on her knees either, not when she's covered in bandages. I'm not prepared to examine what that resistance means. I just shake my head. "That's not why I did it."

"Which brings me back to my original question. Why *did* you do it?"

I don't have an answer any more now than I did earlier. I have lived a very simple life. Even in the orphanage, fighting for food and to keep Pandora safe, things were simple. I didn't have to be smart or cunning; I just had to be brutal enough not to be fucked with. That trend continued in Minos's household. He doesn't prize me for my smarts. He points at a target, and I destroy it.

Things aren't simple like that anymore. Every action, every word, has layers on layers. My life is a fucking onion, and I've always been shit at reading between the lines.

I don't know what I'm feeling, but I don't need to know. I'm a man of action, after all.

The reassurance feels like a fucking excuse to do what I want, but I ignore that and push slowly to my feet. "I'll see you at seven."

Aphrodite still looks dazed and a little lost. "I never said I'd have dinner with you."

"Your place or mine?"

She blinks and finally shakes her head. "Mine. Gods alone know what you have stocked in your fridge. It's probably beer and ketchup."

"I'm a man of taste. There's mustard, too."

Her lips quirk. "Lucky me. No, come to my place. I'll order in." She narrows her eyes, her smile fading far too quickly. "Then you can tell me why you saved my life."

Maybe by tonight, I'll actually have an answer for her.

APHRODITE

MY SISTER SHOWS UP WITHIN THIRTY MINUTES OF THE attack, a mere five minutes after my husband finally leaves me alone. She bursts through the door of my office and looks wildly around before landing on me. "Oh thank fuck, you're okay."

I blink. "Are *you* okay?" Helen looks exhausted. There are faint circles beneath her eyes and her normally impeccable clothing looks like she slept in it. "What's going on?"

"What's going on is that this city has gone mad." She drags a hand through her long hair and shuts the door. "We've had three assassination attempts in the last twelve hours, including yours."

"*Three?*"

"Yeah, some fool tried to drop a shipping container on Poseidon." She makes a face. "They're no longer among the living."

"Oh." I don't know if I want to ask whether or not Poseidon was the one to remove that threat.

Helen doesn't give me a chance to figure it out. She crosses over and crouches down to look at my legs. "Do you need to go to a hospital?"

"No." I barely resist the urge to brush my fingers against the bandage on my thigh, the memory of my husband's gentle touch confusing and disorientating. He saved me. I still haven't had time to process that. Truthfully, I can barely believe it happened, but even more shocking was the quiet moment afterward. The moment where I fell apart and he somehow managed to make me feel safe. I certainly don't know what to think of that.

"Probably for the best." Helen sits back on her heels. "I can't guarantee the hospitals are safe right now. Nowhere is safe, really. This is so fucked."

Her phone trills, its jaunty little tune totally at odds with the seriousness of the situation. I raise my brows as a deep voice says, "*Hey, sexy,*" against the music. "Charming."

"Achilles has a funny sense of humor." She fishes her phone out of her pocket and frowns. "It's Perseus. Hold on." A few button clicks and she answers with video. "Eris is okay."

Our brother's face fills the screen. Anyone who didn't know him would think he looks much the same as ever, but I grew up with him. I recognize the stress deepening the faint lines bracketing his mouth and the fact that he's starting to get the same dark circles beneath his eyes that Helen is.

He looks at me a long moment. "We're locking down."

"That's a mistake." Helen shakes her head sharply. "If we look like we're running scared, the city is going to riot. MuseWatch is already practically salivating over each new attempt. We can't afford to go into hiding."

"I don't give a fuck." He looks at something off-camera and his expression shutters. "I'll be with you in a moment, Hera." A few seconds later, she must leave the room, because he relaxes a little. Hardly matrimonial bliss over there. "We can't afford to lose another of the Thirteen, and none of the three attempts in the last twenty-four hours actually followed the clause's parameters. If one of these attempts succeeds, we're going to either have a violent civilian who doesn't know a single thing about their new responsibility, or we're going to have a vacancy that will take time to fill. Neither of those outcomes is acceptable."

"Or we're going to have another of Minos's minions in the role." Helen makes a face. "Though he's been remarkably quiet since the wedding. I don't think he's behind any of these, and Apollo agrees with me."

"I. Do. Not. Care." Perseus bites out the words. "We are locking down."

"No, Helen's right." I'm still feeling a bit shaky, but I'm not about to admit as much to my brother. "Perception matters as much as anything right now. We can't hide."

"Then give me an alternative," he snaps.

"I need a couple hours, but I can send squads of my people to bolster the Thirteen's security teams." Helen holds up a hand when our brother starts to argue. "Achilles has spent the last three months organizing our people into a fighting force he's confident in. I won't pretend that I'd trust every single one of them with the temptation of close contact with us, but there are enough to form thirteen squads."

For a moment, I think Perseus will shoot down the idea. Helen might have settled into her role as Ares, but it's hard to dismiss the sibling roles that have ruled our lives. She's older than me by a year, but from the time we were children, she's been softer, taking more after our mother than our father.

Our mother wasn't hard enough to survive in Olympus.

Gods willing, our sister will be.

I clear my throat. "Either we trust her or we don't, Perseus."

He curses, slow and steady. Trust our brother not to ever lose his cool, even when he's showing a tiny sliver of emotion. "Fine. Do it." He turns his attention on me. "Your husband is swaying public opinion in his favor, and the time he's spending with Adonis is only adding fuel to that fire. They look like they're commiserating over their broken hearts, and it's garnering too much sympathy."

"I'm aware," I manage.

"This stunt today will only further the fiction he's spinning of being a loving and protective husband. Are you sure he's not involved in the shooting?"

I blink. It's a testament to how rattled I still am that I hadn't even considered this was all a ploy on Hephaestus's part. He *did* show up at my office unexpectedly, but surely he'd be better suited to being a widower than saving my life with only one person as a witness. Sele isn't the most discreet when it comes to gossip, and they won't keep their cards close to their chest this time.

Still, there's no way he could have known that.

Unless he's several steps ahead of me...

Despite myself, I can't help thinking back to how carefully he touched me. Gentle isn't a word I'd associate with the man who came into his title through violence, but there's no denying that he *was* gentle with me. Or that my comments about my father bothered him.

He's not that good of an actor. If he was, he would have proven it before now. Right?

I shake my head sharply. "I can't guarantee anything."

"Hmmm." Perseus steeples his hands before his mouth. "Ares, get the squads in place by this afternoon. No one moves until that happens. Tomorrow, we need to meet and discuss what steps to take moving forward."

I press my hands to my thighs as if that's enough to ignore the way they're still shaking, just a little. "Who's *we*? I assume you don't mean the whole of the Thirteen."

"That's exactly what I mean. We can't effectively face this outside threat until we're unified." He makes a face and sits back. "An impossible feat with our current Hephaestus, but there's a target on his back, same as the rest of us."

Helen sighs. "We're not going to get anything done. It'd be better if you curated the group. Us. Hera. Demeter. Apollo. Athena. I suppose Hades can come as well."

I don't entirely disagree with her, but eight out of Thirteen is not great. "Not Poseidon? Or Hermes and Dionysus?" Artemis and my husband can barely be in the same room with each other, but surely she can see the benefit of unification?

"Poseidon has decided that he's not concerned with mundane subjects like Olympus's survival. He isn't taking my calls." He looks at her directly. "Dionysus was at that party, and I didn't send him there, so we can't guarantee that he's on our side. He's too close to

Hermes to trust. No, it needs to be all of us or none of us. Better to keep shit out in the open than have meetings behind closed doors— and encourage the ones we don't trust to do the same."

"Even Hermes is invited? You still suspect she might be a traitor."

"At this point, it's less suspecting and more that I *know* she is. She was in contact with Minos before he came here. She's intentionally being difficult and not sharing what she knows about his benefactor and the greater threat to the city. That makes her an enemy."

Helen shakes her head sharply. "Forget whoever is paying Minos's way. We can't deal with Hermes as an enemy."

"She's one woman."

I exchange a look with my sister. Perseus isn't foolish or impulsive, but that statement is both. I'm not entirely sure what Hermes's game is, but the fact remains that she's not actively trying to cut down the rest of the Thirteen, so we need to prioritize dealing with the assassination clause first. "Fine. The whole Thirteen will meet. We'll talk more tomorrow."

"Stay safe, both of you." He ends the call.

Helen sighs. "I like how he commands it as if that's enough to make it true."

"It's how he deals with an out-of-control situation." I shrug, feigning a lightheartedness I don't feel. "We'll figure it out."

"Will we?" She stretches her arms over her head and something in her spine pops. "Sorry, I'm being morose. It feels like they're one step ahead of us no matter what we do. Minos and his people might not be actively pulling the strings on these attacks, but they're responsible for the events that got us to this place all the same."

She's right, but I don't like the way her shoulders sag in something akin to defeat. "That's not entirely true. They never wagered on you as Ares." I give a faint smile. "We'd be a whole lot worse off if they had control of the military *and* more of the Thirteen." I'd bet good money that the original plan was to have their new Ares—either my now-husband or the Minotaur— provide security for Minos's little house party. With that in play, they would have taken two or even three more titles.

As bad as things are now, they could be so much worse.

"Yeah, I guess that's true, isn't it?" She holds out a hand. "I'm glad you're okay, Eris. You scared the shit out of me. Let's get you home and—"

"No."

"What?"

"No, I'm not going home." I rise without taking her hand. I love my sister, and I mean it when I say she's a great Ares, but sometimes she still lets her emotions get the better of her. Right now, she's like our brother and only thinking of keeping me safe, rather than of the implications of running home like I'm scared. "I'll finish out the day here and then go home."

To dinner with my husband.

I don't know how to feel about that, so I put it out of my head. "I have appointments today that can't be moved. There are three arrangements on the cusp of engagement, and we can't afford to let them lapse. If we lose support of the legacy families right now..."

She curses. "I hate it, but you're right. Fine. But you *will* keep my squad on you at all times."

"Not in my home."

Helen props her hands on her hips and glares at me. "So if an assassin bursts through the window—"

"I'm on the fortieth floor. If they're coming through the window, they're probably better than your team and it's a moot point. This isn't going away anytime soon. We have to find a way forward that doesn't strip the Thirteen of all agency or they won't agree to the extra security." Not that she and my brother could strip the Thirteen of their agency, even if they wanted to.

It takes another fifteen minutes of arguing before my sister leaves, trailing dire promises of what she'll do if I get hurt because of my hardheadedness. I check in with Sele, who's already ordered a cleanup crew for the lobby, and then walk slowly back to my office and lock the door.

"Fuck," I whisper. "Fuck, fuck, *fuck*."

The shakes return with interest. I take a step toward the chairs, but my legs give out and I sink to the floor. "This is ridiculous." My voice sounds halfway normal even though my bones are currently trying to detach themselves and rattle right out of the room. "I am Eris Kasios and I do not panic over...over..." A pathetic little sob erupts from my lips. "Gods*damn* it."

I pull my legs to my chest and drop my forehead to my knees. It doesn't help the shakes, but at least I feel the tiniest bit in control like this. I can't afford to lose it. There's too much hanging in the balance, and even if my part in the fight might not be vital enough to sink Olympus as a whole... I don't actually know that for certain. I can't take it for granted.

I have to stay ten steps ahead of my husband and his family.

I *have* to.

I *will*...when I regain the strength to stand...in just a few minutes.

HEPHAESTUS

I SPEND THE DAY DODGING CALLS FROM ADONIS AND texts from Pandora. If I talk to them, I have to tell them what happened with Aphrodite, and if I do *that*, then there will be separate fallout to deal with.

In between those times, I try to escape the inexplicable guilt saying I shouldn't have left her alone. It doesn't make a damn bit of sense. She's fine. A few cuts and probably some bruises, but we gave each other worse while fucking. Yes, she was still a little unsteady on her feet when I left, but I'm sure she figured it out fast enough.

Probably.

Then comes the call I was expecting. The one I can't avoid. I stare at Minos's name on my phone for several beats and then accept the call. "Yeah?"

"Update me."

I've never been one to crave a softer touch of parental love—how can you want something you don't even know the shape of?—but there are days when Minos treating me like a soldier wears on me. They come more and more often since my failure during the Ares tournament.

I bite back a curse of frustration. Instead, a question bursts free that I had no intention of asking. "Are you responsible for the attack on my wife?"

He pauses. "Would it matter if I was?"

Yes. No. I don't fucking know. "Answer the question."

"Very well." Minos sighs as if I've disappointed him. "I'm not behind any of the attacks on the Thirteen. They're in a situation of their own making, spurred on by the public that loves them and hates them in equal measure."

"What about the Minotaur?"

"What about him?" His tone goes low and dangerous. "You've never questioned my plans before."

"I'm not questioning them now." I think. "But you stopped informing me of the next steps the moment I became Hephaestus."

"Yes, I did. I don't need you for this part of the plan. When it's time for you to act, you'll know." A weighted pause. "Stop wasting time and energy worrying about things that have nothing to do with you. Your public image continues to deteriorate. They're laughing at you."

"I'm dealing with the public perception thing as best I can, but it will take time."

"Weakness will not be tolerated. Get it handled." He barely pauses, switching to his main focus in a heartbeat. "At the next meeting with the Thirteen, propose stricter regulations over the River Styx crossings. And tariffs."

I hold the phone from my face and stare at it a long moment. "You want me to propose we install tariffs on half the city."

"It only makes sense. The lower city is a leech on the rest of the resources. They offer little in the way of benefits and simply take food from the mouths of those who put in the work for it."

Best I can tell, most of the upper city doesn't do much *work* for their food, either. "No one is going to go for that."

"You'd be surprised." He sounds pleased with himself. "Hades hasn't made many friends among the Thirteen during his term, and now that he's got an heir on the way and Zeus doesn't… It's a fault line, my boy. They might all be Olympians in our eyes, but the citizens don't see it that way. We can exploit that. Even if they don't like you much, there are those among the Thirteen who would agree with this move because they dislike Hades even more than they hate you."

It's fucked up. I've been here long enough to understand that the upper city sees those who reside across the river as another city entirely, but best I can tell, the only difference is that the lower city doesn't preen and primp in public or dance to Zeus's tune.

I've read the reports. Hades is a good leader. He takes care of his people, even when he's at a disadvantage against the rest of the city. By all accounts, his people love him.

How long will that love hold once they start feeling the burden of tariffs and the like?

Something uncomfortable twinges in my chest, but I shove it down. We didn't come here to integrate with Olympian society. We came here to bring it down. I might not know the overarching plan Minos is putting in place—he's not one to share more than he has to—but we aren't the good guys.

I've never been one to concern myself with innocents, but I've also never been in a position where innocents might be affected by my actions. I don't...

I try to put it out of my head like I have every other time I've bumped against shit Minos says or does that I don't like. It's not my place to question the plan. Minos is the one who put me on this path and helped me survive and protect Pandora in the bargain. I owe him too much to question him now. But...I want to question him. I want to ask him what the fuck he's doing. Except I already know; exactly what he promised.

Destabilizing and bringing down Olympus.

It just never bothered me before. I clear my throat. "Consider it done."

"Good. Keep me updated."

"I will."

He hangs up without saying goodbye. The awful sensation in my chest doesn't abate as I check the time. I'm due at Aphrodite's place before too long, and for all her determination to cook or whatever the fuck she had in her head this morning, I'm showing up with food.

It takes thirty minutes to find a place that sounds like something I'd actually eat and another twenty to drive to her building. Most of the Thirteen have chauffeurs, but I don't trust anyone in this city enough to mindlessly let them drive me around.

Doing that shit is a good way to end up dead.

I take the elevator up to my wife's place and let myself in. It feels strange to walk through the empty space and set the takeout on the kitchen counter. I expected her to sweep in the moment I walked through the door, a sharp word and a wicked smile firmly in place.

She's nowhere to be seen.

The small hairs at the nape of my neck stand on end. "Aphrodite?" No answer. I take a moment to check the living room and then start down the hall. "Eris?"

She's fine. This is just another game. Another way she's outmaneuvering me. I poke my head into the guest bathroom and the spare bedroom, not finding anything, and then make my way to the master.

The bed is perfectly made, looking like something in a catalog for rich people, right down to the dozen pillows taking up the top third. I hadn't had a chance to get a good look at it the other night. It's luxurious and so perfectly Aphrodite that I shake my head... and pause. Is that the shower running?

I walk slowly across the bedroom, that sick feeling in my chest getting stronger. There is no way my wife would be in the shower at the time when I said I'd be here. Not after today. It's too vulnerable a position. Even if she meant to seduce me, she'd do it in another way. I'm sure of it.

Feeling slightly absurd but not able to shake off my caution, I crack the door and push it slowly open. The shower is a monstrosity, a huge tiled beast that would probably fit five people without crowding.

My wife sits on the floor, her knees drawn to her chest and her head down, her wet hair creating dark rivers down her bare back. A bruise has blossomed on her hip, turning her pale skin a rainbow of purple and black, fading to green and yellow on the edges.

She looks...small.

I don't remember moving away from the door. It's like I blink and I'm back in the kitchen, my head swimming and my chest too tight. I don't even pause to think. I drag out my phone and call Pandora.

She answers almost immediately. "What?"

"Help."

Instantly, all joking is gone from her voice. "What's wrong? What's going on?"

"Aphrodite." I'm whispering and that's fucking ridiculous, but I can't seem to stop. "I brought her dinner. Someone tried to shoot her this morning, and now she's in her shower and she looks so fucking small, and I think she might be crying."

"*What?*"

"She—"

"No, I heard you. I'm just processing." She curses softly. "Damn it, Theseus, are you really hiding in her apartment instead of comforting her right now?"

"I don't know how to comfort someone."

Her tone goes soft. "Look, I'd come, but I think that just might complicate the situation tonight." She hesitates. "You should call Adonis."

It's a token of how fucked my head is right now that I don't even question if that's a good idea or not. "You're right. I'll call him." Now it's my turn to pause. "You really like her, don't you?"

"Yeah, I do." She gives a choked laugh. "And don't you dare hide and wait for him to show up. Call him and then go, like, hug her or something."

She might punch me in the face if I try, but at least then she won't be crying. The thought of her crying is like someone shoved a piece of glass into my chest, and it grinds against my heart with each beat. I don't fucking get it, not when a week ago I was ready to kill her myself.

I don't want her to cry.

"Come by tomorrow. She'll probably be happy to see you, especially if we fuck this up." I hang up without waiting for Pandora's response. She might agree, or she might argue just to argue because I'm the one who made the suggestion.

I call Adonis next, barely waiting for him to answer to cut in, "Someone tried to kill Aphrodite today and she's kind of fucked up and I think she's freaking out." I'm speaking too fast, but it was one thing to patch her up in the immediate aftermath of the attack. It's totally another to deal with the emotional fallout now. I'm shit at comfort. I punch shit and kill things. I don't hug and cuddle and know the right words to say when someone just survived an attempted murder for the first time. "She needs you. *We* need you."

A pause. When he speaks, he's totally in control. "I'll be there in twenty minutes."

"Thank you."

"Don't thank me yet." His voice goes low and cold. "Because after we take care of Eris, you're going to explain to me why you knew this happened and didn't say a single fucking word until now." He hangs up, which is just as well. I don't have an answer for that. After last night, reminding him that we're not actually on the same side feels like a lie.

If anything, I'm more conflicted than ever. It doesn't make a damn bit of sense. I have my path. I've never strayed. I have no reason to, not when Minos has given me everything I need.

Except...

No. No use thinking about that now. Adonis will take less than twenty minutes to get here, and if Aphrodite's still crying in the shower and I'm standing out here, wringing my hands, it will be a fight I'm not sure I can win.

A fight I don't deserve to win.

Even knowing that, it takes me a solid two minutes to dredge up the momentum to carry me back into the bathroom. Aphrodite hasn't shifted. Steam hangs heavy in the air, making my shirt stick to my chest after only a few seconds. I stop in the opening to the shower. "Eris?"

She moves slowly, as if she's an old woman instead of in the prime of her life, turning just her head to look at me. "I'm not up for dinner." She sounds remarkably normal, which is somehow worse. "Maybe another time."

The urge to flee rises again, but this time I muscle past it. I don't know what to say or what will get that awful lost look off her face, but I can't leave her like this.

I don't know what this pull to make her feel better means. I've never felt anything like it, even with Pandora. It's different and it's uncomfortable, and I want to carve it out of me before I'm past the point of no return. I don't even try.

It's too damn late for that, anyway.

Without thinking too hard about it, I start stripping. She closes her eyes and rests her head back on her knees. I shuck off my pants and step into the shower. There are no fewer than four showerheads going. I step beneath them and have to grit my teeth to keep a muttered curse from erupting. The water is *scalding*.

After a brief internal debate, I awkwardly slide down to the floor and lean against the wall next to her, stretching my legs out. Pandora would have the right words to tell Aphrodite it will all be okay. Adonis would know exactly what she needs to hear.

I'm not good with words. I'm sure as fuck not good with comfort.

But death is something I've become intimately familiar with.

I lean my head back against the tile. "The first time is the worst."

Aphrodite slowly looks at me. Her skin has gone pink from the heat of the water, but she still looks too pale. "What?"

"The first time someone tries to kill you." I inhale deeply, letting the steam warm me from the inside out. "It's never fun. You don't get used to it. But the shock lasts less each time."

She blinks those big dark eyes at me. "When was your first?"

I don't want to talk about this. I'm not sure why the fuck I thought it was a good idea to bring it up. But she's focusing on me instead of the memory of earlier today, so I answer her honestly. "I was fourteen. One of the, ah, priests at our orphanage was showing too much interest in Pandora, so I told him to fuck off. He waited until everyone was asleep that day and then came to my room with a knife."

She lifts her head a little. "He gave you one of those scars?"

"Yeah." I touch the long, ragged one running diagonally across my stomach. "He almost gutted me."

I brace for sympathy or pity or some kind of self-righteous bullshit about how no child should have to defend themselves from adults. It's not how the world works, though, and I don't have time for anyone who isn't already aware of that.

"You killed him."

I blink, half-sure I heard her wrong. "What?"

"You killed him." Her smile isn't anywhere near as sharp as usual. "Right?"

I had. I snapped his neck and then passed out from blood loss. I woke up on my fifteenth birthday in the hospital with Minos standing there, bathed in sunlight and looking larger than life. I still don't know how the fuck he found out about it, but no authorities ever came around asking after the priest's death, and by the time I was well enough to leave the hospital, Minos and I had come to an agreement.

When I checked out, I didn't go back to the orphanage.

I went to Minos's home, and Pandora came with me.

At the time, it seemed like a gift from the gods. Minos was a hard taskmaster, but he was fair, and I never had to worry about his gaze lingering too long on me or Pandora. That alone was worth the cost he demanded. "Yes. I killed him."

"Good." She closes her eyes. "It's not the heroes who slay monsters. They're too honorable. Always giving second chances and…" Her breathing goes jagged. "I have a brother. Another one. Younger. He's a hero, and he almost got himself killed playing white knight. I'm glad he's not here to see what Olympus has become. He wouldn't survive it."

I know about the younger brother. Hercules. A handsome

fucker with bright eyes and the kind of shine that makes me want to dent it on principle. He's nothing like his siblings, nothing like Aphrodite in particular. "Probably not."

"I hate you." She finally moves, inching back to lean against the wall at my side. Her shoulder touches mine and she kind of melts against me.

"I know." After a slight hesitation, I wrap my arm around her shoulders and tuck her more firmly against my side. She lets loose a tiny little sound that might be a sob. Neither of us comment on the way she shakes and presses her face to my shoulder.

I should be happy. This is part of Minos's plan. Introducing the knowledge of the assassination clause to the Olympus population is key to destabilizing things and keeping the Thirteen more worried about their lives than about what Minos might be up to. He hasn't explicitly said that he hopes the various murder attempts succeed, but clearly it would be to his benefit.

If Aphrodite dies, I will be free. No longer married to a woman I didn't choose. No longer the laughingstock of this fucking city.

But the thought of this city without her in it isn't one that brings me joy.

Instead, the thorny feeling in my chest tears deeper.

ADONIS

I FIND THEM IN THE SHOWER. THESEUS LOOKS ALMOST relieved when I walk through the door, but he won't be after I'm through with him. He *knew*. For hours, he's avoided my texts and left me thinking that the most I had to worry about was my heart getting entangled after what we shared last night.

Instead, he'd known *all day* that Eris had been attacked.

She looks weak and scared. Neither is an adjective I would ever use to describe the woman I love, but it's the truth. My stomach drops out and I step into the shower, heedless of the spray. It takes a few seconds to turn off the water and grab two towels from the cabinet. One gets dropped on Theseus's lap, and I use the other to wrap around Eris and lift her into my arms.

"I can walk."

"I know." I don't put her down. I *can't* put her down. Her little tremors reach me, even through the thick fabric of the towel. Gods, has she been like this all day?

Even as I think the question, I know better. "You stubborn

fool. You pushed it down and pretended like nothing was wrong, didn't you? I bet you even took clients."

She ducks her head and presses it to my shoulder. "I have to keep up appearances."

This right here is why I will never reach the heights she has in Olympus. I care too fucking much. My emotions might not rule me, but they *affect* me. Eris has every part of her under such tight lockdown that moments like these, where it backfires against her, are rarer than blue moons.

I don't tell her that she should have called me. I don't call her a fool again, even though I want to. Eris and I have had this fight more times than I can count. As much as I'd like to believe that this new violence would be enough to change her perspective, I know better.

I'm not her boyfriend anymore. There's not a single reason for her to call me, or for us to have that fight for the thousandth time. Showing up here is crossing a boundary, but I don't care. It doesn't matter what we've done to hurt each other or how desolate my future is without her in it.

She needs me, so I'm here.

I set her on the bathroom counter and wrap the towel more tightly around her shoulders. "Don't move."

"I can—"

"Do not move."

She drops her gaze and clutches the edges of the towel. "Okay. Fine."

I hate this. I hate that she feels brittle, like one harsh word could send her crumbling. "If you're not going to take care of yourself, then we're going to do it for you."

"*We?*" She looks up, some of the customary sharpness in her gaze. "You can't honestly think—"

"What I think is my business. Stay there." I stalk back into the shower. As I suspected, Theseus hasn't moved. He tenses, but even as angry as I am, I'm not such a monster to mock his inability to stand. I'm glad he didn't try on his own. The tiles are slippery beneath my feet, which makes for treacherous moving.

I might want to yell at him, but I don't want him to hurt.

Gods, I'm pathetic.

I hold out a hand. "Come on."

"I'm good." He looks at my hand like it's a poisonous snake. Instead of arguing, I just maintain my position until he curses under his breath and slaps his hand into mine. I carefully leverage him to his feet.

Then I shove him against the wall, my forearm against his throat. I lean in until our faces nearly touch. "I don't give a fuck if you're an enemy to this city or what your plans are. Our deal was that Eris would be kept from harm."

"She's living, isn't she?"

Distantly, I'm aware that he's letting me do this, that he'd have no problem fighting back and that we'd be damn near evenly matched if he did. "Don't play with words, Theseus. You're not good at it."

He gives a grim smile that doesn't reach his eyes. "She's shaken up, but she'll be fine. You underestimate her."

I don't know what to say to that, so I drop my arm and take a step back. "Are you staying or going?"

It's only because I'm watching him closely that I see the

indecision war across his rough features. He's in over his head. He has been from the moment he entered Olympus, for all that he successfully murdered his way into being one of the Thirteen.

I knew that, of course. His visit to Hephaestus's office and how he's floundered on the public stage more than proved that he doesn't have a handle on what it means to be a member of the Thirteen. Even when he held me close last night, I never doubted for a second that he was still an enemy.

Oh, my foolish heart wanted to believe otherwise, but no matter what my friends and family think, I know better than to believe the dream that the love of a good man is enough to change the people I care about. It didn't work with Eris, and it certainly won't work with Theseus.

But an enemy wouldn't be worried about Eris the way Theseus is now. He can't lie worth a damn, and he wouldn't have called me, wouldn't have sat with her, wouldn't be hesitating now, if he didn't care…at least a little.

"Do you want me to stay?" he asks softly, his voice almost uncertain.

I open my mouth to say I don't care either way, but it's a lie. I want him here. Gods, I don't know what's wrong with me. I'd like to think I'm not normally one to let my foolish heart lead me into inevitable pain, but my history with Eris more than speaks to the truth. "If you want to."

He huffs out a breath and moves past me, wrapping the towel around his waist as he does. I watch him closely, ready to catch his elbow if he stumbles. He doesn't, but I can tell his knee is bothering him by the stiff way he moves.

We find Eris exactly where I left her, which snaps my priorities back into place. Theseus can figure his shit out on his own tonight. She has to take precedence.

"This isn't necessary." She doesn't lift her head. "I'm fine. Or I'll be fine tomorrow."

I don't doubt it. Eris is a Kasios first, and after growing up seeing the things she did, she's developed nerves of steel. It's a token of how bad it was today that she's this shaken up. I take her shoulders and wait for her to look at me. "Then be fine tomorrow, Eris. Tonight, you don't have to be."

Her lower lip quivers, just a little. "Why did you come here at all? Why are you being so nice to me? I know you're too good a person to wish me dead, but I've prioritized the city over you again and again. I broke your fucking heart, Adonis. Don't lie and say I didn't."

It's true. But my pain is less important than hers right now. Tomorrow, we can go back to awkwardly staring at each other across the chasm of the hard decisions that brought us to this place.

I said I'm here for her tonight, and I meant it.

"Eris." *I love you.* I don't say it. Everyone in this room knows it for truth, but the tiny sliver of pride I have left won't let me speak the words. Not again. "For once in your life, don't argue with me."

Her lips curve in a sad smile. "I guess that's the least I can do."

When I rushed over here, I wasn't thinking about how much it would hurt to be in her presence. Theseus leaning on the bathroom counter just out of reach doesn't make things feel less complicated.

He hasn't bothered to get dressed yet, and I will *not* think about the fact I licked my way down his thick chest last night.

Instead, I focus on Eris. Words aren't going to make her feel better right now, and telling her everything is going to be okay feels too much like a lie.

We have enough lies between us.

Her skin is mostly dry by this point, but I grab a second towel and twist her hair up into it. I can feel Theseus watching us closely, but he's not my problem right now. Eris is terrifyingly passive as I work lotion into her skin. It's not something she often had the patience to let me do in the past, but it's a small act I've always enjoyed.

At least until I get to her legs and start taking off the wet bandages. There are easily a dozen cuts on each leg, ranging from little more than a scratch to one on her left thigh that I'm a little worried might need stitches.

I finally glance at Theseus. "First aid kit is under that sink behind you."

He's got a strange look on his face, and for the life of me I can't tell if he's studying us like enemies or like he wants to memorize exactly what I'm doing so he can replicate it in the future. For all that I'm drawn to this man, a moth to his flame, I don't fully understand him. He's harsh and driven and violent, but there's a raw emotional center there that he works hard to keep locked up. I only get glimpses, but it's enough to make me wonder what kind of man he'd be if given the freedom to make his own choices instead of playing the part of marauder for his foster father.

He pulls out the kit and sets it on the counter between us. Eris sighs. "That's not—"

"It's necessary."

Theseus crosses his big arms over his chest. "You said you would get these looked at. You didn't. Those are the bandages I put on there."

It's hard to tell with her head ducked, but I think Eris flushes. "There wasn't time, and you did a fine job."

I'm not sure what to think about that. Saving her life is one thing, but taking care of her afterward? He hates her—or at least he says he does—but if you hate someone, you don't spend a prolonged time bandaging their wounds. You don't check up on them later that night. You don't call in reinforcements when you're in over your head.

But what am I going to do, accuse Theseus of having feelings for his wife?

I want to accuse him of exactly that.

Desperate to escape the conflicting feelings inside me, I gently touch Eris's knee. "These were caused by glass?"

It's Theseus who answers. "The glass divider thing in the lobby shattered."

Again, the anger that he kept this knowledge from me for *hours* rises, and again I shove it down. "Let's get these bandaged." That, at least, I can do. The action calms the worst of my whirling thoughts, if not my emotions. I never would have considered myself naive, and yet I can't help thinking, *It wasn't supposed to be like this.*

Not Olympus falling apart around us, violence rising with each day.

Not Eris, married to another man—a man who is partially responsible for that rise in violence.

"Adonis."

I hate how small Eris sounds, hate it so much I finish with the last bandage on her right leg before I look up to meet her gaze, giving myself time to control my expression. "Yes?"

Eris opens her mouth, but seems to reconsider whatever she was about to say at the last moment. "Thank you for coming. I know I don't deserve this, but...thank you for being here."

I finish bandaging her second leg in silence. By the time I'm done, she's weaving a bit, clearly exhausted. "Have you eaten anything?" I noticed takeout bags in the kitchen when I arrived, but I'd been too focused on getting to her to investigate.

"No, but I'm not hungry."

I give her the look that statement deserves. "Eat something and then you're going to bed."

She narrows her eyes. "I don't need a keeper."

"Don't you?" I push to my feet. "You're doing a bang-up job of taking care of yourself lately." More words bubble up, ones that have no satisfactory answer. Eris has never had any qualms about the fact she puts this city before everything. When we first started dating, I thought it terribly heroic.

That was before I knew the cost.

"This city is going to kill you," I grind out.

"Maybe." She tucks her hair behind her ears and slides off the counter. "But at this point, we can only deal with the circum-stances we have instead of the ones we want." With each word, she sounds more like herself and less fragile. "I have no intention of dying, Adonis. I can promise you that."

She doesn't bother to keep the towel wrapped around her as

she walks away from us. I know this woman's body as well as my own—the curve of her waist, the dimples at the top of her perfect ass, the two crooked fingers on her left hand from when her father slammed it in a door when she was fifteen and broke them. Everyone thought it was because she fell during ballet practice. I'm the only one she told the truth to.

I have to turn away, but that doesn't help because Theseus is still here, still wrapped in that damned towel, still watching us as if taking mental notes. And why not? I doubt he learned much in the way of comfort and softness in Minos's household.

Things would be so much simpler if I only wanted Eris. I drag my hand over my face and speak softly, pitching my voice to only carry to him. "I am very angry with you."

Theseus nods slowly. "Yeah. I get that."

"You *get* that. I—"

He snags me around the waist and drags me against him. It's similar to the moment when I pinned him against the shower wall, but even with the obvious threat, I can't help staring at his mouth. If he smiled right now, I might punch him in the face, but he just looks vaguely tormented, as if he's not any happier with how things have developed than I am.

Theseus squeezes my hip. "Would you believe me if I said I didn't want her dead?"

"No." But I want to. Gods, how I want to. I want to so desperately, it shakes me. "You hate her."

"Yeah, I guess." His gaze tracks toward Eris's closet. "Feels more complicated than hate these days. She's a monster, maybe even *my* monster. I don't like seeing her declawed."

He sees her. Actually sees her. Not the wild-child party-girl persona she picks up and sheds like clothing. Not the cold Aphrodite who makes calls solely to save her city.

Eris. Woman. Monster.

Mine.

Except she's not mine any longer, is she? She's his.

Having sex with this man was a mistake. I knew it when it happened, but with my foolish heart lurching in my chest as if trying to close the distance between us further, I have to admit exactly how thoroughly I've screwed myself.

I'm falling for my ex's husband.

And I'm still in love with my ex.

APHRODITE

IF SOMEONE TOLD ME A WEEK AGO THAT I'D BE SHARING a tense meal with my ex and my husband, I would have laughed them out of the room. I fully intended to stay as far from Adonis as possible, and the only time I planned to be in Hephaestus's presence is when I'm driving him out of his mind with rage.

He's not out of his mind right now.

He's eating with a single-minded intensity that reminds me a bit of one of Helen's partners, Achilles. As if he grew up not entirely trusting his next meal was guaranteed. It makes me feel strange. More so, it's strange how *domestic* this is. Hephaestus put his jeans back on, but didn't bother with a shirt. Adonis has pulled on a pair of lounge pants left over from one of the many times he spent the night.

Weak as it is, I'm wearing one of Adonis's old shirts, its fabric soft and faded from so many washings. It doesn't smell like him anymore—it hasn't in years—but it's my favorite thing to put on when I'm feeling off-center. If I was stronger, I wouldn't telegraph how much I need the comfort, but they found me curled up in the shower, so it's pretty obvious how not okay I am.

Everything about this situation makes me feel strange. I take small bites, mostly to keep Adonis from pestering that I need calories, but my mind is abuzz with the events of the last day.

I held it together through sheer grit today. Every loud sound or quick movement after the attack had me fighting down a flinch. I've been at home in this city from the moment I was born, and for the first time, it feels like it is the enemy instead of a longtime friend. Worse, I don't see a way through this.

The cat is out of the bag regarding the assassination clause. We can't cover it up, and it's obvious that giving people something to gossip about isn't enough to distract from the temptation of claiming a spot on the Thirteen for themselves. The public might not actively hate us right now, but a quick scroll through MuseWatch gave the surreal impression that they're looking at the attempted assassinations as entertainment.

I can't hate them for it. This is the culture the Thirteen created and fostered. We're reaping what we've sown. Even as they root for us or against us in turn, they won't condemn the assassins entirely.

I hope Perseus has some ideas during the meeting tomorrow... because I don't.

To distract myself, I look at the men. Hephaestus glares at the table like it said something insulting about his mother. Adonis eats in the precise way he does everything, never a bit of energy wasted. They sit next to each other at the bar, so close that their shoulders brush regularly, and there's a...

I stare.

No.

Surely not.

I must be imagining things. There has to be a reason my husband and my ex are so comfortable in each other's presence when they have every reason to hate each other. If I'd been in my right mind, I would have noticed it before. Hephaestus has reason to be here, but Adonis doesn't. Not unless he was called. Not unless *Hephaestus* called him.

But why would my husband call my ex for help?

Unless...

I take a long drink of my water and set the glass carefully on the counter. "So, how long have you two been fucking?"

It's a testament to Adonis's training that he doesn't sputter or get flustered. But I've known this man the better part of my life, and I know his tells. They're there in the way his shoulders shift the barest amount; it's not enough movement to be called a flinch, but on him it might as well have been a shout from the rooftops.

Hephaestus doesn't have the same training, but he's not trying to cover it up. He leans back slowly, meeting my gaze. "Since last night."

I don't expect the blast of pain to my chest. It's so sudden, I actually lift my hand as if I can rub it away. I forgot, for a moment, that we're on opposite sides of a war that is both personal and political. I forgot we're enemies. *Fool.* "Well, then."

"Get that look off your face, Wife. Where were *you* last night?" He rises slowly. "You know the game we're playing."

"A game." Adonis pushes his food away from him. "I see."

I watch in something resembling horror as Hephaestus actually *flinches*. "No. That's not what I mean."

"It's what you said."

"Godsdamn it, you know I stick my foot in my mouth more often than not. Did last night feel like a *game* to you?"

If I had any doubts about it before, I don't now. This is a lovers' quarrel happening in my kitchen. I take a step back and a hysterical laugh slips free. "Right. Of course. Well, congratulations to both of you. I'm sure you'll be very happy together."

Adonis finally looks at me. For the first time since he arrived, he's absolutely furious and not trying to hide it. "No, you don't get to do that. You married another man."

"And you fucked him. Guess we're even." I'm not being fair. I *know* I'm not being fair. I don't give a fuck. What I've done, I did for this city. Adonis doesn't have that excuse. He must have done it simply to hurt me. Or, worse in some ways, he did it because he wanted to. Because he's already moved on.

Can you really say that you only care about Pandora because of the purpose she'll serve?

I'm a hypocrite, but I don't care. There's no way they just randomly fell into bed together. Just like that, the pieces click into place. My husband's miraculous bounce back in the public eye, the way he's seemingly effortlessly switched to the doting cuckold. In the space of twenty-four hours, the write-ups stopped frothing at the mouth to see who I'd sleep with next and started talking about how sad my poor, loving husband is while he waits at home for me to return. I thought it a strange coincidence, but it's no coincidence at all.

It's Adonis's doing.

"You helped him. You told him what to say, what to do."

Adonis doesn't blink. "I had my reasons."

Gods, I might deserve this, but I can barely think past the betrayal coating my throat. "Right. Of course you did. Well, don't let me get in the way of your little spat. I'm going to bed." I start for the hallway.

Hephaestus curses and grabs my wrist. He pulls some move that doesn't even make sense, spinning me into his arms and creating a cage.

I slap his chest. "Let me go."

"That was an impressive exit, but you don't get to make Adonis sad and then prance off."

"I do not *prance*."

"*Theseus*." Adonis is on his feet next to us.

I give a sharp laugh. "Oh, so you call him Theseus? It really must be love."

"Don't be ridiculous, Eris."

My real name is another blow. I've missed hearing him say it, but I don't want to hear it now. Not like this. "No, *you*—"

"That's enough," growls Hephaestus. "Both of you." He spins me around and pins my back against his chest. "Just kiss and make up already."

I go still, but my shock is nothing compared to the way Adonis's jaw drops. He looks over my head at my husband. "Excuse me?"

"You heard me." He keeps one arm banded across my waist and grips my chin with his other hand. "Look at her. So sad. So hurt. Don't you want to kiss her better, Adonis?"

I can't breathe. I don't know if I want to fight or simply melt against him. I am not, and have never been, someone particularly submissive in the bedroom or out of it. But...I am so fucking tired. My heart hurts and, damn it, I'm scared out of my mind. I can barely think about tomorrow and the days that follow and what this new reality might look like.

Maybe I can release that. If only for tonight.

Adonis looks downright tormented, his gaze jumping from me to Hephaestus and back again. "Eris..."

I never wanted to give you up.

I don't say it. Even I'm not bastard enough to voice such an unforgivable thing in this moment. I've *missed* him. I don't deserve him back in my life or my bed, but I don't have the walls in place to stop this.

I don't want to stop it.

Just like that, I decide. I relax against my husband's chest and tilt my head back, pressing my throat more firmly into his palm. "That's why you're here, isn't it? To make me feel better, my perpetual knight in shining armor."

Adonis's mouth goes hard. "You don't have to say it like that."

"But she's right." Hephaestus's words rumble against my back. "You're the good one, Adonis. Better than both of us combined." He drags his thumb up and down my throat slowly. "Leave her in my care and who knows what damage I might do."

Adonis crosses his arms over his chest and glares. "You're trying to manipulate me and you're not even doing a good job at it."

"Why bother being good at it?" He moves his arm by my waist, hooking the edge of my shirt and lifting it a few inches. Not enough to flash anyone, but it's close enough that Adonis's gaze sharpens on my newly exposed thighs. "You want it. She wants it. What's the point in playing games?"

"Because you're fucking with *my* heart."

Hephaestus hesitates. It's only because I'm pressed so tightly to him that I feel his breath hitch. "You aren't the only one with a fool heart tangled up in this. Stop playing the martyr and get on your knees."

I draw a shocked breath, but it's lost in Adonis's obedience. He curses and sinks to his knees slowly before us. "I won't get out of this unscathed, and I resent you using me like a pawn between you."

I need to say something, to stop this or reassure him or... something. This night has taken a twist for the unexpected and Adonis is right. We need to stop. This wasn't simple from the beginning, and it feels like every step we take only makes it more complicated, entangles us further.

But I can't quite manage to speak as Hephaestus lifts my shirt, baring me from the waist down. He's still stroking my throat with his thumb, a possessive and strangely gentling movement. When he speaks to Adonis, he sounds almost tender. "You may have started out like a pawn, but you didn't stay that way for long."

"Don't."

He ignores Adonis's protest. "Last night meant something to me, no matter how messy it is. Now, you know what she needs. Give it to her."

"What she *needs* is a good night's rest and an increased security force."

I can't let that stand. "I know what I need. I don't *need* the two of you to decide it for me."

Hephaestus gives a rough chuckle. "By all means, Wife, use your big-girl words and tell us."

I need to be safe. I need to have one corner of this godsforsaken city where I'm able to rest and not have to worry about a knife in my back, literal or otherwise. I need to stop hurting the people I most care about with every move I make.

I don't say the words. I can't. Not now. Not ever. They might honestly be here to make me feel better, but that doesn't change the fact that both have worked against me in the last few days. I can't trust them.

Gods, I'm so tired.

I close my eyes. For once, the truth works better than any lie could. "I need to come so hard I forget everything that happened today."

Adonis exhales harshly. For a moment, I think he'll start arguing again, but he just runs his hands up my legs, careful to avoid the scattering of bandages. They're both touching me so gently. Adonis and I were together long enough that we tried every flavor of sex we were interested in, so gentle isn't out of the realm of normal for him.

But my husband?

There's no time to spiral into worry about what this might do to the power games between us. Not with Adonis pressing my thighs wide and wedging his broad shoulders between them. I go up onto my toes, but he anticipates me, draping one leg over his shoulder.

Then his mouth is on my pussy and I can't think of anything at all.

Giving up control feels a bit like jumping out of a plane. The ground approaches with each slow drag of Adonis's tongue against my clit, but I don't care, because in this moment I feel weightless and free. I close my eyes and give myself over to this experience. *Gods, I missed you.*

The consequences can wait until morning.

"That's right, Wife. Relax against me." Hephaestus's low voice in my ear makes me shiver. "Doesn't his mouth feel good? Hard to worry about anything with him sucking on your clit."

Adonis responds by doing exactly that. He sucks hard on my clit. We've been lovers for a third of my life. He knows my body as well as I do, and he proves it by pressing two fingers into me and zeroing in on my G-spot in exactly the motion I like best.

I moan. I don't even have time to consider keeping the sound internal. Hephaestus inhales sharply. For a moment I think—I fear—that he'll do something to stop the orgasm rising in gentle waves, urged on by Adonis's tongue against my clit and his fingers inside me. He doesn't. He just tightens his grip around my hips, helping Adonis keep me off the ground. I'm held suspended between them, and another time that would freak me the fuck out, but right now I just want someone else to take control.

"Let Adonis make you feel good." A pause. "He needs it as much as you do."

I tense, my mind trying to fight through the haze of pending orgasm to worry about what Hephaestus is talking about. It's too late. My body has the wheel, and it's intent on its pleasure. The wave crests between one breath and the next, sending me shuddering into an orgasm.

Too good. It's too fucking good.

"Up, Adonis. Let's move this to the bedroom."

I can't think clearly enough to decide whether that is the best idea or the worst. Especially when Adonis scoops me into his arms and it feels like coming home. If I was a little stronger, a little less rattled, a little steadier, I would hold myself apart as much as possible. It's the smart thing to do. Adonis might have come riding to my rescue tonight, but that doesn't change what I've done to him in the name of duty. What's no longer between us because of the choices I've made.

But I'm not stronger, or less rattled, or steady. I'm scared out of my mind and doing my best to keep it locked down. It's the only excuse I have for laying my head against his shoulder and admitting, "I miss you."

He tightens his arms around me. "I miss you, too."

It strikes me, as Adonis walks into my bedroom and Hephaestus follows us in and shuts the door, that I might be playing right into my husband's hands. If he intends to rip my heart out, putting Adonis back in my bed is a good plan.

I don't care. I might never get this again. I'll deal with the inevitable pain in order to have this right now.

Hephaestus's hands fall to the front of his pants. "That was a good start, but you're still thinking too hard. Take off your clothes, Wife. Tonight, the only fight is seeing who can make you come the most."

HEPHAESTUS

I SHOULD LEAVE. THERE'S NOTHING FOR ME IN THIS room. My wife might have leaned back against me so sweetly while she came, but this strange peace between us won't last. We're on the opposite sides of a conflict. That's not going to change, and if I keep fucking her, it makes things...complicated.

Adonis slips his hand into mine. It's a brief contact, there and gone in a moment. Is he looking for reassurance? Confusion alights in my chest. It only gets worse when he stops and looks back at me. Gods, he's beautiful. The kind of beautiful that takes my breath away every time I look at him too long. I know I keep thinking that, but I suspect I could spend the rest of my life with this man and still not get used to it.

He's not who I'm here for, though.

Or, at least...not the only one I'm here for.

Aphrodite has followed my command and pulled off that oversized shirt—I have a feeling it belongs to Adonis. It's obviously well loved, the fabric worn thin from years of use and the print on the front faded until it's unrecognizable. That shirt is a clear representation of their history. They've known each other so fucking long.

Have loved each other for so fucking long.

I don't get that. Or I do, but only in theory. I love Pandora, but romantic relationships are a totally different animal. And now I'm standing here, feeling like an intruder.

"Theseus." Adonis's brows draw together. "Are you okay?"

I could ask him the same thing. There's a tightness to his shoulders that looks like he's about to spring into motion. Like he might run the fuck out of this room. I don't know why that calms me down, makes my thoughts stop spinning.

Maybe they do need me here, after all.

You should use this. They're both vulnerable right now.

The voice almost sounds like Minos. For the first time in a very long time, I ignore it. I don't want to hurt Adonis. I haven't since that first conversation between us. As for my wife? The thought of causing her further pain makes me uncomfortable in a way I'm not ready to confront.

But then, I'm a man of action. "Take off your clothes, Adonis."

He hesitates, but I don't blink, don't give him anything to argue about. It's an order, plain and simple. After another beat, he slowly unbuttons his shirt and shrugs out of it. I turn away as his hands fall to his pants. If I watch him strip, I'm going to lose track of where we're headed.

Aphrodite crawls across the bed and takes up a position leaning against the headboard. She watches me with an expression she's trying to keep locked down. She's not doing a good job of it. My wife is unsure. I wonder if that's ever happened before?

The thought should make me happy, but instead it feels like I swallowed hot coals. She might not be swinging around a sword or staring down the sights of a rifle, but my wife is a warrior. A monster. Until this attack on her life, she's never shown even a hint of uncertainty or indecision. Even when I threw her curve balls, she pivoted smoothly into whatever action or smart-ass comment would take me to my knees.

I want that fiery witch back. This woman is all too human, and she makes me feel strange and soft, like I'm another person entirely. Like I'm not her enemy.

I snag Adonis's hand and tug him to me. Kissing him isn't part of some grand plan. I don't have a fucking plan right now. If I did, I wouldn't feel like the ledge is crumbling under my feet and I'm about to fall into some great unknown. But he's visibly wavering, and there isn't a damn thing I can say to make him sure that this is where he's supposed to be. So I'll show him instead.

He tastes of my wife's pussy.

I lick the inside of his mouth and tug him closer. Yes, this is what we need. His hands grabbing my biceps and pulling me against him. His hard cock jumping against my palm when I press my hand to him. His sweet little moan that I want to eat right up.

We're not here alone, though.

Taking a step back from him feels all kinds of wrong, but I manage it. I move to his back and stare at Aphrodite over his shoulder. If I thought watching us would distract her, I missed the mark. Her eyes are a little too wide, and she's got this look on her face as if she's studying a feast on the other side of shark-infested waters. Permanently out of reach.

Not tonight we're not.

If the gods exist, they're laughing their asses off at me right now. How the fuck did I end up as the person driving this thing? The one who's doing his damnedest to be the glue that gets us through the night? I don't know if that's ironic or just flat-out fucked.

I stroke Adonis's cock, still holding my wife's gaze. "Spread your legs."

Her breath hitches, but she obeys. Her body is fucking unreal. Tits high and tight, topped with rosy nipples I can't wait to get my mouth on again. Waist with the perfect curves for...*our*...hands. Just like that, I know where we're headed.

"I can't see her pussy properly. Can you, Adonis?" He makes a choked sound and I squeeze his cock. "That wasn't an answer."

"No," he gasps. "I can't see her pussy properly."

"Didn't think so." I guide him to the edge of the bed and up onto it. No matter what else is true about my wife, she's got good taste in shit around her house. The bed is massive, the kind of space that can easily fit the three of us, and potentially even more people. I give Adonis a little push to topple him on one side of her and ease myself down onto the other side. We end up pressed to the outsides of her thighs, which gives me the excuse to shift back and guide her legs even wider yet. "Show us, Wife."

Her eyes flash, but she doesn't argue. Instead, she snakes a hand down her stomach and creates a V with her fingers. She parts her pussy, exposing herself to us entirely. "Better," I growl.

"Yeah," Adonis manages. He stares at her pussy for a long moment and then turns his attention to me.

Waiting to see where I'll lead them next.

The rush of power leaves me dizzy. I should question this, but I'm not in the mood to worry about how to spin this to my advantage. No, I just want them to come undone at *my* hands.

I hold Adonis's gaze as I slide my hand up Aphrodite's thigh and press two fingers into her. They both inhale sharply and the shaky ground under me crumbles a bit more. "She's so wet from your mouth." I pump into her slowly, and I'm not even mad when Adonis rips his eyes from mine to watch me fuck my wife with my fingers.

He licks his lips. "Yeah."

"Do you know what I want?" Neither of them answer, but that's fine. Their attention is narrowed on me, waiting on what I say next. I wedge a third finger into her. "I want to feel you like this."

Adonis blinks. "What?"

I pull out of her and grab his hand, lacing my fingers with his. "I want to feel you." I guide our hands to Aphrodite's pussy and press our fingers inside. "Like this."

"Oh *fuck*." Aphrodite fists the sheets and lifts her hips. "Yes. That. I want that."

Adonis's lips are parted and he looks dazed. "Like this." He watches us fuck her with our intertwined fingers. "Yeah." He clears his throat. "Yeah, I want that."

"Good boy." The words feel ripped out of my chest. "Get her ready for us."

This time, he doesn't wait for me to give explicit instructions. He dips down and presses a messy kiss to her clit. She makes a sexy little sound. I watch him eat her out for a few beats and then turn my attention to her. She's slick against our fingers as we keep finger-fucking her, but neither of us are small guys, and no matter how much I hate her most...*some*...of the time, I want this to be good for her.

Another orgasm or two ought to do it.

"Look at me, Wife."

She opens her eyes slowly. Her skin is flushed with desire, and she's squirming as we work her. She's beautiful, but then she's always been beautiful. I don't really mean to shift up and kiss her. Kissing is one of those things that I like in theory, but rarely bother with. That isn't true with Adonis, and apparently it's not true with my wife, either.

It doesn't mean anything. It can't mean anything.

Except those thoughts feel like a lie.

Aphrodite arches up as I get close, taking my mouth even as she makes another of those sexy little sounds. She releases the sheets and digs her hands into my hair, holding me to her. The kiss is messy and rough, but that's us. It's fucking perfect. I lose myself in the feel of her tongue and teeth, in the way her desire makes my fingers slide against Adonis's. I'm so fucking hard, it makes me dizzy.

She sobs against my lips as she comes, her pussy fluttering around our fingers. I break the kiss and look down just as Adonis lifts his head, the bottom half of his face still glistening with her desire. "Now."

He nods shakily. "Yeah. Okay."

I disentangle our fingers and catch Aphrodite's chin. "On our wedding night, you said you didn't care if I wore condoms. Is that still true?"

She blinks and seems to come back to herself. "Yes. I'm on birth control. I, um, haven't been with anyone since Adonis. I was tested before our wedding."

He gives her a sharp look, but I can't really decipher it. "I was tested after we broke up as well."

Yeah, there's a boatload of baggage there. That's fine. They can shelve it for tonight. "I was also tested before coming to Olympus. You've seen the paperwork." If I had won Ares as planned, it would have been required to marry Helen. And obviously Minos had contingency plans, marriage among them, if I lost. I look at Adonis. "Are you comfortable going without?"

He doesn't hesitate. "Yes."

There are a dozen reasons why this is a bad idea, but I don't give a fuck. "Where's the lube?"

Aphrodite gives a breathless laugh. "Right to the point. I can appreciate that." She waves a shaking hand at her nightstand. "There."

I climb off the bed and take the opportunity to shuck off my pants. The lube is exactly where she promised, some fancy shit in a glass bottle. Nothing but the best for my wife. I motion at them. "Turn over, Wife."

She hesitates, but I'm not in the mood for it. We've established our roles tonight, and they need me here to drag them along with me. I wedge a hand under her hip and flip her over to face Adonis. She curses, but I'm already climbing onto the bed and taking up a position behind her. I thrust the lube bottle into her hand. "Adonis's cock is looking lonely."

"You are such an asshole."

"And you're stalling." I lean close and nip her earlobe. "If you don't want to fuck him, then I'll do it and you can sit there and watch."

As I suspected, that gets her moving. She squirts some lube onto her palm and reaches down to coat his length. I like the look of her hand around his thick cock. Almost as much as I like *my* hand around his wide length. When he shines with lube, I nip her ear again. "Now mine."

This time, she doesn't argue. She reaches back and strokes my cock. The lube makes her hand slippery, but the little witch doesn't miss the opportunity to skate her nails along the underside of my length.

I hiss out a breath. "Be nice or you don't get either cock."

"*You* be nice or I might forget myself and bite off something important."

I grin against her skin. *That's my witch of a wife.* I catch her thigh and pull her leg up and out. "You know what to do."

She doesn't hesitate to press my cock to her entrance. With the lube and her being so fucking wet, I slide right in. Pleasure makes my brain short out, but I muscle my response back. As good as this feels, it's about to feel better. I work into her in short strokes until I'm sheathed to the hilt.

"Fuck, that's good." She presses back against me, soft and sweet. "Now Adonis."

They both jolt, but I damn well know they both want this as much as I do. I squeeze her thigh. "It's going to feel even fucking better to have him stretching you, too. Fucking you."

"Yes," she breathes.

I have to shift a bit to be able to see her take his cock as he moves into position, but I sure as shit feel it when his broad head brushes the base of my cock. They both make a frustrated sound when he slides right off us.

I know it doesn't mean they need me. Not in any real way. That doesn't change the fact that I feel needed right now.

I'm not prepared for the sheer wave of emotion that washes over me in response to that realization.

So I shelve it.

I'll deal with it later.

Right now, I have two of the most beautiful, infuriating people I've ever met in my bed and I need to drive them out of their busy minds.

I grab my wife around the waist and tip onto my back, taking her with me. It takes a second to get situated, but I catch her other thigh and hold her legs open. "Now, Adonis. Fuck us properly."

ADONIS

I DON'T KNOW HOW I GOT TO THIS PLACE, BUT I NEVER want this fever dream to pass. Surely it's a dream. I can't possibly be kneeling between Theseus's thighs, looking down to where his big cock spreads Eris's pussy. His balls hang thick and heavy, and I can't help reaching down and cupping them with one hand and pressing the other to her lower stomach so I can brush her clit with my thumb.

She moans and he growls. He glares up at me with those dark eyes. "You're stalling."

Maybe I am. I know this is only sex, but it feels like making a promise I'm not sure I'll survive. Eris almost broke me when she left me. If I taste the possibility of both of them together, I don't know if I'll have a heart left to break.

We've gone too far to go back now. The time to protect myself was back in the kitchen. Instead, I went to my knees before them.

Fitting that I'm on my knees now, too.

I've never been religious, but as I press my cock against

Theseus's and start to work into Eris's pussy, I think their bodies might be an altar I could spend a lifetime worshipping at.

Or a lifetime mourning the loss of.

As promised, the fit is tight. Almost too tight. Sweat glistens on my skin and I'm shaking, and I barely have the head of my cock inside her.

Eris is breathing in gasps, her breasts shaking with each inhale. Each exhale is a quiet, "Fuck."

I thrust a little, sinking deeper. The lube has made our cocks slick, and being pressed so tightly to Theseus's length is enough to have me fighting not to lose control.

"That's right." Theseus's voice is low and almost unintelligible. "Keep going."

I brace my hands on either side of their hips and stare at the spot where I'm sinking slowing into her pussy. Feeding her—feeding them—one slow inch at a time. Theseus's fingers pulse on her thighs and he makes one of those delicious growls again. "Deeper."

"Working on it," I manage.

"*Deeper.*"

"Oh fuck." Eris shakes around us. "Oh shit, I think I'm going to come."

"Then come, Wife."

Every time he calls her *wife*, a tremor goes through me. I can't begin to say if it's pleasure or pain. Perhaps it's a little bit of both. I sink the rest of the way into her with a moan. Theseus doesn't give me a chance to get accustomed to the sensation. He grabs my throat and drags me closer.

Eris's hands find my back even as Theseus takes my mouth. It feels good to be held by them. Too good. Devastatingly good. I try to hold still, but it's as if all the pent-up emotions of the last few weeks have reached a boiling point.

I can't stop.

I don't even try.

I withdraw slowly, earning a muttered curse from Theseus, and then begin a slow thrust. Fucking him. Fucking her. Fucking both of them.

Eris buries her face in my throat. Her body goes tight, and it's the only warning I get before she's coming. She shudders and shakes between us. Each breath sobs from her lips against my skin. I don't mean to meet Theseus's gaze over her head, but it happens all the same.

The look on his face. I don't know how to describe it. Fierce and almost angry, and yet somehow tender at the same time. He releases her thighs and guides her to wrap her legs around my waist. The new position shifts us inside her, and Eris cries out. "Too much. Gods, I think I'm—"

I kiss her. I swallow her words and her cries, wishing I could drink down her fear and relieve her of it entirely. I know better. It will still be there tomorrow when passions have cooled and the real world calls.

Despite my best efforts, this orgasm pulls me over the edge. I moan as I come, thrusting into her harder, my cock dragging against Theseus's. It feels like they drain every bit of seed out of me. I'm shaking and weak, unable to do anything but pant against Eris's lips. She's not much better, her legs loose around my waist and her fingertips gentle on my back.

"Not done yet," Theseus growls.

I don't know how he manages to flip us without dislodging anyone. It shouldn't be possible, but a lot of things shouldn't be possible when it comes to Theseus. He presses a hand to the small of Eris's back, pressing us even tighter together.

Then he starts moving.

I'm so sensitive from coming that I cry out as his cock slides against mine. It's too much. "I—"

"Be a good boy and take it," he growls.

Good boy.

Those words feel like he reaches right into my chest and strums my very soul. With a single sentence, he propels me from being too sensitive to take what he's giving to needing him to never stop. "*Theseus.*"

"That's right. I'm giving this to you right now. To both of you." He doesn't pick up his pace. He just keeps up that devastatingly thorough stroke that seems to go on forever.

Eris's hands find my face and then she takes my mouth again. We're the only two sailors in a storm of Theseus's making. It ends when he says it does, and I'm not certain we'll survive the pleasure he continues to deal. If tonight doesn't ruin us, then whatever the morning brings will.

My heartbreak.

Our consequences.

He thrusts deep and comes with a curse. It feels so good, I can't help thrusting again, which makes him thrust and Eris writhe, and it's as if we're stuck in a loop. We keep moving until he finally drags himself from us and pulls her off my cock.

They collapse half on top of me. Eris snuggles her face against my throat, little tremors still racking her body. Or maybe I'm the one who's shaking. I'm not entirely sure.

Theseus catches my hand and presses my knuckles to his lips. "You did well."

His praise warms me. I'm too tired to worry about the fact that I shouldn't trust this man. It doesn't matter. Not now. Maybe not ever. I care about him more than I could have anticipated.

Eris shifts against me, and I look down at her. Theseus isn't the only one in this bed I care about. I love her. No matter how we hurt each other, I don't know that I will ever stop loving her. I gather her closer with my free arm and she smiles against my skin. "That's one way to comfort someone."

"It worked, didn't it?" Theseus is still a little breathless, his voice rough and tired.

"Yes." She sounds half-asleep. As I watch, her blinks become longer. Within a few minutes, her breathing evens out and the last of the tension melts from her body.

I wait a few beats more. I'm not sure if I'm stalling or if I really can't believe she fell asleep that fast. Even after hours of sex, it usually takes her longer to wind down enough to let sleep take her.

Theseus shifts behind her, and I reluctantly look up to meet his gaze. Nothing about tonight has gone like I expected, but I can't deny that it was exactly what Eris needed.

What I needed.

"Thank you," I say softly. "I know I wasn't gracious about it initially, but thank you for being there for her. This morning and tonight."

He seems like he might want to bolt, but finally sighs and relaxes against her back. When he speaks, he keeps his voice just as quiet as mine. "I thought she had things under control today or I would have called you sooner."

I look down at the sleeping woman between us. "She's gotten very good about masking it when she gets scared."

"Yeah, I got that now." He hesitates. "I am not your ally. Thinking of me as one is a mistake."

"Are you saying that to convince me...or yourself?"

Another of those world-weary sighs. "I can't be, Adonis. You can't rely on me, and you'd be a fucking fool to trust me with anything."

He's right. He's been nothing but honest from the beginning, which is an irony in and of itself. Theseus Vitalis, enemy to Olympus and yet more truthful than anyone else in this blasted city. I don't know what he means to do next in service of his foster father, but he's already done plenty. Trusting him is a mistake.

And yet...

"I trusted you with my body last night." The words are little more than a whisper. "I trusted you with *hers* tonight. That means something."

"Don't."

The temptation to press him is nearly overwhelming. He might be a monster, but I can't escape the gentle way he touched me. Or the fact that he took care of Eris in his own way, first when he saved her life and then again tonight. That means something, too, no matter how obviously uncomfortable it makes him. "What if there was another way? A way to not be standing on opposite sides of this line?"

"There's not." He catches my chin and drags his thumb over my bottom lip. For a moment, conflict shows in his eyes, but then he drops his hand to drape over Eris's body. "There's not," Theseus repeats. "This doesn't end happy with us. When it ends, it's in blood and tears."

APHRODITE

I WAKE UP FEELING MORE RELAXED THAN I HAVE IN months. I know it's a lie the moment I open my eyes and see the two men in my bed. Adonis sleeps in his customary position—on his side. I've always found it odd that the man never moves when he sleeps. But then, Adonis doesn't have the same tumultuous relationship with sleep that I do. I toss and turn, and it slips through my fingers night after night. He simply closes his eyes and lets it take him.

Hephaestus is another thing entirely. He's on the other side of Adonis, sprawled over more than his fair share of the bed, one big arm and leg tossed over the other man.

I shift, and have to talk down the surge of warmth that rises when I realize he's clasped my hip with one hand and that Adonis has one arm draped over my waist.

Last night can't mean anything.

Adonis is my ex for good reason, and my husband is my enemy. It doesn't matter that they took care of me in a truly inventive way, or that it felt particularly cathartic to release some of the pent-up messy emotions between me and Adonis.

In a few hours, we will be standing on the opposite side of the line from each other at a meeting among the Thirteen. I cannot afford to soften to him, or start to think traitorous thoughts about how maybe he isn't that bad. He *is* that bad. It's the entire reason I married him.

My body feels heavy, but it's a lie. I have to get moving. There's a meeting to attend and a destabilizing city to fix. I can't stay here in this strange little alternate reality where I don't really hate my husband and I might have a future with the man I love.

That, more than anything, gets me moving. I learned early on the price of wishing on stars. It doesn't change anything, and the inevitable disappointment can crush your soul if you're not careful. Better to work within the boundaries of what's real instead of what you *wish* was real.

I check the clock, which shows I have plenty of time before I need to be in Dodona Tower for my brother's meeting. Gods alone only know what Perseus has come up with in the meantime.

All he wanted was stability and a better Olympus than our father left us.

Look at us now, being hunted in the streets like prey.

I take a quick trip to the bathroom and snag my robe off the back of the door. I don't know if I'll kick Adonis out or leave him here, but if he's content to sleep... Well, someone might as well get extra sleep. I should let Hephaestus sleep right through the meeting. It's the strategic thing to do. But somehow I'm reaching over Adonis and tapping Hephaestus's shoulder. "You won't want to be late for this meeting. Get up."

"Five minutes." He tucks his face into the side of Adonis's throat. "Just five fucking minutes."

"Suit yourself." I hate how well rested I feel. Two full nights of sleep in a row, both of them spent with my husband in my bed. No use thinking about that. Nothing good can come of it. I slip out of the bedroom and pad down the hall toward my kitchen. I'm never conflicted. I don't have the time or luxury for this kind of spinning out.

A sound brings me up short. There is...someone in my kitchen.

I take a step back before I catch myself. I am not running back to the men and begging them to protect me. This is *my* house. I wrap my robe more firmly around me and duck into my office to grab the first thing I see. It's a massive hardcover book on the history of Olympus—a family heirloom that could crush a small child—and I feel a little ridiculous as I heft it in front of me and start back down the hall. That feeling of ridiculousness only gets worse when I see who's puttering about in my kitchen.

Pandora.

She's wearing a pair of faded jeans and a loose cropped T-shirt that I suspect originated in Hephaestus's closet. It leaves her soft belly exposed and I am struck by the sudden urge to go to my knees and press my mouth there. "Um."

"Morning." She takes in the book I'm holding. "I'd ask how you're doing, but you look both thoroughly sexed and kind of stressed. Apparently Theseus took the old 'when you're holding a hammer, every problem looks like a nail' approach."

I'm...not sure how to act in this situation. Obviously, Pandora knew I was married to Hephaestus—Theseus—but this feels very different than the relationship we've been building to date. The whole point was to keep him out of what Pandora and I have… and then turn around and needle him about it. To let him twist in the wind and worry about what I might be up to with his beloved best friend.

Except he's in my bed and she's in my kitchen.

My stomach dips and I try for a smile. "Morning?"

She props her hands on her hips. "Are you going to hit me with that book?"

"No?"

"Then why don't you put it down and come here?"

I numbly set it on the narrow hall table next to me. My body hardly feels like my own right now. I'm more centered that I was last night, but not by much.

My whole world has gone topsy-turvy.

Even so, it feels so damn right to step forward and into Pandora's arms. She hugs me tightly and I find myself clinging to her and inhaling her flowery shampoo scent.

"I'm glad you're okay," she murmurs against my throat. "I was really worried about you when Theseus called me last night."

Just like that, the pieces click into place. My husband came here, found me—well, the less I think about how he found me, the better—and then called Pandora. "You're the one who told him to call Adonis, aren't you?"

"Yes." She leans back enough to look into my eyes. "Theseus and I would have fucked it up, even if we tried our best. Adonis knows you." She smiles a little. "He loves you. You love him, too. He was who you needed."

"Thank you," I whisper. I search her expression for some kind of hurt, but there's nothing. "This is a very strange situation."

"Welcome to polyamory." She gives me one last squeeze and steps back.

"Just like that?" It seems to defy belief that I can take her at face value. That Pandora wouldn't feel even a sliver of the conflicting feelings coursing through me right now. That she would offer relief instead of piling on the guilt. "That simple."

"There's nothing simple about it. It gets thorny and sometimes the communication is better than other times. But that's life, isn't it?" She shrugs. "What's on the agenda today?"

I follow her into the kitchen. It doesn't even occur to me to lie. "The Thirteen have a meeting about the increased attacks against us. After that, I need to survey the replacement glass divider being installed in my office."

Pandora nods. "You'll need some protein to get you through." She eyes me. "You're the type to fly right through lunch without eating, aren't you?"

Guilt heats my skin, even though I have nothing to actually feel guilt for. "I'm very busy. Sometimes it slips my mind."

"Thought so." She nudges me with her hip. "Sit down and let me feed you. Preferences on breakfast?"

I tuck my robe more firmly around my body and perch on the barstool at the island. "Simple. I usually grab a protein bar or something on the way out the door."

The look she sends my way is so filled with exasperation that my heart gives a funny little thump. I'm going to have to have my chest looked at. All these skipped beats can't be good for my health. Between the three of them, my heart is working overtime.

Pandora starts unloading the grocery bags on the counter. "How about an omelet? Protein and even a vegetable or two."

"That sounds lovely." My heart gives another thump. "But you don't have to do that. Really, I'm okay."

"I know you're okay, just like I know I don't have to do this. I'm not here because I have to be. I'm here because I want to be." She starts moving about my kitchen. It takes her all of thirty seconds to find what she's looking for and get a pan heating up on the stove. She hums under her breath as she works.

It's... I don't even have words.

The surreal feeling only gets more pronounced when Hephaestus and Adonis wander into the kitchen. My husband has managed to pull himself together in relatively short time. His hair even looks combed. He gives Pandora a hug, a quick squeeze of her shoulders, and presses a kiss to her temple. Adonis veers around her easily and gets to work starting a giant pot of coffee. His eyes are half-open, and I'm nearly certain he's not actually awake yet. He never is before his first cup of coffee.

It's *nice*. The four of us in my kitchen. It doesn't feel like the men walked in and ruined the moment. Instead, it's almost as if they're adding to the lovely feeling of domestic bliss.

Hephaestus leans against the counter and crosses his arms over his chest. I notice he gets several steps out of Pandora's way while she cooks, which strikes me as strangely cute. He eyes me. "You look better this morning."

"Yes, well, you fucked me damn near into unconsciousness. It's amazing how little capacity a person has for fear when they're that exhausted from orgasms."

His lips quirk. Not quite a smile, but on him, it's practically bursting into laughter. "A mutual benefit. You're much more agreeable when you're coming. I only thought about strangling you once last night. Twice at most."

"*Theseus.*" Pandora whips him with a dish towel, the snap making me jump. She glares. "What's wrong with you? Don't say shit like that."

Now's the time to drive a chasm between them, to tell her that he's said much worse to me, has actively threatened me. Pandora wouldn't be here if she didn't care about me, and she might have a much longer relationship with him, but the fault lines are right there and ready to exploit.

Except I...don't.

Instead, I sit there and listen to them casually snipe at each other in a way that speaks to a very long history. The rhythm of their conversation has grooves of retread topics, the same way a river carves out a canyon. The words might be sharp, but fondness permeates every syllable.

This can't last. There are too many obstacles in front of us. But I almost wish I was wrong about our little foursome's inevitable collapse.

"Here." Adonis sets a mug of coffee in front of me and takes the seat on my left.

"Thank you." I wrap my hands around it, letting the heat steal through the ceramic and warm my palms.

He leans his elbows on the counter and turns his head to look at me. "Last night…"

"Yeah." It changed everything and nothing. I'm still married to Hephaestus. I still love Adonis. We're still diametrically opposed on multiple different levels. Maybe the three of us worked last night, but that doesn't mean we could ever work in the long term.

Still, I can't not say what I'm feeling right now. "Thank you. For everything. I know this wasn't easy for you."

He gives a ghost of his normal happy smile. "I enjoyed last night. I'm not happy that you're in danger, but it was cathartic."

"*Cathartic.*" A strange word, but it fits. I bump my shoulder against his. "That's a new one."

"With you? Always a surprise."

Pandora spins around and places a plate in front of me. The omelet looks like something I'd order at a restaurant. I raise my brows. "This is impressive."

"Yes, well, he can't cook." She jerks her thumb at Hephaestus. "And I had plenty of free time while Minos had his children, foster and otherwise, dancing to his tune. His cook, Picus, was fond of me and taught me what he knew." Her smile dims. "I hope he's doing okay without us there to feed."

"I'm sure he's fine," Hephaestus rumbles. "Minos sent him to another household to stay busy."

She gives him a sharp look. "That's the first I'm hearing of it."

Adonis clears his throat. When Pandora looks at him, he gives her his best charming smile. I'm faintly amused to see her blink against the force of it. She shakes her head. "Hello again, Adonis. You *would* be as handsome in the morning when you've just rolled out of bed as you are when you're dressed to the nines. Glad to see you've been well in the weeks since I've seen you. I'm assuming you have a request?"

"If I can impose on you to make another plate, I would be endlessly grateful and forever in your debt."

She laughs softly. "No need for the theatrics. I'm happy to cook for you." She slants a glance at Hephaestus. "All of you."

"What he said. Endlessly grateful." On my husband's lips, the words sound almost like a threat.

"Right. Sure." Pandora rolls her eyes. "Sit down and stop lurking. It's distracting."

"I'm good at lurking." He *winks* and ambles around the island to take the stool on Adonis's other side.

I don't know what to do with this side of Hephaestus. I've seen him dangerous and furious and vicious. But in the last twenty-four hours, I've also seen him gentle and playful and dominating in a really sexy way. He was borderline cruel last night, but I can't deny that his motivations were pure. Or close enough to pure to count.

It complicates things in a way I'm not comfortable with. Hating him was so much easier before he took care with my body…and then my heart. Before I saw the tenderness in the way he touched Adonis and the comfortable amusement inherent in his interactions with Pandora.

I drink my coffee and let the moment wash over me. Pandora teasing Hephaestus. Adonis slipping in a comment here and there, his attitude warming as his coffee cup empties.

It's…nice.

It makes me want to stay here in this strange little world forever. I can't, though. I need to get ready, get my head on straight, and go off to the war meeting with my brother.

I turn to Adonis. "I have to go."

"I know." He squeezes my knee and lifts his voice. "Dinner tonight."

It's not a question, but I still find myself shifting sideways to look at my husband. He's more relaxed than I've ever seen him and he nods easily. "Sure, dinner."

Adonis glances at Pandora. Her brows wing up in response. "I get the feeling the three of you will forget to eat if I'm not around. I'll be here."

I want you here for more than food.

Gods, what's happening to me?

I should be the one to take a wrecking ball to this moment, to remind them that none of us are actually allies, and this little group will fall apart at the first hit from the world outside my apartment.

Instead I stand and round the island to hug her. "Thank you for breakfast."

She catches my elbows and looks up at me, her expression going fierce. "Stay safe today, Eris."

My throat goes tight. "I will. I promise."

I hope to the gods I'm not lying to her.

PANDORA

ERIS DISAPPEARS TO GET READY. I WAIT UNTIL I'VE SLIPPED plates of food in front of both the men to lean against the counter and say, "So, who had the brilliant idea to fuck the trauma-tized woman?"

Adonis chokes, spitting out coffee. "What?"

"It was me." Theseus meets my gaze steadily. "It seemed like a good idea at the time, and she's steadier on her feet now. It wasn't a bad idea."

I roll my eyes. "You would think that, wouldn't you?" He's not entirely wrong, though. She must have been in a bad state to make him so panicked last night, but I'm not sure I want to address *that* right now.

Theseus cares about her. I can't tell if he knows it yet, but if he didn't care at least a little bit, last night he would have turned around and walked out of her apartment and never looked back.

That should comfort me—*I* care about Eris—but I know him too well. He won't let something as small as caring get in the way of following orders. Minos has his claws in too deep. If he tells Theseus to murder Eris, Theseus might feel a little bad about it, but he'll do it.

It feels like we're on a runaway train heading straight for a blown-out bridge. I don't know how to slow us down, don't know how to get off the tracks.

The only option is to ride it directly to our ruin.

I shift to look at Adonis. "I expected such nonsense from him. What's your excuse?"

"I don't have one. It just kind of happened." He ducks his head in a really charming way. I understand what they see in him. There's something about Adonis that draws everyone around him. It was evident at Minos's house party, to the point where not even Theseus was unaffected. He's certainly affected *now*.

I eye him. Yeah, he's downright smitten. It's there in the way his body seems pulled in by a gravitational pull Adonis is putting out. Their shoulders keep brushing, and he grabs Adonis's mug to refill when he gets his own coffee.

I've only seen him like this once before, with a guy he had a summer romance with right after Minos brought us into his household. He's soft with me, but it's a different kind of intimacy, born of our shared trauma. We're best friends and I'm closer to him than anyone else in the world, but it will never be romantic.

It will never be Theseus looking like he looks right now, like he's not entirely sure what to do with his hands. He's a warrior. I've seen him move through a series of opponents—one of the training exercises Minos insists on—as if he's water and untouchable. He might not be able to move quite so fluidly now, but he's still grace-ful in his way.

Not right now.

He's moving like he did when he turned fourteen and grew six inches in a few months. His body was new and strange and he had to relearn how to move through the world without slamming into things.

I press my lips together. This is a recipe for disaster. I don't know if the other three aren't aware of it, or are intentionally ignoring it, but there's not much to be done if they are deter-mined to see the course through. I'm not sure they *are* deter-mined to see it through, though. The whole mood this morning feels very unreal, as if it's a bubble just waiting for someone to pop it.

Really, I'm a hypocrite. I have no intention of putting distance between me and any of these people. It's just going to hurt when things blow up in our faces. "Theseus." I wait for him to look at me. "Minos was looking for you this morning."

He meets my gaze steadily. "I'll call him once I'm done with the meeting."

Something like hope flutters in my chest. A month ago, he would have dropped everything to rush for his phone and apolo-gized the moment his foster father picked up. Still, I know better than to believe Minos's influence is waning.

"I see." My best friend is many things, but fickle isn't one of them. It will take more than a pretty face and charming smile to pull him from that poisonous household.

Adonis looks between us. "Should I give you a minute?"

"It's fine." Theseus leans back. "Pandora is worried about my priorities."

I snort. "Only because your priorities are suspect." If I knew what Minos was up to, I might be tempted to go straight to that golden asshole in his tower and use the information to leverage Theseus's freedom.

Except, no, I'm still being a hypocrite. No matter how little I like Minos, I won't do anything to endanger Theseus. There's not a single reason for Zeus to honor his word about not harming Theseus if he married Eris. In fact, there are half a dozen reasons off the top of my head to make his enemy disappear and stick someone he trusts into the Hephaestus title.

"It's no use trying to talk sense into him." Eris appears, looking more put together than she has a right to after being gone such a short time. She's pulled her hair back into a slick ponytail and gone with a minimal makeup look...except for her crimson lips. She picked a fitted black dress that shows off her lean frame, and black heels high enough to make her the tallest person in the room.

"Wife." For once, I can't read the expression on Theseus's face. Or, to be more accurate, there are too many conflicting expressions. Lust, anger, something like tenderness, maybe the tiniest hint of vulnerability. Theseus doesn't know how to feel about his wife.

That makes two of us.

"I'll walk you out." I say.

She looks at me. "That's really not necessary. None of this is."

There it is. The first crack.

Theseus crosses his arms over his chest. "I don't know. Felt pretty necessary to me."

Surprise pulls me up short. Now is the time when he should snarl something and storm out. Not stand there calmly and stare his wife down.

"Fine. It was a little necessary. Your sacrifice has been duly noted, but I have to leave now. You should do the same if you don't want to be late." If I hadn't heard the panic in Theseus's voice last night and then seen the fragility in her eyes this morning, I never would have known what happened yesterday.

Good.

She's too stubborn to show weakness to the rest of the city, and I'm glad of it. Enemies looking for a fracture to exploit will find none.

That doesn't mean I'm content for her stubbornness to apply to me, too. "You and your husband have more in common than either of you will admit. Both of your priorities are misguided." I shake my head. "And you're both too stubborn by half. Let's go."

Eris catches up to me as I reach the door. She's remarkably subdued as we take the elevator down to the parking garage. The doors open and she reaches out to hold them that way. "My priorities aren't misguided. I realize this city doesn't mean anything to you, but—"

"This city will kill you and move on to the next Aphrodite without blinking." I speak too harshly, but it's the truth.

"Maybe." She shrugs. "Sometimes that's the price of being a person like me."

"You'll die for nothing, then." I don't normally let my feelings get the best of me, but she's speaking so reasonably, as if the danger to her is barely worth mentioning. "Surely your life is worth more than being some footnote in Olympian history."

Eris gives me a long look. "What did you think would happen when you came to my city, Pandora?" She says it gently, which somehow makes it that much worse. "Even if you didn't know Minos's plans, you had to know he meant harm to the people who live here. Did you really think the Thirteen wouldn't step up to get between our city and the one who threatens it?"

Guilt flares. Truth be told, I didn't care about the people in this city, any more than I cared about the people on the island we left. The only person I cared about is sitting back in Eris's kitchen, probably flirting with Adonis.

I know what kind of person that makes me, but I made my peace with that a long time ago. I lift my chin. "How many people have you hurt for the good of this city? Including the ones back in your apartment?"

She doesn't flinch. I don't honestly expect her to.

Eris shrugs. "You're just proving my point. The good of the many will always outweigh the need of one person." She makes a face. "I'm not eager to throw myself in front of a bullet, but there's been risk associated with being me since I was born. It's just more explicit now."

"I hate this," I whisper. "I hate that you're in danger and that you're at odds with Theseus."

Her expression goes contemplative. "Maybe we're not quite the enemies we were a few days ago. I don't know if last night actually changes anything." Eris narrows her eyes. "What are my odds of turning him?"

I wish I had better news for her. She might see Theseus as a tool the same way Minos does, but it's not the same. As husband and wife, he and Eris are closer to being on the same footing than him and the stand-in parent he feels he owes everything to. Her turning Theseus and having him dancing to *her* tune wouldn't be ideal, but it'd still be preferable.

It'll never happen.

I turn and look out into the parking garage. It's full of wildly expensive vehicles and shadows. No one around to hear me tell the truth. "Not good. In his mind, Minos saved us. He swept in after a really traumatic event and seemed to give Theseus everything he could have ever dreamed of."

"After that priest tried to hurt you and Theseus killed him, but not before he almost disemboweled Theseus. Made him quite the perfect little soldier-victim for Minos, I imagine."

"What?" I spin back to face her. "How do you know about that?" I had given her the bare details before, but I purposefully kept things back.

"He told me." She's still got that look on her face, the one that says she's seeing a thousand puzzle pieces and considering the best way to put them together. "After I was attacked."

The story of how we came to be in Minos's household isn't exactly a secret, but Theseus doesn't share private stories. Especially not ones that involve me. The people who know why he killed that priest number in the single digits. "Eris."

"Yes?"

She doesn't understand. How could she? I barely understand myself. What happened between them that things have shifted this much? I don't know how to feel. I want him free of Minos, but I truly don't want him to put on someone else's shackles. Not even hers. "If he told you that story, then your odds aren't as bad as I thought. They're not good—Minos's hold on him is too complete—but they're not zero."

She smiles suddenly. "I've worked with worse."

"He's not a toy to be fought over."

"No, he's not." She pauses. "But if he doesn't get out of my way, I will be forced to crush him. I won't hesitate, Pandora. I can't afford to."

"Eris—"

She catches my hands, placing them on her hips. "Come over early."

Nothing I say to either of them is going to change their paths forward. Theseus and Eris are well-matched in a number of ways, including their bullheaded stubbornness to dance to tunes set by other people. She won't thank me for pointing that out any more than he does, and if I keep arguing, it will end things between us sooner than I'm ready to let her go.

So I don't argue. I run my hands up her sides as she steps closer. In her heels, I barely come up to her shoulder, which puts me right at the perfect height to appreciate her breasts. They're truly lovely breasts. I would very much like to get my hands and mouth on them.

I clear my throat, trying to focus. "You're not going to have time for me if you're running around the city putting out fires."

"I'll make time for you." She skates her fingers up my arms and cups my face. "I'll always make time for you. Thank you for breakfast." She presses a kiss to my lips, light and teasing. "And thank you for being the voice of reason last night. Bringing in Adonis might not have gone how you'd thought it would, but it truly *did* help."

I pull her close and kiss her properly. Eris tastes like mint and I'm smudging her lipstick, but I don't care. I think my hands might be shaking, but I can't be sure. When she finally eases back, I'm clinging to her. "I was worried about you. I *am* worried about you."

"I know." She wraps her arms around my shoulders and holds me close. "I know."

Ironic that it feels like she's comforting me when she's the one who was hurt. I've known this woman a few weeks, and I have no business feeling like the world would be significantly dimmer without her in it, but I don't make a habit of ignoring hard truths.

I care about Eris. A lot. Sometime in the last few days, I've slipped right over the edge of enjoying her company and fallen into…falling. Maybe that should bother or scare me, but there's no use railing against fundamental truth. It simply is. And the fundamental truth of this situation is that I'm falling for Eris. "Stay safe today."

"I promise that I'll try." She gives me one last squeeze and steps back. "Feel free to stay at my place if you'd like. As you found out this morning, you have access."

Granting me access to her home was no doubt part of her ploy to seduce me, but it warms me all the same. "I might do that."

"Good." She pulls a compact and tissue from her purse and somehow manages to fix her lipstick in a few swipes. "You stay safe today, too."

I'm about to point out that the entirety of Olympus isn't after *me*, but I don't get a chance before a trio of people in black tactical gear approach. I tense, ready to grab Eris and haul her back into the elevator, but she sighs. "My sister *would* send Achilles as part of my team."

As soon as she says it, I recognize the unreasonably handsome white man in the center of the trio. He's the one who fought the Minotaur in the final Ares trial. It'd been a fearsome fight, going well past the point when the Minotaur was eliminated.

For his part, he doesn't seem any happier with the arrangement than Eris is. He gives her a cold look. "Aphrodite. We're here to escort you." His lips thin. "You were supposed to wait upstairs for us."

"Oh, that." She waves it away. "I needed to have a private conversation with my dear Pandora. I'm sure you understand."

He turns that steely gaze on me. "What I understand is that any danger to you will be eliminated."

I go cold. No mistaking the threat being directed at me. Eris steps between us and drawls, "Aw, Achilles, I didn't think you liked me that much."

"I don't. But if you get hurt, it will make Helen sad. I go out of my way not to make my woman sad."

"Lucky me." She turns and presses another quick kiss to my lips. "See you tonight."

I watch them walk away, my heart in my throat. There's no denying that Ares set Eris up with the best people she had, but will it be enough? When every citizen of this city is a possible enemy, the chances of making it out of this without losing someone I love...

It feels impossible.

HEPHAESTUS

I WATCH ADONIS DO DISHES OVER THE RIM OF MY coffee cup. My wife was right; I need to get moving if I don't want to be late. But I can't leave before I button things up with him.

He seems fine enough, but I don't know if I trust that. He's Olympian. He lies as well as the rest of them, even if he doesn't seem to lie to me all that often. "You good?"

"Not really." He rolls his head, his neck popping. "This whole situation is messy."

"Messy" doesn't begin to cover it. There were a few moments this morning in the kitchen when I forgot all about that, though. It was just nice to be there with Pandora while Aphrodite and Adonis drank their coffee. The casual intimacy relaxed something in me that I can't afford to have relaxed, but I didn't want it to end.

I still don't.

That doesn't prevent me from running my mouth. "You could walk away. We don't have a choice about being here, but you do."

Pandora, too, but I know better than to try to push her again. She'll make her own decisions. She always has.

"I really can't." He finishes the dishes and makes quick work of drying them. "Not from her. Not from you, either."

My stomach does a strange swoop. "Adonis—"

"Be safe out there today."

That makes me pause. "Are you worried about me?"

He huffs out a breath. "Of course I am. The public of Olympus are mostly good people, but the ambitious ones without moral compasses are looking at every single one of the Thirteen and sharpening their knives. *You* are one of the Thirteen."

"No one is coming after me." I say it confidently, even as a little kernel of doubt takes seed. Minos is hardly a caring father figure, but surely he wouldn't put me in a position where it was likely I'd be killed...

Would he?

"You need to go," Adonis says gently. "You can't be late for meetings with the Thirteen. Your position is already rocky enough."

He's right, but I couldn't give a fuck about the Thirteen and their rules and rituals right now. I'm starting to be able to read him better, though. I recognize the stubborn set of his mouth. There will be no arguing with him about this. "Just finishing my coffee." I drain the mug. "This conversation isn't over."

"Wouldn't dream of it." He plucks the mug from my hands and presses a quick kiss to my lips. "Now, *go*."

I go.

Fifteen minutes later, I walk into the conference room where

Zeus has called the Thirteen for what's become a weekly meeting. It's a waste of fucking time. There are alliances within the group, and plenty of them are at odds with each other. If Zeus says the sky is blue, Artemis will snarl that it's purple out of sheer spite.

Not even their hatred for me and Minos is enough to unify them, though you wouldn't know it by the glares I receive from every person in the room when I walk through the door.

Everyone except my wife.

She doesn't smile, but her expression is carefully blank. Might as well roll out the welcome mat for me after the last two weeks. I walk around the table, careful to minimize my limp as much as possible even though my knee aches like a motherfucker.

I'm starting to think that pain will never go away.

I drop into the empty chair next to Eris. I should probably say something to showcase that she spent last night in my bed willingly and doesn't hate me as much as she should, but the words don't come. I'm not on her side, but that doesn't mean I have to kick her legs out from under her when she's trying so hard to keep her shit together.

Zeus leans forward and everyone around the table goes quiet. Neat trick. His cold gaze flicks over me, his eyes narrowing the slightest bit when he sees how close I'm sitting to his sister.

He turns that look on the empty chair in the center of the table. "Where is Hermes?"

Dionysus clears his throat. "She said duty calls and made a last-minute trip outside the boundary."

Zeus doesn't curse. He doesn't so much as blink. "No one sanctioned that trip, Poseidon."

Poseidon shrugs. He's a big fucker with pale skin and deep red hair. "She's Hermes. She doesn't need approval." His deep voice gains an edge. "Unless the laws have changed in the last few days?"

Zeus sweeps a look over the rest of the room. "Then we move on without her. Let's begin."

Before anyone can speak, the doors open and Minos walks in.

Shock makes me freeze. What the fuck is he doing here? He doesn't even look at me, his attention focusing on Zeus as he smiles. "Everyone is so serious. Am I late?"

"Right on time." Zeus doesn't return his smile. "You have our attention. What do you want?"

Minos's brows draw together the tiniest bit in genuine surprise. "I'm sorry? You invited me here today."

"Yes. I did." Zeus leans back. No one seems to breathe. "I tire of these games, Minos. You came to Olympus with an agenda, and I've indulged it. That's finished now. You want something from the Thirteen. Let's stop wasting everyone's time and dispense with the games."

A bold move.

I don't know if it's a smart one, but I keep my mouth shut as I watch Minos. Whatever he thought this meeting was about, he didn't expect this. He also didn't get to this point in his life without learning to think on his feet.

He smiles at Zeus, as if he can beam his charm right into the other man's head. "But you like games so much in Olympus. I've merely been honoring my new home by indulging in them."

"You haven't answered my question."

I flick a glance at Artemis. She's not keeping her expression as locked down as the others. If there wasn't a table between them, she might have tried to attack Minos. I'm so used to her looking at *me* like that after I killed her cousin that it's almost not worth mentioning. The way Hera reaches out and touches her arm beneath the table *is*, though. Especially when Artemis slumps back in her chair in response. I didn't think those two liked each other much.

Minos spreads his arms, every inch a showman. "If I didn't know any better, I would think you're accusing me of being behind those attacks on the Thirteen I keep reading about in MuseWatch."

"Why wouldn't people assume that?" Zeus's voice has no inflection. No anger. No frustration. It's eerie. He glances at me again. "You've done it before."

"As I said, I am embracing the customs of the city that's adopted me and mine." Minos's smile goes cunning. "No one under my command has made any attempts on the lives of anyone in this room. Feel free to verify that information." His gaze cuts to Apollo. "Though I have a feeling you already have."

The way Apollo's jaw clenches verifies that.

Minos had said he wasn't behind the attacks, but I wasn't sure I believed it. Now I am. He's always been a fan of letting other people get their hands dirty while he enjoys his lavish lifestyle without fear of consequences.

The bitterness of the thought gives me pause. I've never been ignorant of the man's faults, but I've never felt this grinding frustration with them, either. He doesn't care that my wife almost died yesterday. Realistically, there's no reason for him to care.

There's no reason for *me* to care, either.

But I do.

I don't want her dead. If Minos was behind the attacks, he could call them off; at least the ones against her. But he's not, which means he's riled up the beast that is the Olympian populace and then he set them loose on those in charge.

There's no controlling it now. Every one of the Thirteen is a target.

Even me. Maybe even especially me.

"Are you done with your baseless accusations?" Minos manages to sound imperial and disappointed, both at the same time. "I have come here out of my feeling of responsibility to you for allowing me and mine citizenship, but if you're going to act as if I'm the enemy, I can spend my time elsewhere."

"You are the enemy. We treat enemies accordingly." Zeus flicks a hand. "You may go."

For a moment, it looks like Minos might argue, but he shrugs. "Very well. I look forward to the next Dodona Tower party." He turns and walks at a perfectly reasonable pace to the door.

It closes behind him. The silence is a barbed thing, threaded through with shock as every single person in the room tries to process what the fuck just happened. Even me. Zeus has more balls than I gave him credit for. I don't know that it'll be enough, but I'm a little impressed despite myself.

I shake my head, and it's as if my movement brings the others to life. Every person at the table starts talking at the same time. Well, every person except Zeus and Hera.

He lets them talk in circles for a few minutes before he raises his hand. It's a testament to his power that it only take a few seconds for silence to fall. Zeus sweeps a look at each of us. "You will all accept secondary security from Ares." He keeps speaking even as most of them protest. "It doesn't matter if Minos is behind the attacks on our people. The security most of you have is not enough."

Hades lifts a brow. "Ares's people are not welcome in the lower city."

Zeus clenches his jaw, a tiny movement, but he might as well have shouted his frustration. "You are making a mistake."

"If Hades doesn't take the security, neither am I." Artemis shoves to her feet. "You should have killed him from the start."

"We cannot afford more changeover." Zeus doesn't raise his voice.

My reluctant admiration for him grows. I don't like the fucker, and he doesn't seem to have a drop of charm in his body, but he gets shit done. It probably won't be enough to balance whatever Minos's next steps are, but he's a dangerous man.

They start arguing again, and I let the conversation roll over me. I won't be taking Ares's people, but there's no reason to speak my intentions. I'll just leave without them when this meeting is done.

Next to me, my wife is doing the same.

I lean close and lower my voice. "Take Ares's security."

"I intend to." Her answer is so soft, it's almost lost in Athena pointing out she has her own security force and Ares shooting back a question on how that helped her against the sniper. "You should take the offer, too."

"I'm not in danger."

She touches my arm. "If Minos is telling the truth...yes, you are. No matter what else is true, you're one of the Thirteen now. One of us."

I almost argue, but stop when it hits me. She's *worried* about me. I search her face for any sign of the sly smile or a lie, but for the first time in our marriage she seems perfectly earnest. "One would think you'd paint the target on my back yourself," I say slowly, testing these new, uncharted waters.

"That's just it, Husband." She smiles sweetly, only the tiniest edge present. "I'm the only one who gets to kill you. I'll bury anyone else who tries."

APHRODITE

THE MEETING GOES ON FOREVER, AND WE AREN'T ANY closer to solutions by the end of it. I understand why my brother insists on getting the whole of the Thirteen together...but I am also starting to see why our father refused to do it.

Thirteen people in power means we'll never be united, even with massive problems knocking on our doorstep. But that's the problem. Some of our number would have to see an enemy surrounding our city before they believed the threat.

Instead, they look at Minos and think they know exactly what he's capable of because he reminds them of the last Zeus. It's a mistake—not that they'll take my word for it.

Things dispel like they always do these days. Someone storms off—Artemis this time—and the rest leave in ones and twos. My brother catches my eye and gives a small shake of his head.

Ah. So we'll be meeting in a smaller group after this.

"See you tonight, Wife." Hephaestus squeezes my arm and rises stiffly. I watch him try to cover his limp as he leaves the room. There's an uncomfortable feeling in my stomach, almost like worry. I meant what I said earlier. I want him to take my sister's offer of security. Not because it's another way to spy on him. Not because I think it will pull him more visibly onto our side.

Because I don't want him to get hurt.

Gods, what is wrong with me? I can't afford to waver now. The worst part is I can't even pretend it's because I know it would make Pandora sad if something happened to him. I didn't even think of her when I was speaking earlier.

Once it's clear that everyone still sitting is invited to this secondary meeting, I look around the room. "No Demeter?" I can understand keeping Hera and Hades out of it. Hera will be only too happy to watch my brother burn, regardless of how it affects the city. I'm honestly a bit surprised she hasn't facilitated an assassination attempt on him already. Hades may or may not have been invited, but he'll be more concerned with the lower city—and his pregnant wife.

"Demeter has prior obligations," Perseus says. He looks as perfectly put together as always, his suit pressed and his blond hair seeming to be recently trimmed. Gone are the faint smudges of sleepless nights beneath his eyes, which only proves that he's gotten better at concealer than he was when we were teenagers. If I hadn't seen him yesterday, I wouldn't know how haggard he looked only twenty-four hours ago.

I glance at Athena and Apollo. She's dressed as impeccably as always in a deep gray suit with a paler silver blouse beneath it. Apollo has on a very expensive, very boring suit and looks like he's swallowed something spiky. It makes sense. He's a man with a plan, and there's no easy plan to get us out of this.

Helen's pulled the same makeup trick Perseus has, and she looks just as pristine as ever, as if she wasn't losing her damn mind yesterday. She's wearing what's become her customary Ares uniform for business—a perfectly tailored black suit with a bright blouse beneath it.

Perseus steeples his hands in front of his face. "We have a problem."

"You can say that again," Helen mutters. She lifts her voice. "Half a dozen attempts were made since we spoke yesterday. Before this meeting started, I got a call that my people interrupted a woman with a knife going after Artemis. They neutralized the situation, but it's not even noon yet."

Interesting. Maybe that's why Artemis was angrier than usual.

Athena taps a single finger against the table. "There's not much that can be done. The information is out. The public won't be distracted by petty feuds and dramatics." She shoots a sharp look at me.

It takes everything I can do not to flush. Petty feuds and dramatics have always worked as a bait and switch in the past, and I'm good at using them to keep the populace's attention where we want it. It's not my fault that we're dealing with something significantly more challenging right now. I'm not about to protest, though. Ultimately, my pride matters less than the problem at hand. "Do you have a suggestion, or is that just criticism?"

Her lips curve. Athena always has liked people who are

prickly. It's why we get along well enough when we're forced to interact. "We kill your husband."

What?

"*What?*" Apollo leans forward to look at her. "How does that help anything? Minos has already leaked the information about the clause. As you said, the cat's out of the bag."

"Yes, there's no taking back the information about that blasted little law." She taps the table again. "Which means there's no reason not to use it to our advantage. You can bet Minos will eventually do the same. He might not be behind the recent attempts, but that doesn't mean he won't be behind future ones."

The latter is nothing more than I've already considered. I look at Perseus, who hasn't said anything yet. There's something almost like panic fluttering inside me. They mean it. They really will kill Hephaestus. "Well? You support this?"

"Don't you?" His gaze sharpens on me. "You hate him. What's more, having that man in that position hurts the city. We rely on whoever holds the Hephaestus title and their people to keep the more technical parts of the city running, as well as come up with new advancements to better the quality of life for our citizens. Even if he wasn't an active enemy, he's not suited to the role and you know it."

I do know it. I've thought the very same things in the past. There's absolutely no reason for me to want to shove to my feet and yell at my brother for suggesting such a thing. There's no reason for it to feel like the walls are closing in.

A few days ago, I would have jumped at the chance to become a widow. This marriage was only meant to serve the purpose of distracting the public and distracting Hephaestus, and it's failed at both tasks.

But that was before my husband knelt in front of me and bandaged my wounds. Before he saved my life. Before he comforted me in his own rough way last night when I was at my lowest. "We gave our word that we wouldn't harm him if he married me."

"It's for the good of Olympus," Helen says softly. There's sympathy in her eyes, but also a steely determination I know too well. "They're right. It's a good call."

I won't have to do anything. Just take the path of least resistance and allow the people in this room to plot to make me a widow. There will be no more vicious arguments that turn into sex. No more trying to outmaneuver each other. No more lying next to his big body, quietly snoring beside me and lulling me into sleep.

I...can't do it.

Pandora said bringing him over to our side was nearly impossible, but it's fully impossible if he's dead. I'll take those odds. I'll take *any* odds right now. "I can turn him," I blurt out.

Athena snorts. "No, you can't."

"Yes, I can." I lift my chin, fighting to keep the uncertainty out of my face and voice. I need to project the cold bitch Aphrodite or they won't trust me. "He's smitten with Adonis, and he's warming to me despite the tumultuous start to our marriage. If I can turn him, his connection to Minos means he'll be a bigger asset than anyone else we can stick in the role."

Perseus might as well have been glazed over with ice. "He's not suited to the title."

"The strength of the title is the people behind it. Hephaestus's senior team has seen three people in that position. One person can't outweigh all that experience." Helen's proven this with Achilles and Patroclus in her corner, but I won't throw her under the bus like that right now, not when she worked so hard to be worthy of the Ares title even before claiming it. Hephaestus's team seems to hate him, but that's beside the point.

If anything, my brother's blue eyes get icier. No one else in the room seems to breathe. Perseus leans forward. He opens his mouth and his brow furrows in frustration. I tense, but he seems to discard whatever he was about to say. He sits back with a sigh. "You have three days."

I jolt. "Three days? That's an impossible task."

"Either it can be done or it can't. The amount of time shouldn't factor into it."

That's not even remotely reasonable, and I'm about to tell him exactly that when Apollo shakes his head sharply. "Surely you aren't entertaining this. He's a murderer."

Perseus turns that cold gaze on Apollo. "Murder isn't an unforgivable sin in this city and you know it. If we can turn him, he'll be an asset in whatever comes next."

"We *have* an asset from Minos's household already."

"Oh?" He raises an eyebrow. "Then you're here to report that your outreach to Ariadne has borne fruit?"

Apollo huffs out a breath. "No. Minos has her under lock and key. She's not even active online right now."

Damn it, I haven't texted Eurydice about Ariadne. I completely forgot in the midst of everything that happened yesterday. I slip my phone out of my purse and type out a quick message asking for an update. It's entirely possible she hasn't made more progress than Apollo, but I need to know.

My phone vibrates in my hand almost immediately. While Apollo and my brother keep speaking, I glance down.

Eurydice: I'm taking her to the club tonight. 😊

Holy shit. She's really doing it.

Me: Keep me updated, please.

Eurydice: Of course. I'll call tomorrow.

I place my phone back in my purse. Eurydice and Ariadne is still a long shot, even if she's making more progress than Apollo on that front right now. Ariadne might have warned Apollo about her father's plans, but that doesn't mean she knows more about what his next steps are than Pandora does.

Offering this information to the gathered people will sign my husband's death warrant. If they think they have another way to strike at Minos, they won't bother with Hephaestus. "There is no other way."

"That remains to be seen." Perseus looks at me. "Three days, Aphrodite."

Helen shifts. "None of that changes the threat we're facing right now. Increased security is in place for all members of the Thirteen who accepted my offer, but it's only a matter of time before one of these attempts succeeds. They might not successfully engage the clause, but they could very well kill one of us. If that happens, it will only increase the frenzy."

"Then ensure it doesn't happen while we figure this out." Perseus says it like it's as easy as that. "Ideas to turn the tide?"

"We need to give them something else to fight." There's a flush in Helen's cheeks from our brother's rebuke, but her voice is steady.

Athena shakes her head. "Yes, but more than that. A common enemy will unite the city."

"A common enemy won't work." Apollo drags his hands over his face. He's been working long hours and it shows. Unlike my siblings, he hasn't bothered to try to hide his exhaustion. "It might bring the majority of people in line, but the majority of people aren't attempting murder right now. The citizens who have always wanted to be one of the Thirteen, have always believed that they deserve it, will keep coming." He sighs. "We have to go public about the barrier. It's the best chance we have."

"No." We all look at my brother as he speaks. His expression doesn't move. "That is not an option."

"It's the *only* option." Apollo glares. "They need to know we have bigger things to worry about than petty power squabbles inside the city. Not even these murderous fools would want to be in charge in the event that the barrier falls."

"Find another way."

Athena sighs. "He's right, Apollo. If they think the barrier is falling, it will only increase the chaos. People will panic. Some will try to leave, which will either be impossible or weaken the barrier further. We don't have the answers for why it's failing, which will only undermine our authority. We can't tell them."

"Three days," I find myself saying. "Give me three days to turn my husband and find something on Minos. Even if you kill Hephaestus, it won't help the overall climate of the city, and it might just make things worse." I look around the room. "Take the next three days and see if you can come up with a better plan."

Perseus pushes to his feet. "I'm sure you all have places to be."

Everyone reluctantly stands. I already know what's coming, so I don't flinch when he says, "Aphrodite, a word."

Helen squeezes my hand as she slips through the door after Apollo and Athena, closing it softly behind her. I cross my arms over my chest. My brother doesn't make me wait long.

Perseus plants his hands on the desk and leans forward. "Are you compromised?"

I flinch. "Excuse me?"

"You heard me."

"Are you really asking *me* that? Of all the people in the room, my loyalty should be beyond question."

"You're right. It should be."

A harsh laugh bursts free. Gods, I didn't expect his doubt to sting quite so badly. "I have done just as much as you for this city. More, even, because your wife is an Olympian citizen and doesn't threaten to murder *you* on a regular basis."

He doesn't blink. "You'd be surprised."

Actually, I wouldn't. Callisto Dimitriou is fucking terrifying.

But she's not who we're talking about right now. My skin

heats, and I do my best to keep my expression as locked down as my brother's. He's always been better at this particular skill set than I have, and he proves it now.

"I am not compromised," I say through gritted teeth. I might be suffering from permanent indigestion and need to have my heart looked at by a doctor, but I am not some naive innocent who will let my tangled emotions color my actions. "I have always done what's best for Olympus, and I will continue to do so."

He stares at me for a long moment. "You really think you can turn him."

I don't know what I think. My husband obviously has feelings for Adonis, and he's treated me with more care than I imagined possible. But Pandora knows him better than anyone and she has her doubts.

Oh well. I've scaled unscalable odds before.

But why? Why not just let Perseus kill him and be done with it?

I don't have an answer to that question. "Before you ask, he's a terrible liar and if I get him on our side, he's not capable of being a double agent."

Perseus sighs. "You're playing a dangerous game."

"We all are." I drop my arms. "If that's all?"

"It is." He straightens. "Don't get killed, Eris. If you do, if Helen does, I'll become the villain they want me to be."

A chill drips down my spine. My brother is not demonstrative and he's certainly not one to let his emotions get the best of him. I drag in a breath and strive to keep my tone even. "If one of us gets killed, you will do what's best for this city just like you've always done."

He turns and looks out the window, shielding his expression from me. "Does the city really deserve our blood?"

The chill gets worse, worming right into my bones. "Perseus?"

"I used to think it did, but now I wonder. The first chance they got, they turned on us like feral beasts. Maybe our father had the right idea about ruling the way he did. I can't manage his level of charm...but fear is always an option."

I cross to him and tentatively touch his arm. "He was a monster."

"We're monsters, too." He's still not looking at me. "We never had a chance to be anything but monsters."

Actual fear takes hold. Our chances of making it through this aren't overly optimistic at this point, but they fall to damn near zero if my brother buckles. I steel myself and shove his shoulder hard enough for him to spin to face me. "That's enough."

For once, he's not glazed in ice. His blue eyes are fiery and furious. "I have tried not to be him. I have tried to work with the other members of the Thirteen. I have fucking *tried* to bring peace to this city." He laughs, harsh and bitter. "You have three days before I take action. If they won't see reason, then I'll give them something to fear."

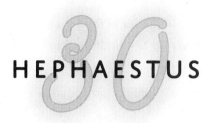

HEPHAESTUS

I MEET PANDORA AT A COFFEE SHOP A FEW BLOCKS FROM Dodona Tower. She's sitting at a corner booth tucked out of sight of the windows to the street. I slide carefully into the seat across from her. "Why here?" It would be more secure to talk in Minos's penthouse... Unless she doesn't want him to overhear this conversation.

Honestly, that works for me.

My head is still spinning from the meeting with the rest of the Thirteen and my wife's concern for me. I want to say she's totally off base with it, but the more I think about it, the less sure I am.

"I didn't want to deal with going back there." She passes a cup of coffee across the table to me. "This is a mess."

"Yeah."

"What are you going to do?"

That's the question, isn't it? The fact that it's a question at all is a problem. I haven't wavered in fifteen years, and I can't waver now. I close my eyes and inhale deeply. It never used to be tricky to remember everything I owe Minos. It never felt like a burden instead of a blessing. "What am I supposed to do?"

"Theseus." She bumps her foot against mine. "You know I'm in your corner, no matter what, right?"

"Yeah." It's never been a question, even if we butt heads on a regular basis. "I know that."

"Good." She sighs. "I'm worried. This plan doesn't make sense. Even if Minos was able to replace the entirety of the Thirteen—which he doesn't have enough people to do—it doesn't change the fact that that ridiculous clause means every one of them will have a target on their back. The people won't follow them."

She's not wrong. The growing unrest in the city almost feels like a physical weight in the air. It's dangerous, and a shit ton of people are going to get caught in the cross fire if these individual attempts on people's lives turn into a mob.

I've only seen a mob once before and that shit gave me a lifetime of nightmares. People stop being people and the violence is enough to make even me sick. If the citizens of Olympus become a mob, there won't be much left of the city.

"He's not trying to replace the rest of the Thirteen. The house party was a one-shot." He's a good enough liar to fool the Thirteen this morning, but what he said matches the conversation I overheard a few days ago. "He's got something else going on. Some shipment coming in through the port. I don't know the details."

She looks at me, her dark eyes troubled. "That doesn't worry you? I know he's the type to keep things close to his chest, but why are we just dancing to the tune he sets? I don't want to see Eris hurt. I don't think you do, either."

"She's the enemy." The words don't have the same ring of truth they did even a few days ago.

"Are you sure?" She presses her lips together. "And even if she is, don't lie and say you consider Adonis an enemy, too. I see the way you look at him."

There's no point in lying. Even if I was good at it, I don't lie to Pandora. "It doesn't matter."

"It matters."

I curse. "No, Pandora, it doesn't. If Adonis isn't smart enough to get out of the way of whatever Minos is planning, then it doesn't matter how I feel about him."

She searches my face. "Are you really okay with that?"

No. "Yes."

"Liar." She drains the rest of her coffee. "How did the meeting go?"

"I don't know how they get shit done in this place. They're like a pack of jackals tearing into each other." Surely they know the threat the city is facing. I've watched Minos deal with similar, smaller-scale conflicts over the years. He simply makes people disappear. It's what they should have done to us the moment the Ares competition ended.

Instead, they offered us citizenship, and half the ruling body showed up to Minos's damned house party without their security and all but offered him their throats.

They deserve whatever comes to them.

The reasoning feels flimsier than ever. I might not like most of those fuckers, but I can't exactly fault them for panicking now that every person on the street could be poised to murder them.

Could be poised to murder Aphrodite.

I drag my hand through my hair. "It's a mess."

"Yes, we've established that." She sighs. "Something has to give, Theseus. She won't be the one to fold."

No, my wife doesn't know how to give up. She'll put on a brave face and keep going until someone successfully kills her. The thought shouldn't bother me, but it feels like sandpaper under my skin. Fucking *wrong*. Frustration makes my voice rough. "So I'm supposed to fold?"

"I didn't say that."

"But you're thinking it."

"Whatever you think you owe Minos, you've paid that price ten times over," she says quietly. "I don't want you to pay with your life, too."

There it is again, that worry that I'll be one of the Thirteen struck down. I want to argue with her. I am not some pampered rich person who doesn't know how to defend myself. But the doubt planted with Adonis this morning is blooming into something ugly inside me.

I glance at her empty cup. "You done?"

"Yes, Theseus." She sighs again. "I'm done."

"I'll walk you out."

Neither of us says anything as I pay the tab and we head out to the street. I call Pandora a car and wait with her while it arrives. She stares at the people walking down the sidewalk, all intent on getting to their destinations. "You should ask him."

No need to ask what she's talking about. I bite back a curse. "Even if I did, I'm not going to tell you what the fuck he's planning.

You say you see the way I look at Adonis, but I see the way you look at my wife."

She gives a faint smile. "I like her quite a bit."

I do, too.

I shake my head. Where the fuck did that thought come from? "It doesn't matter. I'm loyal to him. I know better than expecting that same loyalty from you, but fuck, Pandora. Switching sides?"

"Mmm." Her ride pulls up and she steps off the curb. She opens the door and looks back at me. "I don't want to be any more involved in this than I already am. I'm in this city for *you*." She pauses, dark eyes worried. "But you should know what he's planning, Theseus. You're paying the price for his ambitions—not Minos. If you're going to suffer because of him, you should at least know why."

She's gone before I can form an answer. Really, there's no answer. Pandora's always had faith in me. That I'd stand strong against whatever the fuck the world threw at us. That I wouldn't buckle under the pressure of keeping us safe. For how well she knows me, she's never seemed to notice how fucking scared I was when we were kids.

She was the only thing I ever cared about. Not the beatings. Not being deprived of food. Not the agonizing work they put us through. Pandora. Every day, I saw her fight to keep her light shining, and every day, I was terrified that I'd wake up and see the same haunted look on her face that every other kid in that place wore. I went without to make sure she had what she needed, and if she noticed *that*, she never seemed to register what drove it.

Fear.

I might have protected her up to that point where that fucking priest got ideas, but who's to say I would have kept being successful? We were kids. Too weak to do more than drown in the waves made by people more powerful than us.

Minos changed that. I'm not a complete fool. I know he sees me as a tool to be used. Not a son. Never that. But I've seen the way Minos treats his only son. Better to be a tool than an eternal disappointment.

I stop short. What the fuck am I thinking? I've never doubted him. Not like this. Yeah, I haven't been a naive innocent, dancing to the tune he sang, but I've never questioned him. Not really.

If you're going to suffer because of him, you should at least know why.

"Damn it, Pandora," I mutter. "Damn it, Adonis. And damn it, Eris." One of them, I could ignore, but all three?

I flag down a taxi and give Minos's address. We make it two blocks before the driver's increased focus on me makes my skin prickle. I stop looking out the window and start watching him. His hands shift restlessly on the steering wheel and he's studying me as much as his eyes are on the road. Not in a curious way, either. There's intent there. *It's happening.* He's a nobody, some random citizen, but that doesn't mean he's not a danger.

I lean forward, getting right in his space. "Yeah, I'm Hephaestus. You might have heard the news about that nasty little clause, which means you know why that news was released."

He licks his lips, his temples damp with sweat. "You're the reason we even know about the clause. You killed the last Hephaestus."

Yeah. I did. And I've been regretting it ever since. "That's right." I don't touch him. He's jumpy enough to drive us right off the road, and I don't want to waste my morning with that bullshit. I lower my voice, injecting as much threat as possible. "So you're going to drive me where I need to go, and you're not going to try anything funny. If you do, I'll snap your fucking neck."

He swallows hard. "Yes, sir."

I sit back, but keep my eye on him as he drives the rest of the way to Minos's place. It's only now, sitting here in the back seat of a man who considered killing me to further his own power, that I can't deny the truth any longer. They were right. All of them. And I *was* fucking naive.

I barely wait for the car to stop at the curb outside Minos's building before I toss money at him and climb out. My knee is stiff and painful, but I try to keep my limp minimized as I walk into the lobby and take the elevator up.

Luck—if that's what you want to call it—is in my favor. Minos and the Minotaur sit in his office, their heads together as they examine a tablet between them. They both look up when I walk through the door. Minos opens his mouth to speak, but I get there first. "When were you going to tell me that I was a necessary loss?"

"Excuse me?"

I shut the door and lean against it. "Something's been bothering me." No reason to tell him where that doubt comes from. It doesn't matter for this conversation. "You aren't behind the attacks, but the second you had one of us trigger that clause, it put a target on every single one of the Thirteen's backs—including mine."

"You knew that would be a risk."

Yes, but I hadn't thought I'd face it alone. Somewhere in the back of my mind, I didn't quite believe Minos when he said he wasn't behind all the attacks. Oh, I don't think he's had a hand in the recent ones, but why wouldn't he look to place more of his people among the Thirteen? The days after I took the title were rife with uncertainty; it would have been the perfect time to strike.

Unless he has no intention of a second strike.

Unless he *never* had an intention for a second strike.

"No putting that cat back in the bag, is there? Everyone knows it's a thing now, which means the Thirteen will be hunted for the rest of Olympus's future. Kind of hard to enact plans when you're constantly looking over your shoulder." He doesn't contradict me, just watches me work through it with a small smile on his mouth. Holy fuck, I'm right. "You don't plan on replacing the rest of the Thirteen with your people, do you?"

"*Our* people, Son."

There was a time when, even though I damn well knew better, hearing that word from him was enough to override anything else I could possibly say. A weakness, and one he exploited. "There's not going to be a Thirteen when you're through," I say softly.

The Minotaur gives Minos a long look, but that fucker always plays his cards close to his chest. Even knowing him for years, I can't say for sure if he knew about this before or if he's only hearing about it now.

Minos leans back. "Don't you worry about my plan. I—"

"I think it's time you shared that plan with us." I glance at the Minotaur. "You would have been in the crosshairs, too, if you'd managed to kill Artemis and take that title. Don't you want to know what he's up to?"

He crosses his massive arms over his equally massive chest. "Yes."

Minos narrows his eyes. "All right, boys. I suppose I can let you in on some of the plan you've both managed to fuck up repeatedly." The words sting, but not as much as they used to. He shakes his head slowly. "Olympus is a ripe fruit to be plucked. They have little experience with anything resembling war; peace has made them soft."

"We've heard the spiel." I've never talked to Minos this way before, but the events of the last couple days keep compounding in my head. Adonis's uncertainty. The vulnerable look in Aphrodite's eyes that she wasn't quite able to hide. Pandora's fierce words. The worry all three of them share for *my* safety.

When I came to Olympus, the only thing I cared about was Pandora's happiness and Minos's approval. Now, things feel more complicated.

Minos glares. "One of you was supposed to take Ares. The other was intended to use the assassination clause to take another title. With two in the Thirteen, it would have been enough to start the destabilization process. *You* failed." He turns that furious look on the Minotaur. "As a result, we had to take a different route. The end outcome is the same. The Thirteen fall, and a new leadership rises in its place."

A different route. Something having to do with shipments in the harbor. What is he importing? I glare at him. "You mean *you'll* rise in its place."

Minos blinks, true surprise on his face. "Is that what you think, my boy?" He laughs, the sound filling the room. "No, I prefer proximity to power to taking it myself." He gives me a sly look. "Fewer targets on my back that way."

Targets like the one currently on *my* back. Not that he cares. I've obviously served my purpose, and he doesn't give a shit about the potential fallout. I've never felt more like a fool than I do in this moment. "If not you in a leadership position, then who?"

"My benefactor." His smile widens. "Olympus owes her a debt, and she means to collect."

ADONIS

I'M NOT REALLY SURPRISED WHEN ERIS TEXTS ME AN INVITE to have lunch with her. We'd been hurtling along before she broke up with me and married Theseus. Crashing into each other and away again. I used to be so sure I knew where we were headed before that point, and then when it ended, I was certain it had ended for good this time.

I'm not sure of anything anymore.

Her building looks exactly the same as it has every other time I've come here. There's no way to tell from the street that violence was committed here just yesterday.

I push through the door and smile. "Hey, Sele."

"Hey, Adonis." They tuck a strand of hair behind their ear. "You're looking good."

"Thanks." I examine the new glass divider. If I hadn't spent a whole lot of time in this place, I don't know if I'd notice it's different from the last one. Both have a floral pattern etched into frosted glass. They both even have roses in the design. But it's not the same. "Is she in her office?"

"Yes, she's expecting you." They tap a few keys on their keyboard. "You can go back."

I find Eris standing in front of her desk, frowning at a bag with takeout in it. She glances up at me, and her eyes go soft. "Hey."

"Hey." I wish things could be as easy between us as they used to be, but I'm not sure if it's even possible. It's a mistake to wish for that, too, but I don't care. My heart is already in tatters. Might as well light it on fire. I nod at the bag. "You got us lunch already?"

"Not me." She goes back to staring at the bag as if it's a snake ready to strike. "Pandora sent it, along with a bitingly polite note saying she expects me to eat a proper amount and not skip this meal in favor of working."

I raise my brows. "She knows you well."

"Apparently." She sighs and shakes her head. "Sorry, this just threw me. It showed up right as I was about to order for us." She pokes at the bag tentatively. "There's enough food here to feed a small army, so I think it should work for the two of us."

It's a challenge to hold my tongue as she carefully arranges the takeout on her desk. Silences between us used to be comfortable. Now they're thorny with things left unsaid. Do I apologize? Do I demand *she* apologize? What do we even talk about now? Gods, this is so awkward. It's the only excuse I have for blurting out, "You like her a lot."

Eris freezes. "Yes, I do."

I wait for jealousy or anger or hurt. Instead, all I feel is confusion. We've never had anything resembling a traditional relationship before, but I don't know if we have a relationship at all right now. "I see."

She sits back and meets my gaze. "You like him a lot, too."

Guilt flares, but it's dulled by the truth. "Yeah. A lot."

Her lips curve, but her eyes are sad. "I meant what I said last night. I miss you."

"I miss you, too." But I can't leave it at that. It seems impossible that priorities in my life would shift in just a few short days, but it's happened all the same. "If you've asked me here to convince me to do something to hurt Theseus, I'm not going to do it."

"And yet you were willing to work with him to hurt me." She holds up a hand before I can sputter out a response. "I don't blame you for it, Adonis. I know I broke your heart. I'm sorry for that."

I don't ask her if she'd do anything differently if she could go back. I already know the answer. Eris loves me, but her first priority will always be this city. "So where does that leave us?"

"That's the question, isn't it?" She sinks onto her chair, looking tired. "I'm going to be frank with you."

"When have you been anything but frank with me?"

A small smile is her only acknowledgment of that truth. "We have to bring my husband over to our side."

I shake my head slowly. "I just told you—"

"And *I'm* telling *you* that we have to bring him to our side. In three days."

Three days? I huff out a laugh. "You don't ask for much, do you? That timeline is impossible. You're setting yourself up for failure."

"I'd better not be." She slumps back in her chair. "It's the only way we can keep him alive."

I blink. "Excuse me?"

"My brother is going to kill him if we can't pull this off."

Shock roots me in place. I play her words back through my head, but they don't make any more sense now than they did a few seconds ago. "Impossible."

"You'd be surprised. If Zeus wants someone dead, they're not long for this world."

The tone in her voice makes me think she's not talking about *this* Zeus as much as the last one. Her father. The long shadow that poisoned so much of her childhood. The man who taught her that the only way to survive was to tread others underfoot. I don't blame her for surviving; I'll never blame her for that.

But sometimes, in the dark of the night, I wonder what it might have been like if her mother had lived. If her early years hadn't been a training ground for what Zeus considered good leadership. If she hadn't watched her father marry and then—allegedly—kill two more women.

"Stop that."

I jolt. "Stop what?"

She gives me a knowing look. "You're thinking dark thoughts about my father. He's dead. He can't hurt me anymore."

If only that were true. I shake my head sharply. She's right. This line of thinking isn't helping anyone. I swallow hard. "Your brother can't seriously mean to kill your husband."

"I highly doubt he'll do it personally." She makes a face. "Then again, he's acting out of character, so I can't take anything for granted."

The very idea of Zeus being off the rails is, frankly, terrifying. We survived under the last one because he was more invested in being a charming dictator than actively feared, though fear was an undercurrent to his reign. Perseus doesn't have that charm. He's not the kind of man who can tempt people to flock to his side and curry his favor.

If he goes this route, his only option will be to rule through fear.

"The Thirteen gave their word that Theseus would not be harmed as long as he went through with the marriage to you."

"I know." She drops her gaze. "This is the part where I say they likely won't do it personally, so it's a tiny loophole to giving their word, but... I know."

Her resignation worries me as much as everything else we're talking about. Eris is never *resigned*. She's a fighter to her core, but there's no way she could have anticipated this from her brother. "Tell me that your brother isn't turning into your father."

"He would *never*." Her eyes flash. "All my father wanted was power over others. Perseus wants the same thing I do—for our city and our people to be safe."

Maybe. Probably. But that doesn't change the fact that Eris has already proven that she'll trample individuals for the greater good. The Thirteen are supposed to be equal in power, but it's not the truth. Hades. Poseidon. *Zeus.* They stand above the others as legacy titles. If one of them decides to truly abuse that power... I don't know what would happen. "Eris," I say quietly. "I know he's your brother, but Zeus or not, he can't go around murdering people."

She doesn't look happy. "I think you'll find that he can do whatever he damn well pleases. Especially when he has the support of several key members of the Thirteen." Eris shakes her head hard. "He's not bluffing, Adonis. Whatever my feelings on his plan, the fact remains that we either have to take action or stand by while he makes me a widow."

I drag my hands over my face. I knew having lunch with Eris would be difficult, but not even I could have anticipated the direction this conversation has gone. "I would think that would make you happy. Being a widow, I mean."

"I would have thought so, too." She leans her head back against her chair, leaving the long line of her throat exposed. There's a faint mark there, one she's almost successfully covered up with makeup. I can't begin to tell if it's from me or Theseus, but I recognize the heat that blooms in my chest in response. I'm not overly possessive by nature, but she was *ours* to take care of last night, and there's something truly powerful about that.

"Eris…"

"I don't want him dead." The words burst out of her. She stares at the ceiling. "My life would be significantly simpler if I did. He's a pain in the ass. He's crude and violent and a threat to everything I hold dear."

I wait, but she doesn't immediately continue. Nothing she's said is wrong. I feel the same way, which is why I know there's more to it. "But?"

"But." She exhales slowly. "I'm not one to care about a sob story, but he's got quite the sob story. It doesn't excuse what he's done, but I understand it, and I resent that I understand it. He's very bad at comfort, which is almost a comfort in and of itself, because he tries. With me, a woman he should hate." She lifts her head and meets my gaze. "He also fucks like a dream."

Yes, that about sums it up. Theseus is rough and downright vicious at times, but he's not a one-note individual. "I don't think you can turn him at all, let alone in three days," I say quietly.

"Maybe. Probably." She gives herself a shake. "But apparently I'm not quite the monster I thought, because I want to try. Pandora doesn't like our odds, but she admits there's a slim chance we could do it. Will you help me?"

Yes. Fool that I am, I want to try, too. No matter that he's an enemy, or why he came here in the first place. I care about him and I want to help, and it's enough for me to start to nod before I catch myself.

But I do catch myself.

Because Theseus isn't the only barrier between us and a happy, peaceful future.

"What about you and me? If you manage to pull this off and we save him, where does that leave us?"

"Us." She presses her lips together. "I'd like to ask you a question."

I already know I won't like it, not with her studying me so seriously, but I nod all the same. This is going to hurt, but so much of being with Eris hurts. I'm all but used to the experience. "Okay."

She opens her mouth, pauses, and then seems to force the words out. "Do you think we worked on our own? Really worked?"

It's on the tip of my tongue to say that of course we worked. I love this woman, thorns and vicious ambition and all. I have for a very long time. I will continue loving her until my dying day, whether or not we're together.

But the more I turn her words over, examining them from different angles, the more I wonder if there aren't layers I've been intentionally ignoring for too many years. "What do you mean?"

"Far be it from me to pretend I know what a healthy relationship looks like, but I don't think it's two people crashing together and away again repeatedly over a decade." She looks down at her hands, twisting her fingers in her lap. "I think neither of us were entirely honest with each other about what we wanted—what we needed."

Blaming her for that would be so easy. She never cheated on me, but she also never waited long after our breakup fights to be photographed with others, and I know Eris well enough to know *those* photographs weren't for publicity's sake. She took those people home where the sheets were still warm in our bed.

But was I any different? My time with others hasn't been as blatantly publicized, but I was hardly celibate during our breaks. If I'm going to be honest—and I can be nothing but honest right now—part of me was relieved for that freedom even as I missed her.

"What are you saying?"

She seems to force her hands apart. "I'm saying..." Another of those long exhales. "That neither of us is really built for monogamy, and maybe if we stop trying to cram ourselves into that box, we'll be happier. Maybe if we try something new we can have some semblance of a steady, healthy relationship." She shrugs. "It's working out for my sister. Maybe it would work out for us, too."

Part of me wants to argue. My parents are incredibly happy

and stable without needing to be polyamorous. A lot of people are. But I can't argue because Eris is right. "Last night…"

"It fit." She gives a soft smile. "I don't even like him most of the time, but I can't pretend that it didn't feel like you and I suddenly balanced each other out in a way that I've never felt before."

That's exactly it. It felt *balanced*. There's something deeply ironic about Theseus potentially being the stabilizing glue that holds us together. I swallow hard. "And Pandora?"

"I like her. A lot." That softness on her face becomes more pronounced. "If there's a way we can make it work with the four of us, I would very much like to. I know that sounds naive considering our current climate and the fact that both Theseus and I might be dead before too long, but—"

"You won't die." I refuse to let it happen.

This morning, I was still reeling from being in bed with Theseus and Eris, but it was downright lovely in the kitchen with the four of us, Pandora and Theseus bickering in the way only longtime friends can, Eris relaxed and indulgent, and me… I could be at home there. It felt almost wrong to want that in the moment, but maybe that was because it clashed with what I thought I should have.

"I want it, too. Him with us." I take a deep breath. "But three days to make it happen? That's an impossible task."

"Maybe." She pushes one of the containers over to me. "Eat something and let's talk. We might come up with something brilliant."

"You have a lot of faith in us." I take the container and start to eat. Strangely enough, I'm not even remotely surprised to find Pandora has divined Eris's favorite restaurant and ordered the takeout from there. It might be a manipulation tactic, but I don't think so. She obviously cares for Eris as much as Eris cares for her.

Eris taps her fork against the side of her container. "What if we tie him to my bed and fuck him until he can't think of anything but us?"

A surge of heat goes through my body at the thought. I like what I've shared with Theseus when it's just the two of us, but I like what we shared with the three of us, too. I clear my throat. "That might work, but only until he recovers his senses." We share a look and I surprise myself by laughing. "Eris, we can't keep him chained to our bed indefinitely."

"Pity." Her smile. "I like that. Our bed." She lifts her drink. "Let's make it the truth."

Two days ago, I never could have guessed that I'd be here, contemplating a future with the woman I loved and lost and the completely unsuitable man that I've teetered right over the edge of falling for. Now, I can't imagine being anywhere else.

I touch my drink to hers. "Deal."

APHRODITE

I WISH I COULD SAY I HAVE A PLAN TO BRING MY husband around. I don't. I have the possibility of a plan, but that's hardly the same thing. Everything rides on me—on us—being able to convince him that he's best suited to switch sides against the man he thinks saved him. Some good fucking and a little bit of infatuation isn't going to be enough to combat that. I don't know what will be enough...

But Pandora will know.

Her knowledge isn't what has my heart racing as Achilles drives us into my parking garage and pulls up in front of the elevator door, though. He turns, bracing one arm across the back of the passenger seat so he can look at me. "Two of my people will do a quick walk-through of your place and then you can go up."

"That's not necessary."

He doesn't blink. "We've been through this. Your sister put me in charge of your security and—"

"And you take it very seriously, which I deeply appreciate." It takes more effort than I want to admit to keep my tone light and my frustration nowhere in evidence. Achilles is doing his job, and as loath as I am to admit it, he's quite good at it. Holding it against him just because his presence is necessary is shitty.

I'm not sure I care, though.

"There is no one in my apartment. The security in this building is top-notch." And if Pandora beat me here, I don't want Achilles's people to scare the shit out of her. I reach for the door. "Thank you for today, but I'm leaving now."

"Aphrodite." He waits for me to look at him. "If you don't want us to sweep the place first, then I'm going up with you now."

"But—"

"Those are your only options. If you don't pick, I'm going to pick for you." He speaks just as reasonably as I do, which is why it takes my tired brain a few seconds to catch up.

I narrow my eyes. I know exactly what he'll pick, and I don't like it one bit. "I don't know why my sister puts up with you," I snarl.

"My charm and good looks," he fires right back. "Plus, I'm tall enough to reach the high shelf without her having to climb up onto the counter."

Helen is not *that* short. "And here I thought it was because you're so good in bed."

He grins. "A gentleman never kisses and tells."

Gods, but I like him even when he's being stubborn. I *do* see what my sister likes about him. I prefer my partners with a little less...everything...but Achilles does have a certain charm about him. When he's not being a pain in the ass. "You may accompany me up to my apartment to assure yourself that there are no boogey-men hiding under my bed."

He glances at the other two guards in the car. "Stay here." He doesn't speak again until we're in the elevator heading up, but then he turns to me with an uncharacteristically serious expression on his face. "We're being overprotective, but it's for a good reason. You can't trust anyone, Aphrodite. Not when anyone and everyone could be an enemy."

My stomach drops out. "I'm aware of the risk."

"Then stop fighting and let me do my job." A weighted pause. "For your sister's sake."

Damn it, but he's got a trump card with that and he knows it. No matter how little I like the extra security, I would have agreed to it because Helen insisted. I would have agreed regardless—I'm not a fool, and I *was* just attacked yesterday—but I would have put up more of a fight if someone else suggested their security team.

I sigh. "You're in the elevator, aren't you? I'm not going to wait for you to leave and then take off on my own."

"You know, I wasn't worried about you doing exactly that until you said something." He grins. "But Patroclus *was* worried about it, so he suggested I leave two of my team watching the exits."

"Yeah, yeah." I roll my eyes, even as my chest gives a little pang. Achilles and Patroclus are nothing like my actual brothers—they're not cold and reserved like Perseus or naive and idealistic like Hercules—but in the last two months they've both fallen into a strange sort of fraternal role that I enjoy despite myself.

It doesn't hurt that they look at my sister like the sun rises and sets with her.

It takes Achilles a few minutes to do a thorough sweep of the place and even as he walks to the door, he's got a look on his face like he's not happy. "I'd feel better if you had someone in here with you."

"No." I smile as I say it, though. "I promise to let your people know if plans change and I need to leave."

He shakes his head. "I guess that's what they call compromise."

"Never heard of her."

He grins. "Me either. But we'll make it work." He opens the door. "See you tomorrow, Aphrodite."

"See you tomorrow." I don't bother to point out that he has much more important things to do than play babysitter for me. He's not my personal detail because there's no one else capable of doing it; he's here because it makes Helen feel better. I can't fault him for that.

I've only had time enough to pick a bottle of wine and pull down two glasses when my door opens and Pandora walks through. I pause, drinking in the sight of her. "Did you dress up for me?"

She looks down at herself, dressed in another body-con dress similar to the one from the other night. It's black, cut low on her breasts and high on her thighs, and it hugs her generous body like a second skin.

I want to peel it off with my teeth.

Pandora gives me a pretty smile. "I might have."

"Thank you for lunch." I set the wine bottle down and cross the room to her. "It was really thoughtful of you to do that."

"You don't take care of yourself," she says softly. She slides her hands up my arms as I take her hips. "I figured even if one of the guys got the same idea, better two lunches than none. And let's not pretend you were going to remember to eat on your own."

"I'm very busy." I flush, but I'm not entirely sure if it's with embarrassment or pleasure. There's a little bit of both in there. "Thank you for...taking care of me."

"Mm-hmm." She steps closer, pressing against me. Her expression is soft and open. "I like to take care of the people I care about. It's important to me."

I need to talk to her about Hephaestus, but the words freeze on my tongue. We've had such little time alone together. I don't want to waste it talking about plans and fear and the future. Maybe that's selfish, but I don't give a fuck. "I care about you, too." I release her hip to brush a strand of her hair back and let my hand linger on her throat. "I won't pretend this didn't start a particular way, but I'm drawn to you like I've never been drawn to anyone else before."

"Not even Adonis?" She says it with a playful tone.

I should allow her to tease this into a joke, but I can't quite manage it. "It's different." I trace her jaw with my thumb. "Everything's different with you."

"Eris." She bites her bottom lip and meets my gaze. "We don't have much time before the guys get here."

"We have enough." I lean down. My emotions might be tangled when it comes to my husband, when it comes to Adonis, but it feels so damn clear with Pandora. "Let me keep you."

"I already told you." She smiles. "I'm not the type of person who's meant to be kept."

"Then let me…" Why does this feel so incredibly vulnerable? My instincts demand I retreat, throw up shields between us, but if I do that, I'll lose her. I recognize that, acknowledge this moment is hung in the balance. Pandora might not be for keeping, but I want her in my life.

No matter what else happens.

I kiss the corner of her mouth. "Then let me share time with you. However that looks. I don't want to let this go, but it's becoming increasingly clear that none of us were meant for…a traditional relationship."

"Are you sure?" She searches my face. "It's bound to get messy from time to time."

I laugh a little. "Messier than me marrying your best friend and him seducing my ex?"

"Well… Probably not messier than that."

"Then we can handle it." I hope to the gods I'm not lying to her. I *want* to handle it.

She kisses me before we can talk ourselves out of this. Maybe that would be the smart thing to do because this is so damned complicated. If I was honest with myself, I'd admit I don't see a way through without crashing and burning.

I pull her close and kiss her hard. We only have a short time and I'm not about to waste it. She tastes of peppermint and feels like a dream in my arms. I want…

I want everything.

I always was greedy like that.

It takes effort to draw away enough to say, "I know I said no sex but—"

She digs her hands into my hair. "Don't you go noble on me now."

"Gods forbid." I smile. "Bedroom or closer?"

"Closer," she whispers against my lips.

Perfect.

I move back toward my living room, taking her with me. It's an awkward dance of short steps and bumping into each other, but I don't want to add even an inch of distance between us. So much about my seduction of Pandora has been calculated—at least in part—but there's nothing calculated in this. I'm fumbling like a teenager as I reach for the hem of her dress and work it up over her hips.

We tumble onto the couch in a mess of questing hands and greedy lips. Pandora yanks my shirt over my head and my arms get tangled. I curse and have to move off her to free myself. I take the opportunity to divest myself of my pants as well. "Get that fucking dress off."

"So bossy." She's grinning as she pulls her dress over her head and tosses it away. Pandora doesn't wait for me to say anything to do the same with her bra. There are no panties to speak of.

I have to stop for a moment and just look at her.

"You are so fucking beautiful," I murmur. Her lush body is a present I've been dying to unwrap and now that we're here, I don't know where to start. Her wide hips with their scattering of stretch marks? Her soft belly that looks so damn kissable?

My gaze falls to the tops of her thighs. No. *That's* where I'm starting. I was thinking about her pussy even before she rubbed herself to orgasm against my thigh. "Spread your legs, love." I shiver a little as I hear the echo of my husband's voice in the words, remember how he told me to do the same thing last night. It's different with Pandora, though. The whole dynamic is different and yet no less necessary. I want to fill my senses with her, to get drunk off the sight and smell and touch and taste of her.

She spreads her thighs slowly, teasingly. "Like this?"

"Yeah." I lick my lips. "Just like that." I sink to my knees before her. I don't know if I believe in an afterlife, but surely paradise is this moment, Pandora's soft thighs and pretty pussy. Perhaps I'm finding religion right here, right now.

PANDORA

I FULLY INTENDED TO BE A COMFORT TO ERIS TONIGHT, not to end up on the couch with her mouth between my thighs. Or at least...I think I did. It's hard to think clearly with her clever tongue working my clit. She has the most blissed-out expression on her face, as if she could spend hours in this exact position, wringing wave after wave of pleasure from me. I'm certainly not opposed to the idea.

But not tonight. Not when so much hangs in the balance.

I dig my hands into her long dark hair and tug her up to my mouth. She tastes of me and need. It's too good; I keep expecting it to dispel the way a dream does. I moan against her lips. "We don't have much time."

"Fuck them."

Gods, but I'm falling in love with this woman. It doesn't matter that it's happening far too fast and far too intensely. There's no room for how things *should* be, only how they are. I can't see a way through, no matter which angle I look at the problem from.

That knowledge scares me more than I want to admit. If there's no path through, then this ends in tragedy.

I've never been a fan of tragedies. I prefer romances with their guaranteed happily-ever-afters.

Desperation gives me the strength to flip us, to press Eris back to the couch and kiss her hard enough to make my head spin. She smells expensive, some perfume I could never afford. Not that I'd wear it. I prefer to trail my nose across her collarbone and inhale it right off her skin. "I don't want you to get hurt."

She doesn't waste her time with meaningless words of comfort that we both know would be a lie. Instead, she kisses me hard and delves her hand between my thighs. This time, I don't stop her as she strums my pleasure higher and higher. I tell myself she needs this as much as I do, but the truth is always the same.

I am greedy when it comes to pleasure.

There is so little happiness in this world. Can I really be blamed for grasping the threads of what comes my way and clinging to it with all my strength? It never lasts, but there's sweetness even in the loss. Or at least that's what I tell myself when it happens again and again.

I don't want to lose Eris, though. The thought of her being yet another casualty in the ambitious games of Minos and people like him makes me sick to my stomach. I pull her closer, kissing her as if my mouth can keep her with me, can ensure her safety.

A lie. All of it is a fucking lie.

That doesn't stop me from coming against her fingers, my body shivering and shaking. I barely wait for the aftereffects to ease before I slide down her body and set my mouth to her pussy. She tastes better than I could have dreamed.

I'm starting to discover that's just Eris... Better than I could have dreamed.

She sifts her fingers through my hair and lifts her hips. "Yes, right there." Her low voice is breathy with need.

Knowing *I* brought her to this point makes me downright giddy. I follow her low urging, using the flat of my tongue to rub back and forth on her clit. Her breathing goes choppy and every muscle in her body tightens. "*Don't stop.*"

Another night, I'd leave her on edge. Would see just how far I can push her before her patience runs out and she turns the tables on me. Not tonight. Tonight, I need her orgasm more than I need my next breath.

She cries out my name as she comes, the sound as sweet as the taste of her on my tongue. I give her one last long lick and then lift my head. Desire thrums in my blood, but we don't have time to indulge. Still, I can't stop myself from pressing a quick kiss to her thigh as I sit up.

Eris catches my wrist and pulls me down on top of her. She wraps her arms around me and inhales deeply. "I'm not ready to be done yet."

"I know." I settle against her, letting her hold me as our tensions ease. For how fierce and downright vicious this woman can be at times, she's sweet right now. With me.

She sighs. "Things are going to get ugly tonight. Everyone is so damn stubborn."

"I know that, too." I smile even though it feels bitter. "Though I hope you're including yourself in that list. You're no wilting flower in danger of being steamrolled."

Eris laughs a little. "No, I'm many things, but not that." She sifts her fingers through my hair. "Things might be easier if I was. Let others take the lead and be content with following."

I know she's not intending it as criticism of me, but it's hard not to take it as such. I tense. "Sometimes that's the only way to live. Emphasis on *live*."

"I will never fault a person for doing what it takes to survive," she says quietly. "I've done a lot of things I'm not particularly proud of in the pursuit of surviving... But I always craved more. As soon as I was able to move out of my father's house, I wanted enough power to ensure no one would make me feel helpless again."

I understand that on a foundational level, even if I've gone about things differently. "Was it bad? With your father?"

She opens her mouth, but seems to reconsider whatever she was about to say. "Yes." She shudders a little. "Yes, it was bad."

"I'm sorry." And I am. Even if she's come from an incredibly privileged life, that doesn't mean it was free of harm. Unfortunately, monsters exist in all forms, in all walks of life.

"There's no going back in time and changing things. Even if time travel were possible, there's no one powerful enough to challenge him. Or there wasn't then." She kisses my temple and nudges me to sit up. "It's not like that in Olympus anymore, though the gods only know if that will be to our benefit or detriment."

I understand. No matter how much I hate Minos, I can't deny that he's effective in pursuing his goals. Only someone like him—someone like Eris's father—could come into an enemy city with a small household of people and take the first steps of bringing the entire population to their knees. I tuck my hair behind my ears. "I meant what I said this morning. I don't know if you can convince Theseus to join your side, and without him, I don't see how you have even a sliver of chance of succeeding against Minos."

"Even with him, it's still a long shot." She shrugs a shoulder. "But the alternative is submitting to defeat, which is no alternative at all." Eris's lips quirk. "I fight, Pandora. It's the only thing I know how to do. It might not be in an arena with a weapon in my hand, but it's no less important."

Worry worms its way through my stomach. I'm not a fighter. I run from danger, preferring to let flight be my response to fear. The only people I fight with are those I trust. Realization rolls through me in a slow wave. *Guess we shot right past the falling stage and into* fallen.

I swallow hard. "I don't know how much help I'll be, but I'll try."

Her smile is terrifyingly fragile. "Thank you."

"Don't thank me yet." I rise unsteadily to my feet and grab my dress. "We might as well get some food ordered. Gods know, if Adonis is anything like Theseus, he'll be starving by the time dinner rolls around."

"Pandora." Eris waits for me to look at her to continue, more tentative than I've ever heard her, as if feeling her way through each word. "I don't know what the future brings or what it will look like for the...four...of us, but I'm glad you're here."

I'm glad I'm here, too. I don't know where we end up or what it looks like, either, but I'm caught in the tide of Eris and Theseus and even Adonis. Maybe it's naive to think that the only way through this is together, but I can't shake the belief. I shimmy into my dress as Eris pulls on her clothes.

She hesitates and glances at my dress. "Would you like something more comfortable? I expect this won't be a short night." When I start to frown, she blushes. "I might have ordered in some clothes for you. Um, you know, just in case you wanted to sleep over at some point. I wanted you to be comfortable, and while I *deeply* appreciate the sexy dresses you wear, I know all too well that they're not for lounging around the house."

"You bought me clothes," I say slowly. My stomach dips. It's a sweet gesture, but Eris and I aren't remotely the same size and if she misjudged, that's going to feel...really bad.

Some of her embarrassment seems to flick away. "If you've got that look on your face because I overstepped, then that's one thing, but if you're underestimating me and thinking that I was ham-handed in this gift, then have a little faith."

My throat feels tight. "I'm sure it's a nice gesture, but—"

"Have a little faith," she repeats. Eris slips her hand into mine before I can decide if I want to argue. She tows me down the hall, and I'm both surprised and strangely pleased when she turns to the door before her bedroom. She catches my look and gives a sheepish smile. "I do listen when you talk, you know. I want you in my life, but I'm not going to tie you down or shove you into a role that doesn't feel good. I get the feeling you don't want to play wife to me, and that's okay. I'm happy to give you your space." She pauses. "But I would like at least some of that space to be in proximity to me, no matter how you choose to utilize it."

I don't know what to say. I haven't tried to date much up to this point. People either get the wrong idea about what I want in a relationship, or they have a significant problem with Theseus's role in my life, which really just categorizes them under the first umbrella. There was a lovely person before we left Aeaea who seemed like they might be a good fit, at least in part, but then we left before I could fully realize that.

Eris opens the door and tugs me into the room. It's decorated in similar vibes to the rest of the place, expensive and sensual. The comforter is a deep cerulean and there are a wide variety of pillows on the bed in white and varying shades of blue. Thick curtains hang over the large windows overlooking the city.

She walks to a doorway leading into a large closet. It's mostly empty, but a handful of obviously new clothes hang near the front of it.

That sick feeling in my stomach rises again, but I try to do as she asked and have faith. I cross to the clothes and frown. These certainly aren't Eris's size. A quick look at the nearest tag has my brows rising. "These are my size." I check another two, finding the same thing.

"Of course they are." She sounds a little smug, but I don't hold it against her. Not when she's grinning widely with happiness lighting her dark eyes. "Do you like them?"

As promised, they're comfortable lounge clothing. Expensive, yes, but nothing so overt that it would give me the excuse to refuse the gift. I almost laugh. As if I would. Maybe there are people out there who value their pride more than fancy gifts, but the latter are few and far between in my world and I'm not about to turn them down.

I cross back to her and go up on my toes to kiss her. "Thank you. They're lovely."

A sound from the entrance of her penthouse has her lifting her head. Her frown clears when a deep voice calls her name. "Oh, that's Adonis." She presses another quick kiss to my lips. "Why don't you get changed and I'll get that food ordered?"

"Okay." I turn back to the clothes as she slips out of the room. Impossible not to take this evening as a sign that we could really work. Oh, my rose-tinted glasses aren't so thick that I don't see the wide variety of pitfalls awaiting us, but Eris is one of the most formidable people I've ever met. If anyone can make a nontraditional romantic situation work and keep herself and Theseus alive in the process, it's her.

I get the feeling that Adonis will go where she—and where Theseus—goes. Which leaves us with the last potential wrench in this tangled situation. Theseus. I don't know what he'll do. He's surprised me a few times since he married Eris, but that doesn't mean that he's going to counteract more than a decade's worth of loyalty to Minos.

No matter how much I desperately want him to.

HEPHAESTUS

IT'S THE STRANGEST THING TO WALK INTO APHRODITE'S penthouse and find her, Pandora, and Adonis waiting for me. They've all gathered in the kitchen similar to how we were this morning, but there's less tension in the air. As I watch, Pandora slips past Aphrodite and trails her fingers over my wife's back. Adonis stands a little apart, but his shoulders are relaxed and he's working a cork out of a bottle of wine.

Aphrodite sees me first. I watch in confusion as she walks directly to me and presses her hands to my chest. "Glad you could make it." She even sounds like she means it.

"Glad to be here." I sound like I mean it, too.

Damn it, I *do* mean it. I don't know how the home of the woman I was forced to marry, that I hated above all others, managed to become a haven, but it feels that way. It's not just because Pandora is here. Or Adonis. It's the strange combination of them...plus Aphrodite.

Eris.

She still hasn't moved away, and I can't quite lift my hands to return the almost tentative touch. But I can't leave it unanswered, either. "How did the rest of your day go?"

Her smile is small, but it reaches her eyes. "I only jumped at loud noises a few dozen times, but better than yesterday." She pauses. "Yours?"

Part of me wants to shut this down, to stop even the tiniest hint of camaraderie. I might not like what I've learned of Minos's plans, but I can't just shuck them off. The thought of doing so makes my skin crawl...

Or maybe that's the thought of letting him hurt the woman standing in front of me, her expression open for the first time since she walked down the aisle to me.

I swallow hard. "It was a shit show. Probably for the same reason yours was."

Her smile fades. "It's not ideal that we're on opposite sides of this now, no matter how we started."

How could it be any other way? I don't have an answer by the time she steps back and leads the way into the kitchen. I don't know what to expect, but Pandora presses a quick kiss to my cheek and then Adonis hooks the back of my neck and kisses me hard enough to make my skin go hot. He releases me before I can decide to do anything more about it, though.

My head is spinning. It feels like I ended up in the wrong apartment, with a life that looks familiar but isn't the same. Isn't *real*.

If Minos succeeds in his plans, they'll all hate me. Even Pandora. Maybe especially Pandora. She would never admit to wanting a family, not when she's been suspicious of Minos from the start, but there's no denying how relaxed she looks as she jokes lightly with Adonis and gets him flustered. Something has unwound in my wife as well, though not as thoroughly as with the other two. Even though her shoulders aren't tight, she watches them with the same worry that's worming around in my chest. As if drawn by my attention, she shifts her gaze to mine in a moment of perfect understanding.

We're going to break this.

We don't want to. We will try very hard not to bring harm to this group. But we're both loyal to greater forces. I might be willing to consider peace, at least with Aphrodite, but Minos will never be satisfied with that route. And Zeus won't rest until he's driven us from the city. I'd bet good money on it.

I'm not sure what I'd say if I had the chance. I never get it. Adonis opens the first takeout container and freezes. No one notices it but me, but they sure as fuck notice when he slaps Pandora's hand away from another container.

"Hey!" She rubs the back of her hand. "What the fuck?"

"Eris." He glances at her. "Sniff this."

Aphrodite hurries over and follows his direction, leaning down and inhaling deeply. She curses. "They weren't even trying to be subtle. The leaves are all over the salad."

I find myself closing the distance and looking over her shoulder. "Poison?"

"Yes, though whoever did this didn't choose well. It would take eating this entire salad and then some to get a fatal dose, but I'm not in the mood to be in digestive distress for the next few days." She carefully refolds the top of the box and slides it back into the bag.

"Where did you order from? Who does the delivery?"

She studies me for a long moment. "What does it matter?"

Adonis clears his throat. "I'm taking this out."

Pandora looks between me and Aphrodite. "I'll...go with you," she says slowly. "For protection."

"Protection." He gives a choked laugh. "Right. Good idea."

I barely wait for them to leave the room to start in on my wife. "What the fuck is that supposed to mean? 'What does it matter?' It matters because someone tried to poison us."

"No, they tried to poison *me*. I ordered this before you arrived. There's no conceivable way they would know you're here." She tucks her hair behind her ears. For once, there's no venom in her tone. "That's what you wanted, isn't it? Anarchy in Olympus. Our experienced leaders replaced with murderous civilians who are unprepared for what it takes to rule. Your people are aware that the barrier is fading, and while there's currently no standing army waiting to conquer us when it finally does, I think we both know an army isn't necessary to take a city. Not anymore."

Something sticky and barbed takes up residence in my chest. I think it might be guilt. "War is part of life."

She smiles sadly. "Why are you saying that like you're trying to convince me? I know, Husband."

"It wasn't supposed to be like this." I drag my hands through my hair. "I wasn't supposed to—"

"Care?"

I glare. "I care about people."

"You care about Pandora."

That's not true anymore. Or, what I mean is I still care about

Pandora—she's family—but she's not the only person I care about now. She's not the only person whose safety I worry about. "I don't want you dead," I finally say.

Aphrodite's eyebrows shoot up. "From you, that's practically a declaration of love."

"Oh, shut the—"

She holds up a hand. "I don't want you dead, either. I realize it's horribly cliché to start to fall for your own husband, but here we are."

"Aphrodite..." I clear my throat. "Eris, I—"

Once again, she cuts me off. "Did Minos tell you that he plans to kill me?" She grabs a wineglass and fills it nearly to the brim with red wine. "Because my brother wants to make me a widow. I'm curious if they're following the same playbook when it comes to our marriage."

I tense. "Zeus is going to try to kill me."

"Not him personally." She pauses. "Probably. A few weeks ago, I would say he'd never stoop to murder for fear of turning out like our father, but my brother isn't acting like himself these days."

Hearing that should make me happy. Zeus is unraveling. That's a win for us. Except, as I think of the cold-eyed motherfucker who is Eris's brother, I'm not sure unleashing him will be anything but a danger. I learned early to avoid the cold ones, because when they shatter, there's often an inferno of rage beneath the exterior. Or, in scarier cases, there's nothing beneath but an even deeper freeze. I have no idea which Zeus will be, but I suddenly don't want to find out.

"What a fucking mess, and us in the middle of it." I find myself chuckling, a grim sound that has no joy in it. I'm not remotely surprised when Eris joins me. Her chuckle turns into giggles and she tips until she bumps against my shoulder. Between one ragged laugh and the next, we're clinging to each other and laughing so hard tears creep from the edges of my eyes.

"Absolutely." She leans her head against my shoulder. It feels...nice. Everything about this feels nice. Ironic, maybe, that the only other person in this fucked-up city who understands exactly how impossible the position I'm in is my wife, who's in an identical position, even if it's on the opposite side of this conflict.

We're two soldiers trapped in a trench, and it won't matter who's firing the shots winging their way overhead. A bullet is a bullet. It only takes one well-placed shot to end us once and for all. "What do we do?" I don't mean to ask it, but this moment feels too honest to retreat from. At least not yet.

"I don't know." She rubs her face against my shoulder a little. Tension slowly filters back into her body, and I already know I won't like what she says next. "I'm not going to flip on the city. Are you going to flip on Minos?"

A week ago I could have answered without hesitation. Now, I'm not so sure. I knew I was just a weapon for Minos to pick up and attack Olympus with, but since taking the Hephaestus title, that role has started to feel like wearing someone else's skin. Too tight. Too constricting. And when I'm around Minos, I feel like I can't breathe.

But I owe him so much.

Do you?

Hearing Pandora's voice in my head feels so real, I actually turn to look toward the door, expecting her to be standing there with Adonis.

It's the only reason I see the attack coming.

I get a flash of a broad-shouldered person in black with a mask pulled down over their face. Then the only thing I see is the gun they're pointing at us. I don't think. There's no time for that. I shove Eris toward the floor. "Get down."

The bullet pings over our heads, but I'm already moving. I take one step before my body serves to remind me that my knee is not, and will never again be, able to sustain this kind of motion. I stumble against the counter, barely dodging another bullet.

Out of the corner of my eye, I see Eris moving and curse. She won't be content to stay down and safe this time. The only weapon readily available is the wine bottle. I grab it and fling it at the attacker's head.

They throw up their hand just in time to deflect, but the impact sends the gun skittering across the floor toward the hallway. Still too far away, but *they* don't have it. An opportunity, and one I can't afford to miss. I dive for it. If I can get my fucking hands on it, I can end this now.

They're moving behind me, rushing toward the gun even as I scramble for it. Close. Too damn close. I'm not going to have any range on this, even if I can get there first. My fingertips brush the cool metal right as a boot connects with my ribs. Pain flares, turning my mind hazy and red. I open my mouth, but there's no air to inhale. My lungs have locked up in my chest. Fuck, that hurts.

"No!"

I roll onto my side just as Eris runs at the attacker. "Stop," I rasp. She doesn't hear me, or she ignores me.

Our attacker turns to face her. I catch a glint of metal in their hands and try to shout a warning. My fucking lungs haven't unclenched, though, and it comes out as a garbled yell. The attacker curses. Which is when I see that my wife has one of her kitchen knives in her hand.

"Don't." Again, the word barely makes it past my lips. I try to inhale, but my lungs are still seized up. Fuck, fuck, *fuck*.

The attacker stumbles back. They should be taking this moment to press their advantage, but they're too busy avoiding her strikes. They're good strikes, quick without over-extending her arm. It still won't be enough. I have to get on my feet and I have to do it *now*.

I don't get a chance.

The attacker has backed closer to me and they look down and meet my gaze. My death is in those dark eyes. They ignore Eris entirely and bring the knife down. It'll take me in my chest, maybe my neck, and there's no coming back from that shit. I instinctively throw my hands up.

They never make contact. Eris hits them hard enough to take them both off their feet. The attacker lands on their back beside me, their head slamming against the floor. They lay there for a beat, and I think they might be stunned.

At least until Eris rolls off them and I see the blood.

Not just blood.

Their fucking *knife* is sticking out of Eris's stomach.

"Fuck!" the low voice says. The attacker scrambles back.

Distantly, I register that they're here for me, not for her, but that doesn't mean a single damn thing to the growing puddle of blood around her body.

I manage to crawl to her just as the door opens and Adonis and Pandora walk back into the penthouse. Pandora cries out, but Adonis springs into motion without hesitation. Another time, I'd marvel at how he goes from easygoing charmer to something furious and violent in the space of a heartbeat.

Our attacker never sees him coming.

He punches them in the side of the head and they slump like a puppet whose strings have been cut. Adonis shoves them to the floor and flips them onto their stomach. "Pandora, get the zip ties from under the sink and then bring me my phone." He's all business as he yanks the black mask from their head, revealing a white guy with short dark hair. I've never seen him before, but that doesn't mean a single damn thing.

I press my hands to Eris's stomach and go cold. Too much blood. Too much fucking blood. "Eris. Wife, look at me."

"So bossy." The words are too faint to bring me any amount of comfort.

"*Eris?*" Adonis is by my side in an instant. "Don't move the knife."

"I know not to move the fucking knife," I snap. "Call someone. Now." Desperation bubbles up inside me, burning like acid. I lean down to look into Eris's glazed eyes. "Hang on. Help is coming."

"Stabbed." She gives a pained laugh that cuts off halfway through. "Helen will never...let me live it down." The last bit comes out on an exhale, the words so faint they're almost incomprehensible.

"Then you'd better live so she can yell at you." I glance down and my stomach lurches. My hands are covered in her blood to my wrists. *Too much. She's losing too much.* "Don't you dare die on me, Wife."

She smiles a little but her eyes close. "No promises."

Fear makes me shake. "*Where's that fucking phone?*" I roar.

"Here!" Pandora skids up to us and drops it into Adonis's hands.

It's just as well. My hands are shaking too much to dial. I stare into my wife's eyes as Adonis barks orders into the phone. I barely register his words. I'm too busy trying to will the color back into Eris's face.

I knew I didn't want her dead, but it's not until she passes out in my arms that I realize exactly how much I want her alive and with me.

ADONIS

I'VE NEVER KNOWN FEAR LIKE WHAT I FEEL IN THE TEN minutes it takes for the paramedics to arrive. They're not the same people who help the main population of Olympus; these are a team specific to the Thirteen. It's the only reason I trust them enough to move back from Eris's unconscious body as they sweep in.

That and the fact Zeus followed them in.

He looks like shit, and I don't give a fuck because Eris is dying on her floor and it's *his* fault. I surge to my feet and am on him in a handful of steps. He doesn't bother to fight me as I slam him against the wall. Later, that will bother me. Right now, I flat-out don't give a fuck.

"You did this."

He looks past me to where the paramedics have strapped Eris to a gurney. "I had nothing to do with this."

I slam him against the wall again. "Don't lie to me. I know the ultimatum you gave her."

Zeus finally focuses on me. His blue eyes flash. "Then you

know I gave her three days." He shoves me off, easily breaking my hold. "Then you know I would *never* endanger my sister."

"Not without cause." My heart is in my throat as the paramedics wheel her out of the penthouse just as three people rush in. I immediately recognize Ares and her two partners. She's pale, but takes in the situation in a single glance. "Achilles, you and Patroclus secure the attacker. Alive. I want answers and I want them as soon as possible."

For once, Achilles doesn't have an arrogant remark in response. He moves efficiently to the downed attacker and checks the zip tie I fastened around their wrists. Apparently satisfied, he hauls them up and passes them to Patroclus, who keeps them on their feet with a stern hand on their shoulder.

The lead paramedic pauses. "We won't know the full extent of the damage until we get her into surgery and get that knife out," she says to Zeus and Ares. "Would one of you like to ride with us to the hospital?"

"I will." Zeus straightens his jacket that I rumpled when I slammed him into the wall and turns away from me as if he's not concerned I might attack his exposed back.

I actually take a step forward before Pandora catches my elbow. She shakes her head. "Don't."

"Easy for you to say. I—"

She digs her nails into my skin and narrows her eyes. "Do *not* tell me what is or isn't easy for me to say." She shifts closer. "Fighting right now delays her getting to the hospital. Have your pissing match with Zeus after we know she's okay."

Zeus disappears through the door while she holds me back. I wait a beat and then step away from her. If I hadn't had such a nice chat with her while we disposed of the poisoned food, I would have been here when the attacker first showed up. I could have stopped them.

Ares turns to us, her hazel eyes narrowed. "I'm going to have some questions for all three of you, but it can wait until after Eris gets out of surgery." Her voice breaks a little on the last word.

Achilles clasps her shoulder. "She's going to be fine. Just like Patroclus was fine after the tournament."

Her face goes hard as she looks down to where Theseus is leaning against the wall. "If my sister—" Her voice breaks off and she swears. "I will finish the job I started in the maze."

I tense, fully expecting Theseus to say or do something to escalate the situation. His obvious contempt for the Thirteen is inflammatory, to say the least. But he doesn't say anything at all. He just nods at Ares and watches her sweep out of the room with her men and their prisoner at her back.

The door slamming shut springs us into motion. Pandora and I hurry to Theseus. We go to our knees on either side of him. She reaches for him, but stops before touching him. "Are you hurt? Your knee?"

"No." He struggles to sit up straighter and winces. "Maybe. Not my knee, but that fucker got in a good kick." He gingerly touches his right side. "Might have cracked a rib." He turns his attention to me. "Did you recognize him?"

"No. I've never seen him before." Which only means he wasn't one of Athena's. My stomach drops out. Eris *has* to be okay, but the thought of how close I came to losing them both leaves me shaky. "Let's get you to the hospital, too."

"No."

I blink. "What do you mean, *no*?"

"No." He nods at Pandora and they share a look I can't quite decipher. Theseus clears his throat. "I have something I have to take care of first."

I look between them. "Eris just got *stabbed*. What could you possibly have to do that's more important than coming to the hospital with me?" I knew he was a hard man, of course, but this is another realm entirely. If not for the panicked way he'd commanded Eris to stay with us, I would think he's entirely unaffected.

Pandora presses her lips together, dark eyes worried. "Are you sure?"

I feel like I've missed an entire conversation. "Are you sure of what?"

Theseus ignores me. "Yeah."

"Do you want me to go with you?"

"No. I got it."

Frustration lances my throat, hot and cloying. "What the fuck are you talking about? Go where?" I grit out.

He finally looks at me. "This has gone far enough. I'm going to deal with Minos."

"*Deal* with Minos." Surely he doesn't mean—

"Not permanently." Theseus takes my hand and allows me to leverage him to his feet. "I don't have it in me to do that to him, even if he deserves it. I'll meet you both at the hospital in a little while. Be there for our woman when she wakes up, even if I can't be."

Our woman.

The two words toll through me, changing something forever. He's right, though. Eris is ours. All of ours. I clear my throat. "What are you doing? If you aren't going to kill him—"

He rolls his shoulders. "I'm going to make sure this never happens again. Not to her." Theseus stalks out of the penthouse before I can figure out a response to that. It's only when the door closes behind him that I realize he still had Eris's blood on his hands.

"He can't stop it." I feel numb. It won't last, but it's almost pleasant for this beat of silence before we have to move, before reality comes crashing back in. "He can't stop anything."

"You'd be surprised what Theseus can do when he sets his mind to it." Pandora can't quite mask the worry on her face, though. "Come on. I want to be there for Eris when she wakes up."

I look at the bloodstain on the marble floor. "Go on ahead. I'm going to clean this up."

"Adonis," she says softly.

"I don't want her coming back and having the first thing she sees be a reminder of what happened to her." I can't go back in time and save her. I can't *fix* this, no matter how much I want to. But I can make damned sure she doesn't have to face the memory all over again when she comes home.

She has to come home. I can't allow myself to consider another outcome.

Pandora nods slowly. "Okay, that's smart. Let's do it together."

"You don't have to. I can…"

She's already moving into the kitchen and poking around beneath the sink until she finds the cleaning supplies. It takes us less than ten minutes to remove every trace of blood from the penthouse. It seems like it should be more difficult to erase evidence of such catastrophic events, but my numbness has me in a stranglehold.

I don't think I'm going to breathe until I see Eris and can confirm that she's alive and well. Or as well as can be expected considering tonight's events.

Pandora takes my hand as we step into the elevator. She's startlingly warm, and I'm not ashamed to say I cling to her as the car descends. "She has to be okay." I've said it a dozen times since we started cleaning. I don't seem to be able to say anything else.

"She's going to be better than okay," she says firmly, just like she has answered me every other time. "She's going to come out of surgery spitting mad and ready to make whoever is responsible pay."

I shake my head slowly. "Best I can tell, the attacker wasn't there for Eris. If they were, they wouldn't have panicked when she got stabbed. They would have finished the job. I could be wrong, but I don't think so."

Pandora tenses beside me. "They were there for Theseus."

"I think so." Which means they were sent by one of the Thirteen.

I hate to admit it, but I believe that Zeus isn't responsible. He would wait until Theseus wasn't near Eris to have his people strike. No, this was someone else, someone who didn't necessarily care if Eris—if Aphrodite—was caught in the cross fire.

Maybe even someone who hoped she would be.

"Who sent them?" Pandora looks up at me, her normal happy expression nowhere in evidence. She looks furious enough that I almost take a step back. "You have an idea."

"It wasn't either of her siblings. But there are plenty of people among that group who wouldn't care if she got caught in the cross fire. They wouldn't shed a tear if she dies." Artemis, in particular, has plenty of reason to hate Theseus...and Eris for standing in her way when she wanted revenge for her cousin's death.

"Adonis." Pandora's hand becomes a vise around mine. "Right now, she's alone and helpless on an operating table. Do you think one of them might try to take advantage of that?"

I don't know. *I don't fucking know. Artemis has no overt in at the hospital, but that doesn't mean she's not capable of finishing the job.* "We need to move. *Now.*"

My car is in the parking garage. We hurry to it and then we're flying out the exit and toward the hospital. "Zeus won't let anyone hurt her." Maybe if I say it enough times, I'll actually believe it. He won't let anyone close...except the nurses and doctors and whoever else is needed in the surgery room. "Gods*damn* it."

"What?" Pandora clutches the handle above the door as I fly around a turn, running a red light. "We're not going to help Eris if we die on the way there!"

"Everyone is the enemy." I have to force my foot off the accelerator as we come up against traffic. "That's what your people wanted, isn't it? Look at us now. Some doctor or nurse might decide to kill her right there on the table to take her title."

Pandora looks sick. "It wasn't my plan. I know that doesn't make it better, and it might actually make it worse because I came with Minos even knowing there was something going on. But I never wanted anyone hurt."

It's so tempting to take my anger and fear out on her. It's also not fair. I know how these things work better than most. People at the top make the decisions and tip the dominoes over.

It's everyone else who pays the price.

Ten minutes later, we're screeching into the hospital parking lot. Pandora has to keep me from sprinting wildly into the hospital, though we move at a quick walk that's almost a run. She laces her fingers with mine and provides a steadying presence even though her lips are tight and her eyes worried.

We barely make it two steps inside before we're stopped by two people dressed in black with a patch on their right shoulders of helmet and a sword crossed with a spear. "No civilians. We're having an emergency."

"Let them through," says a tired voice behind them. "They're with us."

Ares's soldiers part to reveal the woman herself. Achilles and Patroclus flank her, both looking just as worried as I feel. She eyes me. "You got here fast."

"We were motivated." I step forward. "Any news?"

"No, not yet. We have *our* team in there, though. The best doctors on the Thirteen's payroll. They'll see her through." Ares speaks in the quiet tone of someone barely hanging on.

"The clause—"

"They are *our people*," she repeats. Her eyes are colder than I've ever seen them. "And they know I'll personally put a bullet between their eyes if they try something."

It's not a guarantee, but it's all we have. I'm not a doctor. I can't perform surgery. I take a shaky breath. "Okay."

Pandora is squeezing my hand so hard, I've lost feeling in my fingers, but her voice is relatively even. "We'll wait with you until we know she's safe." She glances at me, a silent message there that I'm in total agreement with. Neither of us will be sent on our way once Eris wakes up. I don't care if I have to fight Ares, Achilles, Patroclus, or even Zeus himself. I am getting into that room to see Eris with my own eyes and make sure she knows she's safe now.

But she's not the only one I'm worried about.

I allow Pandora to lead me to one of the uncomfortable seats in the waiting room. We sink down and exchange another look. "Will Theseus be okay?"

"I don't know." A line appears between her brows. "Minos has been very careful to use disappointment and praise in turn to keep Theseus in line, but that was when Theseus worshipped the ground he walks on. If he confronts Minos directly, that won't hold. I don't know what Minos will do."

Despite my best efforts, I think back to the final Ares trial. The Minotaur fought Achilles, Patroclus, and Helen at the same time. He almost killed Patroclus, and when Helen eliminated him, he kept fighting and might have killed Achilles, too. I've never seen anything like it. The whole time he enacted such violence, he didn't have any expression on his face.

"If Minos sets the Minotaur after Theseus, what will happen?"

She flinches. "Blood and tears, Adonis. Blood and tears."

HEPHAESTUS

PURE RAGE CARRIES ME ALL THE WAY TO MINOS'S HOME.
I can't stop replaying the attack. I should have been stronger.
Faster. Fucking *something*. The attacker got the drop on us, but
Eris should have stayed down. What was the fool woman doing,
rushing at the fucking assassin?

Trying to protect me.

I can't pretend the cloying feeling in my chest is anything but
guilt. It's sticky and sharp and every breath seems to drive it deeper
into my lungs. She was trying to protect me, her enemy, the man
she only married to keep this fucking city safe.

The city doesn't deserve her. The Thirteen sure as shit don't.

I shove open the door hard enough that it bangs into the wall
behind it and tries to rebound. I catch it easily. "Minos! Where the
fuck are you?"

It takes seconds to reach his office and find it empty. I charge into
his bedroom with the same results. Those are the only two places in
this apartment he spends any time, which means he's not here.

Footsteps sound, but I know before Ariadne rounds the corner that it's not the person I'm seeking. She skids to a stop, her eyes wide. "Theseus. Oh gods, is that *blood*?"

"Yes." I start past her. "Where is he?"

"Shouldn't you, um, maybe wash your hands? Take a breath?"

I don't grab Ariadne and shake her, but the temptation is there. "Where is he?" I repeat. I keep my words so low, they're almost incomprehensible. I don't care. If I start bellowing, I'm going to annihilate this apartment. I want to rip into the walls, to smash and break whatever I can get my hands on and howl to the fucking moon.

None of it will make a difference or ensure Eris lives.

Ariadne hesitates. She looks around and steps closer. "I heard about Aphrodite. I'm sorry."

"Ariadne." I take her shoulders and lean down, getting in her face. "Where the fuck is your father?"

"Are you going to kill him?" she whispers.

I don't ask her if she'd try to stop me. Minos's relationship with her and Icarus is no less fucked than his relationship with me and the Minotaur. It's just a different flavor of fucked. Maybe she doesn't know if she wants to stop me or get out of my way. That's fine. I don't know what I want right now, either. "Where is he? I'm not going to ask again."

"Get your fucking hands off my sister."

I look over slowly to find Icarus in the doorway. He's got a baseball bat in his hands and while he doesn't look like a stone-cold killer, I have no doubt he'd take that damned bat to my head and waste both our time. I drop my hands from Ariadne's shoulders. "My fight isn't with either of you. Tell me where he is and I'll go."

Icarus adjusts his grip on the baseball bat, but doesn't lower it. "She's Olympian, Theseus. Surely you're not going to burn bridges with all of us over your *wife*."

"I am putting a stop to this."

"It's too late," Ariadne whispers. "There's no stopping it."

I give her a sharp look, but I'm not about to fold now. It doesn't matter if we can't stop Minos's greater plan. I don't give a fuck about this city as a whole. But I'll be damned before I let Eris stay in the crosshairs. "I'm not going to ask again." I don't want to hurt either of them, but if they stand between me and their father, I will go through them to get to him.

"He's meeting with the Minotaur downstairs," Icarus says. "In the apartment they're both pretending we don't know about." He rattles off the floor and number.

Minos has a secret residence. Of course he does. He's never one to keep all his eggs in one basket...or to leave incriminating evidence lying around where one of his children might happen on it. The fact he didn't tell *me* about the apartment is just more proof that I am expendable to him. I've played my role and now he has no more use for me.

Later, that might hurt. Maybe. Right now, I'm too fucking furious to worry about it.

I turn and head for the door. Every step sends pain flaring in my knee, but I ignore it just like I've been ignoring it for days. I'll pay for the negligence later. If there is a later.

It doesn't take long to get down to the floor and apartment

Icarus directed me to. It's only as I'm raising my fist to bang on the door that I pause to wonder if he steered me wrong and I'm about to barge in on some innocent.

But when the door flies open, it's the Minotaur glaring at me, his scarred face pulled into unforgiving lines. "What are you doing here?"

Instead of answering, I shoulder past him into the apartment. One look around confirms it's exactly what I'd expect. A command center. There's a desk with several computer monitors set up in front of a fancy chair. No other furniture.

Minos walks out of the doorway leading into a hall. "What's all this?" He almost misses a step when he sees me, but Minos is too good to be thrown off by my presence. "Son, you have blood on your hands."

"Call them off," I tell him.

He raises his brows. "What are you on about? Call who off?"

This is how we're going to play it? I expected nothing less, but I still want to wrap my hands around his neck and squeeze. I flex them, and his gaze falls to clock the move. His brows rise higher. "Looks like you've had an eventful night. Fill me in."

"No."

His eyes flash. "What do you mean, no?"

"I am done playing this game. You set me up to be expendable, and because of that, my wife is on the operating table right now. I don't give a fuck about your plan or your goals. If she doesn't survive the night, I'll kill you myself. Fuck you, and fuck your plans."

Just like that, his charming mask falls. "Check your tone and try that again. You don't get to tell me when you're done. *I* tell *you* when you're done. You're a weapon, if a piss-poor one. Your only job is to annihilate whatever enemy I point you at."

I knew it, but hearing him state it so clearly breaks the last string of his hold on me. "Not anymore."

He takes a menacing step toward me. "The only reason you have that title and power is because I deemed that you should. I can take it away as easily as I gave it to you and put your ass right back on the streets where I found you."

There's a sense of relief in letting go. It will hurt later. Wounds always do. But in this moment, it's freeing. I stare him down. "Fuck the title and fuck the power. I'll resign."

He jolts. "What?"

I hadn't meant to say the words, but now that they've been voiced, they feel right. "I'll resign," I repeat. I find myself grinning. "Yeah, fuck this title." I'm not a good fit for it. I never have been. Not to mention, power isn't all it's cracked up to be. It's brought me nothing but grief, and I'm over it. "Fight your own fucking war. I'm done doing it for you." I turn and start for the door.

"If you walk out of here, you're dead to me." His voice surges into a roar as I keep moving. "Do you hear me, you little shit? You'll be no better than these Olympian vermin and I'll exterminate you alongside them."

I glance over my shoulder. It strikes me that Minos looks… small. Ever since he took me in, he's felt larger than life. The only god I worshipped, the only power I devoted myself to. Now, with his chest heaving and his mouth working while he tries to find the exact combination of words to hurt me enough to make me buckle, he's nothing more than a man, and a pathetic one at that.

I have no allegiance to Olympus. I'm not an attack dog switching sides—switching masters. But I've found my first sliver of true happiness here, and I won't let anyone endanger it. Not even him. "If you touch one of my people, I will come back here and skin you alive. You taught me to do that when I was seventeen, remember? There will be no mercy for you. Don't fuck with me."

Minos, god of my teenage years, flinches.

That's all I need to turn around...and find the Minotaur blocking the door. I stare at him. We've been rivals and enemies and occasionally something that almost resembles friends. There's nothing of that in his eyes now. "Get out of my way," I say softly.

His empty gaze flicks over my shoulder to where Minos is still cursing and throwing threats with enough venom that I'm glad he's not armed. "Might be a mistake." He matches my tone, his words designed not to carry. "Backing the wrong horse."

"I'm not backing any horse." We barely talk, and even then, it's usually about fighting techniques or weapons. Still, after spending half my life at his side, I can't help the desire not to leave like this. "I'm choosing to be happy—if I can figure out what the fuck that looks like. You should do the same."

Another glance at Minos. The Minotaur shrugs. "I'm where I want to be." But he moves slowly to the side and allows me to pass.

I slip out of the room, but I don't take a full breath until I'm back in my car and winging my way to the hospital. My hands won't stop shaking. I think I made the right call—or at least the only call available to me—but there's a pit of loss inside me that's going to be a bitch to wade through when things calm down.

If they calm down.

I park in a hurry, ready to charge into the emergency room and demand answers. Unfortunately, my body is fucking *done* with the abuse I've heaped on it. My knee locks up as I try to climb out. I curse and slump against the side of the car, gritting my teeth and riding out the pain. The hospital is *right there*, but I can't power through it this time. I've been ignoring my limits for days—weeks—and now I'm paying the price.

"Theseus?"

I look up to find Adonis standing a few feet away, his features drawn. He holds up an unlit cigarette and gives a sheepish smile. "Seemed a great time to start smoking."

"Throw that shit away." I try to put weight on my leg and hiss out a breath when all I get for my trouble is a rush of agony. "Bad for you."

He's by my side in an instant. "Your knee or your ribs?"

"Knee. Put it through...too much."

"I suppose fighting for your life and then charging off to confront Minos will do that." He slips beneath my arm without asking, which I appreciate even as I curse. The truth is that I'm not getting into that hospital without help.

"News?"

"Not yet." He doesn't look at me as we make our slow, painful way to the sliding glass doors. "She's still in surgery. They're not even updating Zeus and Ares." A pause. "Are you okay?"

"No." I grit my teeth. "But I will be."

The two people in question stare at us as we move through the doors. Zeus glares at me and I glare right back. This motherfucker better not think he can keep me from my wife. He stalks up to us, and just like every other time we've stood close together, I'm surprised to find he's not particularly tall. He's got a big presence. Zeus eyes me. "Find somewhere else to be, Hephaestus."

Hephaestus. I've fucking *hated* that name since taking it. Maybe I should balk at shucking it aside, but the truth is that it feels like a burden and I'm sick of carrying burdens for other people. "I'm done."

"Excuse me?"

"Consider this my resignation. I'm out as Hephaestus."

He narrows his eyes. "What trick is this?"

"No trick." I see Pandora sitting in a waiting room chair, her knee bouncing nervously as she watches us. I finally understand what she's been saying for years. Gods, it's a miracle she's put up with my contrary ass. I turn back to Zeus. "I'm done. Being one of the Thirteen is a nightmare. You all can fuck right off, just like Minos can fuck right off."

If anything, he glares harder. "If this is some ploy—"

"For fuck's sake, Zeus," Adonis mutters.

I give him a squeeze even as I keep my expression locked down as best I can. "Suspect me later if you want. Right now, you're standing between me and my wife, and I will take you out at the knees if you don't get the fuck out of my way." I seem to be saying that a lot lately, but it's the truth.

He steps slowly out of my way. "You fuck with her, I'll cut your throat myself."

I've spent most of my life getting into fights with dangerous people, so I have plenty of experience when someone's bluffing. Zeus isn't. It makes me like the fucker a little bit. I grin. "I fuck with you, you'll have to get in line, because she'll be the first one to put a blade to my throat."

He hesitates and nods shortly. Then he gets the fuck out of my way. About damn time. I make it three steps before I pause. What I'm about to do is more a betrayal than resigning from the title, but I'm not going to pry Eris or Adonis out of Olympus, which means I have to keep the fucking city standing for them. "Minos has several shipments in the harbor. I don't know if they'll be under his name, but you want to get to whatever that cargo is before he does."

Zeus stares at me a long moment and then gives a sharp nod. As I turn from him, he's already pulling out his phone.

Pandora surges to her feet and rushes to us. She pulls both me and Adonis into a hug, and I manage to hold them to me without it being incredibly awkward. Maybe I'm getting better at this whole comfort thing?

It's easier when I don't have to find words. There's nothing to say. Eris will live. I refuse to believe in any other outcome. Without me as Hephaestus, it means we only have one set of enemies to deal with. Yeah, that means the entire fucking city, but still. We'll figure it out.

We manage to get three seats against the wall and sit there as the seconds tick by, one of my hands clutched in each of theirs. I stare at the door, willing the doctor to arrive with good news. I do it for so long, that when she finally does, I almost don't believe it.

She's a curvy exhausted-looking woman with light-brown skin and her hair hidden under a cap. She eyes us. "She made it through surgery. *Two* of you can go back." She holds up two fingers. "If you make a fuss about it, none of you can go back. She needs to rest, and I'm not going to have you fighting in my hospital."

"I'll go." Zeus steps forward. I fully expect him to take Ares, but he turns those cold blue eyes on me. "You coming?"

For a second, I think he couldn't possibly be speaking to me, but Adonis gives me a squeeze and then he stands to help me to my feet. "We'll be right here when you're done."

I take a deep breath, feeling weirdly adrift as I walk away from them, but Adonis and Pandora aren't the ones who need me right now.

My wife is.

APHRODITE

GETTING STABBED HURTS LIKE A BITCH. I DO NOT RECOM-
mend it. Maybe I should have agreed to the extra pain meds the
nurse insisted on, but my brain is already foggy from whatever
they gave me to keep me under during surgery. I'm alone in this
hospital room, and virtually helpless. I'm not going to make it any
easier on someone who wants me dead.

Gods, I'm tired.

I close my eyes. Just for a moment. Just to give me a break
from spinning my mental wheels trying to see a way forward. It
feels like I've been churning for my entire life and yet I'm really no
better off than I was as a child.

All the freedom I fought for. All the power. And yet here I am,
once again the target of the violence I fought so hard to escape. It's
not the same as growing up in my father's house. It's not *remotely*
the same.

I feel just as trapped.

The door opens and I jolt. "Fuck, that hurts."

I expected the nurse, or maybe a doctor. I didn't expect my brother and my husband to enter the room without bloodshed. They both look like shit. Perseus probably hasn't slept in days. Theseus has blood stained in the creases of his fingers.

I have never been so glad to see two people in my entire life. My lower lip quivers, and I can't seem to make it stop. "Is that blood?" My voice comes out strange. I want to blame the drugs, but I feel small and weak and unforgivably glad to see my husband. "Are you okay?"

He looks down at his hands and curses. "I thought I got it all."

"Shitty at your job as always, Theseus."

I glare at my brother. I know his bitchy attitude spawns from worry, but that doesn't mean I'm going to lie here and let him drive the wedge between me and my husband any deeper. "He is Hephaestus, and you will refer to him as such."

"No, he's really not." Perseus says it without any inflection. "He resigned his title less than an hour ago. It was all very dramatic." He glances at Theseus. "While I appreciate the tip about the ships, you were too late. They were unloaded sometime last night. Poseidon has no idea what was inside them."

"You have all the resources of Olympus at your disposal. I'm sure you'll figure it out."

The words don't make sense. Not the resignation, and not whatever ship they're talking about. I know I should care about the latter, but I can't get past the former. "You resigned?"

He gives Perseus a dirty look and rounds the hospital bed to sink gingerly into the chair next to me. "I have some things to say, but I'll wait until this puffed-up parakeet leaves."

My brother crosses his arms over his chest. "I left my sister alone with you, and she's been almost shot and successfully stabbed. Anything you want to say to her, you can say in front of me."

Theseus's jaw goes tight, and I can't help tensing. The tiny movement sends a fresh wave of pain through me. I should have expected it, but it catches me by surprise and I whimper. He looks back at me and takes my hand. "Do I need to get the nurse?"

"No." My voice is hoarse. "No, I'm fine."

He narrows his eyes. "You refused more pain meds, didn't you?" My brother starts cursing, but neither of us look at him. Theseus squeezes my hand slowly, almost like he's not sure if it's the right move. "We'll talk, and then you'll take your meds, Eris. Promise me."

"It's not safe," I whisper.

"I'll watch over you. No one will get close."

It's a testament to how weak I am right now that I want to look into those words, to mine them for proof that he cares about me as much as I've started to care about him. I close my eyes for a moment, fighting to think instead of just feel. It doesn't work. I've been in a state of fight or flight for days, and my body just gives out and goes limp with relief knowing he'll stand between me and anything that comes through the door. I wet my dry lips. "What did you want to say?"

He leans forward, as serious as I've ever seen him. "I'm done with this city and its power games, with Minos and his bullshit. I'm done being a weapon. Your brother is right; I resigned from the Hephaestus title." He gives a self-deprecating grin. "I think we both know I was shit at it, and the cost is too damn high."

"But…" I find myself gripping his hand as if I have the strength to keep him with me. If he isn't working for Minos and isn't one of the Thirteen, there's nothing to keep him in Olympus. He hates this city; he's never been shy about expressing that. "You're leaving?" "What? No." He shakes his head. "Pandora's not going anywhere, and I can't really picture a life without Adonis. Not anymore."

I give a trembling smile, all too aware of who he didn't list. It's okay. I married him for politics, not for love. For *power*. Funny how that rings so hollow right now when my heart feels like it's turning to dust. "Adonis does have that effect on people he cares about."

"Yeah, he does." He looks down at our linked hands. "Besides, you've more than proven you can't protect yourself. If I'm not Hephaestus, there's only one target in our household, and I think we can figure out a way to keep you safe."

There's not enough air in the room. "What?"

Theseus squeezes my hand again, surer this time. "You're my wife, Eris. I haven't wanted to strangle you in nearly a week. That's love, don't you think?"

"Don't joke. Not right now. Not about this," I whisper. There's a horrible burning in my throat and behind my eyes. *I am a Kasios and we don't cry.* I instantly make a liar out of myself when something wet slips from the corner of my eye.

"I'm not joking." My brother scoffs, but Theseus just leans closer and lowers his voice. "I won't pretend I know what proper love looks like. I'm just feeling my way. I want Adonis in my life. At my side. I want the same with you. I want you to feel like you can be with Pandora, too."

It's too good to be true, and yet all I can see are pitfalls. "We'll never be safe. The city is coming down around us, and Minos isn't going to stop."

"He's not going to stop," he agrees. Now, he finally looks at Perseus. "Find out what he had in those ships and you'll get an idea of what he's planning. He's going to continue to destabilize the city. Probably has something up his sleeve for the barrier, too. The enemy isn't at your gates today, but you can bet your ass they'll be there the second they can get access to the city. At the rate you're going, there won't even be a fight. They'll show up, off you and whoever is left standing, and take over. All they need is a good story and the public will welcome them with open arms."

"I am aware," my brother bites out. "If you have nothing more to offer by way of information and you're no longer one of the Thirteen, what's to stop me from making you disappear? You've caused me and this city nothing but problems."

"*No.*" It hurts to raise my voice, but I do it all the same. "Don't you dare."

He looks frustrated enough to rip out his hair. "You *know* the cost, Aphrodite. The city comes first. Before our personal happiness. Before everything. That man is a threat to Olympus, and he needs to be removed before he can cause more harm." When I just glare, he curses. "Even if we don't kill him, you have to get a divorce. You're Aphrodite. If you're married, you need to be married to someone with power. If he's not Hephaestus, he's no one."

He's right. I hate that he's right. I stare at my hand linked with my husband's. Right now, the thing to do is free myself and declare that I want a divorce. To rise from the ashes of this catastrophic relationship and set my sights on someone who will help stabilize the power structure in Olympus as much as possible. One of the scions of a powerful legacy family. Someone who will be firmly in my pocket and whose alliance will benefit the city.

I...don't want to.

Theseus runs his thumb over my knuckles. "Aren't you tired of being a weapon they pick up and use until it's beaten and broken? I sure as fuck am. You've sacrificed so much for this city, and the first thing they do to thank you is try to kill you and take your power for their own." His voice goes low and fierce. "They don't deserve you, Eris."

"Shut the fuck up," Perseus snaps. "You don't know what you're talking about. What we're trying to accomplish."

"Trying and failing from where I'm sitting."

"Stop it. Both of you." I don't yell, but they both obey. I look at my brother, at the blatant evidence of the price the city demands written across his face. He won't bend, and he won't break, but he might do exactly as he threatened and turn into the monster the city requires.

If someone asked me a week—even a few days—ago, I would have said I have the same resolve as Perseus. That I'm willing to pay whatever price Olympus demands as long as the city benefits. Maybe I was naive, but I never expected the burden to be so heavy.

"What if I wasn't Aphrodite?"

Perseus flinches. "Aphrodite—"

"Her name is *Eris*."

I don't look at Theseus, even as my heart feels like it just sprung wings. Instead, I hold my brother's gaze. "We can't lose

Helen as Ares—she's too formidable and she's proven to be a good fit—and you're Zeus. But with three of us in the Thirteen, it's put some of the legacy families on the outs with us. We need them if we're going to unify and survive this."

"Don't."

I clear my throat. "I won't pretend this isn't selfish, Perseus." I gingerly touch the bandage on my stomach. It was very foolish to skip those pain meds, but at least my mind is clear. Even if it feels like I'm free-falling. "I'm so tired. I was suited to battles of public perception, not ones with guns and knives." My throat burns and I swallow a few times. "Please don't make me do this. *Please*."

"Oh, Eris." He's at my side in an instant. He doesn't take my hand; we're not that kind of family. But he does shift down until our faces are even. "I'm not him. I won't make you do anything."

Him. Our father.

Against my best efforts, another tear slips free. "I'll still help."

"I know."

"I might be able to do more this way."

His lips curve the tiniest bit. "I expect nothing less." Perseus's attention shifts to Theseus for a long moment. "I want formal resignations from both of you on my desk by the end of the week. The sooner, the better. It will take some time to get the Hephaestus competition moving." He nods at me. "Do you have a successor picked?"

I hadn't, but in the end, it's the easiest choice in the world. "Sele. They've worked for the Aphrodite office for as long as I have. They're formidable and good at their job, and they come from the Baros family, which is one of the ones who've been waffling over recent events. It will bring them back into the fold."

"Very well." He straightens. "I'm glad you're okay, Eris." Perseus drags a hand through his hair. "I'm also selfishly glad that I won't have to worry about more attempts on your life if you're no longer Aphrodite. No one's getting close to Ares with Achilles and Patroclus in the way."

"And you?"

He gives another of those small smiles. "I can take care of myself." Then he's gone, slipping out of the hospital room and leaving me alone with my husband.

I can't quite believe what just happened. All my life, it felt like I was heading in a single direction, reaching the pinnacle of the Thirteen and then using that power to serve the city that is my home. It's silly to think that I don't know who I am if I'm not Aphrodite—I held the position for less than year—but I feel a bit empty.

Maybe it's shock.

I swallow hard and look at my husband. "Did you mean it? All of it?" It seems impossible that we've reached this point, considering where we started. The small, political part of my brain whispers that I need to release his hand, to take away any indication that I might care just as much as he does, but I ignore it.

We will always have power for the sake of who we are, but that doesn't mean it has to own us and our actions. We get to choose now. I want to choose him. To choose Pandora and Adonis.

I want them to choose me, too.

I want *Theseus* to choose me.

"You know I can't lie worth a damn." He grins suddenly, the expression light and almost giddy. "I know we're not free, but fuck, it feels like it."

I slowly realize that he's right. That strange emptiness is a weightless feeling I barely know how to comprehend. It's as if I've been carrying around an anchor for most of my life without realizing that setting it down was an option. Without it, I feel like I could fly. "What about—"

The door opens again and Adonis and Pandora spill into the room. They rush to my side and there are several chaotic minutes while they try to ensure I'm okay and Theseus finally brings everyone up to speed.

It's...nice. Really nice.

This isn't what I thought my life would be, but I can't deny that having the three of them here feels so right I might cry. Again.

Pandora presses my knuckles to her lips. "I'm so glad you're okay."

"Me, too."

Adonis stares down at me, dark eyes serious. "You really mean to resign as Aphrodite?"

There's a wealth of history and pain in that question. Why am I doing it now when I wouldn't have done it for him alone? Why did I take this position in the first place? It's hard to meet his eyes. "Yes. I..." I take a deep breath. "I'm sorry. I'm sorry for all the pain I put you through, and I'm sorry for pulling you into this mess."

"Speak for yourself." Theseus still looks downright giddy. "I'd do it all again and then some to end up here."

Adonis nods slowly. "You were right before. We weren't quite a good fit with just the two of us." He looks at Theseus. "Maybe things needed/to play out this way to get us here."

It's such a purely Adonis thing to say that another damned tear slips free. "I love you."

"I love you, too." He clears his throat. "Let me go find the doctor and see if we can make a plan for getting you home."

Pandora turns to Theseus. "You really mean it? You're resigning the title and cutting off Minos?"

Some of his joy dims a little. "You've been saying I should find my own way for years. I should have listened."

Far from condemning him, she laughs. "One day you'll finally admit that I'm smarter than you and also have better perspective."

"Yeah." His gaze tracks to me. "You saw the value in Eris before I did."

"Yep." She takes my hand again. "Gods, but I'm happy that you're okay. I was so fucking worried."

Far be it from me to miss an opportunity. I give her a sweet smile. "Does that mean you're moving in? Both of you?"

"Yeah." Theseus laughs. "Yeah, where the fuck else would I go?"

Pandora raises a single brow. "This isn't going to be one of those things where I move in with you and you suddenly expect monogamy, is it?"

"No." I shake my head. "I meant it when I said I won't try to shove you into a box. I can't pretend there won't be hiccups and missteps, but if you want to bring people back to the apartment—"

"No," Theseus cuts in. "It's a security risk."

"If you want to bring people back to the apartment," I talk over him, "then that's more than fine. I want it to feel like home to you, whatever that means."

Pandora snorts. "Theseus looks like he's about to hog-tie me, so let's table this discussion for later."

"Deal." The fact that there *will* be a later is still processing. I touch my bandage again. I'm alive. More than that, I have a future that I barely dared dream about. One I thought completely impossible for me.

Adonis slips back into the room and gives us a quick update. We'll be here for a bit. Apparently stab wounds aren't something you can just check out of a hospital with the same day you're admitted...especially if they're stomach wounds.

"Eris."

I focus on Theseus. "Yes?"

"You don't have to." He looks markedly uncomfortable, which means he's about to try to be sweet or comforting. "Resign, I mean. I can't pretend I know your whole history, but you fought hard to get that title. You shouldn't have to give it up."

That's the thing. It doesn't feel like giving up anything. It feels like a release. "You said Minos made you feel like a weapon. My father did the same." Gods, why is this so hard to say? "I'm done being a weapon for other people. I'm not going to pretend I won't keep fighting for Olympus, but I...don't want it to be this way. Or the way I was. I want something else. I want you. All of you."

For the first time in my life, I want love.

Not power.

More, I *can* have it. With these three. Together.

EURYDICE

THE MUSIC IS A DEEP, THROBBING BEAT THAT SEEMS TO soak into every molecule of the room, inciting the occupants to sin. Or, if not inciting, then at least smoothing away any lingering worries about clinging to the perception of purity that the upper city values so highly.

We're not in the upper city now.

I glance at my phone for the fifth time in ten minutes and curse under my breath when the text I'm waiting for finally comes through.

Ariadne: My dad put us on lockdown. I'm sorry, but I can't come tonight.

I've spent three weeks and half a dozen failed attempts trying to get Ariadne into Hades's kink club. Lying through my teeth about how no one will know who she is. Feeling guilty for coaxing her into what is essentially a trap when she shows all evidence of being a lovely person. That guilt has faded thanks to the events of the last month.

People are dying and the fault lies with the Vitalis family. With *Ariadne's* family. Her father might be the one pulling the strings, but the little hints Ariadne gave Apollo at that house party six weeks ago weren't enough. She knew this was coming and she didn't warn us.

That makes her the enemy.

An enemy that's not walking into my trap tonight. I sigh. Not that this is much of a *trap*, exactly. It's more that I've been tasked with attempting to coax her over to our side. If that's not possible, then I suspect someone will just flat out take her, but I'm the carrot in this situation.

Not that anyone knows it.

I look around, my guilt flaring for a completely different reason. I've been in my brother-in-law's sex club half a dozen times in the last couple months. I have no doubts that Hades is aware of it, though I'm careful to only show up when I know he and Persephone won't be presiding over the activities.

This is the first time I've come alone.

It feels weird not to have Charon as my ever-present shadow. He wouldn't have approved of tonight's activities, so I snuck out without telling anyone where I was going. The club manager, Hypnos, has seen me around enough now that the bouncers didn't stop me when I walked through the door. Zir doesn't know my arrangement with Charon, which works well enough for me. Charon initially allowed me access to the club, with one caveat: I'm only allowed to watch. He's loosened up the rules a bit, but it's hard to be comfortable indulging when he's looking over my shoulder.

But Charon isn't here right now.

The room is a true den of iniquity, all artfully designed to seduce the senses. The lights are always low when the club is open, but a cleverly hidden waterway around the edge of the room throws dizzying reflections onto the ceiling, giving the impression of us being underground. I've seen the furniture arranged in a dozen different ways, but tonight it's the traditional layout with couches and chairs and cushions situated to allow plenty of space for conversation and, well, fucking.

I inhale the scent of sex and smooth my hands down my tight mini dress. My body thrums in response. It's been...so long. I haven't been with anyone since the events of last December, and somehow nine months have gone by. For a long time, I was focused on putting one foot in front of the other and not letting the pain of Orpheus's betrayal break me.

But now?

I look around the room. Every other time I've come here has been with Charon babysitting me. I don't know if Hades put him up to it, or if he's taken it upon himself to be my guide to the lower city, but I was hardly going to indulge with him looking over my shoulder. He's made comments more than once about how I could if I wanted to, but it felt too strange. I still haven't decided if it was a *good* strange or a *bad* strange, though. Either way...he's not here tonight.

"I've seen you around, always watching, never participating."

I jolt and turn to find a man has taken up a spot against the wall next to me. He's a very attractive South Asian man who's about my height with a slim build and smiling eyes. He also looks incredibly familiar, and not just because I'm sure I've seen him a few times during my visits here.

He holds out a hand. "Thanatos."

Recognition clicks as I slip my hand into his. "You're Hypnos's brother." Now that I say it, I see the similarities between him and zir. Same medium-brown skin tone, thick dark hair, and refined features. They also both have incredibly sensual lips. Not that I've noticed. Except I have.

"Guilty as charged." Instead of shaking my hand, he raises it to press a light kiss to my knuckles. It should be cheesy, but his dark eyes invite me to indulge him.

I find myself smiling as heat stirs to life low in my stomach. It's been so long since I've even *wanted* to indulge… No, that's a lie. But it's been a very long time since I've encountered someone who was safe to indulge with. Someone who I could spend a fun night with and not worry about shattering a relationship I value in the process.

One-night stands aren't usually the way I operate—I get attached very quickly once sex enters the picture—but perhaps it's time to make an exception. "It's nice to meet you."

Thanatos lifts his head, but doesn't release my hand. He holds me in a light grip I could break at any moment, heat licking into his dark eyes. "It strikes me that you haven't had a proper introduction to the delights of the club."

He's flirting with me. I don't know why that surprises me so much. I suppose I've become so used to blending into the background that I expect it to be the default. *It certainly is with Charon.* The man treats me kindly, but it's clear he's never felt the same flicker of desire that plagues me in his presence.

I've learned the hard way what happens when you give your heart to a man who doesn't cherish it. I refuse to do it again.

Thanatos isn't asking for my heart. He's not asking for anything at all right now. I take a slow breath, inhaling the evocative scent of his cologne. He's still holding my hand. I find myself smiling. "By all means. Introduce me."

His grin is bright and charming. "It would be my pleasure."

I ignore the guilt that clings to me as he leads me to an empty couch near the wall farthest from the door. I'm not certain if it's intentional or not, but I appreciate the sliver of privacy the location offers. There's an unspoken rule that what goes on here isn't mentioned outside these walls unless my sister and her husband wish it to be so, but that doesn't mean I want to risk the gossip getting back to *them*.

They wouldn't understand. Oh, maybe Hades would, but Persephone? Never. To her, I'm her baby sister to be protected at all costs. She never stops to think that maybe the blanket of protection she and our other sisters provide is suffocating me slowly. If she knew I was here, she would sweep in with all the rage of a vengeful goddess to strike down anyone who dared look at me.

And should they *touch* me?

Unthinkable.

Except Thanatos is touching me now. He sits close enough that we're pressed together and turns over my hand to trace the fine veins of my wrist with the tips of his fingers. "You've been here many times in the last few months."

I lift my brows. "Have you been watching me?"

He shrugs, completely unselfconscious. "Everyone watches

you, Eurydice, and not just because you're beautiful." His fingers trail up to the inside of my elbow. "You're absolutely captivating."

I'm aware that he's trying to seduce me. He might not be the one I want if I'm being truly honest with myself, but what's the harm in allowing myself to be seduced? He has kind eyes. Maybe what I need to get over Orpheus once and for all isn't a great love to sweep away everything that came before. Maybe what I need is a string of kind lovers who don't stir my heart but are more than capable of stirring my body.

Thanatos certainly is doing a good job of it. His touch isn't anything that would be inappropriate in another public setting, but I find myself holding my breath as he continues to trace light patterns over my skin, each sending a zing of desire through me.

I relax slowly against the back of the couch and look up at him. "You're quite captivating yourself."

His smile takes on a self-deprecating tone. "I'm not too shabby." His fingers trail slightly up my bicep, the backs of his knuckles brushing against my breast. He holds my gaze. "May I?"

I can't quite catch my breath. I don't know what he's asking, but I want it all the same. "Yes."

Thanatos leans in, closing the last little bit of distance between us, and kisses me. It's a good kiss. It's light and intentional, a test and a seduction, all wrapped into one. It makes me shift in my seat, but my heart stays unfeeling in my chest.

Perfect.

At least until Thanatos leans back and I catch sight of the previously unoccupied chair across from us. It's not unoccupied any longer. Now it's been claimed by a large white man with intense blue eyes, shoulders that fill a doorway, and dark hair that reaches nearly to his shoulders. My heart gives a horrible thump in my chest.

Charon.

Thanatos goes still in response to my tension. He turns to follow my gaze and seems to stop breathing. "Charon."

"Thanatos. You're overstepping." His voice is calm. It's always calm. I once overheard Hades speaking with my sister, expressing concern that Charon had lost his customary humor in the last year. Persephone had responded that he'd grown up a lot because of the events that continue to destabilize Olympus. I think they're both wrong. He's still got humor, but it's become a dry thing that flies right over my head at times.

He doesn't look like he's laughing now.

In fact, he looks almost murderous.

Thanatos shifts away from me. "I'm sorry. I didn't realize she was yours."

"She's not." He doesn't move, doesn't take his gaze from the other man. "But she's not for the taking."

ACKNOWLEDGMENTS

THIS SERIES CONTINUES TO EVOLVE IN THE MOST delightful of ways, and I cannot thank my readers enough. None of this would be possible without you, and I am so incredibly humbled by your support.

Endless thanks to Mary Altman for always "Yes, and"ing my wild plans. This is my most ambitious book to date, and I would never have dared try it without your support. Can't wait for the next one!

Thank you to my agent, Laura Bradford, for continuing to champion this series!

To Pam Jaffree and Katie Stutz for being the best publicist duo an author could ever want! You wrangle my chaos, and I deeply appreciate it!

Thank you Dominique Raccah and Todd Stocke; Rachel Gilmer, Jocelyn Travis, and Susie Benton; Diane Dannenfeldt and Carolyn Lesnick; India Hunter and Heather Hall; Tara Jaggers, Stephanie Gafron, and Dawn Adams; Brian Grogan, Sean Murray, and Elizabeth Otte.

Endless love and appreciation to Jenny Norbak and Melody Carlisle for being the best group chat a person could ever ask for. I don't deserve you! Thank you to Nisha Sharma for always having my back and talking me through some truly ridiculous situations. Thank you to Piper J Drake and Asa Maria Bradley for dragging me out of the house to a writing retreat that was one of my favorite experiences this year!

To Tim... Man, look at us now. I still can't quite believe that this is our life now, but you never once doubted that we'd get here. Your faith in me has gotten me through some tough shit, and I wouldn't want to be on this journey with anyone else.

ABOUT THE AUTHOR

Katee Robert is a *New York Times* and *USA Today* bestselling author of spicy romance. *Entertainment Weekly* calls her writing "unspeakably hot." Her books have sold over two million copies. She lives in the Pacific Northwest with her husband, children, a cat who thinks he's a dog, and two Great Danes who think they're lap dogs. You can visit her online at kateerobert.com or on TikTok @authorkateerobert.